SOMEWHERE
TO HIDE

MEL SHERRATT

Also by Mel Sherratt

Taunting the Dead

FT
Pbk

For Chris, for being you and for making great tea. Love you to bits, fella.

ACKNOWLEDGMENTS

To my treasured friend, Alison Niebieszczanski. For listening to me, encouraging me, believing in me and for never being able to get a word in edgewise at times. Who stuck by me every year, through thick and thin, and makes me proud to know her. Same too, for my wonderful friends, Maria Duffy and Talli Roland. For comfort and reassurance, chats and laughter. For always being there. I really can't thank you enough and I hope there is much more to come.

The crime ladies for their continuous friendship and support – Mari Hannah, Rebecca Bradley and Pam McIlroy. For murderous conversation during the many get-togethers as well as over the phone. Nothing is too much trouble.

The crime fellas who keep me sane in real life and on Twitter – my big buddy David Jackson, Will Carver, Keith Walters, Emlyn Rees and Mark Edwards.

For people I've yet to meet or don't meet often enough – Caroline Smailes, Cath Bore, Louise Voss, Elizabeth Haynes, Jacqui Rose, Rachel Abbott, Sarah Watts, Fanny Blake, Tammy Cohen, Michele Gorman, Janet Brigden, George Allan, Jill Clarke, Julie Green, Jane Casey, Mandasue Heller.

Strong women who inspire me with their music – my lady, Pink, who I feel depicts my writing style perfectly within her lyrics, Lady Gaga, Amy Winehouse, Adele, Jessie J and Katy Perry. And the guys – Plan B, Paul Weller and Take That.

For all the writers who have helped me in any way. For all the readers who have sent me messages, whether by email, tweets or Facebook, thank you so much for your kind words. Each one makes me believe a little bit more.

For my mum – for being the strong woman that made me into what I am today.

Finally, to my husband, Chris. Thank you for your unwavering support, love and honesty. For raising me up when I'm feeling down – and for twisting my twists just that little bit further. And for not complaining too much at the amount of times I burn our meals. I could never do, and wouldn't want to do, anything without your love.

PROLOGUE – ONE WEEK EARLIER

The White Lion public house stood forlorn in the middle of the Mitchell Estate. Before the recession, it had been a thriving business. Now all that was left was a boarded up building with a For Sale sign hanging haphazardly by one nail. Rubbish bags sat alongside two single mattresses, a few wooden pallets and a settee in the car park, the low wall around it missing many of its bricks.

Austin Forrester had been watching it for three days before making his move. During this time, he'd seen only one other loner like himself. The youth was in his early teens, scraggy and unkempt, wearing clothes that hadn't seen water in months.

That afternoon, he watched him leave and disappear out of view before leap-frogging the wall and legging it to the back of the building. He felt around the edges of the windows until he found the metal sheeting that had been jemmied open. Within seconds, he pushed himself through the gap and jumped down to the floor inside.

Once his eyes adjusted to the shadows, Austin moved quickly. A door creaked as he pushed it open to find what used to be the kitchen. He walked on further and the building opened up into a lobby. Coming to a flight of stairs he chose to go up two steps at a time, his speedy heartbeat the only sound he could hear. He came across a room with a single mattress on the floor. A grubby sleeping bag lay on it, the zip opened and pushed wide. Empty beer cans and takeaway cartons were piled high on top of a beer crate serving as a coffee table. Austin breathed through his nose, the pile of clothes and trainers at the foot of the mattress adding to the stench inside the room.

Less than ten minutes later he was out again, leaving no signs of his presence. So when he went back at midnight, the youth didn't stand a chance. The first he knew of anything was when Austin pinned him to the bed, his gloved hands squeezing tightly around his neck. Sensing he was fighting for his life, the youth struggled to pull his arms free of the sleeping bag and thrashed them about, clawing urgently at Austin's gloves. His breath came out of his nostrils in fits and starts. Austin moved with him, holding him down and avoiding his knees pushing up, trying to flip him off balance. Finally, the youth's arms and shoulders flopped.

Afterwards, Austin lit a cigarette and inhaled deeply. Funny how things work out, he thought, glancing around the room again. This place couldn't be a more perfect hideout for him to watch and wait. He'd be in the thick of things but inconspicuous when he needed to be.

He took another long drag and stared at the corpse beside him. For a moment, he wondered why the youth was here, what his story was, and his background. Had he been dragged up through the system too?

Although he felt the anger brewing inside, he knew he had to bide his time for the next few months. Besides, it wouldn't take long to put his plan into action. He already knew the date it would all come to a head. The fifteenth of August 2012.

Everyone on the Mitchell Estate would know his name by then.

ONE

Liz McIntyre woke up with a start when she heard the front door slam shut. She looked at the clock to see it was just past midnight. A further glance around assured her that the room was tidy. She jumped to her feet and rushed into the hallway.

'Hi, had a good night?' she asked her husband tentatively, knowing that so much depended on his answer.

'No. It was shit.'

Liz's heart sank as he pushed past her. She watched him drop heavily onto the settee.

'Make us a drink,' he said without looking her way. 'Coffee will do.'

In the kitchen, Liz's hands shook as she filled the kettle with water. She hated Kevin when he was sober. Sober Kevin was crueller than drunken Kevin. Quickly, she reached for his Super Dad mug.

'I'll have some toast while you're at it,' he shouted through to her.

When she went back into the living room, Kevin was flicking through the television channels. Liz placed the mug and plate on the coffee table. She glanced at the clock again: half past twelve.

'Is it okay if I go to bed while you eat that?'

'No. You can stay here until I tell you otherwise.' His eyes flicked up to rest on hers and he patted the empty cushion. 'Right here, next to me.'

Liz willed her legs to bend and sat down. Fifteen minutes later, Kevin had finished his meal, finished his drink and finished with her as he fastened his trousers again.

'Not very exciting, but at least you're clean and tidy,' he said, standing up.

Liz pulled her dressing gown around her body. Maybe now he'd let her leave the room. But then she felt his eyes on her. After a moment, she looked up, her sense of dread escalating.

'Why did you do that?' he snapped. When she didn't reply quickly enough, he grabbed her roughly by the hair. 'I'm talking to you!'

Liz gasped as he pulled her to her feet. His eyes were menacing, saliva glistening on his lower lip.

'Answer me!' he said.

'I – I don't understand what –'

'The minute I got off you, you covered yourself up. Do I repulse you that much?'

'No! I was cold, that's all.'

'You lying bitch.' Kevin pulled harshly at the belt of her dressing gown. 'You don't look so good yourself.' Through the thin material of her nightdress, he squeezed her breast, causing her to gasp out in pain. 'Look at you. Not even a decent handful. You're nothing but skin and bones. I wonder what other people would think of you. Take it off.'

A moment's hesitation.

'Take it off or I'll rip it off.'

Liz shrugged off the gown, letting it drop to the floor.

'And the rest. I want you naked.'

'Please, Kevin.' Already feeling vulnerable, she didn't want to go any further.

'Please, Kevin,' he mimicked cruelly. 'Take it off.'

She removed the nightgown. Standing naked before him, she covered her breasts with a forearm.

Kevin pulled her roughly by the elbow, marching them both into the hallway. 'Let's see what other people think of your pathetic, skinny body,' he said as he opened the front door.

With a shove Liz lurched forward, landing heavily on the front path. The gravel embedded itself into the skin of her palms and knees but she stayed quiet.

'Down on all fours. That's a great pose for you,' Kevin sneered behind her. 'You're nothing but an ungrateful bitch anyway. So if you act like a dog, expect to be treated like one.'

Hot tears welled in Liz's eyes but she had to keep calm. It was the middle of March and although it wasn't too cold outside she was vulnerable. She had two people to think of right now and she didn't want Chloe to wake up. If she didn't play it cool, Kevin would make her stay outside all night. As if that wasn't bad enough, from the corner of her eye she noticed a curtain moving in the bedroom window of the house next door.

Pushing her humiliation to the back of her mind, she sat up on her stinging knees and turned back to face him. She knew what she had to do.

'I'm sorry,' she whispered, tears coming freely now. 'How can I make it up to you?'

Kevin leant on the door frame, one foot crossing the other. His arms were folded: his eyes seemed to be mocking her, daring her to come back at him and stand up for herself. Then all of a sudden, he came outside. Liz flinched as he drew near but gently he helped her to stand up again. He turned over her hands, checking the bleeding palms.

'Ouch, they look sore.' He smiled. 'Come on in and I'll see to them.'

He marched her into the kitchen and sat her at the table. While he rummaged around in the kitchen cupboards, she sat shaking violently in terror but unable to move for fear. Finally, he found what he was looking for and held it up triumphantly.

'TCP.' His grin was almost manic. 'It'll hurt but it's for your own good.'

Fear gripped Liz as she realised his intention. He was going to make her hold her hands in the liquid. They would go numb, she was sure, and then she would be completely helpless. Instinctively, she moved away but he grabbed one of her hands, turned it palm up and poured the liquid in it.

By now an expert on pain from slaps, punches, even the odd bite, Liz braced herself. Waves of heat radiated through her hand and up her arm. She did the worse thing possible. She screamed.

Kevin slapped her, the whole weight of his body behind it. Her head reared to the right, knocking her off balance and she fell to the floor. She scrambled towards the door. Kevin grabbed her ankles and pulled her back towards him. She kicked out, still thinking she could get away if she was quick. But the pain in her palm was nothing like the pain of his heel digging into the top of her hand. She screamed again. She couldn't help it.

'Shut up,' he warned. Then he kicked her in the stomach. 'If anyone alerts that stupid bitch from the housing association, you'll get more like this.' He kicked her again.

'Please, stop,' she sobbed. 'Think of the baby. I don't want to lose our baby!'

As his fists started to fly, Liz curled up into a ball. Suddenly her hands didn't sting anymore: everything did. She fought for breath with every blow but she knew what she had to do. She had to keep quiet until it was over. It was the only way she knew she would survive.

Forty miles away, Becky Ward had also been woken up by the sound of a front door slamming. She knew it would be a while yet before her bedroom door opened but, even so, she slid her hand underneath the pillow and curled her fingers around the handle of the knife.

Above the sound of her drumming heartbeat, she heard the television go on and the sound of bottle tops being removed. Cupboards opened, the smell of chips wafted up the stairs and then silence as her dad and uncle settled down to watch the television.

She glanced at her watch: just gone midnight. She'd bet her new trainers that Uncle James would come creeping in before half past twelve, with his sweet words and his stale breath, his roaming hands and his heavy body. But this time there would be no more defenceless Becky. No more giving in until it was over. This time, she would fight for both of them.

Her fingers gripped tighter round the knife handle as she

recalled the first time it had happened. She'd been eleven, too young to push him away when he'd slapped her hard. James had been thirty-five, two years older than her dad and, as the older brother, he thought he could do what he wanted. He'd threatened her with much worse if she told her dad what was going on. But now she was going to get her revenge, which in turn would give her the proof she needed. Then she would tell her dad.

A long twenty minutes later, Becky heard the living room door open and heavy footsteps came up the stairs. She held her breath as they stopped at the top of the landing. They moved to the bathroom but were back within minutes. Becky flicked open the knife. As the door flew open, she pushed it underneath the mattress.

James Ward stood in front of her, the belt to his jeans hanging loose. Like Becky, he was tall and thin, but with the added advantage of plenty of bulk to hold her down. Blue eyes darted backwards and forwards as they tried their best to focus.

'Switch on the lamp,' he slurred. 'I want to see you.'

Becky did as she was told, silently praying that she'd have the strength to go through with her plan.

James lifted the corner of the duvet and leered at her.

'Take them off.'

She took off her pyjama top and dropped it to the floor; she watched his eyes widen as she removed her pyjama trousers and dropped them too. Wearily, she lay there as he looked her up and down before getting in beside her.

'This is still our secret,' he told her as he kissed her neck. He pressed hard on her firm breasts. 'No one would believe you anyway, would they?'

He'd said the same thing every time he visited. Over the years, the words had changed, become less aggressive because Becky had given up fighting. When she was eleven and frightened that he would tell her father, Becky let him do it because she didn't know any better. When she was thirteen and a little taller, she'd started to fight him off but the punches back had hurt. When she was fifteen, the first time she'd been pregnant, she'd succumbed to him. If she didn't protest, it was over and done with quicker. But now, this time was different.

James kissed her on the lips, the face, the neck, big sloppy kisses and rancid breath. Becky felt her body stiffen at his touch and willed herself to give in for just a few more seconds. She closed her eyes tightly as she felt the weight of him, almost dead heavy. He ran rough hands over her body, lower, lower. He pushed her legs apart and rolled on top of her.

As soon as he'd slithered his jeans down to his knees, she reached for the knife. With all her strength, she thrust it into the side of his leg.

'Get off me,' she said, still holding the knife in her hand.

James put his hand to his leg. It came away covered with blood. 'What have you done, you stupid little bitch!'

Becky watched his eyes roll around in their sockets. Sensing no resistance, she pushed him away and got out of the bed. Breathing heavily she stood in the middle of the room, listening as he cried out in agony; watching while the blood running from his leg made a pool on the sheet. She wanted it to soak through to the mattress. That was the evidence she needed. To say he'd been in her bed.

Suddenly James flopped sideways, his shoulder taking

his weight against the wall. His eyes closed, his body stilled.

Becky left it a few seconds before she dared prod him in the chest. James didn't move. She prodded him again.

'Uncle James?'

Still no response.

'Uncle JAMES!'

Oh shit! She must have killed him. Her breathing took on a life of its own. When he didn't move a minute later, and the pool of blood became larger, she picked up her pyjama top and wrapped it around the knife. Then she gathered together some clothes, dressed quickly and shoved a few things into a holdall. All the time James didn't stir.

Oh, God. Oh, God. OH, GOD! Her plan to soak the blood into the mattress had worked but she hadn't meant to kill him.

She had to get out of there, and fast. Trying not to hyperventilate, she reached for her jacket from the back of the door and ran. But something made her stop halfway down the stairs. The living room door was open. Her dad was still awake! He must have heard it all. She'd never be able to get out of the door without him seeing her. She'd have to get in first, explain her side of things.

'Dad, I need to –'

Becky stopped mid-sentence as she walked into the room because her father *was* asleep. His eyes were closed, his head rested back on the chair, and he was snoring heavily. She frowned. She could have sworn he'd been awake.

'Dad!' She tried again but still he didn't move.

Looking down at him, for a moment Becky's life was suspended. She wished she could wake up and find out this was all a nightmare. She wished she had a father who she could talk to, spend time with, when he wasn't down the pub. She wished her mother were still alive. If she had been, none of this would have happened. She wished she had an uncle who looked out for her, not did…

Becky gulped back tears. She closed the door quietly and went into the kitchen. She took biscuits, a few cans of coke and packets of crisps and shoved them into her holdall. She crept back across the hallway. Then, without a backward glance, she opened the front door of her childhood home, closed it quietly behind her and ran.

TWO

Life on the Mitchell Estate was never dull. Cathy Mason lived in Christopher Avenue, on the bottom half of the estate. She'd answered the door to many a strange request since her husband had died three years ago. A knock on the door at nine am could mean a number of things. It could be a bailiff with an eviction warrant pending. It could be someone wanting to administer a slap or a punch to a person inside. It could mean an early morning raid by a drugs squad or even, on one occasion, armed police. Several times, it had been a husband returning from an all-night bender wanting to speak to his estranged wife – or a wayward teenager the worse for wear after a night on the tiles.

This morning she pulled back the bolts, keeping the chain in place before removing it when she saw who was standing on her doorstep.

'Morning, Josie,' she smiled. 'To what do I owe this pleasure? Or is this a business call?'

'It's always a pleasure to see you, Cath. But I do have business to discuss as well. Is that the sound of the kettle boiling?'

Cathy closed the door behind them and followed Josie down a brightly lit hallway into the kitchen.

For a Mitchell Housing Association property, it was certainly a step up from the norm. For starters, the rubbish was in a bin: it hadn't been chucked to the floor and left to rot for months. The top of the dining table wasn't piled high with a metre of dirty washing. Worktops were clear: there wasn't a single food product festering in a dish, no congealed greasy residue in the sink, no pyramid of used teabags that threatened to reach the ceiling. And it smelt of something lemony, with a slight hint of bleach, and...

Clean: it smelt clean.

'Hey,' Cathy flicked on the kettle, 'do you know anything about that boy whose body they found in the canal last week?'

'I'm sure decent people discuss the weather when they sit down to make small talk,' replied Josie. 'Whereas we talk dead bodies.'

'Yes, but that's because you know everything that goes on around here.'

'More is the pity.' Josie sighed. 'He was only in his late teens, poor kid.'

'Anyone we know?'

'Too early to tell. There was no ID found on him. Mind you, it is a strange one. Apparently, he had cigarette burns all over his cheeks. It looks like whoever killed him strangled him first, used his face as an ashtray and then dumped him in the water.'

'First?' Cathy frowned. 'Don't people usually go doo-lally *before* they kill someone?'

Josie shrugged. 'You know the Mitchell Estate. It's had its fair share of weirdoes over the years.'

'Yeah, and you've visited most of them.'

'It gives me a chance to send the worst of them to you though, doesn't it?'

'Don't I know it?' Cathy tutted. 'My hair is turning grey far earlier than it should. You'll have me old before my time.'

Josie doubted that. Cathy Mason was one of the few women on the estate who took pride in their appearance. Looking far younger than her thirty-nine years, with long dark hair and enticing brown eyes framed by the longest of lashes, she was slim with clear, almost radiant skin. Hardly a wrinkle underneath her natural-look make-up and wearing immaculate yet simple clothing, Cathy wouldn't have it said but she put a lot of women on the Mitchell Estate to shame.

And she never missed a thing.

'Heavy caseload?' Cathy asked, noticing Josie's drooping shoulders. She handed her a mug of tea and sat down at the table.

Josie nodded, following suit. 'Not enough hours in the day, as ever. How's Jess?'

'Jess is Jess.' Cathy huffed. 'That girl will always think of herself and no one else. Did you hear what she did last week? She whacked one of the Bradley twins.'

'Oh dear.' Josie grimaced. Gina Bradley was another of her tenants. She had three out of control children but the twins, sixteen-year-old girls, were by far the worst.

'I had their mother on the doorstep after my blood. That Gina thinks those girls are blameless, the silly cow. They're always in the thick of things but she won't have it.' Cathy pointed at Josie. 'You should do something about it.'

'You're right. I wish I could get rid of the whole Bradley clan. I can't understand how we allowed them to take on so many properties in the same street. We should have been savvier and split them all over the estate. Now I can't go down Stanley Avenue without getting accosted by mother, father, sister or grandmother. Come to think of it, even their bloody dog doesn't like me.'

Josie Mellor was thirty-six and had been at Mitchell Housing Association for seventeen years. She'd started off working on the main reception at their head office in Stockleigh before moving over to work on the estate. Even though she was small in stature and didn't look like she was capable of standing up for herself in any type of sticky situation, she'd been a housing officer for the past seven years. More recently, she'd been splitting her hours between ongoing cases and working in the community house set up by one of the residents' associations.

'Then she came home bladdered again last week,' Cathy continued, 'making all kinds of racket. Archie Meredith was over like a shot the next morning. Honestly, I have more visitors than Crewe Station. It's pathetic. And they never see the good in anyone. They should try looking in a mirror once in a while.'

Josie smiled her gratitude. 'What would this estate do without you, Cathy Mason? You are one special lady. Not everyone would do what you do.'

'Stop trying to get on my good side. I know you're buttering me up for something. What brings you to my humble abode so early in the morning, anyway? I haven't seen much of you lately.'

Josie tucked shoulder-length mousey hair behind her ears. 'I need a favour,' she replied.

Cathy raised her eyebrows.

'Okay, I need *another* favour. Remember when I asked you if you'd be able to take on a woman with a young child, when she was ready to admit defeat?'

'Bloody hell, that was some months ago.'

'Liz McIntyre came to see me yesterday. She was in a right state and had the remnants of some pretty nasty bruises. I've put her and her daughter up in a hostel overnight but I was wondering…'

Liz McIntyre was one of Josie's tenants that she suspected was being abused by her husband. Several times, Liz's neighbour had rung showing concern over the goings on next door. Several times, Josie had visited Liz only to be told to mind her own business. Over the past couple of months, Josie's visits had become more frequent.

'And she's after somewhere to stay?' Cathy questioned.

Josie took a sip of her drink before nodding. 'It's only until I can fix her up with a place of her own. But it's better than her returning to him, which I know she will do if she has to stay in the hostel.' She paused before continuing. 'I'd feel so much better knowing that she has somewhere safe to stay. I've already asked her to move away, maybe to another area, but she won't leave the estate. I know I can trust you to look out for her and her daughter, Chloe. She's only eight. And you have room at the moment, don't you?'

When Rich died three years ago, Cathy's life had changed dramatically. Dragged up through her childhood, her marriage had been volatile, sometimes to the brink of nasty and back, but Rich had grounded her with his love. She'd been his wife for sixteen years. If it wasn't for that one stupid mistake she'd made, life until he died would have been more than she had expected.

She'd been thirty-six when it happened. As if that wasn't bad enough, she was made redundant the month after and again six months later with the next job. Around that time, her friend's daughter, Nicola, came to stay. She wasn't getting on with her parents at home so it was a good idea all round. They had peace, quiet and assurance; Cathy had someone to look after, company in a quiet house. It hadn't all been fun: some of it was hard work. Nicola's mood swings were volatile but when she was happy, Cathy had enjoyed her company. Once Nicola felt able to return home and try again, Cathy decided to see if there was any kind of fostering she could do involving younger, perhaps vulnerable, women. It hadn't been easy but Josie managed to persuade the right people and she hadn't looked back. It had given her something to work at; something she was good at; something to ease the pain. Her eyes welled up with tears.

'Don't worry,' said Josie, noticing her distress. 'Let me do the rounds with the hostels again.'

But Cathy shook her head. 'There's no need. I'll be fine. Besides, have you ever known me to let down a sister in distress?'

'I'm sure Liz will be grateful for your help.'

'I meant helping you out, you dope,' Cathy smiled.

'Shit!'

Cathy ended the phone call and sighed in spectacular fashion. Not only was Josie's request about to end her peace and quiet, but also it seemed there was a sixteen-year-old girl in need of her help. Jess was going to be furious.

Seventeen-year-old Jess Myatt had been with Cathy for near on a year now. She'd managed to keep her at school for the last few months of her final year but since then Jess had been reluctant to get a job. Cathy kept encouraging her to enrol for college in September but Jess wasn't keen. Well, what chance did she stand nowadays with so many skilled workers on the dole? She'd come away from school without an exam to her name, in steep competition with a lot of her friends who had achieved nothing either. And, as she rightly said over and over, who would take her on? There were only so many small back street shops and factories that would employ cheap labour.

In her eyes, someone older than Jess coming to the house, and with a young child, would take away the top spot she'd gained due to the length of time she'd been here. Cathy had to be prepared mentally for the inevitable ructions that the next few days would bring. She had to prepare Jess too. It wouldn't be fair to blame everything on her, despite her big woman attitude.

'Jess.' Cathy knocked on the bedroom door before entering. 'I need to talk to you.'

'Jesus, Cath. It's only quarter to ten,' a voice could be heard from beneath the duvet. 'What do you want?'

Cathy drew back the bedroom curtains, staring out onto the street for a second before turning back. 'I've had a couple of calls today. One from PC Baxter and one from –'

'There's someone coming to stay, isn't there?' The duvet was pulled back to reveal a scowl.

'Yes,' Cathy replied. 'But it's not someone. There are three people.'

'Three!'

Jess had the face of a cherubic angel, clear, innocent and fresh but had the temper of a devil. Inside, she was like a coiled spring. She sat up in bed, short red hair looking as though it didn't need much styling.

'I've had more than this before, and I'll do it again if I have to.'

'But –'

Cathy sat down on the edge of the bed. 'There are no buts. We have other people coming to stay. You don't have the monopoly on me, even though it seems like you've been here forever now.'

'If things carry on the way they are,' Jess retorted, getting out of bed, 'it looks like I'll be moving out anyway.' She pushed past Cathy. Moments later, the bathroom door slammed.

Cathy flinched at the bang and sighed. She wasn't really worried. They'd been in this situation many times over the months: Jess always came around eventually. But it wasn't pleasant to witness her reaction.

When it was clear that she wasn't going to run back and put her point across more poignantly, Cathy pulled the duvet from the floor and back onto the bed. Then she glanced at her watch. Not yet ten o'clock and already she could feel a headache coming on. No wonder she felt like the weight of the world was on her shoulders at times. And if past experiences were anything to go by, three people arriving at the same time meant a whole raft of problems coming with them. Life wasn't going to be quiet for the foreseeable future.

'Hi, Cathy!' Josie's voice rang out with false brightness as she stood on the doorstep less than three hours after her last visit. 'I'm so sorry to put pressure on you, but you know this game by now. Like buses: there isn't one for ages and then two at the same time – or rather, three. This is Becky Ward. Please say that Andy has warned you to expect her.'

'Yes, he rang about an hour ago. Hi, Becky.'

Cathy held the front door wide open and ushered the two women inside. They went through to the kitchen.

Cathy pushed Becky gently down into a chair and tilted up her chin. 'Lovely blue eyes you have there but I can't see them for the swelling. You've got a great shiner coming too. What did you do to get that?'

'Nothing.' Becky jerked her head away.

'She was caught shoplifting at Shop&Save last night, over on Vincent Square,' said Josie. 'Andy – PC Baxter, I mean – tried to caution her but she legged it and gave him the slip. He spotted her again just after six this morning when he went back on duty. She was walking up Davy Road.'

'I can speak for myself,' Becky muttered before folding her arms.

Cathy didn't doubt that for a second. She also reckoned that Becky would clam up the moment any awkward questions were asked of her.

'Have you eaten?' she enquired.

Becky shook her head.

'Would you like some toast? And a cup of tea?'

Becky shook her head again. Then she changed her mind and nodded slightly.

Josie checked her watch. 'No tea for me, Cathy. I've got an appointment in ten minutes. No rest for the wicked, I suppose. Can I leave Becky in your capable hands while I make enquiries?'

'Enquiries?' Becky's eyes widened and she sat up straight. 'What kind of enquiries?'

'Just to see where you can stay. Cathy can help for now but we have a duty of care to put you somewhere more permanent. You're sure you can't go home?'

'Yes! I'm never going back.'

Cathy's heart went out to the young girl sitting at her table. Becky Ward might be sixteen but she had the look of a middle-aged woman who'd seen more than her fair share of worry. Her skin was pale, except for the odd blemish and group of spots. Wavy, blonde hair rested halfway down her back, looking in desperate need of a good shampoo. Yet, other than the mud stains on the knees of her jeans, her clothes were clean. She didn't look like she had been on the streets for long.

Cathy glanced around. 'Haven't you got a bag?' she asked. 'Or anything to call your own?'

'She's only got the clothes she's in now,' Josie explained when Becky didn't. 'No possessions, no bags, no spare knickers and toothbrush.'

'Well, it just might be your lucky day.' Cathy smiled warmly at Becky. 'You can stay for a while, if you like?'

Becky shrugged.

'I thought you could speak for yourself,' she teased, nudging her playfully. Then she looked up at Josie. 'Leave

31

her with me. She can have the room next to Jess.' She turned back to Becky once she'd gone. 'I'll tell you the same as I tell everyone else when they come to stay. I'm here for you if ever you need me. But there are certain rules that I like to be kept. Break them too often and you're out. Understand?'

Becky began to cry. Cathy pulled up a chair and waited until her tears slowed and her body stopped shaking so much. Then she reached across the table to a box of tissues and handed a couple to Becky.

'I always find a good cry helps me feel better,' she told her.

'I'm so screwed.' Becky blew her nose loudly. 'I don't know what to do.'

'About what?'

'Everything.'

Cathy smiled at her theatrical tone. 'Have you fallen out with your parents?'

'No.'

'Mother? Father?'

'No.'

'That's the reason why most young girls end up here. Take Jess, for instance. Her mother kicked her out because she couldn't cope with her mood swings. She's a feisty soul but treat her like an adult and she's not much to handle. I suppose your mother thought the same of you, hmm?'

'My mum's dead.'

'Oops. Trust me and my big mouth. I'm not known for my tact.' Cathy decided to change the subject. 'Where's that accent of yours from? Manchester?'

Becky nodded. 'Salford.'

'So why did you come to Stockleigh?'

'It was the first bus that left from the station on Saturday. I – I didn't know where to go really.'

'Was that when you left home? On Saturday?'

'No, eleven days ago. I stayed around Salford but I started to get pestered by this creepy guy.'

'Don't worry. You're safe here for now.' Cathy didn't want to push Becky into too much talk so early on. She knew it was vital that she gained the girl's trust as soon as possible but prying too deep too soon was one lesson she'd learnt during her first few months taking young girls in. She ran her right hand subconsciously over the scar on her left. Sarah Draycott had taken a pair of scissors to her after she'd asked her one question too many.

'You would have been better going south of Manchester rather than north,' she continued. 'This estate wouldn't have been my first choice – not my choice at all, actually.'

The Mitchell Estate consisted of 1,500 houses. Some were owner-occupied, some were rented from the local authority and the majority of the remaining ones belonged to Mitchell Housing Association. It was split down the middle by a main road, Davy Road. Known locally as The Mitch, the bottom half housed families who tried hard to keep their properties respectable. Gardens were tended, rubbish put in the bins, their cars were taxed and parked in their drives or by the kerbside. Tenants usually felt safe popping to the shop for a loaf of bread. Some of the neighbours greeted each other with a wave and a nod. Most of them watched out for each other when strangers were on the prowl.

The top of the estate, however, had a reputation for being the worst place in the city to live. It was referred to as The

Hell. There the cars were lucky to have any wheels left in the morning. Abandoned vehicles on the lawns were more prominent than garden shrubs. The rubbish piled up in the middle of the roads and tenants fought to be heard over the thud, thud of the music – that's if they weren't fighting among themselves. Neighbours would rob you before they'd ask how you were. Even the stray dogs wandered around in threes.

Becky went quiet and Cathy relented. 'It's not that bad, you know. It's just that I've been born and bred here. The place is ripe with the usual social housing problems – drugs, fighting, single mums with no control of their kids, thieving. You don't ever go to the shops after dark by yourself or you're asking for trouble. Other than that, it's a great place to live.' She forced a smile. 'You could have done much worse, though.'

Becky looked like she was going to cry again so Cathy stood up and opened the key cupboard. 'Your room is number two. It's the smallest one I have but it'll be fine. You don't have to use the key but if you feel safer that way, it's up to you. If you leave during the day, the key stays here, understand? You need to be in by eleven: midnight at the weekend if by prior arrangement.' She paused. 'I know Josie asked this but I'm going to ask again, while she's not here. Is there any chance of you going back home at any time?'

Becky shook her head. Cathy knew she wasn't going to get any more talk out of her. The girl needed some space. There were bound to be more tears before the day was out.

'Right then,' she said. 'Let's get you settled. I bet you could do with a bath and a sleep. I'll introduce you to Jess later. She's stormed off out so you'll have a bit of peace and quiet while she's not here. But be warned. The minute she's back, she's bound to create an atmosphere. She's really good at it.'

THREE

The next morning, Liz McIntyre woke up in unfamiliar surroundings. Disorientated, she sat up quickly before flopping back down on the bed. The room at Cathy Mason's house was welcoming, its walls painted a calming lavender. Besides the double bed she and Chloe were in, there was a wardrobe, a dressing table and an old school chair on the far wall. Cathy had added a small blue vase filled with white carnations but other than that and a couple of framed paintings, the room was sparse. Yet although she didn't relish the thought of sleeping with her daughter, Chloe, every night, Liz was grateful for any bed away from the hostel she'd briefly stayed in a couple of times.

She turned her head slightly to check on Chloe. She was asleep for now but had woken up three times during the night, screaming out about a monster coming to get her. Liz hoped she hadn't woken anyone else: she'd tried to calm her quickly each time. Yet as Chloe had drifted off after each occasion, soothed by her mum's arms, it had taken ages for Liz to drift off again afterwards.

She stared at her daughter, her gentle snores the only sound in the room. Sometimes Liz had so much love in her heart for Chloe that it frightened her. How was she going to protect her? Maybe they could just stay away from Kev long enough for him to move on without them. But she knew her wishes were futile. How could she think she could escape from his clutches, just like that? Then again, other women did, didn't they?

Wide awake now, she slipped out of the bedroom quietly and went downstairs. It was six thirty: no one would be awake this early, surely?

But Cathy was already in the kitchen. She smiled when she saw her.

'Morning. Did you sleep much last night?'

'A little.'

'And Chloe?'

'On and off.' Liz thought better of sharing the story of the nightmares. 'I thought I'd come downstairs, make a cup of tea and go back before she wakes. Do you always get up this early?'

'Yep.' Cathy closed the washer door quietly and reached for the powder. 'It's always the bloody same, isn't it? When I was younger I never wanted to get out of bed when the alarm clock went off at six for work. Now I don't even use an alarm clock.'

Liz moved to the left, away from the glare of the early spring sun streaming through the large window at the far end of the room. Cathy had the same standard fitted kitchen that Liz had left behind in Douglas Close but that was its only similarity. The white wooden units looked clinical there but here, beside the huge notice board covered in photos of young teenage girls, and the sunset yellow walls, they looked homely.

She sat down at the pine table, wondering how many women had done the same with Cathy. How·many had told her their secrets. How many lives she'd helped to mould, hoping to send women off in another direction entirely than where they'd thought they were heading. Josie Mellor had told her that Cathy took in female teenagers but she would also take on anyone if she thought she could help. Liz doubted she'd be able to help her though. The average age of the girls in the photos was just that, girls. She was twenty-eight.

Cathy joined her at the table. She was dressed in dark bootleg jeans, a white long-sleeved T-shirt and a multi-coloured scarf knotted at the nape of her neck. She wore make-up; her hair looked as if it had been straightened that morning. Liz's shoulders drooped. How did she find the energy? She barely had the strength to get Chloe ready and off to school.

'How long have you lived on the estate?' Cathy asked her. 'I can't say I've noticed you around.'

'I was in Douglas Close for eight years,' Liz explained. 'We kept ourselves to ourselves. We didn't know the neighbours.'

'And your fella? Married, were you?'

Liz nodded. Cathy sensed an invisible wall being erected in seconds.

'I've been around here since I was sixteen.' She sat down opposite Liz. 'The estate's got worse since then but I wouldn't live anywhere else. It was where I met Rich – my late husband. When he died, I thought of moving away but I just couldn't. I had a lot of good people rallying around me. No matter what people say about the Mitchell Estate, there are some good ones here. It's just the trouble makers that make it worse for everyone else.'

'It's a dump,' Liz retorted. 'If I could leave, I would.'

'Really?' Cathy didn't sound convinced: hadn't Josie said that Liz hadn't wanted to move away? 'Most people who say that have no intention of doing anything about it. Better the devil, and all that.'

'But there's not much to do around here, is there? I mean, is it any wonder the kids are bored? The clubs have closed down; most of the shops and the pubs are boarded up. I'm surprised everyone hasn't moved away. There must be more to life than this wretched routine all the time.'

Cathy nodded. 'There's plenty going on at the community house. I'm a volunteer there. Josie Mellor helps to run it. We do all kinds of sessions, like job interview techniques, basic computer skills, that type of thing. Do you work?'

'No. My days were filled with cleaning the house,' Liz replied bitterly. 'Everything had to be shipshape and perfect. Everything had to be just so.'

Cathy was tempted to add in the words *or else* when Liz stopped. That awkward silence filled the room again.

'How long were you married, Cathy?'

'Sixteen years. Rich died three years ago, when I was thirty-six. He fell down a flight of steps on his way back home from the pub one night and suffered fatal head injuries. Can you believe that? It was so bloody senseless. What about you?'

'We married in 2004. It was the year Chloe was born.'

'I met Rich when I was seventeen. He was my real first boyfriend.' Cathy pointed to a photo in the middle of the notice board. 'That was taken a few years ago, when he was best man at a wedding.'

Liz looked across to see a picture of two people who seemed very much in love. Rich was marginally taller than Cathy and stood proud in a dark three-piece suit. Hazel eyes smiled back at Liz as he posed, Cathy's arm linked through his as they stood in front of the church. Cathy looked striking in a navy blue and cream shift dress and a wide-brimmed hat.

'You look so happy together,' said Liz.

'Oh, we weren't always happy,' Cathy reflected. Then she grinned. 'You need to ask Josie about the goings on at Rich and Cathy Mason's house. Time and time again I'd tell Rich to sling his hook when he'd come home from the pub absolutely blind drunk. He always said he was going out for the last hour, in the days when last orders meant eleven pm on the dot – and he'd always end up late, at some lock-up or another after hours.

'I do miss him still,' Cathy added before silence invaded the room again. 'It was really hard work at times but the more we were together, I suppose, the more it seemed to click.'

'Did the rest of your family like him?'

'I don't have any family. My father left me and my mother when I was six and my mother took to drink. She died when I was sixteen and I was put into a hostel for homeless teens.'

'Oh... I...' Liz sensed she'd put her foot in it again. She quickly changed the subject. 'Josie mentioned that you don't have any children, is that right?'

'Yes, that's right.' Cathy sighed, realising that it was time to stop the questions coming. She always tried to open up to new women so that they felt they could share their stories too. But some things she didn't want to talk about, didn't want to be reminded of either.

'So now that you've learned all there is to know about me,' she said, 'when you're ready to talk, I'm always here to listen. I've seen and heard everything in this house but what is said in these four walls stays in these four walls. You have my word. So if you ever need a shoulder to cry on, someone to rant at or a bit of friendly advice, don't be afraid to ask. I'm only here to listen, not to pass judgement. There are things about my life that aren't so rosy either. I'm sure –'

'I can't believe it's only quarter past seven,' Jess said, barging into the room. She marched across the floor, her dressing gown flying wildly behind her, and pointed at Liz. 'That brat of yours has been snuffling for the past few minutes. She's kept me up half the night as well. Can't you gag her or something?'

'Hey!' Cathy snapped. 'We'll have less of that talk in here. Chloe is entitled to make as much noise as she wants to. Besides, you're seventeen and you make far more noise than young Chloe. You don't hear me complaining now, do you?'

'I'd better go to her,' said Liz, quickly finishing her drink.

'Yes, do.' Jess made a shooing gesture. 'Run along and tend to the young miss before I knock her bleeding head off.'

Cathy watched Jess give Liz an evil glare as she scuttled away.

'You'd better watch your step,' she told her once Liz had gone. 'And if your sleep is so important, where were you until midnight last night?'

'Out.' Jess folded her arms and rested her back against the work top.

'Out where?'

'Oh, for God's sake. It's like being back at school.'

'You know you should be in by eleven.'

'Rules, schmools.'

'They protect you as well as ensuring that you show consideration to others.'

Jess sighed. 'I'm sick of having to do this every time someone new arrives.'

'Then you know what to do about it, don't you?' Cathy challenged.

Later that morning, Liz walked with Chloe along Adam Street heading for the primary school. The weather was overcast and a tiny bit drizzly. She pulled her coat into her chest as it billowed in the wind. Her eyes flitted over the crowd of parents gathered at the school gates, praying that she would spot Kevin if he was there so she could be ready to react. Even though she knew he was on the early shift at work and would most likely be waiting for them in the afternoon, her heart still pounded in her chest. She held on tightly to Chloe's hand.

'Will you be okay on your own today, Mum?' Chloe asked when they arrived at the entrance.

Liz ran a hand over her head. Chloe had a similar shade of mousey hair to her own, the same button nose and chubby cheeks. Unfortunately, Chloe had her dad's deep-set eyes. A constant reminder. They were looking up at her now.

'Of course I will, sweetheart.' She smiled. 'And I'll be here to pick you up as usual. There's nothing to worry about.'

'I could look after you. I'll make you some dinner and lots of cups of tea.'

Liz squatted down to her daughter's level. 'Please don't worry, Chloe,' she said, giving her a reassuring hug. 'I'll be fine and back before you know it.'

Liz waved until Chloe was out of sight. Even then she didn't want to move. She sighed. They would get through this mess, she tried to reassure herself. It was only a matter of time.

'That's a huge sigh,' said a voice by her side.

Liz turned to see Sue Rothbourne standing next to her. She was in her mid-thirties with short, bleached hair, far too much make-up and wearing the Shop&Save uniform of garish green trousers and tunic with matching ballet pumps. Liz saw her often because her daughter, Abby, was one of Chloe's friends.

She tried to muster a smile for her.

'Oh, dear. Rough weekend?'

'You could say that.'

'My two have been playing up all morning,' Sue went on to say. 'I couldn't separate the little buggers from fighting over the free gift in the cereal. I tell you, a piece of red plastic that's supposed to be a dog. I –'

Out of the blue, an arm encircled Liz's waist, warm breath next to her ear. Liz jumped as Kevin kissed her on the cheek.

'Hello, darling,' he smiled icily. 'Sorry I missed you this morning. I didn't realise you had to leave so early.'

43

Liz felt every tiny hair on her neck stand on end. She gasped involuntarily. Aware that Sue was waiting to be introduced, she had to look at him. But not directly in the eye.

'This is my husband, Kevin,' she said, trying to keep the tremble from her voice.

'I'm very pleased to meet you.' Kevin gave Sue that charismatic smile that had worked its magic on Liz all those years ago. 'It's Sue, isn't it?'

Sue ran a hand through her hair and beamed. 'That's right,' she nodded, a little too enthusiastically. 'I'm Abby's mum.'

'Ah.' Kevin nodded in recognition. 'She's a pretty little thing, isn't she, Liz?'

Liz managed to nod back but she needn't have bothered. She watched as Sue's face and neck flushed under Kevin's constant stare. Couldn't she see that he'd read the name from her work badge? That he hadn't got a clue who she was? That he was just using his charm to make her feel special?

After a few seconds of small talk that felt like hours, Liz was left alone with him. Most of the other parents had been and gone: there was only the odd one or two who were still rushing in late.

Kevin grabbed her wrist tightly and swung her round to face him. Liz flinched, still not daring to look him in the eye.

'So, my lovely,' he hissed. 'Where the fuck did you disappear to?'

FOUR

Cathy was in the back garden pegging out a load of washing. She jumped at the sound of the side gate slamming shut violently. When she looked around, Liz was leaning against it. She went over to her as quickly as she could.

'What's the matter?'

Liz stared at her, tears welling in troubled eyes as she fought to catch her breath. 'My husband was waiting for me at Chloe's school. I thought he was on the early shift today. He – he must have been hiding somewhere until Chloe had gone inside. At first he was all nice, like come home babe, we can sort things out.' A sob escaped her. 'But when I said no, he started shouting. He said – he said –'

'Did he hurt you?'

Liz shook her head and sniffed. 'I just didn't expect to see him. I was going to go in and see Chloe's teacher, explain what had happened and see if I could collect her earlier for a few afternoons. I was hoping it would settle her a little bit before I had to deal with him.'

Cathy gently manoeuvred her to a bench at the side of the garden and they both sat down.

'How did you get away?' she asked.

'One of the teachers came out to lock the gates. She took me inside but I could see his car. It was still there twenty minutes later. That's when the secretary gave me a lift home. I had to duck down in the back seat so he couldn't see me.'

'You'll have to face him some time.' Cathy wasn't one to jazz up the future. 'Do you think he'll be there tonight?'

'I'm not sure – most probably, if he hasn't gone to work. I'm picking Chloe up half an hour early. But I'm scared that he'll follow me here afterwards.'

'Don't you worry about that. I've dealt with far worse than him on my doorstep, on numerous occasions. That's why I'm linked up to a twenty-four-hour alarm system. If I have any type of trouble, the police will respond as soon as possible.'

'What if they don't come quick enough?' Liz looked horrified at the thought.

'They've never let me down so far.'

'But they might. They're always going on about it on the television. Most of the time they're too late. And if he follows me here, where will I go then? I don't want to spend my life on the run from him, always having to look over my shoulder.'

Cathy didn't know what to say to that. She knew from past experience that Kevin would probably arrive on her doorstep if not today, then tomorrow or the day after. It was usually during the first week. She always tried to prepare herself for it. Apart from one man who'd held a knife against her throat until she'd told him where his wife was, she'd never had cause to worry. The men were only interested in getting their women away to hurt them again. They didn't want to hurt Cathy, just get past her. But still, she'd stand her ground as always.

46

'How's Becky?' Liz blew her nose on the tissue that Cathy handed to her. 'Have you seen her today?'

'No, she hasn't come out of her room. I'm not sure yet what she's so scared of.'

'I wonder what her background is.'

'She'll tell us in her own time. It usually takes a few days before I can gain their trust. I'll have to watch her with Jess though. Becky doesn't seem very streetwise whereas Jess... But I can only do my best.'

'Why do you do this?' Liz asked, all of a sudden. 'It can't be an easy job, looking after waifs and strays with all the problems that we bring with us.'

'I have my reasons.' Cathy smiled, knowing full well that she wouldn't divulge the real one.

'You could have got a job doing anything.'

'Around here?' Cathy shook her head. 'I enjoy this, most of the time. I get a different challenge every day.'

'Some days are more challenging than others, no doubt,' Liz said, attempting a smile.

'At least I get to work from home. I save a fortune in petrol. Without any shops nearby to tempt me, I don't spend much money. And without having to pay for all the booze and fags that Rich got through, I'm quids in. It works out quite well.'

'But don't you ever get lonely? You're too young to be on your own.'

'Who would have me, with a house full of hormonal women?' Cathy looked up as something caught her eye. Spotting Becky standing in her bedroom window, she waved, but Becky moved out of sight again.

'Thanks for listening,' said Liz. 'I haven't had anyone to talk to for ages.'

'He hit you, didn't he?'

Liz nodded, tears welling again.

'Often?'

Another nod.

Cathy took her hand and gave it a quick squeeze. 'You did the right thing to leave him. Did Chloe ever witness it?'

'No. We kept it away from her.'

Cathy studied Liz's face as she looked away then. Liz had clear skin but prominent dark rings around each eye. Her brown hair, to her shoulders in length, was tied back off her face with a red band. She wore no make-up. Cathy wondered when she'd stopped making the most of herself and whether it was her choice or Kevin's.

'You might want to think about going to some of the courses run at the community house,' Cathy said when Liz looked her way again moments later. 'I'm helping Josie out with those too. She's a fabulous housing officer is our Jose; she has such a way of bringing out the best in people. She's really – oh hi, Jess.'

'Don't speak to me.' Jess slammed the gate and marched up the path.

Cathy wondered if she'd have any gate left by the end of the day. She sighed as she looked down at Jess's bare feet.

'What happened to your shoes?'

'Those bleeding Bradley twins nicked them. Twenty quid I paid for them and they've thrown them into the canal.'

As Jess stood in cut off denim shorts and black footless tights with red painted nails and dirty feet, Cathy wondered where she'd found the money to buy them in the first place.

Then she glanced at Liz, who was trying to keep a straight face.

'Don't laugh at me.' Jess pointed at Liz. 'Especially you. You've only been here five minutes.'

'I've told you already to back off and take your anger out on someone else.' Cathy's tone was sharp.

'What? Like you, you mean?'

Cathy stood up and pushed her gently away. 'Come on, hopalong,' she said, easing her along the path. 'It's not Liz's fault that you go around taunting people all the time.'

'But it wasn't my fault!' Jess protested.

'No,' said Cathy, not believing her for a second. 'It never is.'

From her room, Becky watched Cathy and Jess until they disappeared from sight. She stared down at Liz, wondering why she had turned up here. Why would anyone bring someone as young as Chloe to Cathy's house? They must be running away from something too, she realised all of a sudden. Maybe she wasn't the only one who had a secret. Maybe that's why they were all after somewhere to hide.

Becky couldn't believe she was still free. She couldn't understand why there was no one coming after her: Rebecca Louise Ward wanted for the murder of James Michael Ward. Even though it was nearly two weeks since that awful night, she'd watched *Central News* last night but there hadn't been anything so far about a murder. She'd scanned the local newspaper but they weren't running the story. There wasn't even anything in the small print. Perhaps she was too far away now. Her photograph must have been circulated everywhere but at least she'd had the sense to dump the knife. There was no way she wanted to be found with that. Even so, she didn't dare risk going out yet in case the police were still after her.

Her eyes followed Cathy as she came to sit with Liz again. She'd brought out a tray with biscuits and two hot drinks. Becky longed to go outside and warm herself in the sunny spell they were experiencing but she was stuck in here. Liz could go wherever she wanted. So could Cathy. And Jess. They weren't murderers.

She crashed down on the length of the bed, her eyes flicking around the tiny room. It was barely big enough to hold the single bed, wardrobe and chest of drawers. But then again, what had she to put in the room? What had she to hang up in the wardrobe? She glanced down at the pink T-shirt and black jeans that she was wearing. Cathy had given her two bags of clothes when she'd shown her to her room: apparently they'd been left behind by some other girl.

To alleviate her frustration, she pummelled the mattress over and over.

'What are you doing that for?' A voice came through the half open door. 'If you really want to vent your anger, you need to kick something and damage it.'

Becky looked up to see Jess standing on the threshold.

'How old are you?' she questioned.

'Sixteen.'

'What're you here for?'

'Murder.'

Jess snorted. 'Don't make me laugh. If the force of that punch is anything to go by you haven't got murder in you.'

Becky played with a loose strand of cotton on the hem of the curtains. 'That's what you think.'

Intrigued by the comment, Jess ventured in another step. 'Okay, then. Tell me who you're supposed to have killed.'

'My uncle.'

'What did you do to him?'

'I stabbed him.'

'NO WAY!'

'Yes way.'

'You're lying!'

'Want to try me and find out?'

Becky cursed herself as soon as the words were out. Stupid, stupid cow. The last thing she needed was to bring attention her way. What if Jess went to the police and told them where she was hiding? She'd end up in prison, or worse, on the run again.

'Look,' she said quickly. 'I'll give you something if you'll keep your mouth shut.'

'Like you've got anything that I need!' Jess sat down beside her on the bed. 'You came with nothing, remember?'

Becky disappeared under the bed and pulled out a Nintendo game consol. 'Here. It's worth fifty quid at least.'

Jess laughed. 'You obviously haven't lived on the streets.'

'I have!'

'How long?'

'Eleven days.'

'That's nowt.'

'Well, how long did you live on the streets then?'

Jess looked away. She changed the subject, knowing when she was beat. She'd never even had to sleep rough for one night because of Cathy. She picked up the Nintendo.

'This won't be worth more than a tenner. Where did you get it? Did you lift it?'

'Yes,' Becky lied. If Jess thought she'd stolen it, she wasn't going to confess to finding it underneath the floorboards. She'd caught her foot in the carpet and on closer inspection had come across a hidey-hole. She wondered if it belonged to the girl that she'd heard had been sent to prison.

'Give it to me then.' Jess snatched at it but Becky moved it from her grip just before her hand clasped around it.

'Promise me you won't say anything?'

'Promise.'

Becky handed it to her. Jess glanced at it and stood up quickly.

'Piece of shit this is. I suppose it'll get me a fix or two.'

'You're not meant to sell it!' Becky tried to snatch it back. 'Give it to me, if you don't want it.'

'I didn't say that.' Jess was at the door by now. 'I don't suppose you want to make yourself a few quid by stealing to order?' When Becky looked confused, she continued. 'People tell me what they want, I'll tell you what to nick and give you a fair price for it. It's easy money.'

Becky shook her head. There was no way she was going into town. What if she were spotted by the police?

'You'll soon change your mind. You'll have to find something to do or else Cathy will have you making coffee at the community house every day. Besides, when you've been here for a few days, you'll get fed up of doing nowt.'

'I'm not going out ever again.'

'You can't stay in here forever.'

'What's there to go out for? I'm not getting caught and going to prison. I'd kill myself first.'

'Ooh!' Jess raised her hands and wiggled her fingers. 'Such big talk for such a small person.'

'I'm one metre sixty-five if you must know.'

'Skinny thing though, aren't you?'

'I won't be soon.'

Jess's mouth dropped opened. 'Don't tell me you're up the duff?'

Becky gnawed her bottom lip and looked away.

'Oh, you stupid bitch. Have you never heard of using a condom?'

'Leave me alone,' Becky retorted. 'It's got nothing to do with you anyway.'

'It has if you want me to keep quiet about it.' Jess ran a finger over her top lip. 'What's it worth for me not to tell Cathy? She'll have you out in a flash. You can't stay here if you're preggers. She won't allow it.'

'Then I won't tell her.'

'If you think you can keep that to yourself, you're more stupid than I thought. It's a baby we're talking about not a Nintendo that's been hidden beneath the carpet.'

Becky frowned.

'I knew it was there, you silly cow. I know that hiding place. Me and Cheryl, the last girl who stayed here, were like this.' Jess waved two crossed fingers at her. 'So don't think you're so special.'

'Piss off and leave me alone.' Becky turned her face towards the wall.

Jess grabbed her hair and pulled hard, yanking back her head. 'Don't turn your back on me, you silly cow.'

'Ow! Let me go, you bitch!'

Jess shoved her forward and, as Becky turned, slapped her hard around the face.

'Don't mess with me,' she told her. 'I can make your life very uncomfortable if you don't play ball. So you're either with me or you're not.'

Becky rubbed her cheek to help ease the sting. Oh, God. This was getting worse. All she wanted to do was lay low for a while until she could move on to somewhere better, away from this dump. Resigning herself to her fate, she nodded as Jess continued to stare at her.

'I think you and me need to get to know each other better. We shall go out tonight and have some fun. Be ready for eight and I'll introduce you to some people.'

'I don't want to go out.'

Jess shrugged a shoulder. 'I'm not really bothered what you want to do.'

'But I –' Becky lowered her eyes as Jess glared at her again.

'Tell Cathy that you have a headache and you're going to bed. I'll knock on your door when I'm ready. We'll probably have to shimmy down the drainpipe. Cathy will be watching the front door like a hawk. She'll never suspect that I'll be going out with you though. I should have thought of it sooner.'

Only once she'd heard Jess go running down the stairs, followed by the kitchen door slamming, did Becky fall back on the bed and let the tears fall. How the hell was she going to get out of this one? She couldn't say she was ill because Jess would come into her room and see that she was lying. If she stayed downstairs with Cathy, then she would be for it when she was in on her own. Either way she'd be toast.

There was only one thing to do. She would have to play the game. Be ready for eight o'clock and see where Jess took her. Maybe it would be fun.

Becky cried even harder then. Who was she trying to kid? This was her life now, her nightmare. She would have to toughen up or be eaten alive. She only had herself to rely on.

But that was the thing that scared her the most. She wasn't sure that she *could* rely on herself. Look at the mess she'd landed herself in lately: sixteen-years-old, pregnant and wanted for murder. If Cathy found out that she was up the duff, she'd send her packing and what would happen to her then?

Becky shuddered, the truth too uncomfortable to bear. How the hell was she going to survive this?

'Cathy, are you going to fetch me from school every day now?' Chloe asked as she skipped into the house holding on to her hand.

'Oh, I don't think so, poppet,' Cathy replied. 'I wouldn't have time but I thought I'd make a special effort today. And I've bought you a cake, with lots of strawberry jam and pink icing.'

'Why? It isn't my birthday until next year now. I'll be nine in March. Mum says I can have my ears pierced when I'm nine.'

'I said you *might* be able to have your ears pierced, Chloe,' Liz said, a little sharper than she'd intended.

55

'Emily Baker had hers done last summer,' Chloe continued regardless. 'She's in my class.' She turned to her mum excitedly. 'Mum, Mum, can Emily come for tea at Cathy's? Can she, please?'

Liz was barely listening to her daughter. She was trying to swivel her head 360 degrees to look for Kevin along Christopher Avenue. So far, thankfully, she hadn't seen him. Maybe he had just changed his shift to catch her this morning and was at work now.

'Of course she can come for tea,' Cathy told Chloe. 'You should treat my home like your own. Everyone's welcome, as long as I know in advance.'

A few minutes later, they were inside and out of sight. So Liz didn't see the blue Ford Focus that drove slowly along the adjacent road.

FIVE

Later that evening, Becky agonised over what to wear as she rummaged through the bag of clothes she'd been given. She finally picked out a long-sleeved pale T-shirt with a red love heart emblazoned on the front and a pair of faded jeans that were a bit too long. She wore her own trainers and knew she looked scruffy but what did she care? She didn't want to go out anyway.

A few minutes before eight o' clock, Jess barged into her room. She wore skinny jeans, black heels and a short-sleeved lemon and pale blue checked shirt with a white vest underneath. Her red hair was spiked to perfection.

She took one look at Becky and gasped. 'Jesus Christ, you look like a ten-year-old,' she cried and left just as quickly as she'd arrived. She returned moments later and threw a red top at her. 'Put that on. You've got to look presentable if you're coming out with me.'

Reluctantly, Becky stripped off the blue top and replaced it with the red one. This one was short-sleeved, with a low, sweetheart neckline, and a black skull-and-crossbones emblem sewn on beneath it. Becky reckoned it looked like a designer brand but it could well be off a market stall for all she knew about labels.

Jess looked her up and down, frowning when she spotted her footwear. 'What size shoes do you take?'

'Five.' Jess ran to her room again and came back with a pair of black high heels. 'I can't be seen with you wearing those manky trainers. It would ruin my street cred.'

Becky tried them on as Jess opened the window and took her own shoes off.

'Climb down onto the porch roof. Then use the sill on the window and jump onto the garden. It's easy. I've done it loads of times.'

'In these?' Becky pointed to her feet.

'Dur!' Jess tutted. 'Don't be stupid. Throw them onto the roof like I've just done. Once you get there, throw them onto the grass.'

Jess disappeared and Becky stuck her head out of the window. Seconds later, she watched her jump onto the grass. Seconds after that she joined her, picked up her shoes and sneaked over the back fence into the alley behind.

She glanced around taking in her new surroundings as they reached the main road. Davy Road looked like a row of identical houses, parked cars squashed into every available space alongside the pavements on each side. Some of the gardens were tidy, some unkempt. Some of the properties looked spotless. Then every now and again, a doss hole would reveal itself, mostly hidden behind overgrown hedges, piles of rubbish along the path, yellow netting – or closed curtains that were too small for the window, trying to hide God knows what inside. Still, from what she could see it didn't look as bad as Cathy had mentioned.

'Where are we going?' she asked, more out of nervousness than curiosity.

'You and me are going to get lashed,' Jess told her. 'We'll have to go to Shop&Save first to get some vodka.'

'I haven't got any money. Have you?'

'We don't need money, now, do we?'

Suddenly the penny dropped. Jess wanted her to shoplift.

Becky turned to her in a panic. 'I can't. I nearly got caught there when I first arrived.'

'So? That was ages ago. You'll be okay. Anyway, it's your initiation test to join the gang.'

'What gang?'

'Our gang – you and me.'

Even though the night wasn't too cold, Becky shivered. If she got caught and the police were called, she'd be in big trouble. She pulled away from Jess.

But Jess wasn't happy. 'What's up with you?'

'I'll do time if the police catch me.'

'Don't come on with that tall tale again. The police are no more looking for you than my parents are looking for me and they only live around the bleeding corner.' Jess grabbed her arm and kept a firm hold. 'Come on, it'll be a laugh.'

Minutes later, Becky's heart pounded inside her head as she stood in front of the alcohol shelves inside Shop&Save. Most of the expensive liquor was behind the till, out of their reach. Jess walked up and down the aisle pretending to look for something, really watching the woman behind the till.

'Now!' she whispered loudly as the woman reached for a packet of cigarettes for a young boy who didn't look old enough to smoke. Becky grabbed a bottle of vodka and shoved it under her top. She held it in place with her arm by her side and moved away quickly.

'Have you got any cheese and onion crisps?' Jess shouted.

Heart beating fit to burst now, Becky made her escape as the woman showed Jess where they were. She walked out of the shop and across the car park, faster and faster, not looking back until she'd crossed over Davy Road again.

'Hey! Wait up!' Jess joined her a minute later. She took the bottle and swigged a huge mouthful, then passed it to Becky. Becky did the same but coughed at the burning sensation in her throat.

Jess eyed her suspiciously as she wiped her mouth. 'Don't tell me you've never got bladdered before,' she questioned.

'Of course I have,' Becky lied. Apart from cans of lager, there had never been any alcohol in her house. Her dad was always at the pub so there was no need to buy anything stronger. Trying to hide her naivety, she knocked back another large amount, trying not to choke this time. 'What shall we do now?' she asked.

Jess checked her watch. 'We're meeting Danny Bradley in fifteen minutes. I said I'd be here about nine. He's coming to pick me up.'

'Is he your boyfriend?'

'I wish.' Jess urged Becky to drink some more vodka. 'He's not interested in me. I'm too young. He says he likes his ladies to be more, how shall I put it, experienced. I told him I'd had experience but he meant experience that comes with age, I suppose. I've given him the odd blow job but that's all he's interested in. I'll keep on trying though. He's gorgeous. You can see for yourself soon.'

'Does he have any friends?' Becky asked. It was a valid question: she'd be lonely if Jess was to cop off with Danny. And already she was starting to feel a bit queasy. She wondered if she could get him to drop her off back at Cathy's.

Jess laughed. 'None that would be interested in a virgin like you.'

Becky lowered her eyes. It looked like Jess didn't believe that she was pregnant.

Both girls turned as a car peeped its horn and came screeching to a halt inches from the kerb at the side of them. An electric window dropped down. Jess moved forward and Becky followed, intrigued to see who had captured Jess's heart.

'Hey, Danny,' Jess smiled, pushing her chest out as she leaned on the car door. 'Feel like a good time tonight?'

'What're you drinking?' he asked.

'Voddie.' Jess threw a thumb over her shoulder. 'The new girl lifted it. Want some?'

'I've got my own stash.' Danny flapped his fingers. 'Move out of the way; let me have a look at her then.'

Jess huffed but did as she was told. She pulled Becky nearer. Becky practically fell through the window with the force.

There were two men in the car. The passenger was about eighteen, with a skinhead and a bad case of acne which was just as well because Becky couldn't take her eyes off the driver. His hair was cut short and he sported a goatee beard. His skin was olive, his eyes as dark as the moodiness he was trying to portray. As he smiled, Becky noticed that one of his front teeth was chipped. She felt her cheeks burning as he stared at her. She also felt Jess's eyes boring into the back of her head.

Suddenly she was pushed aside. Jess ran a hand across the paintwork of the car. 'Nice motor you've thieved.' She leaned further forward this time. 'Where're you off to?'

'Around.' Danny revved the engine. 'Are you getting in or not?'

Jess didn't need to be asked twice. She opened the back door and slid along the seat. Becky followed suit but Danny turned, his hand on the back of the seat in front.

'Not you, lovely one. You can sit in the front with me. Parksy, shift your arse into the back.'

Cathy flicked on the kettle and glanced at her watch again. It only revealed what she already knew since she'd looked at it a minute earlier. It was twenty minutes past eleven. She'd swing for Jess when she finally came home.

Why hadn't she thought to check on Becky before half past nine? She'd knocked twice with no reply either time before going in on the third. When she had found the room empty, she had checked the window. Behind the curtain was the tell tale magazine. It was an old trick of Jess's so that the window looked shut but could in fact be pulled up on her return. She thought she could sneak in as if she'd been there all along. How stupid did Jess think she was?

Cathy had been on tenterhooks ever since. Where would Jess take Becky? And would she keep her out all night? She wouldn't put it past her to try and get Becky into trouble straight away. And why had they sneaked out in the first instance? Yes, she would have lectured them if they had gone out the front way but she wouldn't have stopped them.

She had no right to do that even if she wanted to. Despite what had been thrown at her over the past three years, she was no one's keeper.

Aware that she wasn't going to settle until she knew they were home safe and sound, she parted the curtains and stood staring out into the street. Across from her was her friend, Rose's, house. The house was all in darkness: Rose was in Kos for a fortnight. She'd been gone for ten days of the two weeks that she would be away. Already, Cathy missed her so much. She'd been the first person Rose had met when she'd moved here with her husband, Arthur. She and Rich had been messing about in the street after a heavy snowfall as the other couple were moving into Christopher Avenue. Seeing Rose and Arthur struggling with a double bed, they'd rushed over to help. Rose had extracted the estate's gossip from Cathy during the next few minutes and a loyal friendship had begun. Twenty-six years her senior, Rose had become the mother Cathy had always wanted. She dreaded the day when anything happened to her. Trust her to be away now when she needed calming down. Still, she'd be back in three days with a deep tan and a large bottle of Bacardi for her.

Cathy hadn't really known her mother, Carole. Even before her father had left them when she was six, she'd learned to fend for herself. School was only two streets away, no main roads to negotiate, so she was capable of making the short journey alone. She made jam sandwiches for her lunch, soup for tea, then oven chips and fish fingers as she got older. Her clothes were always shabby, always worn that extra day before they were washed. Socks were grey, shoes were scuffed and she was teased for it at school.

Reeking Riley she was called by the kids in her year. By the time she was ten, she was known as the quiet one.

As the years went on, Cathy managed to look after herself more. It became routine to get up early, clean the house, leave her mother in bed while she went to school. Afterwards, she would wash and iron and cook tea before starting on her homework. If Carole was home for her return, she'd more than likely be sleeping off a hangover before going out again. Carole Riley turned to drink to blot out her non-existent life and her daughter turned into herself to block out hers.

After the third spell in hospital, Carole's liver failed. Cathy was sixteen when her mother took her last breath. The housing association claimed their house back and moved her into a block set up for homeless teenagers on the Mitchell Estate. The rooms were filled with girls, two in each. A woman in the flat downstairs was meant to look out for them. She was a type of warden, if Cathy remembered rightly, but she didn't do a very good job of things. Still, it was here that she met Tina Unwin.

Tina Unwin told Cathy she was only intending on staying for a few weeks until she got her life sorted. But five months later, she was still there. Cathy settled in too and they became friends instantly, which she really enjoyed. It was nice to have someone to laugh with, cry with, come home to and care for even. Yet in some ways, they were the worst months of Cathy's life. It could be quite rowdy at the block. Cathy learned to fight to defend her few possessions. There was a huge turnover of tenants so there were always ructions as another girl moved in and tried her luck in becoming top of the pile. She'd been there for six months when she met

Rich. Rich Mason was nineteen and one of the Mitchell Estate's notorious scallies. He was known for getting his own way. He would fight for it, steal for it. Some people said he would kill for it, but Cathy never saw that in him.

Three months later, when Tina decided to try her luck with a guy she'd met in Preston, Cathy moved in with Rich and life had been good for a few months. Until he'd been sent to prison for three years for robbery. She was evicted from his place and had gone off the rails but they'd still kept in touch. When he came out of prison after serving just over two years of his sentence, they hooked up again and married a year later. And in all that time, she'd never told him that she'd had a baby and given it up for adoption. It had been one of the worst decisions she'd ever made and even now, when she found herself alone, she'd often wonder what could have been if things had turned out differently.

She sighed loudly and glanced up the street again but there was nothing. She wondered what was worse: having her own children to worry about or having someone else's.

At half past eleven, Becky held on to Jess for dear life as she negotiated her way up Christopher Avenue.

'Watch out, you stupid cow!' Jess said for the umpteenth time as Becky fell forward, taking her along too. She fell to the pavement, grazing her knee on the kerb. 'Ow. Anyone would think you've never had a drink before.'

Becky dropped with a thump too. 'I can't go any further,' she slurred. 'I don't feel very well.'

'Oh, God.' Jess took a step away. 'Not more puke. I'm never going to look Danny Bradley in the eye EVER again. You made a right mess of the car. It's a good job he dumped it.' She laughed. 'I bet the owner wouldn't want it back. Do you think they'll catch you because of your DNA in the spew?'

Becky threw up. Then she began to cry.

'Jesus Christ,' Jess moaned. 'I can't believe you have anything else left in you.'

A window opened across the road. 'Will you two shut your bloody mouths and get off home. Some of us are trying to sleep!'

Jess turned and raised her middle finger. 'Wind your neck in, Archie Meredith,' she shouted. 'Weren't you ever young, free and single? Why don't you get a life?'

'Why don't you get a job, you scrounging cow? I work a ten-hour shift to pay for the likes of you to lie in bed all day and get pissed every night.'

'Ooh, chill out fat bastard and cop a load of this.' Jess pulled up her top and flashed her bra. 'There you go. Think of me while you get yourself off.'

'Jess!' Cathy whispered loudly as she walked up to them. 'That's enough!' She placed a hand on Becky's back. 'Where the hell have you two been?'

'Don't... feel... very well,' Becky managed to slur. 'My head's spinning.'

'She's such a light-weight,' said Jess. 'I wish I'd never bothered with her.'

'You shouldn't have taken her out at all,' Cathy hissed.

'She's making all the noise, not me.' Jess was unaware that she was shouting too.

'Move them on, Cathy, or I'll ring the association tomorrow,' a voice yelled across again.

'I'm doing my best, Archie,' Cathy replied. 'Go in and I'll deal with them.'

'Yeah,' shouted Jess. 'Run along to wifey.'

'Enough, Jess!' said Cathy. 'Will you get in the house, right now!'

Jess staggered a few steps further. 'Okay, okay,' she muttered. 'I'm going. You can bring cheap-date along. I can't believe she can't take her ale. She's sixteen.'

'And you're seventeen. Neither of you should be drinking yet!'

Cathy pulled Becky up onto her feet. But Becky wasn't co-operating. She dropped to the floor again.

'I can't,' she sobbed.

'Yes, you can.'

'No, I…'

Cathy pulled on Becky's arm, trying to coax her up on her feet. 'You'll have to help me, Jess,' she said.

'Who do you think I am?' Jess marched off as quickly as she could. 'I'm not her bleeding babysitter.'

Cathy sighed and struggled with Becky on her own. 'Come on,' she encouraged as they made it to the gate. 'Nearly there.'

'I'm sorry.' Becky was crying loudly now. 'I didn't mean to get into trouble. I've never dr–drunk vodka before.'

Cathy finally got her into the house, closing the front door behind her with a sigh. She guided her up the stairs and into her bedroom, all the time wondering if she would get a phone call or a letter from the housing association. She hadn't had either for a while so it was bound to happen soon. Not all of the residents in Christopher Avenue were thrilled about Cathy helping out young girls in trouble.

She pushed open the bedroom door and Becky collapsed on top of her bed. Cathy took off her shoes, pulled the duvet from underneath her and covered her up. She ran a hand over Becky's forehead. The poor child was white, her lips dry. Mascara ran in lines down her cheeks; red lipstick was smeared around her mouth. She watched her for a few moments before heading back out of the room. One thing was certain: she'd be having words with both of them in the morning.

She'd reached the door when Becky screamed.

'Don't leave me! I feel sick again.'

Cathy sighed loudly, wondering if she'd ever get to bed that night. 'You need to calm down, Becky. You'll be fine once you've slept it off.'

'No... I...' Becky suddenly sat upright, a look of horror contorting her face. 'My baby! Oh, God, I've killed my baby again!'

Cathy froze. Did she just say – oh no. Please, not that.

'Lie down,' she told her, 'and get some sleep.'

'But my baby! Have I hurt my baby?'

As Becky sobbed uncontrollably, Cathy held her close. Knowing that she'd been in a similar position herself, memories tried to come flooding back but she pushed them away, back to the depths of her mind.

She didn't need reminders. She lived through the pain every day – just as Becky would if she decided not to keep her baby too.

SIX

Cathy had just drifted off to sleep when she was awoken by a loud noise. She listened: there was someone banging at the front door. In her experience it could mean only one thing. She flicked on the light. For Christ's sake: it was two am.

'Liz!' Another bang. 'Liz! Get down here now.'

Cathy flung her bedroom window open and peered down. 'Will you stop making that bleeding racket!' she whispered loudly. 'It's Kevin, isn't it?'

'So what if it is?'

'She doesn't want to see you.'

'Well, I want to see her.' Kevin peered up. 'And who the fuck are you? Where's my daughter? CHLOE!'

'Be quiet or else you'll have the whole street awake!' From her position up high, Cathy could see exactly how Kevin McIntyre could intimidate his wife. He was tall, broad and very capable of his bad boy role, his angry temperament ready to take on the world. In his drunken rage, he was neither attractive nor unsightly, just plain old nasty.

'I don't give a stuff if I wake up the whole frigging universe! Liz! LIZ!'

'Will you lot ever shut UP!' The window opened across the street again. 'I've got to get up at five thirty. At this rate, it won't be worth going back to sleep.'

'Mind your own business, you nosy bastard!' Kevin yelled across to Archie Meredith. 'I'm staying here until I see my wife. LIZ!'

'I'm warning you, Cathy. I'll be on the blower tomorrow. I'm sick of this every bloody night.'

'Look, Archie. I –'

'Piss off, you wanker!' Kevin shouted and then turned back to Cathy. 'Tell her to come down or I'll kick the fucking door in.'

'Come back in the morning when it's light and you're sober.'

But Kevin wasn't going anywhere. He pulled back his head and yelled.

'LIZ!'

'I'll have to go down to him. He won't let up until I do.'

Cathy turned to see Liz standing in her pyjamas, a cardigan clutched tightly around her middle.

'No, he's really drunk at the moment. Maybe you'd be better speaking to him tomorrow, when he's calmed down.'

Liz shook her head, close to tears. 'He knows where I am now. He won't give up until he's seen me. And I don't want to get Chloe upset. She's still asleep but she won't be if he carries on.'

Cathy threw on her dressing gown. 'I'm coming down with you but you're not to open the door.'

'But –'

'You know full well what he's capable of. Don't give him the chance.'

'But if I don't see him now, he'll come back again and again. Then where will I go?'

'I've told you, you can stay here for as long as you want. I've dealt with his kind before and –'

Kevin shouted through the letterbox, making them both jump. 'I know you're in there. I just want to talk.'

Before Cathy could stop her, Liz was down the stairs and opening the door the inch the chain allowed.

'Liz! Wait!'

She followed quickly behind to see the door shooting out of her hands as Kevin kicked it hard. He grabbed Liz by the throat and slammed her up against the wall.

'You bitch!' he seethed. 'You can't fucking leave me!'

Liz put her hands over his, trying to loosen his grip. 'Stop it!'

'Let her go!' Cathy grabbed the hockey stick that she kept behind the door and whacked it across the back of his knees.

Kevin's legs buckled and he sank to the floor, letting go of Liz.

'You mad bitch!' he cried.

Liz gasped for air.

Cathy stood with the stick poised to strike again. 'Just thought you'd like a taste of your own medicine. It hurts, doesn't it?'

Kevin stepped towards her but Cathy stood her ground.

'Come any nearer and I'll use it again,' she warned. 'You can't control me like you've controlled her.'

Kevin rushed towards Cathy and she swung the stick again, this time cracking him on his shoulder.

Liz stood rigid, her back against the wall as she watched Kevin stumble. She stared at Cathy in awe. Where the hell did she get her strength?

'Are you going or am I calling the police?' Cathy addressed Kevin, again poised to strike with the stick.

Kevin used the banister to pull himself upright. 'I'm going,' he said, rubbing at his shoulder. 'But I'm warning *you*,' he shot round to look at Liz, 'I'll be back and when I do I'm not leaving without you or my daughter. You have no right to take her from me.'

'I have every right!' Liz screamed suddenly in a rush of adrenaline. 'I won't let you see her.'

Kevin smirked nastily. 'You can't watch me every minute of the day.' In a flash, he grabbed Liz's arm.

'Mummy!' They all looked up to see Chloe. She was sitting on the landing, her arms wrapped around her knees. Tears were pouring down her face.

Kevin hid his anger towards Liz in an instant and smiled. 'Chloe! Come down here and give your dad a kiss.'

Chloe shook her head fervently, her eyes squeezed shut.

Liz pushed past Kevin and ran up the stairs. 'Please leave us alone,' she said as she took Chloe into her arms. 'Look at what you're doing to her. She's so traumatised by what's happened that she's having nightmares.'

Kevin raised his arms in exasperation. 'I'm going,' he said. 'But I will be back. You can count on that.'

'I wouldn't count on anything,' Cathy retorted. She held open the front door. 'Time to leave, I think.'

Twenty minutes later, after checking again on Becky, Cathy lay in her bed, wondering if that would be the last time she'd have to get up tonight. What a week, and it wasn't over yet. Thank God it was Thursday tomorrow. There was nothing more grounding than a visit to the cemetery. Maybe she should take Jess and Becky with her, she thought as she turned over. If they continued to behave as they had done tonight, either one of them could be joining her husband six feet under.

She switched off the bedside lamp and lay awake in the darkness, relishing the silence. The room was lit by a pale glow from the lamppost outside the bedroom window. It gave everything an eerie glow but she didn't care. All she wanted to do was sleep.

Despite the nocturnal goings on, Cathy was still up at six thirty the following morning. She frowned when she spotted a letter on the mat inside the front door. It was too early for their postman to have completed his round.

As she drew nearer, she noticed it was an envelope. She turned it to both sides but it was blank. Inside, a note was written on white paper with blue lines, the kind found in any newsagents or stationery shop. The message was clear and simple, written in capital letters.

'I AM WATCHING YOU'

Cathy frowned again: just four words but with a hell of a meaning behind them. She wondered how long it would be before Kevin McIntyre would give up the fight. In her experience, some men didn't bother coming after their women at all. Some caused trouble for a few nights. Very occasionally it took longer, involving the police and intervention from the courts. She had a gut feeling that this was going to be a long drawn-out affair and decided to hide the note for now. She lodged it inside her diary and pushed it to the back of the kitchen drawer. It wouldn't be wise to let Liz see it yet: she'd been through enough last night.

Another hour later when she heard floorboards creaking upstairs, Cathy left for the cemetery. She wanted to be alone with her thoughts before drowning in everyone else's, once their days started and they unburdened their problems onto her.

But the quiet roads gave her more time to think about last night. She couldn't stop seeing the anger on Kevin's face as he had his hands around Liz's neck. Equally, she couldn't rid herself of Liz's sheer look of terror.

Finally, she arrived at the church and parked up. Emerging into the graveyard, she breathed in the unmistakeable smell of freshly cut grass. It had become customary for her to count the rows as she walked slowly along the pathway, turning right at number seven. Rich had been laid to rest in the sixth grave along.

'It's another lovely day, Rich,' she spoke aloud with no awkwardness. 'We're having quite a run of them for April.' She dropped to her knees in front of the gravestone, cleared away last week's flowers from the base, rinsed out the steel water holder and carefully arranged the fresh blooms in their place, all the time chattering on.

'We've got a really lively bunch in the house right now,' she added. 'I'm beginning to feel nearer to sixty years of age than forty – I'll be grey before my time at this rate with all the worry. Still, I must admit I was feeling low when Cheryl got sent down – you remember, she got six months – but now it seems I might have bitten off more than I can chew. Becky is barely sixteen, and do you know what she told me last night? She's pregnant! Then there's Liz. She has a daughter Chloe, who's only eight. She's such a quiet little girl. Her father has been handy with his fists. I don't know all of the details – I don't want to know them really – but I have to be there to listen if needs be, don't I? And sometimes that means asking awkward questions, but still. I suspect he's been hitting Liz for a long time, the bastard.' She paused for a moment before grinning. 'I gave him a good seeing to last night. No one messes with Cathy Mason, now do they?'

Her thoughts out in the open, Cathy kneeled for a while in the peaceful surroundings. Looking around, she noticed quite a few people now. A couple with a baby in a pram walked past and she smiled at them. How she wished she were still part of a couple.

As the light wind played around with her hair, it almost seemed as if Rich was standing right beside her. She often turned her head expecting him to be there; expecting him to reach out and place a hand on her shoulder. Cathy wished she could talk to him just one more time, so he could tell her that everything was all right – that what she'd done was only to protect him. Only Rich could put her mind at ease. After all, there were no secrets between them now.

Half an hour later, Cathy stood up. She raised her hand to her lips, kissed her fingertips and gently touched the top of his headstone.

'I'd better be getting back and see what those girls have to say for themselves about last night's escapades. Wish me luck. I have a feeling I'm going to need it.'

SEVEN

It was half past ten when Becky showed her face later that morning. She sat down at the kitchen table across from Cathy and Liz. After a lot of thought on the matter, Cathy had decided to give her a second chance. It had been her first night after all and she knew Becky was only partly to blame.

'You look a little green,' she said. 'Are you okay?'

Becky nodded. 'Sorry.'

'You should have told me you were going out.'

'I forgot.'

'And have you forgotten now that you had a drink? And that I had to put you to bed because you could barely stand up?'

'I told Jess that I'd drunk vodka before and I hadn't.' Becky began to pick at the raffia placemat on the table. 'It wasn't her fault.'

Cathy raised her eyebrows. 'And how long did it take you to think of that when you woke up this morning? I know Jess put you up to it. The one thing I can't fathom out is why you did it. You have a tongue in your head. You should have told her to back off if you didn't want to go out. Or you should have come to me.'

The room descended into an awkward silence, except for

the sound from the small television over on the far wall. Liz pointed at it as the news came on.

'I knew he was guilty,' she said. 'He has the look of a serial killer. I'd love to get my hands on him. What he did to those –'

At the mention of killer, Becky burst into tears.

'What's the matter?' Cathy tried again to get her to talk. 'There's obviously something troubling you and the sooner you get it out into the open the better, don't you think?'

'Oh, you mean the baby?'

'Baby?' Liz paled. 'Oh my god. You're not pregnant?'

'Is that what I told you last night?' Becky wanted to know.

'Was there something else that you might have meant?' asked Cathy.

Becky gulped. 'Oh, God, I... I –'

'Whatever is going on inside that screwed up head of yours, you shouldn't be drinking if you're pregnant!' Liz raised her voice. 'How irresponsible can you be? Do you know the damage that you could cause to an –'

'That's enough, Liz,' Cathy tried to calm her, slightly alarmed at her outburst.

'No, it isn't! You might have to be soft with her but I don't. I can't believe –'

'I said that's enough! If you can't find anything constructive to say, then I think you should leave and let me speak to Becky in private.'

'Fine,' Liz snapped and left the room without another word.

Once she'd gone, they sat in silence. Becky's tears had stopped but she looked scared to death about something.

And if Cathy's instinct was right, it was more than the baby.

'Do you want to tell me about it yet?' Cathy coaxed her gently a few minutes later.

'About the baby?'

'About anything really.'

'I think I'm three months gone.'

'Right. And does the father know?'

Becky shook her head.

'Are you going to tell him?'

Becky shook her head again.

'Is that why you ran away?' As Becky went to shake her head for the third time, Cathy intervened. 'This needs to be a two-way conversation. You can't keep hiding behind the fact that I don't know anything about your background. You have to trust me or there's nothing I can do for you.'

Another silence.

'The housing association will find you a placement soon. If you work with me, I can let you stay here until you find your feet. But you have to let me know what's happened to you or else I won't be able to fight your corner.'

'I don't know who the father is,' Becky said at last.

'You don't know because you've been sleeping around or you don't know because you're afraid to tell me who it really is?'

'I don't sleep around.'

Another silence.

'So was it only the once?'

'No.'

'Was it someone that you know from school?'

Becky shook her head.

Cathy could feel her frustration building up. Why

wouldn't she tell her? Then a hideous thought struck her.

'Becky, someone didn't force you to have sex, did they? I know some boys can be frisky but you have a right to say no. And if you did say no and he continued, then that's a different matter entirely.'

Becky wondered whether she should confide in Cathy. She hadn't heard anything on the news so maybe she hadn't killed her uncle after all. But she wasn't sure she wanted to divulge that much information. Would Cathy keep it to herself if she did tell her? Murder, or even stabbing if she hadn't killed him, still came with a hefty sentence. She had maimed someone: it wouldn't matter what he had done to her.

'Have you decided whether or not you want to have the baby?' Cathy tried another approach when Becky froze up again.

'Cathy,' Becky leaned forwards suddenly, 'will you promise to keep it to yourself if I tell you a secret?'

'That secret had better not be about me,' Jess snapped as she barged into the room. She reached for a mug before turning back to Becky with a look that said 'just you dare say anything'.

'Can you leave us for a few minutes?' Cathy asked calmly. 'We're having a private conversation. It won't take us long to finish.'

'I'm entitled to get a cup of coffee. And besides, I had a good long chat with Becky last night. I know her secret too.'

'You do?' Cathy frowned, knowing that this could be dangerous.

'Yeah. So anything that's being said can be said in front of me, now can't it?'

Becky could feel the hate emanating from Jess. She sat on her hands to stop them shaking, hoping that she hadn't told her everything when she was drunk.

'I'm never going to drink again,' she said quietly.

'Which brings me to my next question,' said Cathy. 'And if you did know Becky's secret, I'm appalled at you, Jess, for letting her get into that state. Why did you sneak out last night? I specifically told you to leave Becky alone but you couldn't resist, could you?'

'It wasn't my fault! Did she say it was my fault?'

'Actually, she didn't. But I'm not stupid. I won't let you have your own way. I told you the other day to watch yourself or else.'

'God, you're worse than my bleeding mother at times.' Jess banged down the mug noisily.

'Where did you get the money for alcohol? I didn't know that you had any.'

'Look, I'm sorry, all right! I messed up. I shouldn't have taken Becky out with me, but believe me, it won't happen again. I can't stand snitches.'

'I didn't snitch!' said Becky.

'You must have. She knows far too much.' Jess walked off.

'Sit down,' said Cathy.

'No, I'm not staying for another bloody table meeting.'

'I said sit down!'

Jess dropped heavily into the seat and folded her arms.

'You are not going to take advantage of Becky now that she's come to stay,' Cathy said once she had Jess's attention again. 'I have a duty of care towards her, just as much as I do to you and I will not tolerate any late night escapades.'

'Yeah, yeah. I hear you.'

'I mean it, Jess. If Archie Meredith gets onto Josie, I'll be in trouble. So I want you in at eleven for the next two weeks – even weekends.'

'But –'

'No buts. Eleven o'clock or it's back to your mum's. I need Chloe to settle as well as Becky so I can't have you thinking that you can come and go as you please. I have my livelihood to think of too. I don't want any more nights like last night.'

'But we weren't the only ones making a racket,' Jess retorted angrily. 'I heard that man shouting for Liz. He made as much noise as us.'

'I know he did and I can deal with that. But this is about you. Both of you. Is that clear?'

Becky nodded straightaway. Cathy continued to glare at Jess until she gave in and nodded too.

'Can I go now?' she snapped, standing up again.

'Yes. And try stopping off at The Academy,' Cathy shouted after her. 'At least make an effort to look like you want to do something.' She turned back to Becky. 'Right, where were we? Weren't you just about to tell me something?'

'It doesn't matter.' Becky clammed up. 'What's The Academy?'

'It's a community college we have on the estate. It might be useful for you to pop in there if you're sticking around.'

'Is it okay if I go back to my room now?'

Cathy watched her forlorn figure as she left. She sighed into the empty room. What was eating at her? Becky seemed to be worried about something far more than the fact that she was pregnant, as if that wasn't enough. Ever since she'd arrived, Cathy had wondered why no one was looking for her. Someone should be missing her. Or else they didn't want anyone knowing that she was gone. Whatever it was, she vowed to get to the bottom of it before too long. Secrets destroyed the soul: she should know.

She stood up and gathered together the dishes. Then she smirked. What had she been saying to Rich earlier? My, she had a happy house now: Liz was probably sulking after her outburst, Becky would be wondering if she should have said more and Jess wouldn't give a stuff if she'd said too much!

Women, Cathy thought. All of us are different, yet in a way we're all the same.

EIGHT

Later that morning, Cathy's day suddenly became a whole lot brighter.

'Yoo-hoo!' a voice shouted through the open back door. 'I'm home. Have you missed me?'

'Like a hole in the head,' Cathy teased Rose, giving her friend a hug. 'Oh, it's so good to see you.'

'I hear you've been having a few late nights?' Rose sat down at the table.

'Moaning Archie Meredith got to you already, then?'

'He couldn't wait. I'd hardly set foot out of the taxi and he was across the road harping on at me. It's not me you want to moan at I told him.'

'I know, I know. It's all my fault.'

'I told him that too but he wouldn't listen.'

'You should stick up for me.' Cathy nudged Rose as she sat down next to her. But she was smiling. Just the sight of her friend had made her feel contented again. It had been a hard two weeks without her. Cathy felt she could get through most things if Rose was around. She would always listen to her. She'd tell her when she'd been too lenient: she'd tell her when she'd been too stern. And it was these things that Cathy always needed to hear, that made their friendship so special. Rose was her rock.

Rose Clarke was sixty-five years old yet looked at least

ten years younger. She would never let herself be known as one of 'those pensioners that looks twenty years older than they are', and took great care with her appearance. She had short, white-grey hair, blue eyes framed with trendy, red-rimmed glasses, not an ounce of extra flab around her tiny frame and never a cigarette past her lips. She wore the simplest of make-up, most of it unseen on tanned skin at the moment, with a white T-shirt and cream linen trousers, despite today's rainy weather.

'Come on then, spill the beans,' she urged Cathy. 'What's been going on since I left to go to sunnier shores?'

'It's been eighty degrees here every day,' Cathy fibbed.

Rose flapped a hand in the air. 'Ha-ha. At least I got to wear my bikini over there. Can you imagine old Mr Percy next door if I wore it here in summer? He'd have a heart attack if he saw me with everything hanging out.'

'Everyone would have a heart attack if you had those out on display.' Cathy pointed to Rose's chest. 'I mean, look at them. They're huge.'

'You're only jealous,' said Rose smugly.

'I am indeed.' Cathy looked down at her less significant chest with resignation.

'Have you seen anything of Alan this week?' Rose asked when she'd caught up with everything. Alan was the new community warden over at Hardman Court, a sheltered housing block for the elderly. Thinking he was perfect for Cathy, Rose had accosted him, asking him to do a few odd jobs for her friend. So far Cathy hadn't been tempted, no matter how hard Rose tried to encourage her.

Cathy shook her head. 'Not since he fixed the lock on my door when Liz's husband kicked it in. Why?'

'Oh, nothing.'

'Rose!' Cathy chided. 'Give over!'

'Oh, come off it. He fancies the pants off you. And from what's been going on here, you sound like you need some fun. A good snog will do you the world of good.'

'As the saying goes, Rose, I'm just not into him.'

'You'll never be into anyone if I don't encourage you.'

'Look,' Cathy tried to appease her. 'I promise you'll be the first to know when I meet the right man.'

'And when will that be? You hardly ever go out: you're tied to this house. It's not good, you know.'

Cathy raised her hands in mock surrender. 'Ten minutes you've been back and already you're giving me grief.'

Rose reached across to squeeze her hand. 'It's for your own good. I don't like to see a young, beautiful woman like you all by herself.' She laughed then. 'I still can't believe you hit that man with your hockey stick. You haven't used that in a good while.'

'No one messes with Cathy Mason.' Cathy grinned.

'What do you plan to do about Becky?' Rose asked moments later.

'About the baby you mean? She can't stay here if she decides to have it – which is a shame as I'd like to help her.'

'You'd like to help everyone.'

'She's vulnerable, Rose, not hard-hearted like Jess. I don't know what life has thrown her way but I suspect something terrible happened to her. I just wish she'd open up and let it all out. I think she'd feel better if she could. But then again, that doesn't always work in my favour, does it?'

'What happened wasn't your fault,' Rose was quick to reassure her. 'You can't help everyone, especially the

Cheryl Morton's of this world.'

Cathy knew Rose was right. Cheryl had been sent to prison for six months for possession of drugs and soliciting. Cathy had tried to help her clean up on numerous occasions. Cheryl would be okay for a few days, weeks sometimes, but the slightest thing would trigger her off and she would go into self-destruct mode. This was her second spell inside, even though she'd insisted that she'd never go back after the first time.

'I'd rather have her here causing chaos than in a prison cell,' said Cathy.

'Cheryl is a liability. Some people you just can't help and she's one of them. She'll be out soon anyway. Do you think she'll come back to see you?'

Cathy shrugged. 'Part of me would love to see her. Part of me would rue the day. She made me so ill, worrying like that. She's such a live wire.'

'She's wired up, more like,' said Rose.

'I know but she's still a kid.'

'A kid with a record now.'

'I warned her so many times.'

'And it always fell on deaf ears. Stop worrying.'

Cathy knew she should but sometimes she couldn't help herself. She felt responsible for the girls put in her charge. She didn't want to let them down.

She smiled then. 'It's so good to see you again, Rose. I haven't half missed you.'

'You mean you've missed my shoulder to cry on. I don't know how you do it. It would drive me batty.'

'You already are batty, my friend,' Cathy taunted.

Austin lit a cigarette and took a deep drag of it. He glanced up and down the road again before checking his watch. Twenty to one: Danny Bradley was late. Still, if it meant a free lift, he'd give him another ten minutes before he left.

It had worked out well for him hooking up with Danny. He'd met him at the dole office as he'd registered for benefits. Danny had been mouthing off while they'd both filled in another set of forms. Austin had liked his attitude enough to start a conversation. Over the past few days, Danny had become his unofficial driver. The more he saw of him, the more he realised that the youth was in awe of him. And why? Because he liked the sound of his background. Danny couldn't work out the peppered truths from within Austin's elaborate lies. It was the one thing he enjoyed about sleeping rough. No matter which town he turned up in, he could be whoever he wanted to be.

A car horn peeped. He looked up and Danny flashed the lights on a clapped out Vauxhall Astra. He hid his look of contempt well as he climbed into the passenger seat with a yank of a stiff door handle.

'All right, mate?' Danny nodded.

Austin nodded back. 'Surely you haven't nicked this?' Before he got in, he pushed aside empty cigarette cartons, crisp packets and cans of lager so that there was somewhere to put his feet.

Danny patted the steering wheel. 'This heap is all mine. I use it when I can't be arsed to get anything else. And I've lifted a twenty off the old lady so I've filled her up a little. What's the plan for today?'

Austin frowned, annoyed that Danny expected to spend

time with him for the honour of being his driver. He swallowed down the words ready to spew out of his mouth. He needed to keep Danny on side, for a little while at least.

'No plan,' he said.

They turned off Alexander Avenue and onto Winston Road. Austin stared at the properties they passed.

'You robbed any of these doss holes?' he asked.

Danny changed gear noisily before replying. 'No, don't tend to shit on my own doorstep. I go on to the private estate – far more for the taking there. I do have a fence on here though, Mick Wilkinson. He takes most things from me.'

Austin made a mental note to find out more about Mick Wilkinson and his outfit. It might be worth his while to get involved with some of the locals, though if everything went to plan he'd have to scarper pretty quickly afterwards.

Danny sped up as a young girl tottered across the road in front of them. Austin sniggered. Her shoes were too high for her, unintentionally making her wiggle provocatively.

'Hey, Becky,' Danny shouted to her as he drew level. 'Fancy a ride and I don't mean of the motor?'

Becky stuck two fingers up to him.

Danny laughed. 'What a cracker, and so ripe.'

Austin watched as Becky continued on her way. She didn't seem much older than sixteen or so with her blonde hair tied away from her face. When she turned back and saw them still looking, she pulled up the collar of her denim jacket to conceal her face. Austin frowned: she seemed like she was hiding something – or hiding from someone.

'I fancy some fun with her,' Danny added, staring after her as well. 'She'll most probably be up for it too. She's the new girl at Cathy Mason's.'

'Who's Cathy Mason?'

'She takes in all these homeless girls. Great for us single boys. They're always gagging for it. Most of them are already hooked on drugs so we get a fair trade off them as well. And if they aren't hooked, they usually are by the time they leave.'

'Sounds like a shit place to live.'

'I reckon it's okay. Cathy Mason's a right looker too. I'd give her one anytime. Her old man copped it a few years back. I've never seen her out with another bloke since so I bet she's gagging for it too.'

'She sounds more like my type.' Austin was still following Becky's form though.

Danny grinned. He papped his horn loud and long and waved as Becky looked back before disappearing around the corner out of view. 'She'll do for me. I'll have her by the end of the week.'

As Danny sped off up the road, Austin remained silent in thought. For now he would let Danny keep Becky warm for him. Then when the timing was right, Becky would be his. She would do just fine.

Sitting on her bed, Liz logged on to her email account and sighed when she saw three more emails from Kevin. None of them had a subject heading but each of them had the same content in the body. She flicked onto the first one and scanned it quickly. *You will come back... I need you here with me... you won't stop me from seeing my daughter...*

She flipped down the lid of her laptop, wondering if he'd eventually get fed up of harassing her. Earlier that morning, she'd been researching domestic violence. This obsession he had with her could go on forever. She couldn't bear the thought of it. What gave a man the right to do that to a woman? Yet again she wished she'd noticed the signs before she'd married him. What she'd seen as gestures of love and affection were really ways of controlling her, possessing her, making her into his own. From the first day she'd met him, Kevin had been protective. When was it that everything had gone wrong? All she had wanted was to be loved, not controlled. Not bullied, not owned.

As she looked down, she noticed Chloe's pink Barbie notepad tucked under the mattress. She pulled it out and flicked through the pages, smiling at the handwriting of a child who was trying hard to make it look grown up. There were lots of loops and letters joined together to make it more exciting.

But just as quickly, her smile dropped as she read the words on one particular page:

> My dad has found out where me and my mum are living. Cathy, that is the lady whose house we are living in. She hit him with a sport stick. I wish my mum had hit my dad with a sport stick. I wish my dad would leave us alone and let mum be happy again. Mum used to smile and laugh. Now Mum is sad. I hear her when she cries at night. She thinks I am asleep but I am not. I think my mum is very brave. Mrs Johnston at school says that mums and dads are splitting up all the time but she didn't say that dads hit mums. Mum does not know I have seen mum and dad arguing a lot of times. Dad shouted at Mum all the time. Mum tried

to make everything happy but nothing was right for Dad. I hate my dad. I wish he would leave my mum alone. I wish we could stay at Cathy's house for ever.

It took Liz a long time to stop crying after she had finished reading. She knew without a doubt that her daughter's words would haunt her forever. What image of marriage could they have caused her to carry through her life? How could they have let their lives have such an impact on her? There was no way she could go back to Kevin now. She needed to be strong for Chloe's sake.

She glanced around the bedroom. It had been a week since they'd arrived and despite the lack of space, it had become comfortable to her already. She felt safe here. When she had been with Kevin, there was nowhere to hide. Here she could deal with it. As long as he couldn't get his hands on her, maybe she would grow stronger every day.

Maybe he would get fed up of hanging around for her. And if he didn't then she would move to somewhere else. Chloe was her future, just as her future plans needed to be for Chloe.

Liz wiped her eyes and prayed that she could follow through with her thoughts. Despite feeling safe, she also knew they'd have to move out soon. Josie Mellor said that she'd find her something as quickly as she could and indeed she was grateful for that. Chloe needed stability after what had happened recently. That essay certainly said as much. She read the words again before slipping the notebook back into its place. Then she thought about what to do next.

Should she confront Chloe? She wondered if maybe she'd wanted her to find it. It would make sense that she'd want to talk about it. But Liz had tried to talk to her about things last night and she'd said she was tired and wanted to go to sleep. She ran her hand through her hair, recalling how secretive she'd been as a child. It might do more harm than good if she were to admit to reading it.

She decided not to do anything for now. She'd concentrate on dealing with Kevin as quickly as possible. At least she hadn't had to dodge him on her way back this morning. For the past few days, Liz had hidden behind anyone she could so that Kevin couldn't see her, or if he did, she would be with someone else to stop him threatening her.

Secretly she wished, hoped and prayed that he'd get tired of hanging around the school gates. And as long as she didn't give him the chance to get her alone, she would be okay. And the longer she stayed away, the stronger she would become.

Wouldn't she?

She stood up and wiped away her tears. She would go and visit Josie at the community house – see what help she could offer. And maybe now was the time to start joining some of the courses they were running.

NINE

It didn't take long before Becky found the courage to venture out again after her recent visit to Shop&Save went without incident. As she began to explore her new surroundings, it was obvious now, even to her, that she hadn't killed Uncle James as she'd originally thought – or if she had, her father must have buried him in the garden and said nothing, which was even more unlikely. Yet it was really weird that she hadn't heard anything.

She wondered if her dad was missing her. It had been nearly a month since she'd legged it that night. In the next breath she doubted that very much, but she still liked to think he would. Because, funnily enough, she still missed him. No matter what he did – or didn't do – he would always be her flesh and blood. But then too, so was Uncle James. She shivered. Maybe it was best not to think about either of them.

After yesterday's mission to the shops and back, Becky headed across there again. She walked along Davy Road for a few minutes and then across the grass and down the steps, through the middle of two blocks of flats and past the community house out onto Vincent Square. Thankfully she noticed when she walked into Shop&Save that she didn't know any of the women who were working that shift. By the time she came out, her bag had a few edible goodies inside it that she'd lifted. She was getting quite a dab hand at it now.

'Excuse me, Miss,' a voice said from behind. 'May I check your bag?'

Becky froze for a second. Oh no! Then she ran.

'Hey, wait up, you daft cow! I'm only messing.'

She turned to see Danny Bradley grinning at her. He looked cool in a Bench T-shirt and narrow grey jeans and, despite what Jess had said about her making a fool of herself the other night, his eyes lit up as if he was pleased to see her.

'God, you mad fool.' She pressed a hand to her chest. 'You nearly gave me a heart attack.'

'You should be more careful.' Danny threw her a smile. 'I couldn't take my eyes off you in there. With a face like that, you're not going to go unnoticed. Where's your loopy mate?'

'She's not my mate.' Becky assumed he was referring to Jess. 'I haven't seen her this morning. I'm sorry about the other night. I didn't mean to be sick on the seat of your car.'

'That's okay. It wasn't my car anyway, remember? You're not the only one that's good at nicking things. Where are you off to?' Danny took her hand and walked on with her. 'Anywhere exciting?'

'No, not really,' Becky managed to say. She felt the blood rush to her cheeks.

'How about doing nothing with me for a bit then?'

'I wouldn't have thought walking was your style.'

'It's not, most of the time. But sometimes I want to do something different.' He looked at her pointedly. 'And most of the time, I get to do what I want.'

He leant forward and kissed her lips so lightly that Becky thought she might have imagined it.

'Do you fancy going for a ride somewhere tonight?' he asked afterwards.

For a split second, she stalled.

Jess would kill her.

Cathy wouldn't be too impressed either.

She glanced up, enough to see the flicker of want in Danny's eyes. An idea popped into her head: maybe she could kill two birds with one stone. She smiled shyly and nodded before she could change her mind.

'Cool,' Danny grinned.

Becky felt butterflies flapping around inside her tummy. She'd never been on a date before. She couldn't wait, even if there would be hell to pay if she was caught. He kissed her again as she made her plan to escape. Even if she had to shimmy down the drainpipe by herself, she would get out to see Danny tonight. After all, she'd only been in trouble that one night so Cathy would think it was Jess that had led her astray.

'I feel like I'm starting school again,' Liz told Cathy as she followed her up the path towards the community house. 'I'm so nervous.'

'It'll be fine,' Cathy soothed as she opened the front door. 'Josie will sort you out. Besides, it's usually quieter in here around lunch time.'

Liz left her nerves in the street and headed in after Cathy. The community house had originally been two semi-detached properties. Doorways had been knocked through from kitchen to kitchen, giving the house six rooms and two bathrooms upstairs, two kitchen areas and two meeting rooms downstairs. The inner wall between the hallways had been removed making a double staircase with one entrance.

Liz spotted the signs on the wall in front of her: *Kids* with an arrow to the right and *Adults* with an arrow to the left. She could hear the deep thud of the base music in the background as they went through the door on the left.

'Hello, ladies,' said a young man with short, spiked hair and an abundance of tattoos and piercings. He was sitting behind a desk.

'Hey, Justin. Is Josie in? She told me she'd be around this morning.'

Justin pointed to a table by his side with a drinks machine. 'Help yourself and I'll get her for you.'

Liz sat down on one of two settees pushed back against the wall, a computer terminal at a desk to her right. The room was painted a pale yellow, making it welcoming but not hiding scuff marks here and there, and causing her to wonder how many people came through it every day. Over the fireplace, a notice board advertised local college courses, imminent meetings and places to find advice. A radio played low in the background. Above the door in this room, the sign said *No kids allowed.*

A few minutes later, Josie clicked across the laminate floor towards them.

'Liz!' She smiled as she drew level and held out a hand. 'We've finally got you here.'

'Hi.' Liz shook it timidly, unable to stop shaking.

Josie clasped her other hand around Liz's. 'Hey, no need to be nervous about anything while you're here,' she reassured. 'We're one big happy family.'

'Actually, she's right.' Justin joined them again. 'She's like my mother – a bloody slave driver.'

Josie raised her eyebrows. 'I suppose you've met the apple of my eye.'

'Apple of your eye, my arse,' Justin quipped. He grabbed a ringing phone. 'Good morning, you're through to the community house. How may I help you?'

'Right,' said Cathy. 'I'm off next door to see what's going on.' She checked her watch. 'See you back here in half an hour?'

'What can I do for you?' Josie asked Liz after they'd gone upstairs into her office and made themselves comfortable. 'Please tell me you want to attend one of my women in crisis sessions.'

'Is that okay?' Liz asked. 'You don't do them in batches, do you?'

'No, you can join in whenever you like.' Josie took a folder from a drawer in her desk and handed it to Liz. 'I made the course that way on purpose. You can also come for one week or one hundred weeks. It's up to you.'

'Will I have to talk about anything in particular?'

'Oh no. Not unless you want to.'

'It's hard sometimes.' Liz looked out of the window for a moment, concentrating on a young mum walking by, dragging her toddler along by the side of another child in a pushchair. 'God, I'm so embarrassed, having to say all of this,' she added.

Josie sat forward. 'Please don't be. Once you get to know some of the women here, they'll open up and tell you their stories. The important thing is that you're not the only one that something bad has happened to. And I think it'll do you good to hear that. And to talk to people who've been through it. I'll introduce you to Suzie: she'll tell you her story. It's a heart-breaking tale but Suzie has come out fighting. She's a different woman from the one I met last year.'

Josie paused a minute. 'I'm glad you came at last.' She smiled warmly when Liz didn't speak. 'I knew something was going on, even though you couldn't tell me. I remember the last time when I visited –'

Liz held up a hand for her to stop. There were tears in her eyes as she recalled the situation Josie was referring to. Josie had been called out from the housing association because someone had complained about the noise again. She and Kevin had been arguing then too. But when he answered the door, Kevin had denied everything being suggested. Liz heard Josie ask to see her and eventually Kevin called her through. Her face had clear marks where his fingers had pressed into her cheeks. Luckily for her, Josie had known better than to question Kevin there and then.

'I'm sorry,' said Josie. 'I didn't mean to stir up bad memories.'

'I just don't want to be reminded of it,' Liz explained.

'Then are you sure you're ready to come to the sessions? Sometimes they can be pretty distressing. Very up-lifting as well, but often heart-breaking. Will you be able to deal with that?'

'I have to. I need to build up my confidence. I'd like to get a job, something part time maybe, to work around Chloe's school hours.'

'This will certainly get you on that road to recovery.' Josie smiled. 'Is there anything else that you need to know?'

'Yes, one thing. I'm sure when I move from Cathy's that Kevin will find out where I am. And I'm bloody well not moving out of the area. So...' Liz glanced down for one split second before sitting upright with assertion. 'How do I go about getting an injunction or a harassment order or whatever?'

Later that evening, Becky stood in front of the tiny wardrobe mirror in her room checking her appearance meticulously. She wore Jess's lipstick. She wore Jess's mascara, Jess's blusher and eye shadow and she had Jess's black and white top on too. She also still had the shoes that she'd been lent. The only thing she could call her own was her trashy underwear.

She pulled up the top and stared down at the once-white bra, one of the only items of clothing she'd arrived at Cathy's with. It certainly wasn't seducing material: she'd have to remember not to take off her top. Either that or she'd have to whip her bra off if Danny did.

Thinking of Danny made her recall the kiss they'd shared that morning. She knew from its intensity that he wanted more. So everything had to be just perfect if she was going to have sex with him tonight. If she didn't look her best, she knew he'd swap her for the more experienced Jess in an instant. Her hands shook as she ran her fingers over her hair again, trying to tame down a few unruly hairs. Had she got enough guts to go through with her plan? It was quite simple really. She would sleep with Danny and then she would forget everything her uncle had done to her. The memory would be erased. Then maybe she wouldn't feel so cheap.

Hearing a horn peep outside, she ran to the window. She

caught sight of Danny pointing to the end of the street as he drove past quickly. Becky opened the window and jumped out onto the roof. Despite the trouble she'd be in with Cathy, there was no way she wanted to be seen by Jess. She'd risk a telling off.

TEN

Cathy was in the living room that evening when Liz joined her. She noticed her weary footsteps, her pale skin giving her a sickly flush. In need of a wash, her hair was tied back from her face, almost hidden out of the way.

'Has Chloe gone to sleep?' she asked her as she flopped down beside her on the settee.

'She's in bed but she isn't asleep. I've left her reading a book, although I know she should be settled by now. Where is everyone?'

'Jess is out, probably causing havoc somewhere, and Becky's in her room.' She pointed to an open bottle of red wine. At Liz's nod, she poured her a glass and they sat in companionable silence while *Coronation Street* came to its conclusion.

'Has Chloe said anything about Kevin lately?' Cathy opened the conversation again.

Liz sighed long and heavy. 'I've been trying to talk to her tonight about it.'

'And?'

'She says she doesn't want to see him. She says he's a monster.'

'Hmm – she got that right.'

'I miss my home,' said Liz. Then, 'I didn't mean –'

Cathy raised her hand. 'Don't mind me. I try my best with this place but it can only be a temporary substitute. Home should always be a special place.'

'Please don't think that I'm ungrateful,' Liz tried to explain. 'I can't thank you enough for taking us in. If you hadn't, I don't know what would have happened.'

'I do. You would have gone back, taken a little bit more and then found another way out. And another until you'd got away again.'

There was silence for a moment.

'He turned into a –' Liz struggled for words to describe Kevin, 'a – a monster. Chloe was right. It's the perfect description.'

'I bet he didn't want you to go to work either?'

Liz shook her head. 'He said he earned enough for me to stay at home and look after Chloe.'

'So he had control over the money?'

'He gave me just enough for the shopping. He paid all the bills though.'

'Did you ever go out?'

'Not as a family. Kevin used to meet up with his friends but I lost touch with all of mine.'

Cathy nodded knowingly. 'He controlled you. That's a form of domestic abuse in itself. Some men get their kicks out of it. It makes them feel superior, taking their inferior thoughts and hiding them away so that no one can mock them for being a coward. Because that's what they all are, cowards the lot of them.'

Liz took a sip of wine before replying. 'I didn't have any choice. If I let him have his own way, then Chloe was sheltered from it. It worked until a month ago.'

'Were you with anyone before you met him?'

'Not anything long term.'

'That's a pity. If he's the only one you can compare a marriage to, then it's no wonder you stayed with him for so long. Do you think he'll ever leave you alone for good?'

'I doubt it. Though if I'd had the courage to leave sooner, I probably wouldn't be in this mess. I wish there were more places like this. Instead, all battered women get are scummy bed and breakfasts. They were worse than being with Kevin. No wonder women go back to the life they know yet hate.'

'And is that the only reason you would go back?'

'That and the promises he'd make.' Liz looked shamefaced. 'I believed him because I wanted to go home, get Chloe settled again. When Josie said that a hostel might be our only choice, I was halfway out of the door. Then she suggested you might be able to help.'

Cathy smiled. 'I'm glad to be of assistance. I've told you before, you and Chloe can stay here for as long as you want. My house is always open to you – although I can't promise there will be a bed for you if you leave. Unfortunately someone else will probably want it.'

'All the same, it's good to hear. I do need to find somewhere else soon but for now I'm staying put. I want to feel safe before I can think about what to do next. A few weeks here will let me clear my head, make me stronger. The more I keep away from Kevin, the better I'll become. His hold on me will weaken. It will, won't it?'

Cathy sighed. 'I hope so. We can try and help you – me and Josie – but you have to do the hardest part of it yourself. Then again, I think you already know that, don't you?'

'I was pregnant,' Liz said all of a sudden, her eyes

103

brimming with tears. 'The last time he hit me. I was pregnant and he knew.'

'Was?'

'I lost it. He took my baby. I can never forgive him for that.'

'Is that why you were so upset about Becky?'

'Yes.' Liz sniffed. 'How can she be so thoughtless when all I wanted was another child?'

'She didn't know you had lost yours.'

'But she talked about it as if it wasn't real. She –'

'She's just gone sixteen. And don't tell me you haven't noticed she has some sort of secret. God knows, I've been trying to get it out of her since she arrived.'

'What do you mean?'

'Something isn't right, but she'll only tell me when she's ready to. Unless… could you try and get it out of her?'

'I doubt she'll confide in me.' Liz shook her head.

'It was just a thought.'

'You'd think she'd want to talk to Jess with them being about the same age.'

'Are you mad? She's more mixed up than Becky ever will be.'

Liz smiled a little but it soon faded. 'I just wish I could get through to Chloe. I know she's protective towards me but I don't really know what that's doing to her. She doesn't want to talk about it.'

'Maybe she feels allegiance towards you and doesn't want to talk badly about Kevin.'

Liz stayed quiet while she thought this over. She supposed Cathy could be right. It seemed far easier to talk to a stranger and bare your soul.

'Shall we try a different approach?' Cathy offered.

'What do you have in mind?'

'You try and talk to Becky, see what you can find out. And I'll have a chat with Chloe?'

Liz shrugged. 'It's worth a shot, I suppose.'

'Smoke?' Danny reached in the glove compartment for his cigarettes.

'No, ta, not for me,' said Becky.

'Never tried it more like.'

'No, I –'

Danny started the car engine. 'Chill out, woman. I wish I'd never started. Tried to stop loads of times but I never have the balls.'

'Where're we going?' she asked, after they'd been driving along a main road for a few minutes.

'Just along the lanes, by the fields off the estate. We can find a quiet spot. No one will interrupt us there and we can have a bit of fun. That's what you want, isn't it?'

'If that's what you want too,' she replied, trying to sound self-assured.

'Sure. And don't worry, I won't be rough.'

'I'm not bothered.'

'Could have fooled me.' Danny stopped at a junction before turning right. 'By the look on your face, you're shit scared. You're not a virgin, are you?'

'God, no!'

'Shame. I like a challenge.'

'Well, you're not going to get one.'

Becky tried to look sexy but really she didn't know how. Instead, she leaned over and placed her hand at the top of his thigh. Danny moved it to his crotch and pressed down hard. He groaned.

'See what you've done to me already?'

Becky pressed her hand down harder. 'Plenty more where that came from,' she said, her nerves hidden behind a faint smile.

As they continued on their way, she prayed she'd got the courage to go through with her plan. If she hadn't, she realised she would have a long walk home. Danny Bradley would almost certainly dump her. She couldn't play around with his feelings: she'd heard girls at school being called dick-teases. This was for real now. Besides, Danny Bradley was more of a man than a boy. He wouldn't want to be messed around. Hadn't he already told her that he got what he wanted, when he wanted it? Imagine how he'd feel if she told him to stop.

In the midst of her panic, Danny turned down an unused dirt track, switched off the engine and turned towards her. He ran a finger over her lips, her chin, down her chest. It stopped at the seam of her top.

'It's a perfect spot here,' he told her. 'No one will see us, don't worry.'

Becky felt herself relax into their first kisses. Her skin tingled more at his touch. Her mouth responded to his as he probed with his tongue deeper and deeper. Her hands roamed over his clothes, inside his clothes, urging him closer.

But within seconds, she felt the customary terror rise up inside her. She closed her eyes but images of Uncle James made her quickly open them again. She had to get this over with, rid herself of those ugly memories. With urgency, she reached for Danny's belt and tugged at the buckle.

Danny gently eased away her hand and put it behind his back again. 'No rush, little one,' he said, not taking his eyes from hers. His hand then found its way up the front of her top.

Becky couldn't help herself. She froze.

Danny stopped kissing her and opened his eyes. 'What's up?'

'Nothing.' She pulled him near again.

How could she tell him what was flashing through her mind as he touched her skin for the first time? How another one had been there before but hadn't been so gentle?

'Let's go into the back,' Danny whispered moments later. They climbed over and lay out on the seat. The night was warm, the air in the car was hot with anticipation.

Becky blinked away tears as he pushed into her. She turned away as he thrust, moving quicker and quicker. Then she grabbed hard onto his buttocks, pushing him in deeper and deeper. It hurt, God it hurt. But maybe that would make him come quicker. Still he continued for longer than she could bear.

When he was all but there, she lashed out. 'Wait a minute,' she cried, trying to push him off. 'Wait!'

Danny started thrusting into her quicker and quicker. He grabbed her flailing hands and held onto them until he bucked for one final time. And then it was over.

But Becky had seen the look on his face. She'd seen it on her uncle James, that look of disgust as she'd allowed him to use her.

'Didn't you like it?' she whispered, trying to stop her bottom lip from trembling.

Danny frowned. 'Whatever gave you that idea?'

'I saw the look on your face, as you, you know.'

Danny grinned. 'That was my sex face. Maybe I'll see yours one day. You didn't come, did you?'

Becky shook her head, unsure if she had reached her peak or not. How would she know?

'Have you never?'

'Of course I have,' she muttered, pulling down her top.

'Yeah, right.' Danny shoved his hand up her skirt but Becky pushed it away.

'Piss off!'

'Hey, don't get stroppy. I was only asking. Because if you haven't, I could do something else that would *guarantee* that you would.'

Becky had had enough for one night. She felt the wetness between her legs and tried desperately not to gag.

'I just thought...'

As Danny touched her lightly on her shoulder, she jumped and inched away from him.

'Whoa!' He moved his hand back. 'Jesus, you look really scared. What the hell has happened to you?'

'Nothing.' Becky tried to smile, hoping to throw him off the scent. The less people that knew about her problems, the more she could keep them a secret. 'I just got scared, that's all. I did like it.'

Danny reached for his fags. 'Thank Christ for that. I thought my reputation was going to get trashed!'

Later, after she'd said goodnight to Danny, Becky ran upstairs and locked herself in the bathroom. She stripped off quickly, stepped under the shower and began to scrub at her skin. She felt dirty, trashy, cheap. In frustration, she began to cry. Rubbing until it was sore to the touch didn't make her feel any better. She could hear her uncle taunting her, calling her names; she could hear him laughing at her.

She tried hard to push away the memories but she couldn't, recalling one time in particular when James slapped her so hard that her neck had hurt for days after. She'd skipped school for two weeks until the bruising on her face had gone, trying to keep it from her dad too. Not that she needed to do that: he hadn't really been around enough to notice.

She scrubbed at her chest, letting the water cascade over her head as she tried not to scream out loud. Why couldn't she have enjoyed sex with Danny? All she could see was James's face when he ran his hand over her breast, when he'd forced himself into her. Would she always be haunted by what he'd done? Always feel disgusted, like she did now, every time someone touched her? Would she never be able to fall in love because men would repulse her? Never be able to touch another man and not think of her uncle?

Her skin was still stinging when she went back to her bedroom. She changed into pyjamas, wondering if her tears would ever stop. Suddenly she heard a rap at her window. She pulled back the curtain to see Jess standing there.

'Let me in!' she whispered loudly.

Becky opened the window wide enough for her to climb through. 'Do you know what time it is?' she said. 'Cathy's going to kill you.'

'She's locked my window, the stupid old fart.' Jess yanked down her denim skirt. 'What's the matter with your face? Have you been crying?'

'No!' Becky wiped at her eyes.

'Where did you get to tonight? I was going to take you out with me. You missed out on some gear. I've had loads to drink and I've had some Whizz.'

'Whizz?'

'Billy?'

Becky looked on blankly.

'Phet?' Jess tutted. 'Speed, you dozy moron!'

'Oh.'

'God, you're so naïve.'

Becky clicked in. That was the reason Jess was being so nice. And why she hadn't realised she'd been wearing her top and shoes.

'Can you feel the love tonight,' Jess began to sing loudly. 'If you want a feel, I'm you…our…rrrrssss!'

'Be quiet!' Becky pushed Jess towards the door. 'You'll get into trouble, remember. You go to bed and I'll say you were with me last night, until I ran off or something. I'll say you were looking for me.'

Jess grinned at her. 'Would you do that for me?' she said. 'Aw, you're so sweet.'

'You have to be quiet though,' Becky warned. 'Cathy's still up. You don't want to start her off.'

Jess put a finger on her lips. 'I will be oh so quiet,' she whispered loudly. She took another step then turned back. 'Will you be my special friend, Becks? I need a special friend.'

'Yes, but go to bed.'

'I would, if I could remember where my room is.' Jess snorted. 'Oh, what am I like?' She sat down on Becky's bed with a thud. 'I can sleep here.'

'No, you can't.'

Becky pulled her to her feet again with so much force that Jess fell forwards, nearly knocking both of them over.

'Watch out!' She instinctively put an arm across her stomach. Luckily Jess kept moving forward. Becky heard her bedroom door open and bang shut a few moments later, then peace resumed again.

She glanced down and splayed her hand over her stomach. All of a sudden the realisation was sinking in. The baby growing inside her meant that she'd be stuck with what that monster had done to her for the rest of her life, and in more ways than one.

'Why did this happen to me?' she sobbed quietly.

Half an hour later, Cathy got up from the kitchen table and tipped the dregs of tea down the sink. Damn Jessica Myatt, she fumed, running the cup under hot water before leaving it to soak. Hearing her thump about upstairs, she realised she must have sneaked in the back way and up to Becky's room while she'd been sitting up waiting for her. What was she going to do with that girl?

She was just about to call it a day when she heard a noise outside. She groaned: not tonight, please. I need to sleep too.

Grabbing the hockey stick, she hurled it high and opened the front door. 'If that's you, Kevin McIntyre, I'm giving you fair warning that I'll swing for you again!' she yelled. 'Leave the poor woman alone.'

'Cathy!' A familiar voice rang out. 'Chill out, will you! It's only me.'

'Cheryl?' Cathy's eyes adjusted to the darkness outside. 'Is that you?'

Cheryl Morton emerged from behind the privet hedge. If Cathy was shocked by her gaunt figure, her sallow skin and her lank greasy hair, she did a good job of hiding it. Cheryl's hands were tucked into the pockets of a black top, the hood up and pulled tightly around her face. She wore dark skinny jeans and flat pumps: the black holdall flung over her shoulder gave her the look of a cat burglar.

'Hiya, Cathy.' Cheryl smiled faintly, dark rings prominent underneath her eyes. 'You couldn't make me a cup of your lovely tea?'

ELEVEN

Becky was still asleep when Jess launched herself into her bedroom the next morning.

'Where are my shoes?' She stooped to pick her top up from the floor. 'And what the fuck is this doing next to your bed?'

'You said I could borrow it,' Becky fibbed, rubbing at her eyes as she levelled with her. 'Remember, last night? You brought it in to say thanks for letting you in.'

'No, I didn't!' Jess grabbed Becky's hair and dragged her to the floor.

'Ow, stop it! Get off me!'

'You lifted it, you thief! I never said you could go in my room. I never said... that's my mascara too, you bitch.'

'I didn't take them!' Becky gasped as Jess pulled harder. 'You gave them to me.'

'No, I didn't! I'm warning you. You touch my stuff again and I'll do more than grab you by the hair. Don't you –'

'Still picking on the young 'uns, I see.'

Becky felt the tension on her hair relax. From her knees, she looked up to see a shockingly thin girl, her rough life seemingly written all over her face. She glanced away quickly for fear of retaliation if she was accused of staring.

'Chez!' Jess gasped. 'What are you doing back?'

'Got out yesterday.' Cheryl folded her arms and stood in the doorway. 'So I say again. What are you up to? Want to pick on someone your own size?'

Jess blushed. 'I was only messing, wasn't I, Becks?'

'Is that right?' Cheryl asked Becky.

Becky nodded her head slightly, holding on to it where it had been pulled. The girl standing in her doorway looked scarier than Jess.

'Are you back at Cathy's then?' asked Jess.

Cheryl sighed. 'What does it look like?'

'I mean, you know, for good.'

'Yes. Cathy says I can stay as long as I want. So, you stupid bitch,' suddenly she was across the room and pulling Jess by her hair, 'touch the young kid again, and I'll floor you. Got it?'

'Ye – yes.'

'I said got it!' Cheryl pulled a little harder.

'Yes! Ow! For fuck's sake, let me go!' Tears sprang to Jess's eyes. Satisfied, Cheryl looked over at Becky. 'You definitely okay?' she asked.

Becky nodded.

Cheryl shoved Jess away. She landed on the floor with a thump.

'Back off or else you'll have me to deal with. You know I hate bullies.' Cheryl stared at Jess long enough for her to redden again before leaving the room.

'I thought she was your friend,' Becky said to Jess, once the two of them were certain Cheryl was out of hearing range.

'She was. I don't know what's up with her. She's gone all weird. Look, maybe you and me should stick together while she's around? She's a right nutter at times is that Cheryl.'

'But I thought you said you were like this.' Becky couldn't resist crossing her index and middle fingers.

'We were! That's before she was locked up for dealing and prostitution.'

Becky's eyes widened. What made anyone of that age have sex with lots of men? She had trouble doing it with just the one.

'So are we mates then?' Jess continued.

'Not if you're going to be nasty. Barging into my room like that and attacking me.'

'Sorry.'

'And you need to stop pulling hair.'

'Okay!' A pause. 'Well?'

Becky shrugged a shoulder. Like hell would she give in.

But Jess sensed victory anyway. 'Good,' she said. 'Then you can help me to get off with Danny Bradley later.'

Cathy was tending to the flower bed around the border of the lawn when she spotted Cheryl in the kitchen window. She waved, beckoning for her to come outside.

'I heard you sorting Jess out,' she said when Cheryl arrived.

'She's a bully.' Cheryl sat down on the bench.

'Even so –'

'She needed sorting.'

Cathy smiled a little. 'She is a loose cannon, that one. Anyway, how are you doing?'

Cheryl shrugged. 'Okay, I suppose.'

'It wasn't too rough an ordeal then?'

Cathy watched the young girl struggle with her emotions. She would have been a bright thing if she hadn't got mixed up in drugs. Abandoned by her father at an early age, Cheryl's mother had then gone off with the first available man that took an interest in her. Cheryl hadn't been part of the bargain so had been left with her grandmother. Two abortions, three suicide attempts and a two-month prison sentence followed quickly by this last stint inside and Cheryl looked the part completely. Her blonde hair was shoved behind her ears away from her shiny, spotty skin. She wasn't wearing any make-up and hardly any clothes: a denim mini skirt was barely covering her dignity, along with flat pump shoes and a white vest top that had seen better days. The sleeves of her long cardigan were pushed up above her elbows. Unlike Liz who hid the bruises of her scuffles with Kevin McIntyre, Cheryl didn't hide the scars of self-harm and needle misuse. They shot up her arms like a game of noughts and crosses.

'Actually,' Cheryl continued moments later, 'it was horrible. I hated being locked up. There was nowt to do but try and score. It took me ages to get my head around being locked in a cell again. My cell mate was a right mardy cow as well, always crying and saying that she'd done nowt to be locked up for.' She made a circling motion against her temple. 'Like I believed that. We were all there for a reason.'

'You weren't meant to enjoy it,' Cathy pointed out.

'I'm never going back.'

'I'm glad to hear it. You just need to stay drug-free now. That's one thing that was good, cleaning you out.'

Cheryl turned away then. Cathy didn't notice her look of

resignation as she pulled at a stubborn weed.

'If you're planning on staying this time until the housing association find you somewhere of your own, I want you in by eleven each night, no later. Is that clear?'

Cheryl folded her arms. 'Okay.'

'And as much as I like Jess getting her come-uppance, don't get too heavy handed. She isn't as streetwise as you and I'd like it to stay that way if possible. I don't want her to get in any deeper than she already is. And Becky is only just gone sixteen and... well, she's fragile at the moment.'

'Okay, okay! I heard you the first time.'

'Well, just you adhere to it then. If you leave on bad terms again, I won't allow you to come back.'

Cheryl stood up. 'Fine,' she snapped. 'Christ, it's like still being in juvie. Don't do this: don't do that. I didn't –'

'You came back here because you had nowhere else to go,' Cathy reminded her with a look that said she wasn't born yesterday. 'So I'm just telling it like it is.'

Cheryl sighed. 'I just want to have a peaceful life, Cath.'

'So do I.' Cathy watched her until she disappeared into the house. 'So do I.'

'Are we going to stay at Cathy's for a long time?' Chloe asked her mum as they turned into Christopher Avenue on their way home from school.

'I'm not sure,' said Liz. 'Why?'

'I like it at Cathy's.'

'Don't you miss your room? And your toys?'

'Toys are for babies, Mum. And I can have new clothes when I need them, can't I?'

If only it were that simple, Liz thought. But now that she

wanted to include Chloe in more decisions, and she'd had a word with Josie who had boosted her confidence tremendously, at least it gave her the opportunity to discuss another idea she'd mentioned.

'Would you be okay if I went to work? Only part-time, while you were at school?'

'So you can still walk with me?' Chloe began to skip at her side.

'Of course,' said Liz. 'And it means that we might be able to have a treat every now and then. Things are going to be tight now that Dad isn't around.'

Chloe took hold of Liz's hand in her own small one. 'We'll be okay, Mum. Just you and me.'

Liz held back tears as they walked the last few yards to Cathy's house. With such an old head on young shoulders, she was frightened that Chloe's childhood had gone already.

The footsteps from behind were upon her before she had time to react. A hand on her shoulder pulled her back with force. Liz barely managed to stay on her feet as she was spun round, coming face to face with Kevin.

'What do – do you want?' she stuttered.

Kevin ignored her. Instead, he smiled and reached down to tweak Chloe's chin. But Chloe moved her head out of the way.

'What's the matter? Not scared of your dad, are you?'

'No,' said Chloe sharply. 'And neither is my mum.'

'Chloe,' said Liz. 'Run along to Cathy's and I'll be with you in a minute.'

'But I don't want to leave you.' Chloe looked on in concern. She took her mother's hand again.

Liz gave it a reassuring squeeze. 'I think Cathy said she

was making cakes to sell at the community house. Maybe you could help her?'

'I'll be back in five minutes if you're not there,' she said, reluctantly walking away.

'What do you want now?' said Liz, for a moment feeling brave.

'You know what,' he replied. 'I want you to come home, both of you.'

Liz shook her head. 'I can't. Especially after what happened the other night.'

'That woman is a lunatic.' Kevin rubbed at his shoulder. 'You should see the bruise I have.'

'It's probably similar to the ones you left me with.'

'What did you say?'

'I... I...' Liz pushed her hands deep into the pockets of her coat so that he couldn't see how much they were shaking.

'I told you I was sorry, what more do you want me to do?'

'And that makes it okay? I lost my baby – our baby.'

'We can make another one.'

'It isn't like a Lego building. We can't just pick up the pieces as if nothing has happened.'

Kevin faltered. 'I miss you, and Chloe. I promise it won't happen again.'

'You followed me here and tried to strangle me.'

'I was drunk,' Kevin gave by way of an explanation. He bowed his head. Liz took the opportunity to glance down the road towards Cathy's house, hoping that Chloe was safely in the garden. Cathy was standing at the gate, looking on. It made her feel so much better. She turned back to Kevin.

119

'I won't let you hurt me ever again.'

Kevin grabbed her arm. 'Who the hell do you think you are with your threatening tone?' His spittle peppered Liz's cheeks.

'You killed our baby.'

'I DIDN'T KNOW YOU WERE PREGNANT!'

'Would it have made a difference?'

'You always push me too far, don't you?' Kevin gripped her arm harder still. 'It's your fault that I react the way I do.'

Liz couldn't speak. He was too close for her to feel comfortable anymore.

'It's time you stopped messing about. I want you home by tomorrow. If you're not there by the time I get off the late shift, then there'll be trouble like you've never known before.'

'Everything all right, Liz?' Cathy's voice came from behind as she drew near.

'Mind your own business, you nosy bitch,' said Kevin, but he let go of his grip on Liz.

Cathy ignored him and linked her arm through Liz's. 'Come on.'

'You can't hide forever,' Kevin shouted after them.

Liz could almost feel his eyes burning a hole in the back of her head. She tried not to run as she drew closer to the safety of the gate, all the time struggling to hold back tears. Just being near to him again had brought back all the fear, all the pain, all the control he'd had over her. How could she think she was able to stand up to him?

Jess and Becky were in Jess's bedroom getting ready to go out. Since the Cheryl episode, they'd spent a bit more time together. Becky knew Jess was using her but she didn't mind so much. Jess didn't scare her as much as Cheryl, so she'd rather not be on her own anyway.

'Can I borrow your white T-shirt, the one with the punk woman image on it?' she asked her.

'No, I'm going to wear it.' Jess stopped straightening her hair for a moment. 'I'm going to shag Danny tonight. I've decided to make myself as accessible as possible. I'm fed up with just dishing out blow jobs.'

Becky frowned. 'I didn't know you were still doing that!'

'Well, not for a while. I think he's got another bird anyway. He's been a bit distant with me lately.'

'Me too,' admitted Becky. Still reeling from Jess's admission, she didn't realise what she was saying.

'What do you mean, distant with you? He doesn't even know you.'

'I know, but –'

Jess smiled knowingly. 'You fancy him, don't you?'

'No!'

'Then why are you blushing? Jesus, you're practically the same colour as my red lippie.' Jess turned back to straightening her hair.

Becky did indeed feel her skin colouring up. Oh my God, what would Jess do to her if she found out that she had slept with Danny? She'd probably have no hair left by the time she'd finished with her. Still, even though she couldn't tell her, Jess might be consoled by the fact that Danny had barely looked at her since the night they'd slept together in his car. That's what she'd meant by him being distant. Just yesterday, he'd papped his horn and driven past when she'd been going to the shops. She thought he might have come back to ask her out again but no. She'd watched his car until it turned out of view.

'I think he treats women like shit anyway,' she told Jess. 'I bet he shags them once and then loses interest. His type usually do.'

Jess laughed. 'He would if it was you he was sleeping with. Whereas me, well, I've got hidden talents. I'll get him one day. And I bet he's sooo worth the wait.'

Becky sighed, staying silent as Jess rummaged through a pile of clothes on her bedroom floor. She watched as she sniffed the armpits of a blue T-shirt before throwing it at her.

'Try this one, but spray plenty of perfume on it. It reeks of smoke.'

'I haven't got –'

Jess gave her a bottle of Thierry Mugler's eau de parfum. 'It's Angel. It's my favourite. I think he should bring one out called Urban Angels, don't you reckon? It's a good name for us down and outs.'

'I'm not a down and out,' muttered Becky.

'Of course you are. That's why the likes of Danny Bradley won't have us. We're too common. Not that he'd have you anyway. It's getting more and more obvious that you're up the duff.'

Becky glanced down at her stomach as she sat down on the bed. Jess was right. She'd noticed that her jeans were getting tighter: she was having problems fastening the zip. Another week and she'd have to abandon them. Keeping her pregnancy a secret was going to become harder still over the next month. But then, she knew if she could get Danny interested again, he wouldn't be bothered about a bit of weight on her belly. All he'd want is what was between her legs, there for him to take whenever he fancied it. Because she would let him if he wanted to – again and again. One of those times must erase the memories. Surely the more she did it and the more men she did it with, she would finally replace its power.

A car horn beeped and they both rushed to the window. Danny Bradley drove past slowly.

'Suppose we'd better go out the front way tonight,' said Jess. They heard the horn again, longer this time. 'Come on, or else he'll be on his way without us.'

Giving herself the once over in Jess's wardrobe mirror, Becky turned sideways and ran a hand over her bump. It wasn't too noticeable yet but it wouldn't be long. She pulled down the blue T-shirt just as Jess grabbed her hand.

'Come on!'

'Where are you two off to in such a hurry?' Cathy asked as they whooshed past her in the hallway downstairs after hanging up their keys in the kitchen.

Becky stopped in her tracks. 'We're going …'

'… out for a walk,' Jess finished off for her.

'Yeah, for a walk.'

'Behave yourselves this time. I don't want any more trouble brought to my doorstep. I've had enough grief off the housing association lately over the noise.'

Jess rolled her eyes before leaving in a clatter of heels.

Cathy watched them both as they ran down the path, Jess nudging Becky and Becky nudging her back as they raced to get to the gate first. She smiled half-heartedly. It was good to see the two of them getting on so well but that in itself was a worry, especially after what had happened to Cheryl recently. Becky was so delicate right now: Jess could either turn out to be a great friend or drag her down a path that she wouldn't wish anyone to follow. To a certain extent, Cathy had to sit back and let them make their own mistakes. But it was so hard to say nothing.

Becky's pregnancy hadn't been discussed again since she'd mentioned it either. Cathy needed to broach the subject before it was too late. And by the look of Becky's tight clothing, she'd have to do it sooner rather than later.

TWELVE

When the girls got to Danny's car, Becky would have been annoyed at Danny's lack of interest if it wasn't for the youth sitting in the passenger seat. Lush was the perfect word to describe him: tanned skin due to the recent spate of warm weather, brown hair, deep blue eyes and a fashionable amount of stubble. He wore black denims, his light blue T-shirt the only smidgen of colour that she could see. As he turned towards them with a smile that did things to her heart, she noticed a faint scar down the right side of his cheek. It was about two inches in length, serving to add a little bit more to his bad boy image. She wondered how he'd got it.

He winked as he caught her staring. Becky looked away immediately, her skin reddening as she slid along the seat. Tonight Danny was in a different car, another old wreck. Jess said he'd nicked it but she couldn't understand why. It didn't seem any better than his own.

'Budge up, Parksy,' Jess told the youth in the back seat. 'Make room for two little ones. Hi, I'm Jess.' She leaned forward to inspect the new arrival, pushing out her chest. 'And you are?'

'Austin.' He looked behind her. 'And you are?'

'Becky.' She smiled shyly.

Danny screeched off and they rode around the estate for a while before heading up towards Stockleigh city centre. But twenty minutes later, he pulled the car over to the side of the road and banged his hands on the steering wheel.

'Not again!'

'What's up?' said Jess.

'Run out of petrol.'

'What are we going to do?'

Becky looked out of the window. On one side there was a row of non-descript terraced houses, on the other, a large area of painted boards showing coloured murals. She wondered what they were hiding: she hadn't seen them before. In fact, she hadn't got a clue where they were. They could be miles away as far as she knew.

'Got any money on you?'

Jess shook her head.

Danny turned to Becky. 'You?'

'No.'

He banged his hands on the steering wheel again. Sheepishly, he turned to Austin. 'I don't suppose…?'

Austin smirked, knowing he had a twenty in his pocket. 'I've only got a fiver and you're not having that. You'll have to get another car and make sure it's got a full tank this time.'

'A fiver between us?' Danny laughed loudly to hide his embarrassment.

They sat in silence while the radio blasted out some dreary tune. Suddenly, Danny opened his door. 'Come on, you lot!'

Becky and Jess wriggled across the back seat and into the cool night air. Parksy followed. Danny retrieved his crow bar, tucked it inside his jacket and the five of them stood on the pavement.

'Are you going to do another one?' Jess asked, wide-eyed with excitement.

Danny nodded and strode off up the road. 'I'll have to. I don't get my giro 'til later in the week so unless I can thieve a bit off the old lady again, my car's got to stay put.'

They all followed behind. Danny finally spotted a small hatchback parked in the alleyway between two rows of terraced houses. He pointed at it.

'This'll do,' he said. 'No one will see me if I'm quick.' He pulled the crow bar out from underneath his jacket. 'You two carry on walking,' he told the girls. 'We'll meet you around the corner.'

'Do you think we should be doing this?' Becky said to Jess as they walked towards the end of the street. 'Cathy will kill us if she finds out.'

Jess linked her arm. 'Relax. No one will find out.'

'It's not nice, though. To have your car nicked.'

'Needs must.'

Becky wasn't sure she liked Jess's attitude. If they nicked a car, someone would miss it.

'Danny's done it lots of times,' Jess told her. 'It's not as simple now though. Most of the modern cars have alarms and immobilisers. That's why he picks older models. He'll run this one around for a while and drop us off.' She grinned. 'Well, drop you off actually. I'm hoping to stay with him. I'm going to have me some fun, if you catch my drift.'

'That Austin's a bit of all right,' said Becky, trying not to blush as she said his name.

'Isn't he just! Actually, I might try him out and you can have Danny, if you like.'

'Jess, I need to tell you –'

Danny screeched to a halt beside them in the stolen car. 'Get in,' he said, looking directly at Becky.

'It's that easy?' Becky was shocked.

'Of course it's not *that* easy. He just does it all the time.' Jess made for the door handle first.

'Not you,' said Danny. 'You're going nowhere. Parksy, you can get out as well. Becky, you can get in.'

'But I –'

'Couldn't you at least drive us home first?' Parksy pleaded. 'We're miles away from the estate.'

Danny leaned over and patted his friend's stomach. 'The walk will do you good,' he grinned. 'Besides, you might be able to kop off with her, if you're desperate.'

'I heard that!' said Jess.

'You were meant to. Now come on you lot, get your arse into gear. I'm not in the mood to get caught tonight.'

'No, just laid, you dirty bastard.' Parksy glared at Austin. 'So why does he get to stay? He's only been around for a few weeks and already you're –'

The look Austin gave Parksy made him get out of the car.

'What did he mean about getting laid, Becky?'

Becky tried to shrug it off. She glanced at Austin. He ushered her forward so she climbed back in.

'Becky!' Jess pointed at Parksy. 'You can't leave me with him!'

Becky moved to get out but Danny slammed the door lock down.

'Oy! Let me out!' she said. 'I thought you were joking. I'm not staying without Jess.'

Danny looked at her with a mixture of lust and menace. Then he laughed and after a quick glance at an irate-looking Jess, he screeched off again.

'Ciao for now,' he shouted through the window.

'Stop!'

Becky looked back as they rode away, this time heading down the main road and away from the city centre. Jess could hardly be seen in the distance.

'Let me out of the car,' she cried.

'Quit whining.' Danny flashed a glare through the rear view window.

'I will not. Let me out!' Becky's mind started to work overtime. Not only was she stuck with Danny who she knew would expect sex, but there was another man in the car. Someone who none of them knew well at all. Danny had said he'd only just met him. If he was nasty, two men could do anything to her. Fear flew through her veins. For a second, she thought about opening the door and flinging herself into the road to escape. Stupid, stupid cow to get herself into this situation.

But then Austin turned and gave her a smile. She wasn't sure why but its warmth was reassuring. She settled down again. Danny was trying to work the CD player.

Austin held up a ten pound note. 'Found this in the glove compartment.'

'Cool!' Danny took it from him. 'There's enough petrol in this one so we can get a few cans.'

Austin snatched the note back. '*I'll* decide what to do and what not to do with it.'

'Of course, boss. Whatever you say.'

They stopped off at an off-licence store and Austin went inside. He came back out minutes later with a few cans and they sat outside while she and Austin drank it. For all his hard boy attitude, Danny wouldn't drink and drive. He'd rather have his freedom.

By this time, Becky had begun to calm down and once the booze was finished, she felt in control of the situation again. She was beginning to have a bit of a laugh until Danny drove off towards the disused track they'd been to before. Once there, he stilled the engine and climbed into the back with her. Austin got out, lit a cigarette and walked a few yards in front.

Danny began to kiss her and for a short while they did nothing else. She became increasingly turned on as he pushed his tongue into her mouth, exploring her deeply. His hand went up the back of her T-shirt, his fingers teasing the bare skin up and down her spine. She followed suit, pulling him towards her so that there was no room between them. He shoved his hand down the front of her jeans. And that was when the panic began to take over. If she let Danny do this, then what would Austin want?

Danny's hand moved further down, cupping her, trying to get his fingers inside her.

'No! Stop!' Becky said breathlessly.

'Ah, come on, Becks. Don't do this again. You'll get a rep as a dick-tease.' Danny pressed her hand down on to his erection. 'You know you want it really.' He sniggered, glancing at Austin who had walked back to the car. 'You know you want it from both of us.'

Becky suddenly became very sober. 'Leave me alone.'

She pushed Danny away and with the force of a tornado, she lashed out. She punched; she kicked; she slapped.

Danny grabbed her wrists and held her down. 'What's wrong with you? You were quick to give it away the other night. I'm only after a repeat performance.'

'No, I –'

Before she could protest again, Danny was lifted from her and thrown from the car. He fell to the ground on his back, scraping across the gravel.

'What the –'

'Leave her alone.' Austin stood over him. He flicked open a knife.

'Whoa!' Danny retreated a few feet backwards. He held his hands up in surrender. 'There's no need for that, mate. She's my girl, you know. I don't just shag anyone.'

Austin turned to Becky with a look in his eyes that she would never forget. It was danger personified. She held her breath as he stared at her.

'Is that right?' he asked her. 'Is he your man?'

Becky shrugged slightly, not wanting to admit anything. She didn't want to spoil her chances with him. But she flinched as he took a step towards Danny.

'Yes!' she cried. 'Yes, he's my man.'

Austin stood still for a moment. Then he put the knife away and helped Danny up as if he'd simply tripped over.

'I suggest you treat your girl with a little more respect.' He clasped Danny's shoulder. 'Take her home. I think she's had enough for one night. And I need this car for something else later.'

*

'You're home early,' Cathy said looking up from her magazine as Jess flopped beside her on the settee and folded her arms in a strop. 'It's only half past nine. Are you feeling okay?'

'No. I've had a crap night, if you must know.'

'Where's Becky?'

Jess shrugged her shoulders.

'But you left with her. Where did she get to?'

'*She* got into a stolen car with Danny Bradley, leaving me to make my own way home.'

'What?' Cathy put down her magazine.

'I would never have done that. Mates don't leave other mates behind. And she knows I fancy Danny Bradley. She is so dead when I get hold of her.'

'But you shouldn't have left her on her own! Where did you last see her?'

'I've just told you,' Jess snapped. 'She got into a stolen car with Danny Bradley and some other bloke called Austin. How the hell should I know where they took her?'

'But I trusted you to look after her and –'

'This isn't my fault. I told her not to get into the car but she ignored me. And then they left me to walk home! Do you think I wanted to walk miles? My feet are killing me.' She took off a shoe. 'Look at my blisters. I won't be able to walk tomorrow. But what sympathy do I get for doing the right thing? All you do is moan at *me*.'

Cathy touched her arm gently. She was wrong to take her anger out on Jess.

'Sorry,' she said. 'I'm just worried about her. I never expected Becky to go off the rails.'

'Like me, you mean.'

'No, of course I didn't mean you! I wasn't even –'

'If you're so bothered about your precious bloody Becky, then maybe you'd better start looking for her.'

Cathy stood up. 'I think I just might do that.'

She was outside in the driveway when a police car pulled up in the street. Cathy flew into panic mode. An officer got out of the driver's seat. Luckily, it was PC Andy Baxter.

'I believe I have something – or someone – that belongs to you.' He opened the rear door. Becky climbed out.

'Where the hell have you been?' cried Cathy.

'I'm not late,' Becky retorted.

'I picked her up not far from where a stolen car was abandoned,' Andy explained. 'We'd been following it for a while: two males and a female inside it. Looked suspiciously like Becky but she's denying it.'

'It wasn't me!'

'She won't tell me who was driving it and I didn't get a good look at him. But I have my suspicions about that too.'

Becky gulped. This was all she needed. After the mix up with Danny, they'd been on their way to drop her off. It was when they were driving past Vincent Square, heading for Christopher Avenue, that they'd first heard police sirens. Through the back window, Becky noticed an unmarked car, only a few feet behind them. Danny had raced around the estate for several minutes trying to lose them. But in the end, he'd driven into a large fenced yard and he and Austin had got out. They'd legged it up and over a row of garages and dropped into the field behind. Becky had sneaked through a privet hedge and ended up in someone's garden. She'd run down the path and was out in the street when Andy had collared her.

Now she was in big strife and not only from Cathy. She could see Jess watching from the doorway, running a finger across her throat as if she were threatening to kill her.

'Jesus Christ, Becky,' said Cathy. 'Every time you go out, you bring home trouble. I –'

'I didn't have any choice! And – and Jess left me, you should be mad with her too!'

'Don't try and put the blame on me, you cow!' said Jess.

'Well, you –'

'Ladies!' Andy nodded towards the house. 'Shall we go inside? Dirty laundry and all that?'

Becky marched past Cathy to go into the house. But Cathy pulled her back. She grabbed Becky's chin and sniffed.

'I thought so. You've been drinking! I told you to be careful in your state. You shouldn't be drinking at all. What were you thinking of!'

Andy didn't look at all shocked by the news that Becky was to become another teenage statistic.

'You don't look pregnant,' he told her. 'When's it due?'

'Never if it's got anything to do with me.'

Cathy squeezed her arm roughly. 'I could slap your stupid face, do you know that? I wish you weren't so… so… You can ruin your own life, Becky, but you have someone else to think about right now.'

'I don't want to be pregnant,' said Becky tearfully.

Cathy calmed a little at this remark. Maybe this could be an opportunity to get to the bottom of her little secret.

'Kitchen. Now,' she demanded but her tone was a little bit lighter. Andy followed them in. Close on his heels was Jess. Cathy stopped her in the doorway.

'I'll handle this.'

'But –'

She closed the door, leaving her protesting in the hall. Then she sat down beside Becky at the table.

'You and I need to talk,' she said. 'And I'm willing to sit here all night if I have to.'

'I've got nowt to say!'

'I have.' Andy sat down next to Cathy. 'I'm going to let you off with a caution this time,' he took out his notebook, 'because you're new around here and because, technically I can't prove whether you were in the car under your own volition. But if there is *one* more next time, I won't be so lenient.'

'Thanks, Andy,' said Cathy, knowing that she owed him once more.

'But it wasn't my fault! They locked the doors. I –'

'Will you shut up and listen to him! He's giving you a second chance. Not that you deserve one but –'

'Are you going to be seeing Danny Bradley again?' Andy interrupted, addressing Becky.

'Not if she wants to stay here,' Cathy answered for her.

Becky stood up, scraping her chair noisily across the floor. 'Leave me alone, both of you. I don't need your help, or your concern. I can look after myself, and my baby. I'll go to the housing association first thing tomorrow, get myself a flat and move out of here. You can wash your hands of me. That's what you want to do, isn't it?'

'Of course it's not.' Cathy touched her arm.

'No, I mean it! I'll pack my things now. You won't see me again after tomorrow.'

As she stormed out, Cathy left her to it this time.

Andy shook his head. 'I still don't know how you do this, Cath. You have far more patience than I'll ever have.'

'I don't always feel patient but I have to keep my wits.' Cathy sighed. 'What else is out there for them? I can only take in four of these girls at a time. God knows what happens to the ones that I miss.'

'I wish Becky would see that.'

'She'll come round,' Cathy said, more confident than she felt about it happening.

Becky paused momentarily when she saw Jess waiting outside her bedroom door.

'You're dead when I get you on your own,' Jess told her. 'Don't think you can treat me like a piece of shit.'

'Leave me alone.'

Becky pushed past her and into her room. Jess grabbed for her arm but she was too quick. In a flash, the door was shut and locked. Sliding down to the floor as Jess hurled a torrent of abuse from the other side of it, she held her head in her hands. What was it with her lately? Is this how her life was going to pan out? Getting into trouble all the time and then what? Drugs? Prison? If she carried on like this, they'd take her baby into care. Then she'd be alone again. She rested a hand on her stomach. That was laughable really. What could she give a baby when she couldn't look after herself?

More to the point, what had got into Danny Bradley? Becky might have let him shag her but he didn't own her. And now Austin thought they were an item, it looked like she'd lost her chance with him. He was much cooler than Danny Bradley. God, she would have to toughen up.

Exhausted and emotional, she dragged herself across to the bed and flopped down onto it.

'Stuff you all,' she said. 'Stuff the lot of you. I don't need anyone else.'

Then she burst into tears.

THIRTEEN

'I will not tolerate this kind of behaviour,' Cathy repeated to Becky over breakfast the next morning. 'It's bad enough that you came in drunk and woke up the whole street when you first arrived but to be brought home by the police? Well, it just raises eyebrows and I don't want any of that.'

'But I told you, it wasn't my fault,' Becky cried. 'They wouldn't let me out of the car. They left Jess behind.'

'*They* left you behind to take the blame.'

'*They* are going to kill you when they get hold of you,' said Jess as she joined them in the kitchen.

'I never grassed them up!'

'You're both as bad as each other,' said Cathy. 'I was so sure that you two would become firm friends.'

'Just because we're both teenagers doesn't mean we'll get on.' Jess slumped down next to Becky and rested her chin on the heel of her hand. 'And friends would look out for each other, not leave them in the lurch to walk miles home on their own.'

'I'm sorry, okay! I didn't know they'd leave you behind.'

Cathy sighed. All she wanted was a bit of peace every now and then. But while she had the two of them together, it seemed a perfect time to keep the conversation going.

'I just want you – both of you – to start thinking of other

people for a change and show some respect,' she said. 'It isn't much to ask.'

'I don't know why you've dragged me into this,' Jess remarked. 'It wasn't me who was brought home by the plod last night.'

'Not this time, but it has been on occasion.' Jess opened her mouth to complain but Cathy didn't give her the chance to speak. 'You know I can't settle until you're home because I worry. What do you want me to do? Buy a notice board and get you to write on it where you are and what time you'll be back?'

'I'm not doing that. It'd be like being at school.'

'If you act like children then I'll treat you the same. This talk is again to remind you of the rules.'

'Not those frigging rules.' Jess folded her arms. 'You don't have control over our every waking minute, you know.'

'Of course I know that,' said Cathy. 'But while you are here, you will show me some respect. You came in late the night before last and I turned a blind eye as you were coherent.'

'So?'

'Put yourself in my position. I have a full house now that Cheryl is back. I have five people to think of and worry about all the time. Can you imagine what that is like?'

'Six,' said Becky quietly.

'What?' Cathy turned towards her.

'There are six of us to look after.' Lightly, she ran a hand over her stomach.

'You keeping it then?' Jess nudged Becky.

Becky blushed. She nodded, although she wasn't sure.

'At least you'll get out of here quicker that way. Single woman with child gets further up the list. You'll have a flat in no time when some other poor slapper does a runner. That Josie Mellor will be round here soon, trying to move you on.' Jess pointed at Cathy. 'That's what she likes to do, move you on so that you're someone else's problem.'

'That's a lie!' Cathy banged her hand down on the table. 'You know I always do what I think is best for you – the best for you all.' She pointed at her. '*You* had better watch your step and be a good friend to this one, and you,' she pointed to Becky, 'need to get streetwise pretty sharpish or you'll be shat on from a great height and used for God only knows what.'

'Like me,' said Jess.

Cathy gave her a sarcastic smile. 'Yes, like you.'

'I've had enough of this. I'm getting out of here.' Jess scraped back her chair and stormed out of the room. 'Be sure to tell Cheryl about the rules again when she gets out of her pit.'

The kitchen door slammed and finally there was peace.

'You won't make me leave, will you?' Becky asked.

Cathy shook her head. 'No, I won't. But you, as well as Jess, need to show some respect. I can only do so much to protect you. You've been here a while now and for the most part of it, you've behaved yourself. But I don't want you getting in too deep with the wrong crowd.'

'I don't really know a crowd.'

Cathy gave her half a smile, not sure if she was trying to make light of the situation or not. 'All the same, I don't want to ruin my relationship with PC Baxter. It's a good job I have him. Do you hear me?'

*

Cathy pulled her arms high and stretched. It was one am. She felt exhausted but was glad that she'd managed to see the end of the film. She switched off the television and listened. Silence. The house was quiet and there was nothing going on out in the garden.

Since their little chat this morning, both girls had been behaving themselves. This evening, Becky hadn't gone out at all but had stayed in her room and Jess had come in about ten, not a whiff of alcohol. She'd apologised for her outburst that morning and they'd talked a while before she'd gone off to bed. Even Cheryl hadn't come home in a stroppy mood. All in all, it had been a better day.

She sat still for a while. This was her favourite time of day, when everyone was home, safely tucked up in their beds, and she could switch off completely. Ten minutes later, she yawned loudly. She got up and went to draw the bolt across the front door. But her high mood was short lived. There was another envelope on the mat.

Cathy ripped it open. Just like the last one, it was blank on both sides. Again there was a piece of cheap lined paper, the writing on it the same as the first note.

'YOU WILL NEVER BE SAFE'

Stupid, stupid man. Cathy screwed up the note in anger. How dare Kevin McIntyre put her in this predicament! He must have sneaked up to the house while she was watching the film. She shuddered: what a creep.

But just as quickly she smoothed out the paper. Now there were two of them, the matter became a little more serious. What should she do? Should she show it to Liz or

141

would it have the desired effect of putting the frighteners on her? Liz was trying to get on with her life: it was just a shame that stupid prick of her husband wasn't.

Cathy sighed. She couldn't decide what to do about it now. She'd speak to Rose about it in the morning. Maybe talking it through would make more sense of it. Maybe between them they could decide.

Over coffee at Rose's house the next morning, they discussed the matter.

'What do you think I should do?' Cathy asked.

'If you don't want to show Liz, then you should show them to Andy,' said Rose. 'He'll know what to do with them. He'll probably tell Liz to take out an injunction or whatever it is she needs to do.'

'Yes, she did mention doing that a while ago.' Cathy sighed. 'But she seems to be finding her feet, even though she's still a nervous wreck whenever she goes out or there's a knock on the door. I don't want to worry her any more than is necessary.'

'You're getting too close, Cath,' Rose pointed out gently. 'She has a right to know.'

'Yes, but –'

'How would you feel if someone had kept it from you?'

Cathy looked down at the table. Rose was right: she knew she'd be mortified.

'And what if there are more to come? If he thinks they aren't being taken seriously…'

'I don't follow.'

'If he thinks that the notes don't bother Liz, then,' Rose shrugged a shoulder, 'who knows what else he might do.'

'God, you have a point there.'

They sat in silence while Cathy mulled it over.

'I still don't know what to do,' she said eventually.

'Yes, you do.' Rose patted her hand. 'It's Liz who needs to decide. You should show them to her.'

Once they'd finished their conversation, Cathy took Rose over to the shops on Vincent Square to pick up a prescription. They headed into the newsagents afterwards. While Rose was over at the till paying for her lottery tickets, Cathy flicked through a magazine.

Someone nudged her. She turned to see Josie and smiled warmly, pointing at the female model she'd been looking at.

'I was just looking to see how I could give the impression of being twenty years younger in a day. I mean, what do they do with these models? Believe me, no amount of Botox or tummy tucks would get rid of the crisps and chocolate that I stuffed down me last night. Mind you, it did give me some exercise this morning. I had to run to the loo several times because I ate that much. Oh, hello…'

Cathy looked on in embarrassment when she noticed that Josie wasn't alone. The man standing to her right was tall, thin but not to the point of being skinny. His hair was dark, receding slightly and cropped short, his clothes clean and stylish. Cathy noted that he could easily fit in the magazine alongside Miss Twenty Something Trollop, although it would have to be a spread on sugar daddies: he looked like he was in his mid forties. As well as the upturn of his lips, bright blue eyes were smiling at her too. All at once Cathy felt heat rise from her chest, up her neck and spread swiftly across her face.

Josie noticed it too and grinned. 'This is Matthew Simpson – Matt,' she introduced. 'He's the new maintenance officer I was telling you about.'

Cathy thrust out her hand. 'Pleased to meet you, Matt.'

'Likewise,' Matt replied, letting his hand linger in hers for a second longer than necessary.

'Those youths have been hanging around again, Josie,' said an elderly lady carrying a small dog underneath her arm. She pushed past them all to grab the three-for-a-pound chocolate bars on offer. 'It's been chaos in my street since. How many times do I have to complain before anything gets done about it?'

'We do our best, Mrs Weston,' Josie replied, rolling her eyes when she knew the woman wasn't looking directly at her. 'But sometimes it's hard to get the right results for everyone.'

'And you're no better,' Mrs Weston vented her anger on Cathy next. 'That bloody girl of yours, that Myatt girl, has been causing trouble too.'

'Oh, wind your neck in, Vera,' Rose answered sharply as she joined them. 'Your grandsons aren't so perfect.'

Aware that she was going to get back what she'd given, Mrs Weston walked off muttering to herself.

'Wow, is it always this eventful when you buy a bag of crisps?' Matt wanted to know. 'There seems to be so much happening on this estate.'

Cathy and Josie shared a smile.

Rose snorted. 'Wait 'til you've been here for a month, love. You'll soon want to go back to where you came from. Which is where, exactly?'

'Buxton.'

'And you chose to come and work *here*?'

Matt laughed at the outlandish look on Rose's face. 'It's not that bad, surely?'

'Ever watched *Shameless?*'

'Yes.'

'And *The Sopranos*?'

Matt nodded slowly, his eyes flicking quickly between them.

'How about *Dexter*?' Cathy smirked.

'Who?' asked Rose.

'*Dexter*. It's an American series. He works in forensics and he's a serial killer.'

'Oh. I was thinking more along the lines of *Bad Girls.*'

'Or even *Taggart*. There's always a *mur-da* going down on the Mitchell Estate.'

Josie nudged Cathy sharply. 'Bugger off, you two. You'll scare him away before I've told him the rest.'

'The rest?' Matt's eyes widened but he finally realised he was being had when the three women burst into laughter.

'You're playing with me,' he grinned. 'Right?'

'Actually,' said Josie, 'I'm afraid we're not.'

FOURTEEN

'We've just been across to the shops,' Rose told Liz when they got back to Cathy's house. 'We bumped into Josie Mellor. She had that new maintenance officer with her.'

'And?' Liz was stirring a saucepan of soup over the cooker.

Rose tried to whistle. 'I wish that I was twenty years younger. What do you say, Cath? Did you like him?'

Cathy nodded. 'He was certainly a sight for sore eyes.'

'Talk, dark and handsome, that's what I would've said in my day,' Rose continued.

Liz laughed. 'What do you think we would say now? Hot, fit and hunky?'

'Yes, exactly that.'

'I don't believe you,' said Cathy. 'You're too old to think of men that age. Unless you want a toy boy?'

Rose roared with laughter. 'Listen, you two. I'm not too old to give you a run for your money.'

'No, just too ugly.' Cathy smiled sweetly at her.

Rose slapped her wrist in a playful manner. 'Speak for yourself. I'm up for it.'

'Yes, but would all your aches and pains be up to it? You keep harping on about your bad back.'

'Oh, I don't see that as a problem. I reckon I could find a

way around it that would mean I didn't have to do all the work.'

'Rose Clarke!' Cathy feigned shock. 'If only your Arthur could hear you now.'

'Why should I care?' Rose said fondly. 'He was probably the cause of it in the first place.'

Liz smiled. 'You two argue like an old married couple.'

'What I was going to say,' Rose directed the comment to Liz, 'is that he's just about right for Cathy.'

'Please.' Cathy waved away the comment. 'A man's the last thing I need in my life, don't you think?'

'Why?' said Liz and Rose in unison.

Cathy frowned. 'Because – because they complicate things.'

'Well, you do fancy him,' said Rose.

'I do not!'

'You should have seen the colour of her cheeks.' Rose winked at Liz and pointed a finger at Cathy. 'Blood red in a matter of seconds.'

'They were not!' said Cathy, knowing full well that she had felt them burning at the time. 'Besides, he'll probably be spoken for if you think he's that good looking.'

Rose leaned forward and patted her hand. 'I'll make it my job to find out for you.'

'You'll do no such thing!'

'Come on, Cathy Mason. How long is it since you had a man between your legs?'

'Change the subject, will you!'

Rose sniffed. 'I think you're mad not to follow up on him. He's one gorgeous man. And it'll heal up soon if you don't use it. It's not natural to go without for so long.'

'You two are worse than Jess and Becky at times,' Liz said, sitting down beside them with a steaming bowl of tomato soup.

'Yes, but we love each other really,' said Rose. 'Don't we, Cathy?'

Cathy huffed. 'That's what you think.'

'Still,' Liz sighed, 'I wish I'd had a friend to grow up with.'

'There must have been someone you were close to,' said Rose.

'I had a few acquaintances when I was at school and when I worked at the post office for a few months but when I hooked up with Kevin, I didn't see them much more after that.'

'You should always make time for friends. Don't you have any close family?'

Liz was just about to take a mouthful of soup but put down her spoon instead. 'I had a really lonely upbringing. When my sister was born six years after me, it was like I didn't exist. She was the pretty one: I was always the clever one. She's always been the favourite. The sun has always, and always will, I'm sure, shine out of her backside, very, very brightly. The year after I had Chloe, my parents moved to Devon. A year later, my sister and her family moved there too and I haven't seen them since.'

'That's such a shame,' said Rose. 'I'm really close to my sister. I could murder her at times but she's always been there for me. And my girls get on well together most of the time.'

'Don't get me wrong, I find out everything that my sister does in my mother's emails,' Liz explained. 'She can't wait to gloat. And she rings me every few months, though I think out of duty. She mostly goes on about how well Shauna's doing and how she goes out with her family all the time. She doesn't realise how hurtful it is. Last year, my parents even came to stay with friends in Congleton but they didn't call to see us.'

'Do you think it was because of Kevin?'

Liz shook her head. 'I know they never wanted me to marry him. They made it perfectly clear how much of a mistake I was making. But it's not that. I'm just not the favourite daughter. It's really that simple.'

'It does explain why you stayed with Kevin for so long though,' Cathy said. 'Did your father ever hit your mum?'

'Cathy!' cried Rose.

Cathy turned towards her quickly. 'What?'

'Sometimes you can be a bit too blunt.'

'I know, but I –'

'It's okay,' Liz told them. 'I don't recall anything. All I can remember is a very oppressive atmosphere. Which is why I needed family stability, I suppose – even though, you're right, it was far from stable with Kevin.'

'Well at least you're out of it now, thank goodness,' said Rose. 'Which is why the saying goes that you can pick your friends but you can't choose your family.'

'I agree with that one entirely.' Cathy shook her head. 'Can't think why I possibly ended up with a friend like you then.'

Rose tutted. 'I've never liked you that much anyway.'

Liz smiled: she found it hard not to.

Becky lay on her bed, one knee on the other, her foot swinging to and fro, her hand resting on her tummy. While she urged her baby to move, she wondered how big it was. And was it okay in there? Was it safe to have sex or should she stop Danny from touching her? That was when she could stand him pawing at her: her breasts were swollen and sore to touch which made it unbearable at times.

After she'd scarpered from the stolen car, Danny had texted her to apologise for his actions. Becky had sulked for a while before making up with him. Without Jess and Cathy knowing, they'd met up again and they'd had sex, four times so far. Twice she'd closed her eyes and imagined that it was Austin Forrester kissing her, Austin Forrester touching her, Austin Forrester riding her. Austin Forrester with his smouldering eyes, his strong features, his sexy bum she'd been staring at the other day when he'd been checking the oil on Danny's old wreck.

She wondered – if she had sex with Austin, would everything be okay? Would the memories of Uncle James fade quicker? Was it just because Danny was rough and he wasn't the right one for her? Or maybe he was the right one for her. How would she know?

There was a knock on the door. Becky looked up to see Liz.

'I thought you might like this.' She came into the room and handed her a book. 'It's a bit old but it has some useful tips and such.'

The paperback was called *Baby Knowledge – From Conception to Birth*. Becky took it from her, wondering if she had secret psychic powers.

'And if there's anything that isn't in there, just ask. I bet there's something you'd like to know. There's a lot happening to you right now.'

At Becky's continued silence, Liz turned to leave.

'Does it hurt a lot?' Becky whispered softly.

'Like hell,' Liz nodded. 'I can't tell you otherwise. It wouldn't be fair.'

'How long did it take?'

'Just over eight hours.'

'Will it take me that long?'

Liz sat down on the bed beside her. 'Everyone's different,' she said. 'When I went to the baby clinic, I spoke to a woman who only realised she was having the baby when she went to the loo and saw the baby's head coming out.'

Becky paled in an instant.

'Sorry.' Liz grimaced. 'I'm not helping, am I?'

'I want to know though.'

'Anything else?'

'How big will it be now?'

'Do you know how far gone you are at all?'

Becky shrugged. She'd only assumed she was pregnant because she'd had the same symptoms before. 'Just over three months, I think.'

'It'll probably be about the size of a kidney bean.'

'Is that all?'

Liz nodded. 'That's why it's so important to look after yourself. The baby needs you at the moment. You are its lifeline. Whatever you do now could possibly have a profound effect on its future.'

Becky looked up, drinking in Liz's every word.

'It's you it's relying on,' she continued. 'You and no one else. Do you understand what I'm trying to say?'

Becky nodded and smiled. Liz was right. This was her baby: *her* responsibility. She would look after it as best she could, make sure that no one hurt it. Eager to learn more, she opened the book and began to flick through the pages.

Liz stood up. 'Why don't you read some of it and then see if you have any questions afterwards? I'm always around for a chat.'

Once she'd gone, Becky lay back on the bed, her legs flat on the mattress this time. No swinging her ankles about like a trapeze artist. Until she'd checked the book, she was going to stay in this position.

An hour later and she was clued up enough to know that things had to change. From now on, there would be no more drinking. No more risk-taking in stolen cars. No more fags here and there that could easily turn into a bigger habit. She would do nothing that would harm her baby.

The book said that having sex was okay too. So if she wanted to do it with Austin, she'd have to do it quickly before she decided who to have as her boyfriend. She liked Danny but she really liked Austin. Maybe he would be the better father, if he was boyfriend-staying-around material.

And he was so mature. Look how he'd sorted Danny out for her when he'd gone too far. That was the trouble with Danny. He didn't know when to stop, when enough was enough. But Austin, well, Austin was more of a man. She recalled his face, something that had played a big part in her dreams over the past few nights. She remembered every little detail: fiery eyes that often glanced up and down her body, the silver loop earring hanging from his left ear. Yet again she wondered how he'd acquired the scar on his cheek. So far she'd been too shy to ask him.

She rested her hand on her stomach again as she considered how to go about her plan. She had to sleep with Austin soon or else he'd guess that she was pregnant. She wouldn't be able to keep it to herself for much longer, even if she wanted to anyway. It didn't take much to work things out. She was bursting out of her clothes even more now, especially her jeans – she couldn't fasten the waistband at all. Cathy had bought her some maternity leggings and a few baggy T-shirts but she didn't want to wear them yet.

But how would she tell Danny that she didn't want to see him anymore? And how was she going to tell Austin that she fancied him when he was always with Danny?

Becky pondered for a while. Maybe it would be better to keep things sweet with Danny in case Austin didn't like her as much as she thought. Although from the looks he kept shooting her way, she doubted that very much.

She smiled. It was then that she realised, despite being sixteen and scared stiff, she wanted to have her baby. And she wanted to keep it. So what if everyone thought she was young and naïve; she'd show them she was mature and ready for anything.

She turned to page twenty: having sex while pregnant.

As Becky lay on her bed with her hand caressing her stomach, Austin lay on top of his filthy mattress with his hand around his cock. The joint he'd smoked earlier had made him pleasantly sleepy and along with the vodka he'd lifted, he was in a good place. Even in this shit hole pub. Everything seemed to be going to plan.

As his hand moved up and down his shaft, he imagined Becky's mouth around it, running her tongue up and down the length before taking him deep into her throat. He closed his eyes. If only it was time to put his plan into action, he could have sex on tap with her. But the timing had to be just right.

Still, there wasn't long to wait now. And he'd seen the looks Becky had been giving him, the glances, the stares, the hair fiddling, the hand on her chest. She was his for the taking. He didn't mind Danny keeping her warm until he was ready. Because he wouldn't have her that long anyway.

FIFTEEN

Cathy was running late for her session helping out at the community house. At the last minute, she'd decided to wash and straighten her hair. She'd also tried three outfits on before she settled on her favourite flirty-swishy skirt, cream wedge heels and a knitted sleeveless top. The recent run of unseasonably warm weather had continued into May, long enough for her to gain a bit of a glow to her skin which the top showed off as subtly as a tiny bit of cleavage. Now she was frantically searching for her car keys. She slapped her forehead more firmly than she'd intended.

'Think, think!' she told herself. 'Where did you have them last?' She cast her mind back to the day before, as if her mind had wandered far from thinking about Matt Simpson after they'd been introduced.

Oh, yes: they'd just come back from the shops. She raced over to the fruit bowl. There next to the apples, oranges and bananas was a bunch of keys.

'I'm off out, girls,' she shouted through to the living room. 'I've left a list of jobs for you to do before I get back. Make sure they're done.'

Checking herself one last time in the hall mirror, she rushed outside. Then she stopped abruptly.

'Fuckity, fuckity, fuck!'

There was a huge scratch down the near side of her car. Both tyres had been slashed, the wing mirror had been kicked off and slung onto the grass. She rushed around to the other side, only to find the same had been done there.

'My car!' Cathy gulped back tears. 'Who did this to my car?'

Rose, who was putting rubbish into her wheelie bin, came rushing over. 'Oh, no.' She gasped. 'That's such a mess. I didn't hear anything out of the ordinary last night either.'

'I – just – I –' Cathy ran both her hands through her carefully prepared hair and pulled it enough to hurt. 'Why me, Rose? Why is it always bloody me?'

Rose walked around the car slowly. 'It might not be anything to do with you. Though it is probably because of you,' she said as she inspected the damage. 'I reckon you must have a list a mile long of culprits. Well, because of whom you have staying with you, anyway.'

'But that's pathetic. I'll kill that Kevin McIntyre when I get my hands on him. He has no right to do this to my property.'

'You can't prove it was him.'

Cathy shook her head, exasperated at the audacity of it all. 'Of course I can't.' She rummaged around in her bag until she found her mobile phone. 'I'll have to ring Josie and tell her I'm going to be late. And I'll have to change my shoes. I can't walk quickly in these bloody things.'

Half an hour later, Cathy rushed into The Den at the community house. She found Suzie, another volunteer helper, in the kitchen.

'I'm sorry I'm late,' she said, plonking her bag down in a flurry. 'My car's been vandalized and I've –'

The small, blonde woman held up a hand. 'It's okay. Matt's told me all about it. Not too much damage caused, I hope?'

'Matt?' Cathy was taken a bit by surprise. 'Jeez, word travels fast.'

'Josie reckons he's good with cars so she thought he might be able to help out. He's calling in a bit later, once the rabble quietens down.'

The rabble Suzie was referring to began to arrive in dribs and drabs during the next hour. The Den was frequented by approximately fifty youngsters from the estate. They were teenagers like Jess, Becky and Cheryl who had recently left school without qualifications, had no aspirations and no chance of ever getting off the Mitchell Estate to improve their outlook.

For every one of them who came through the door twice a week, Cathy saw a little bit of hope. At first when The Den had opened six months ago, the kids on the estate had avoided it, teasing anyone who had the audacity to attend a session and generally blackballing the place without even stepping over its threshold. But as the buzz about the place intensified and The Den became the place to be, a place to meet up, catch up and get a free mug of coffee and a seat to crash down on, Cathy had seen the numbers slowly increasing. Once she'd got them on side, she'd then been given funding for laptops and set up meetings writing CVs, creating simple IT sessions and gradually raising awareness that there was more to life than sitting back and waiting for it to bite you. Some of the teenagers had responded well, gone on to get themselves jobs and moved on with their lives. Some of them had stayed exactly the same as the first day they'd walked in. But the main thing was that they were still coming every week. And, surprisingly, the laptops hadn't been stolen. Cathy had no doubt that she would crack some of them eventually. Success breeds success, she hoped.

Today, if she hadn't been running late as well as having her nerves trashed, Cathy would have done a session on what to wear for a job interview but there was no time for that now. Besides, she didn't feel like she could stand up and present anything positively today. Instead, the group would have to be content with the usual drop-in session with no particular structure other than coffee and a catch up. It would have to do.

As promised, Matt came by about eleven. Cathy brightened at the sight of him walking towards her and gave him a wave. She glanced down at her feet, now sporting ballerina pumps and sighed. Why didn't she bring her shoes with her to change into? What a wimp she was, not being able to manage fifteen minutes brisk walking in them.

She was sitting at the table, encouraging Katie Stedson to have a go at taking her GCSE maths again. Cathy was prepared to help out as much as she could, although that wouldn't be a great deal as maths hadn't been her strong point either.

'I hear you've had a spot of trouble?' Matt said.

Katie looked up, waiting to get all the details. Cathy pointed towards the door.

'There might be a better place to discuss things.' She spoke to Katie next. 'Think about what I said. It would be good for you to have something to focus on other than baby Teagan.'

Katie looked a little disgruntled as Matt and Cathy left. They went upstairs to Josie's office, open to anyone when she wasn't there. Cathy unlocked the door with her key.

'Sorry about that,' she referred to their earlier conversation as they sat down. 'But news travels fast around here. I don't want too many people to know that my car has been vandalized.'

'I'm sorry, too. I'm not used to the estate etiquette yet.' Matt smiled, the skin around his eyes wrinkling.

Cathy smiled too: she couldn't help it. Then as the air crackled with expectancy, she felt colour rising in her cheeks again. What was it about this man? But of course she already knew. Her hormones were telling her.

'Josie mentioned you might be able to help me out.' She opened the window and wafted a hand in front of her face, hoping that he'd think she was flushed because of the weather. 'I'm lost without my car.'

'Yes. I have a small trailer. If you like, I can remove the tyres and take them to be sorted. The mirrors I can fix back and replace; same too with the wipers. But I have to draw the line at a re-spray. I can't get scratches out. Unless they'll come out with a bit of elbow grease?'

Cathy shrugged. 'I can't remember how deep they are. I was so angry that I didn't take too much notice.'

Matt checked his watch, giving Cathy a glimpse of downy hairs on his tanned forearm. 'Shall I pop by after work tonight? Say fourish, if I can get off that early?'

'Would you?'

'Sure. I'll ring around during my lunch break for some

prices; see if I can get a good deal anywhere. Then I can –'

There was a knock on the door and Josie walked in. She smiled when she noticed the cosy situation. 'Suzie told me you were here, Matt. When you have a moment, could you change the strip light in room seven please and see if you can do something with that squeaking door in the kitchen?'

Matt stood up and saluted Josie. 'Yes, boss. I'm on my way.'

'Later will do,' Josie grinned, 'if you're busy now.'

'No, I –'

'We were just finished,' said Cathy, feeling her cheeks burning again.

Matt turned to her. 'See you later.' And then he was gone.

Josie perched on the corner of the desk. 'You're blushing like an infatuated teenager,' she said.

'I am not!'

'You are too! He is gorgeous, though, isn't he?'

Cathy nodded, knowing better than to think she could hide her feelings from Josie.

'So would you?'

'Would I what?'

Josie winked. 'You know, touchy feely. Hide the sausage?'

Cathy picked up a ruler from the desk and rapped Josie on the thigh. 'Don't be so childish.'

Josie leaned towards her and whispered. 'I'm not the one playing games.'

Before Cathy had a chance to reply, Josie was gone too.

*

Cathy had ironed a pile of clothes for Rose and had taken them over to her house. She was pretending to listen to Rose prattling on but really she was thinking about Becky getting into trouble, about Jess leading her astray. She was thinking about Cheryl who was staying away more than she was back. She was thinking...

'Stop worrying,' Rose told her.

Cathy sighed. 'I can't help it.'

Rose peered over the top of her newspaper. 'You have mentioned those notes to Liz, haven't you?'

Cathy looked uncomfortable as she shook her head. 'I just can't find the right time. She seems a bit more content lately.'

'Kevin McIntyre won't just go away.'

'Maybe not. But it has been two weeks since the last one. I was hoping there wouldn't be any more.'

'It isn't your call,' Rose said sharply.

'I can't get everything right.' Cathy frowned. 'I can only try my best.'

'I think you should have been straight with her from the start.'

'And send her right back to him because she'd be too sacred of what he'd do to her if she didn't?'

'You have to leave her to make her own mistakes.'

'And Chloe?' Cathy snapped, annoyed that Rose should even question her judgement. 'Does she have to live with the mistakes too?'

'I was just saying –'

'Well, save it. I'm not listening. Is it my fault that Liz needed help and Josie chose me to look out for her?'

'No, but –'

'I do what I think is best for her – for them all when they live with me – and if that's not good enough for you, Rose Clarke, then I suggest you do your own ironing in future.'

'Don't be so pig-headed. Cathy!'

Cathy stormed down the path and across the street to her own house, seething inwardly. How dare Rose suggest that she didn't have Liz's best interests at heart! Wasn't that her problem, really? She was always thinking too much about other people, how they would react and how she could protect them from more pain. Yet by sheltering them, she chose to give the pain to herself in wondering what to do for the best.

If she told Liz about the notes and Kevin didn't come around, then she would have upset her for nothing. But if she didn't tell Liz about the notes and Kevin did come around and mentioned them, Liz would be angry with Cathy for *not* saying anything. She could scream at the unfairness of it all. Whatever she did would be wrong.

An hour later as she and Liz dished out dinner, and another missed opportunity to discuss the notes had passed, Cathy heard a scream which made the hackles stand up on her neck. Liz tore across the kitchen and up the stairs and she followed quickly behind. Chloe was standing outside her room. Her baby doll had an arm missing.

'What happened, angel?' asked Liz, but Chloe was crying too much to tell her.

Cathy barged into Cheryl's room but it was empty. She could hear Becky singing in the bathroom so knew it couldn't have been her. But Jess was in her room.

'Just what the hell do you get off on?' She grabbed Jess

by the arm and dragged her out onto the landing.

'Get off me!' Jess tried to shrug her off. 'You're bleeding mad! Let go!'

Cathy pushed her in front of Chloe and picked up the doll's arm from the floor. 'Is this your doing, you peevish cow?'

'No! I never touched it.'

'Then who was it?' Cathy twirled round 360 degrees in comical fashion. 'I don't see anyone else around here that would do such a cruel and thoughtless thing.'

'I told you, it wasn't me. You're always blaming me. What would I want with breaking her stupid doll?'

Without thinking, Cathy raised her hand. Then she stopped in mid air. It shocked her that she would want to slap Jess. She calmed herself for a moment.

'You are such a bully,' she told her. 'Sometimes I could knock your block off.'

'I'd like to see you try,' Jess goaded. 'I'd have you reported in a shot.'

'If I was your mother –'

'Well you're not, so shut your fat gob and leave me alone. And I know you won't hit me. You haven't got it in you.' Jess shrugged Cathy off.

Before anyone else could speak, there was another scream. But this time, it was more of a wail, like an animal in distress; a long and harrowing sound which stopped them all in their tracks.

Becky emerged from the bathroom, one hand at her chest clasping a towel covering her torso, the other clutching her stomach. 'My baby!' she sobbed. 'I'm bleeding.'

Cathy looked down at Becky's legs. There was a line of

blood trickling down the inside of her thigh. Liz rushed across to help while Jess hovered around in the background and Chloe stood in the doorway of her bedroom.

Becky clung on to Cathy. 'Please don't let me lose my baby.'

'Let's get you to your room. Can you walk?'

'I –' She folded over in agony, collapsing on the floor.

Cathy stooped down and ran a hand over Becky's forehead. She was hot and clammy.

'We need to get you checked out,' she said. 'Let's get you into my car.'

'Stuff the car,' said Jess. 'Won't she need an ambulance?'

'Ambulance!' Becky looked fraught with fear. 'But that book says –' She looked up at Liz. 'That book says it's the first sign of a mis – miscarriage.' She looked at Cathy then. 'Please help me! Please stop the pain!'

Cathy on one side and Liz on the other, they helped Becky to climb down the stairs. They were nearly halfway down when there was a knock at the door. Jess ran to open it. Matt stood on the doorstep.

'Hi, is Cathy in? I've got a number for someone who says he can look at her car. He reckons – what's happened?'

'It's Becky. She's bleeding,' said Jess. 'I think she's having a miscarriage.'

'NO!' Becky gave out another loud scream and dropped to the floor again.

'Come on.' Cathy tried to pull her back up. 'We're nearly there.'

'Let me help.' Matt moved past Jess and gently scooped Becky up in his arms. 'Hang on to my neck,' he told her.

He carried her down the stairs to his car, Cathy following close behind. They both helped her into the back seat. Then Matt held the door open for Cathy.

'I'll drive you there and you can sit in the back,' he said. 'She needs you with her.'

Without a moment's thought, Cathy kissed him on his cheek. 'Thank you,' she smiled. Then she dived into the car. But not before she saw Matt's face break out into a smile.

SIXTEEN

It had been three days since Becky had lost the baby. After she'd returned from the hospital, she'd been inconsolable for the first twenty-four hours, and lay on the settee in the living room. After that, she'd refused to come out of her room. Cathy had taken food and drink up to her but hardly any of it had been touched. She wished she could help her more, knowing only too well the feelings of loss that she would be going through. But she knew Becky would have to deal with it in her own way. Grief affected people differently.

Along with it, Becky's miscarriage had brought painful memories of loss crashing back into Cathy's head. She'd tried to push them away, instead concentrating on looking after the distraught girl who had turned into no more than a child herself. But still they kept coming back.

At lunchtime, she placed a sandwich and a mug of coffee on a tray and went upstairs. She knocked on Becky's bedroom door before she went in. Becky was lying on her bed curled up in the foetal position. She held a pillow in her arms. Greasy curls were stuck to her pale face, her eyes were puffy and her nostrils red and cracked. She glanced at Cathy then looked away just as quickly.

'I've brought you something to eat,' Cathy said, using her best sing-song voice.

'I'm not hungry.'

She slid the tray onto the bedside table. 'I'll leave it here for a while, just in case.'

'How can I eat when my baby is DEAD?'

'Bloody hell.' Cathy visibly jumped. 'You nearly gave me a heart attack, shouting out like that.'

'S – Sorry.' Becky paused. 'I don't know what to do now that... now that...'

Cathy sat down beside her and pulled her into her arms.

'Why is it always me?' Becky sobbed. 'I'm not a terrible person.'

'Of course you're not. Sometimes it's just nature's way. There must have been something wrong with the baby that meant it couldn't survive.'

'But that means it's my fault.' Becky's sobs became louder. 'Did I reject it? Why would I do that?'

'I didn't say that.' Cathy tried to back pedal. 'I meant that maybe it would have suffered if it had been born.'

'But they can do so much these days. They've got cures for most things. They could have saved it, those doctors. But they didn't because it was me. They looked down their noses but they don't know what I've been through. I wish I'd died as well.'

'Please don't speak like that.' Cathy held Becky closer, as if she could protect her from the pain. 'Life is too precious: it will always improve.'

'It won't.' Becky sniffed.

'It will. I know how you're feeling. I –'

'No, you don't! And you haven't got any children so tell me how you know?'

'I –'

'It was *my* baby!' Becky began to cry again. She pushed Cathy away.

Knowing when she was beat, Cathy stood up. Her hand hovered over Becky's head as she contemplated trying again but she dismissed the thought as soon as it happened. She couldn't reach her yet. Instead she went to her own room. By the side of the bed, she dropped to her knees and pulled out an old-fashioned toffee tin from underneath it. She sat down and, with a deep breath, took off the lid.

The tin was full of mementos. Photos of times gone by, birthday cards, anniversary cards, tickets for her first concert to see Take That and tickets for last year's concert to see Take That where she'd nearly lost her voice by shouting 'I love you, Gary'.

The first photo she came to had been taken on her wedding day. As she picked it up, a lone tear rolled down her cheek. Although she could clearly see his smile, clearly hear his laughter, she couldn't remember Rich's touch. She ran a finger over the image. The picture had aged but the twinkle in his eye was still plain to see. She was so grateful that he hadn't got a clue what had been going on when he'd been inside.

When he'd died, one by one, all their friends had dropped away. Friends she'd thought would stay around forever had deserted her. It had hurt at first: had they only come to see her because of Rich? Why did everyone love Rich and not her? But then she'd come to realise that they were just uncomfortable around her now that she was no longer part of a couple. They'd done so much together that it was hard for people to accept her alone. Without him, she was a reminder of what had been and his friends couldn't cope with it. It was easier for them not to acknowledge her, she could see that now. But it still hurt and three years later, it left her with no one to confide in. That's why she'd ended up so close to Rose.

Quickly, she flicked through the box to find something that would make her smile. She found another photo of Rich. Bare-chested, he was sipping a beer at a beach café. They'd been in Ibiza. Cathy closed her eyes for a moment, almost feeling the breeze rustling through her hair as she recalled the two of them running along the beach hand in hand, getting drunk on sangria and skinny dipping at midnight. With so many dreams and wishes, they'd planned their lives down to the finest detail. At least some of it had turned out as they'd expected.

Rich's memorial card was next to surface. The funeral service had been a mixture of pride and pain. Pride for the man she had spent most of her life with: pain because losing him had torn her in two.

There was nothing of Cathy's childhood in the tin except her birth certificate. She picked it up. Underneath it was what she was looking for. Folded up inside an anniversary card was another birth certificate. Inside that was a small photograph. She gazed at it sadly before flicking it over to read the three words she'd written on the back of it when she was eighteen.

Simon, my son.

The blue ink of the lettering had faded over time but the image was as sharp now as the day it was taken. It was her most treasured possession, a photograph of her baby provided by the hospital. Simon's tiny hands were up by the side of his head. He had a bush of dark hair, her long fingers, and her stubby nose. Painfully, she recalled she hadn't had time to notice anything else before he'd been whisked away.

Why hadn't she told Rich about him? It had been her one stupid mistake and it haunted her now just as much as it had then.

Cathy's tears wouldn't stop this time. She cursed. Why had she made herself look at the photos? Hadn't she cried enough over the past few days?

But really she knew why she had opened the tin. It was because, as she'd gone through Becky's trauma with her, she'd been thinking that now was the right time to do something about making amends for her mistake.

She was going to look for Simon.

Liz awoke with a start. She sat up in bed, sweat glistening on her brow, half expecting to hear a baby cry. Chloe stirred by her side but didn't wake.

It was one fifteen. She pulled back the duvet, crept out of the room and across the landing to the bathroom. There she sat on the edge of the bath and let her tears go.

Since Becky's miscarriage, Liz had been having recurring nightmares of losing her own child. Her baby would have been eighteen weeks old now, as big as an orange. It would have had eyelashes, eyebrows and maybe even some hair. It may have been able to hear her singing in the shower. It would have been growing rapidly and she would have been growing with it. She rested her hand on her empty stomach. It had been too soon to know if it would have been a boy or a girl, but either would have done for her. She'd wanted another child so desperately.

She ran a hand through her hair, hating herself for even thinking it but secretly she was pleased that Becky had lost her baby. It would have been agony if she'd had to stay at Cathy's and watch her grow, watch her give birth, see her walk around with a child that she didn't want.

Liz ran the cold water tap and swilled her face. How selfish was she? She knew how much Becky would be hurting because she'd been there. She could still feel the longing to sense the baby move, to wish that it were still part of her. She'd tried talking about it to Becky but twice she'd been rebuffed. She couldn't blame her for being angry. She had felt angry too, still did.

Flashbacks of a fist plunging into the soft flesh below her chest made her gasp and she began to cry again. Why had he done that to her? What had she done to deserve such treatment? Kevin should have loved her, protected her. He shouldn't have killed their child.

She swilled her face again and then went back to her room. Chloe was still asleep, her arms above her head on the pillow. Liz got into bed, trying not to disturb her. She lay there, gazing at her child, feeling the pull to hold her, protect her from the outside world. At least there was one thing she could be grateful for. She had Chloe, she would always have Chloe. No one, not even Kevin, could take her away.

Early the next morning, Jess knocked softly on Becky's bedroom door.

'Do you fancy coming out today?' she asked, standing on the threshold. 'We could go shopping. Or do anything that you want to.'

'No.'

'Well, how about coming downstairs for a cuppa before I start off on my exciting day of doing nothing?' Jess tried again.

'Please leave me alone,' whispered Becky.

'I'm only trying to help.'

'I know, but you can't. No one can.'

Jess took a step nearer. 'But you're young, Becks. You can have another baby when the time is right. I mean, let's face it. Getting pregnant at sixteen isn't exactly a blast. It sucks up your life forever. You need to live a little before tying yourself down with a kid. That's what I'm going to do. I'm going to be...'

Becky squeezed her eyes tight and pulled the duvet over her head until Jess finally got the message.

Jess stormed downstairs to moan at Cathy. She found her in the kitchen with Liz. They were washing and drying dishes.

'I don't know what to do,' she said to them.

'About what?' said Cathy.

'About Becky. She won't talk to me. She won't come out of her room. I've even offered to take her shopping.' She shrugged her shoulders. 'But I can't get through to her.'

'She's had a terrible loss. It's not like breaking a leg or having a stomach ache.'

'But she was too young to have a baby. I keep on telling her that.'

Liz reached a wet mug from the draining board. 'It's not a question of whether she wanted it,' she couldn't help saying. 'It's a question of losing something that was a part of you and now isn't. You need to realise that.'

'Says the voice of experience,' mocked Jess. 'Just

because you're older than me doesn't mean that you know everything. You've never lost a baby, so how would you know?'

Cathy saw Liz get ready to defend her corner. 'That's enough, Jess,' she interjected, not wanting another argument to start. She threw a tea towel at her. 'You can help to dry the dishes while you're sitting doing nothing.'

'Oh, that's so not fair. Why do I –'

The door opened and they all turned to see Becky standing in the doorway. Her skin was blotchy, her eyes barely visible due to the dark circles beneath them. She wore an over-sized, over-stretched T-shirt and slippers, a cropped cardigan pulled close as if trying to keep out the pain.

Cathy was the first to react. She ushered her into the room and sat her down at the table.

'Would you like a warm drink?' she asked. 'Jess, flick the kettle on and then be on your way.'

'But –' Jess complained.

'I thought you were going shopping.'

'Not on my own.'

Cathy raised an eyebrow.

'Fine. I know when I'm not wanted.'

Ten minutes later, coffee and toast had been made. But Becky hadn't touched either.

'I...' She looked up at Cathy through watery eyes. 'I... can I talk to you?'

Liz saw this as her cue to make herself scarce. 'I'd better get going. I need to –'

'No, please! Will you stay?'

Liz sat down at the table with them, trying not to look too surprised that Becky wanted her there as well.

It took Becky a few moments to compose herself and then it all came tumbling out.

'My baby was the only thing I had that was mine. I can't rely on my dad. I'll probably never see him again.' She glanced up at them both. 'I bet you've been wondering why he hasn't come after me?'

Cathy nodded, unable to tell her that fathers hardly ever came after the girls that she looked after.

'My mum died when I was seven and I went to live with my granny.' Becky smiled. 'I never knew my Pops but I loved my granny, she was the best. I saw my dad every Sunday. He always came around after he'd been to the pub and most of the time he'd fall asleep when he'd had his Sunday dinner. But I didn't care. When she died, I had to go and live with him.'

'How old were you then?' asked Cathy.

'Eleven. That's when everything changed for me. It was like… like living with a stranger. I spent most of the time on my own. My dad would be either at work or at the pub. All of my friends from school lived too far away for me to visit so I used to be in my room a lot. Then Uncle James started coming around.'

Cathy froze as she feared what was coming next.

'He used to make such a fuss of me at first. I remember him buying me lots of nice things – toys, comics, sweets. Then one night when they'd both come in from the pub, he came up to my room. I was asleep and he woke me up when he tried to get into bed with me. I just thought he was drunk and I pushed him away but he kept trying to kiss me and run his hands all over my body. Then he grabbed my chin really hard and told me to shut up or else he'd tell my dad how naughty I was. That was the start of it all. It just got worse from there. I –'

'You mean –' Liz started, 'you mean, he *touched* you.'

Becky laughed, a cackling sound that made Cathy inwardly cringe.

'He did more than touch me,' she said. 'Whose baby do you think it was?'

'Oh, I didn't mean it to sound as if it wasn't true.' Liz sounded distraught.

Cathy gave Liz's arm a reassuring squeeze as Becky continued.

'The first time I thought I might be pregnant, I chucked myself down the stairs because I didn't want to have his baby. I was only fourteen and he'd been coming in to my room once a month since that first time. I didn't have anyone to talk to then either but I just knew.'

'Didn't your dad suspect anything?' asked Cathy.

Becky shook her head. 'I hardly ever saw him, remember? So it was easy really. I stayed away from school while he was at work sometimes anyway, so I just stayed off a little longer. But I hurt my arm when I fell and it was so painful that I went to the hospital. Before I had it X-rayed, I told one of the nurses about the things that were happening to my body. She asked me how old I was. I said I was sixteen. They did some tests and she told me that I wasn't pregnant anymore. I never told anyone else.'

'Oh, Becky.' Tears streamed down Liz's cheeks.

'When I thought I was pregnant again, I knew I had to do something about it. So I got a knife.'

'Dear God!'

'I wasn't going to hurt myself,' Becky explained. 'But I

was going to make sure he never came near me again. On the night I left home, I stabbed my uncle in the leg and then I made a run for it. I thought I'd killed him.' She shuddered. 'That's why I was so scared to come out of my room when I first got here. I thought the police would be looking for me. I swear he was dead when I left him. But he must have been so drunk that he passed out. I took off because I thought he'd stopped breathing. I couldn't have killed him though, because it would have been on the news, wouldn't it?'

'Becky,' said Cathy gently. 'None of it was your fault.'

'It was! Don't you see? I could have stopped him doing it but I was a coward. I thought he'd tell my dad and then I'd have to go into a home because there was no one else to look after me. I didn't want to go into care. Look what's happened to Cheryl. She scares me: her mind is definitely twisted. So I stayed quiet. I did try once or twice to stop him but he made sure that I didn't try again. He was too strong for me.'

Cathy grimaced. How could this still happen? There were supposed to be laws to protect the young innocents but every time she opened a newspaper, every time she switched on a radio or television, she'd hear about another victim. She wished she had enough money and a bigger house to help them all.

'I meant what I said,' she reiterated, knowing that she had to get the message across. 'It wasn't your fault. This was some pathetic, useless bastard of a man who used and abused a child for his own purposes.'

'I – I should have stopped him.'

'You were raped.' Cathy reached across the table for her hand and gave it a squeeze. But Becky pulled it away.

'No! I *let* him do those things. Don't you see? I let him do it to me again and again and again. He said... he said it was all I was good for.'

'Did you ever talk to your dad about it?'

Becky paused, her memory flicking back to the night she had left her family home. The night she saw her dad pretending to be asleep. She shook her head.

'I didn't think he'd believe me.'

She started to cry then, her sobs ringing around the kitchen, getting into the bones of both women. Cathy rushed around to her and it was in her arms that she finally gave in.

'It was horrible. And every time I think of my baby, I think of what he did to me. That's why I was punished. That's why I lost my baby!'

'It wasn't your fault.' Cathy held her close. 'You had no control over things. You were taken advantage of, clear and simple.'

'No... I...' Becky's words became inaudible.

'It wasn't your fault. And it will never happen to you again. Do you hear me? Never!'

SEVENTEEN

Eleven thirty that night, Cathy was curled up on the settee. The television was on in the background: she hadn't watched it since switching it on an hour ago when Jess had come in. Rose had come to her rescue at eight thirty, arriving on the doorstep with broad shoulders and a welcome bottle of wine. Becky had been in her room for most of the night. Cheryl wasn't in yet though.

Even though she'd talked it through with Rose, Cathy was still disturbed by Becky's revelations that morning. She'd thought she'd heard it all over the past three years but what Becky finally told her had really shocked her. How could her father condone what was happening? Her own uncle was abusing her while, it seemed to Cathy, reading between the lines, her father knew perfectly well what was going on. How could he let someone, his brother, violate his daughter? And from such an early age, and for so long. No wonder Becky had been hard to crack since she'd arrived. First her mum had died, then her granny. Since then, it didn't seem like she'd had anyone to trust. Plus she also carried with her the fear that no one would believe her even if she did confide in someone.

Cathy recalled how it had shocked Liz too. She'd caught her crying an hour later, wondering how Becky's father could have turned a blind eye. Put his child at risk. Cathy had to agree. If he were standing in front of her now, she would gouge his eyes out. No, more than that, she'd like to knee him in the balls and then ram her elbow in his back. Then, while he was on his knees, she'd like to bring back her foot and kick him in the face as hard as she could. Then she'd cut off his brother's dick with something serrated, taking her time to extend the pain.

In reality, what she really wanted to do was contact Becky's father and get her uncle charged with rape of a minor. It was obvious to her now that he hadn't been in touch because of the problems it would cause. His brother would be known as a sex offender. Becky would be dragged home and most probably through the courts as well.

But, Cathy sighed and stretched her arms high above her head, it wasn't up to her. It was Becky's choice and she'd chosen not to do anything. Put it all behind her now that the baby had gone. Poor kid. Maybe there was something else she could do for her. She would put her thinking cap on and see what she could come up with.

When Rich had died three years ago, part of Cathy had died with him. She knew that looking after these women gave her a purpose to continue. But the worry it caused her sometimes became too much.

'Am I doing the right thing by these girls, Rich?' she whispered into the room. 'Do I do enough for them? Or is it what they do for me? I hate myself for what I did. I gave up on Simon. Why did I do that, Rich? Why?'

Cathy sat in silence, waiting for an answer that wouldn't come. But she knew the reason why she did this. It was because she'd never turn her back on another person.

*

It was nearing the end of May and it had been a while since Liz had seen or heard from Kevin. Cathy kept thinking that every extra day he kept away was a bonus. After the notes however, which she still hadn't mentioned to her, she doubted that he would leave things be. Even so the banging on the door that evening took them both by surprise.

Liz jumped up from the settee. 'Oh God, he's here again. What am I going to do?'

'Liz!' Kevin rapped hard on the living room window next. He cupped his hands and peered through. 'I can see you! Get your arse out here, right NOW!'

Cathy opened the front window slightly. 'I thought we'd seen the last of you. What do you want this time?'

'Keep out of this, you interfering bitch.'

'Oh, please, if I had a pound for every time someone called me that, I'd be worth a small fortune now. Go home.'

'You can't keep her from me forever.'

'I don't want to talk to you,' Liz appeared at Cathy's side.

Kevin held up Chloe's bike. 'I've come to bring this actually. My Chloe loved this bike.'

'Men often do this,' Cathy whispered to Liz. 'Bring something for the child to make the mother feel guilty. Leave it on the front,' she shouted to Kevin. 'I'll get it later.'

'No, I want to give it to her.'

'She's in bed,' said Liz. 'I'll come and get it.'

Cathy closed the window. 'I'll go. He might be playing the wounded father but he is still capable of hurting you.' She pressed the red emergency call-out button at the side of the telephone unit. 'Let's see if there's anyone on shift that can help us first. Maybe Andy is around.'

Kevin banged on the window again. 'Liz!' he yelled. 'Where are you? What are you doing in there?'

'I'm coming!'

'Liz, wait!' Cathy cried.

But Liz was out of the front door before she had time to pull her back.

Kevin threw the bike down on to the ground and grabbed her arms. 'You think you can say what you like because you're hiding in there, don't you?' he hissed.

'Let her go!' said Cathy.

Kevin forced Liz to her knees. 'Back off,' he told Cathy. 'You're nothing without the stick.'

'I can get it if you want to meet it again. My stick loves cowards. Now get your hands off her.'

'I'll do as I wish.' Kevin leered at Liz.

'Let go!' said Liz. 'You're hurting me!'

'Dad!' Chloe screamed as she appeared in the doorway. She ran across the garden, arms out in front, her pink nightdress flailing around her legs. 'Leave my mum alone.'

At the sight of his daughter, Kevin let go of Liz immediately. Chloe ran into her arms and burst into tears. Liz held on to her tightly.

'Hey.' Kevin bent down to Chloe's level. 'Me and Mum were only fooling around.' He opened his arms wide. 'Haven't you got a kiss for your old dad?'

'Get lost,' sobbed Chloe. 'I'm not a baby. I know you're trying to hurt Mum and I won't let you.'

'Christ, what have you been telling her? She can't be scared of me. I'm her father.'

'I haven't said anything to her,' said Liz, truthfully.

'She's old enough to see things for herself,' said Cathy.

'Yes, but –'

'Go away!' shouted Chloe. 'I hate you. You hurt my mum.'

As she turned her head away, Liz stared at Kevin with a mixture of fear and hate. Fear of what he might do to her when he eventually did catch up with her: hate for the man she had given her heart to at such a tender age and all he'd done was pummel into it and knock out all her hopes and dreams for a happy life.

Cathy glanced at the road as a police car stopped at the kerb. Moments later, PC Mark White got out of it.

'You called the cops!' Kevin glared at Cathy. 'What the hell did you do that for?'

'You can't keep coming around and threatening her. Liz has to move on with her life and so do you.'

'Like hell I do.' Deciding to change tactics, Kevin walked slowly towards Liz. 'Please come home. Listen to me. I'm nothing without you. I'll change.'

'You said that the last time.'

'But I promise! I'll –'

'– stop bothering her.' Mark came through the gate. 'That would be a good place to start. Hi, Cathy, nice evening.'

'It was until he showed up.' Cathy smiled, relieved to see Mark standing in her garden. 'I wonder if you might sort out a little problem we have.'

'I don't know why she called you,' Kevin pointed a finger at Cathy, 'but there was no reason to. I'm having a quiet conversation with my wife and then I'm going home.' This time he looked pointedly at Liz. 'Alone again.'

'Do you want to go with him?' Mark spoke to Liz.

Liz shook her head. Chloe was still holding on to her for dear life, her tiny frame shaking as she sobbed.

'Then I think you'd better call it a night.' Mark indicated the gate with a nod of his head. 'Be on your way.'

'I'm not going yet,' said Kevin. 'I don't see why I should.'

'You'll have to stay outside all night then.' Cathy walked over to join Liz and Chloe. 'Because we're all going in now, aren't we?'

Liz nodded. 'Come on, Chloe. Let's get you back into that warm bed of yours.'

But Chloe clung to Liz's waist. 'Not until *he* goes.'

'Chloe!' Kevin reached out to touch her but Chloe screamed. She continued to scream until he held up his hands. 'Okay, okay, I'm going.'

'Finally, he gets the message,' Cathy said sarcastically. 'And I wouldn't bother coming back too soon either. If at all.'

'You can't stop me.'

'You're right.' PC White reached for his notepad. He walked to the gate and pointed to a blue car. 'Is this his?' When Cathy nodded, he noted down the number plate and then addressed Kevin again. 'I can't stop you, but a harassment order can. And I think I have enough evidence to get one against you. You're harassing your wife, you're scaring your daughter and you're making a general nuisance of yourself in the street.' He glanced around. 'There are three people that I can see watching what's going on.'

'That's because they're all nosy bastards.'

'Swear again and I'll lock you up. You might be able to

get away with it when I'm not here but now that I am, you can add breach of the peace to your list, if you're not careful. Now, move! I want you out of this street or I'll arrest you.'

'I'm going,' Kevin snapped.

Cathy shook her head as she followed Liz indoors. What the hell had got into her? She'd told her not to go outside yet she'd deliberately ignored her warning. Stupid woman, putting herself in danger like that.

As soon as Liz came downstairs again after settling Chloe, Cathy ripped into her.

'The next time he comes here – because there will be a next time,' she told her angrily, 'I don't want you to go running out to him. You know what he's capable of. Whatever possessed you?'

'Sorry.' Liz wouldn't look at her.

'I have an alarm system for a reason. I have back up from the police for a reason. When I say do not go outside, I mean do NOT go outside. That should never have happened. You put yourself in danger.'

'You don't know him like I do. He won't give in until he's done what he came to do. He would have been outside all night if I hadn't gone out to him.'

'No, he wouldn't. The police would have moved him on. Instead you let Chloe see him attack you. Mark's right. You should think about getting a harassment order or you're never going to get rid of him.'

'Don't you think he'll get tired of it soon?'

Liz was after reassurance but Cathy couldn't give it to her.

'I don't know,' she replied. 'I thought he'd gone when he

184

stayed away for so long since the last time. Now he's back on the scene. Unless something drastic is done, he'll just do it all the time.'

'I should never have said anything to him.'

'No, you shouldn't have.'

'I – I just felt brave because I thought he couldn't get at me. Now I've antagonised him again, I've left myself open.'

Cathy could see how upset Liz was so she held her tongue. 'Look, I'm – oh, God, what's that racket now?'

Cathy and Liz followed the noise to its source. There were loud bangs coming from Becky's room. When Cathy opened the door, she saw Becky standing on the roof outside her window. She was pummelling on the glass.

'Cathy!' Becky banged hard again. 'Cathy, let me in!'

'Be quiet, will you!' Cathy pushed up the window and reached for her arm. 'I thought you were already in here.'

'Nope… I snuck out.'

'Can't I ever have a night of peace?' She managed to pull Becky through the window.

'That bitch!' Becky slurred, pointing at the windowsill. 'I left a book there, so I could get in again. She must have moved it.' She peered down at the floor, swaying as she tried to remain upright.

'What are you wittering on about?' Cathy sat her down on the side of the bed.

'That Jess. I left the window open.'

Cathy wafted her hand in front of her face. 'What have you been drinking? And more to the point, where did you get the money from?'

'Who needs money when I have pockets?' Becky laughed at her own joke. 'I have *biiiiiiiiiiggg* pockets.'

Cathy sighed. 'Let's get you into bed before you do anything else.'

'I shagged Pete Freeman tonight. Around the back of the old White Lion.' Becky waggled her little finger. 'That's what I think of Pete Freeman. What a weenie.'

Cathy wanted to tell her that she shouldn't be having sex yet, that it was too soon after the miscarriage, but she knew Becky wouldn't take anything in. She was too drunk. Instead, she pulled off her shoes while Liz removed her jacket. They tried to get her into bed but Becky had other ideas. She began to sing.

'*Baby you're the one. You still turn me on. You can lick my hole again!*'

'Becky, that's enough,' Cathy scolded.

Behind them, they heard Chloe giggle.

Liz went to her. 'You should be in bed, young lady, or I'll never get you up for school in the morning.'

'Chloe?' said Becky, trying to focus on the small figure standing in the doorway. 'Chloe, is that you?'

'Hiya, Becks,' Chloe said before being whisked away by Liz.

'Chloe, don't let the boys touch you. They'll do evil things to you and fu –'

'Becky! That's enough now. Show some respect. Chloe is just a child.'

'But you said I was only a child, didn't you?' Becky stopped. Suddenly the drunken giggles turned to tearful wails. 'You mean baby, don't you? My baby, I lost my baby. Cathy, Cathy, why did I lose my baby?'

EIGHTEEN

Cathy always enjoyed her time at the community house, both in The Den with the teenagers and helping out with the adult courses. It was a time when she felt she could leave all her cares and worries behind at the front door, for a few hours at least. She'd usually be too busy to think about anybody else.

Out of everything, she enjoyed the self-assertiveness courses best. She loved to see someone change from a caterpillar into a butterfly as the weeks attending the courses flew by. Some sessions were for anyone to attend but some were just for the women to discuss and share their different stories. Sometimes they were harrowing; sometimes inspiring. So wherever possible, she and Josie would ensure there was a bit of light-hearted fun within a serious message. This week there'd been a volunteer teaching the women simple self-defence moves.

'I wasn't really expecting to learn anything,' Josie said afterwards as she and Cathy tidied up the room. 'But you never know when you might have to defend yourself in day-to-day life.'

'I don't often go out after dark, if I can help it.' Cathy stacked a chair on top of a pile underneath the window. 'But some of those things would be useful if I didn't feel safe.'

'And there were so many tips. I particularly liked the one where she said to yell fire if you felt threatened. How many people would come running then rather than if you just screamed?'

'Do you need any help in here, ladies?' Matt popped his head around the door.

'I think we can manage to move a few tables,' Josie teased. 'After what we've just been taught, we no longer feel the weaker sex, do we, Cathy?'

Cathy grinned.

'Oh, you've just been to the self-defence class. Tell me more.' Matt came into the room. 'You have me intrigued.'

Josie gathered together two plastic cups that had been left on a table and put them in the bin. 'Shall we show him what we've learned?'

Cathy pursed her lips, trying to stop the grin from looking maniacal. How come she always acted like a tongue-tied teenager whenever Matt came on the scene? It had happened when he'd called to sort out her car again after the vandalism. She'd gone bright red every time he'd spoken to her. In the end, after handing him a cuppa, she'd headed back indoors for fear of making a total idiot of herself. She glanced at Josie.

'Shall we show him the elbow jab?' Cathy moved to Matt's side, pulled her left elbow up high and across towards her right shoulder.

'Move your hips too,' said Josie.

Cathy gave a slight nod and swivelled her hips, allowing her elbow to move further to the right. Then with all her force, she swung it round towards Matt. She caught him straight in his chest.

'Fuck!' Matt grunted and dropped to his knees.

'Oh my God!' Cathy bent down to his level. 'Are you okay? I thought I'd swing and miss you.'

Josie had a hand over her mouth. Suddenly she lost control, laughter bursting out raucously.

Matt clutched a hand to his chest, his breathing rapid. 'Jesus, I wouldn't like to cross you in a dark alleyway. I'm going to have a right bruise there.'

'I'm sorry.' Cathy tried to look concerned, but it was impossible as Josie was still laughing at the top of her voice. She felt a smile forming and gnawed at her bottom lip to try and stop it.

'It's a good job she didn't catch you in the temple or the throat as we were shown next,' Josie managed to say between sniggers. Tears were pouring down her face. 'She could have killed you.'

'I didn't realise he was that close,' Cathy hissed, embarrassment creeping in.

Matt raised a hand. 'It was my fault,' he explained. 'I saw a piece of cotton on the back of your jumper. I doubt it will still be there with that force,' he added as Cathy checked her sleeve.

'Sorry, Matt,' Josie said, wiping at her eyes. 'I haven't laughed so much in ages. It was the look on your face.' She started to giggle again.

Matt stood up slowly. Still holding on to his chest, he spoke to Cathy. 'You owe me one for that. I reckon you need to suck up to me big time.'

Josie burst into laughter again. Cathy blushed. Matt looked bewildered. But then his eyes began to twinkle and his mouth twitched.

'Ah, yes, sexual favours will do nicely. Your place or mine?'

Cathy lowered her eyes from his intense stare. God, how could she get out of this one! Quick, think.

'Coffee!' She pointed to the door. 'I'll just go and make a fresh batch.'

Later that evening, Jess had gone into Becky's room. She was trying to get Becky to come out with her but so far she'd had no luck.

'Come on,' she coaxed. 'It'll do you good to get bladdered and forget everything for a while.'

'I got bladdered two nights ago and that didn't help.'

Jess giggled. 'The Pete Freeman night. Crap lay, isn't he?'

'Oh, have you –?'

'Yeah. Not much to talk about there. Anyway, forget about Pete. We might bump into Austin Forrester. I know how much you fancy him. Now that you're not, well, you know, you can enjoy yourself more, can't you?'

'I don't want to.'

'I'll blag some vodka.'

Becky stared at herself in the tiny mirror on her dressing table. She'd do anything to get rid of this empty feeling. It was as if her life had come to a halt, a crossroads even. She didn't know what she was going to do next.

'It might block out your pain, make you feel better.'

'I doubt it.'

'Please!' Jess pulled out a small plastic bag from her pocket. 'You can have some of this.'

Becky eyed it warily. 'Is that what I think it is?'

190

'Yep. It's Whizz.'

'What does it do again?'

'It makes you feel happy, more lively, like everyone is your friend.'

'But aren't all drugs dangerous?'

'I suppose so but this is tame, really. I try to keep away from the heavier stuff.'

Becky gasped. 'You mean you've tried other things?'

Jess nodded. 'I've done ecstasy loads of times and coke a few times. But Whizz doesn't make me as angry as coke. You should try them all – see which one suits you the best.' She dipped her finger into the bag and held it out to Becky afterwards.

'Go on,' she urged. 'You'll love it. It will make the night more interesting.'

Becky gave in. Tentatively she dipped in her index finger and copied Jess, running it over her top gums. She stood there for a moment.

'What?' said Jess, moments later as Becky remained rooted to the spot.

'I don't feel any different.'

Jess sighed. 'Give it a chance. You'll feel it soon.'

'If I come out with you, can I wear your red shoes?'

'Red shoes, no knickers,' said Jess, grinning.

'What?'

'It's a saying or something.'

'I thought that was fur coat, no knickers.'

'Oh, yes. I think you're right.'

Becky smiled.

'So you'll come out then?'

Half an hour later, they headed for Vincent Square and

joined the throng of kids huddled around Shop&Save car park. Becky became louder and louder as the night wore on. She giggled, she laughed, she danced, and she drank whatever she could scrounge.

Danny, Austin and Parksy strolled up an hour later. Becky was singing an Adele song at the top of her voice. She stopped as they walked past, noticing Austin looking as suave as ever. He smiled with his eyes only. She couldn't work out if he was pleased to see her or sick of the sight of her so she turned her attention to Danny instead.

'Hey, Dan,' she smiled seductively. 'Do you fancy a little bit of hanky panky?'

As Danny turned back with a grin, Jess nudged Becky sharply. 'Oy! Behave yourself, slag.'

'Piss off. I can have whoever I want. It's not up to you.'

'Back off, Becks, or –'

'Ooh,' said Danny, thrilled at the attention. 'There's a fight brewing, lads.'

'Shut up,' said Jess.

'Chill out, woman. I'm stocking up on booze and then going for a drive. Want to come?'

'Did you hear about Pete Freeman?' Danny asked later when the five of them were driving around the estate in his car. Austin had taken the passenger seat again. Becky and Jess were squashed in the back with Parksy.

'No, what happened?'

'He got beat up. He's in hospital. Broken nose, broken arm. His ankle had been stamped on so much that it needed plating.'

Jess and Becky started to giggle.

'Did they catch who did it?' Jess eventually asked after

they remembered that the matter didn't warrant their laughter.

'He never saw who it was. He said he came out of the pub and was ambushed.'

'Ambushed.' Jess and Becky giggled again.

Austin looked back with a smirk. 'You two pissed already? Or are you on something else?'

'Us?' Jess feigned disgust. 'Becky and I would never partake of such a thing!'

'Yeah, right. And my dick is two inches long.'

'Two inches!' Jess shrieked. 'I bleeding hope it's longer than that.' She nudged him. 'Fancy showing me later?'

'In your dreams, wild one.'

Jess pretended to swoon. She nudged Danny. 'I prefer to dream about you, though.'

Becky bit down hard on her bottom lip. She had to remain calm, make sure she didn't spit out her secret while she was loaded. She also prayed that Danny and Austin wouldn't let it slip either. Luckily they didn't. Danny pushed Jess's hand away as she leaned forward.

'How about you, Becks?' Parksy joined in. He grinned lasciviously and pressed his hand to his crotch. 'Who do you dream about?'

'Not you, that's for certain.' She heard Austin snigger. Then he turned around and looked at her.

'Do you dream about me, Becks?'

'Would you like me to?' she dared to say.

Austin ignored her question. 'Do you?'

'I might do.'

'I wouldn't blame you. I am worth dreaming about.'

Their eyes stayed locked together as if no one else was in

the car, as if time had stood still and there were only the two of them.

'Oy!' Danny turned to Austin with a scowl. 'Sloppy seconds your style, then?'

Austin turned towards him, very slowly. 'Shut the fuck up, Bradley.'

Jess looked on in confusion. 'What does he mean by sloppy seconds, Becks?'

The next evening, Cathy was finishing off her coffee, wondering whether to stay up or go to bed. It was past midnight and Becky was late home. Jess had come in at eleven, saying that she'd left Becky with some lad or other. She'd stormed off to bed in a huff after Cathy had tried to question her more.

She washed out her mug and left it to drain while she wondered what to do next. Would Becky simply burn herself out in a matter of weeks and then get back to normal? Or was this going to be the start of a life of drunken antics, followed by the harder stuff? She prayed she wouldn't end up hooked like Cheryl.

But yet what could she do about it? Leave her to make her own mistakes or try and talk to her, calm her down, show her that she would burn out if she weren't careful. It was a tough decision. People thought her 'job' watching over these girls was easy but no one really understood the true heartache she faced. The decisions that she made – had she a right to make them? Really she should tell Becky that if she had one more week like the last one, she was out. But where would she go? Cathy wouldn't just give up on her after a couple of months, no matter what her rules said.

And why should Becky listen to her? Why should she do anything that Cathy asked of her? She couldn't help everyone just to alleviate her own guilt, to wipe out her own mistake. It didn't work like that.

She heard a key in the front door. She stayed very still as Becky came in, making such a noise while telling herself to be quiet.

There was a bang and a groan. Becky must have bumped into the hall table – which meant that she was drunk again.

'Where have you been until now?' Cathy went out to her.

'Frigging hell!' Becky was bending down pulling off a shoe. Unbalanced, she staggered towards her. 'You shouldn't creep about like that.'

'I'm not creeping around. I'm waiting up for you. You're late.' Cathy sniffed. 'And you're as drunk as a skunk again.'

'So?'

'So you're not going to drink away your pain. It doesn't work like that.'

Becky pulled off the other shoe and threw them both to the floor. 'I'm not in pain,' she slurred.

'And where the hell did you find the money to get drunk? Is it from Danny Bradley?'

'No.' Becky laughed. 'I don't need money to pay for anything.'

'What do you mean?' Cathy paled. Surely she couldn't be talking about sex?

'Leave me alone.' Becky pushed past her forcefully. 'I can look after myself. I'm sixteen, not six.'

'But you have to be careful after a miscarriage. You could easily become infected.'

'I said leave me alone!'

'Someone needs to care about you as you certainly don't care about yourself. You don't have to be a sheep and follow behind every low life on the estate.'

Becky frowned, trying to understand.

'If you're not careful, you'll end up like most of the girls around here – used and abused. I don't want that to happen to you.'

'It's a bit late for that,' Becky snapped, tears in her eyes. 'I've already been used and abused.'

'I wasn't referring –'

'I just want the pain to go away.'

Becky turned towards Cathy with such a sorrowful look that she almost felt her heart lurch towards her.

'I hate my life,' she continued. 'The only thing I had to look forward to has been taken away. What am I supposed to do now?'

'Let me help you.'

'Leave me alone. You can't help me. No one can help me.'

Cathy watched her go up the stairs and into the bathroom. She sat on the bottom step for a moment. Running a hand through her hair, she let out a huge sigh. Not so strong now, am I, Richard Mason, she thought, imagining him laughing at her. Only Rich had seen the real Cathy: tough on the outside, susceptible on the inside. If he were here, he'd tell her she was being a soft old bird. But she couldn't help worrying about them. It hadn't been two weeks since Becky had lost her baby. The chatter that she'd overheard confirmed the rumours that they were still hanging around with Danny Bradley and that Austin fella but what could she do about it?

A thought crossed her mind. Was Becky grieving so much for the loss of her baby that she'd get herself pregnant again? Cathy hoped not. Not so soon after she'd miscarried and definitely not with Danny Bradley. Danny Bradley was a thug, a well-known thief on the estate and a no-good layabout. If Becky got mixed up with the likes of him, then Cathy wouldn't be able to stop her getting in deeper and deeper. She was certain it was Danny that had got Cheryl hooked on drugs – she hadn't come home for two weeks either. Still, it was no use worrying about her too. There was only so much of Cathy's mind that she could occupy with other people.

Minutes later, she heard a door upstairs open and close. Sighing loudly, she made her way to bed. Maybe, just maybe, she could get through a night without being dragged out of it again.

At the top of the stairs, she could see Becky's bedroom door slightly ajar. She crept up and pushed it open slightly. Already Becky was gently snoring. She listened for a while before closing the door softly behind her. Then she stood in the silence for a moment.

Her chest began to rise and fall rapidly. She placed a hand on her heart, felt its thump-thumpety-thump, the panic building up inside her as she gasped for air.

Sometimes the responsibility of it all was too much for her to bear.

After a thankfully uneventful morning at the community house, Cathy had hardly set foot on the driveway before Jess and Becky were out of the door and running towards her.

'We've been robbed,' Jess told her.

Cathy's heart sank. She rushed into the house expecting to see a mess but nothing seemed to be out of place.

'I thought you said –'

'Nothing's been touched downstairs except the photo of you and Rich.' Jess handed her the photograph in the frame. The glass was broken, the corner of the frame hanging together by a small tack. 'And the tin that you keep all your notes in.'

Cathy frowned. 'How did you know about that?'

'I've always known about it, since I moved in.'

'Ever taken anything from it?'

'No!' Jess fibbed indignantly.

'Me neither,' added Becky quickly, telling the truth. 'But it's empty now.'

Cathy went through into the kitchen. The drawers on the unit were all open, the contents thrown across the floor. She stepped carefully over to the tin. Lifting the lid, she saw it was empty.

'Damn and blast!'

'It's that bloody cow, Cheryl, isn't it?' Jess answered herself with the nod of her head.

'Don't call her names, Jess. She's ill and desperate.'

Cathy hurried upstairs only to find Cheryl's bedroom had been trashed again. Cathy swore under her breath. This wasn't the first time Cheryl had roughed everything up. The covers had been stripped from the bed, the mattress heaved to the floor. Drawers from the dresser were thrown on top of them. Pages from magazines had been torn and scattered like rose petals awaiting a bride on her wedding day.

'Jeez, what a smell.' Jess covered her mouth and nose with her hand. 'Has someone died in there?'

'Shut up,' said Cathy. 'Have you both checked your rooms?'

'I've got eighty quid missing,' Jess said quickly.

Cathy rolled her eyes. 'Nice try, but you're not getting that from me. Besides, where would you get eighty quid from? And what about you, Becky?'

'No. But I've got nowt to take really.'

'What about Liz's room?'

'It's locked. There's a muddy footprint on the door. Well, a bit of one anyway.'

Cathy thanked the Lord for small mercies and rushed into her own room. But nothing had been touched there either. She picked up the huge toy rabbit that sat on the bed. Rich had bought her that. To everyone else, Roger the Rabbit was just a stuffed toy: to Cathy, Roger the Rabbit was where she stashed her rainy day fund. She had four hundred pounds tucked away in the pocket of his blue trousers. Luckily, no one had found that hiding place yet.

'I hope you give her a good leathering when you next see her,' Jess moaned behind her. 'It's because you let her get away with things that she thinks she can do what she likes.'

'Sounds like someone else I know.'

Jess tutted.

Cathy went back downstairs. 'Come and give me a hand,' she shouted to them. 'Help me clear up this mess.'

'Oh, no.' Jess put her arm out in front of Becky. 'You and me aren't setting foot in the kitchen until the plods are called. Our DNA will be over everything and then who will she blame?'

Becky stopped in mid step. She wasn't sure why.

'You've been watching too much television.' Cathy

shook her head and picked up a pile of papers from the floor.

'Aren't you reporting it?' Jess sounded bewildered.

'No.'

'But she'll do it again and again.'

'And I'll cover for her again and again.' Cathy looked up at Jess. 'Just like I would do for you, until I've had enough and can't take any more. But that has to be my decision.'

Jess turned on her heels. 'Mad, the lot of you. But if you think I'm going to clean up after some junkie... anyway, we're off out, aren't we Becks?'

Two days later as Cathy and Liz were on their way home from the community house, Liz dropped a bombshell.

'Moving out?' said Cathy. 'Aren't you happy staying with me?'

'Yes, of course,' said Liz. 'I just think it would be good for Chloe to settle down somewhere now.'

'I know, but –'

'She needs her own room, her own space.' Liz looked on with pleading eyes, willing Cathy to understand. 'She can't have that at your house.'

'But what about Kevin?' Cathy thought back to the last time they'd seen him. 'I'm sorry if I was sharp with you. I just didn't want him to get the upper hand. I don't want you to leave because of it, though.'

'Don't be silly. That hasn't anything to do with my decision.' Liz shook her head. 'Kevin will find me wherever I go. But I've spoken to Josie and she's setting us up in a flat. She's going to reinforce the doors and locks as part of the domestic violence program initiatives. She's also going to set up a telephone system like yours so I can contact the police if I need to.'

Cathy was astounded. 'You've certainly thought it through,' she said.

'Yes, but only because you gave me the confidence to do so. You've become my friend, I hope, as well as my confidante. And if you're up to it, I'm going to need your friendship much more when I leave.'

Cathy felt herself blushing at Liz's straight-forward talking. She wasn't used to compliments: that someone liked to spend time with her. She smiled. Putting aside all selfish thoughts of how she'd enjoyed having the two of them around, she hugged Liz.

'You don't get rid of me that easily,' she told her, holding back tears. 'Has Josie got anything lined up for you?'

'There's a flat just come empty in Preston Avenue. It's near to Suzie Rushton, you know, from the community house? Josie says we can keep an eye out for each other.'

'That's great.' Cathy tried to sound enthusiastic but if Josie had a flat empty, she knew the system. Liz would have to be out of there within a fortnight.

'Would you like to come with me to view it?' Liz asked. 'I'm going tomorrow afternoon, half past two. I'd really like your opinion.'

Cathy nodded. 'Sure, why not?'

Later back at home, Cathy sat quietly sipping hot coffee. In just under three months she'd watched Liz start to believe that a life without Kevin was possible. That she could do this by herself – fend for herself and Chloe. Still, she might have helped her to gain confidence, but inwardly she cursed herself. It had been great having Liz around to talk to. She was nearer to her age than anyone else. She could have a laugh with her; discuss stupid, light-hearted things, like the men in their shorts when there was only football on the television. Or the latest gossip in *Heat* magazine and last night's episode of *Modern Family*.

More importantly, she'd really enjoyed having Chloe around. That little girl had brought extra rays of sunshine into the house. She was everything that Cathy would have hoped for in a daughter: bright, intelligent and caring. Chloe was always asking Liz how she was, always using her manners. Her parents might not have got along but between them they had done a great job of bringing up Chloe. If only Liz could keep Kevin from getting his claws into her, she might not be too damaged by what she'd been through so far.

Yet although she didn't doubt for a second that Liz thought she was confident enough to live alone without Kevin's interference, Cathy had seen it all before. She'd helped no end of women who had moved on from there to a new place, only to let their men move back in with them again. A few of them had learned the hard way, ending up with more bruises and mental scars. A few had even come back to stay before moving on again. Each time the women were adamant that their men were going to change; most of the time they never did.

Still, Cathy stood up and stretched her arms above her head. No matter what happened in the future, she would be there for her.

A few minutes later, Liz joined her. She turned to Cathy with a smile and held up a box of chocolates. 'Got these for tonight. And I thought I could treat you to a takeaway?'

Cathy rubbed her hands together. 'Fantastic. As long at it all comes with a bottle of red, I'm good with it.'

Liz laughed. 'You and your bloody wine. At least I won't turn into an alcoholic in my own place.'

'Just promise me that you won't let that useless shit back into your life, once my back is turned.'

Liz tried to look insulted at the suggestion but broke out into a smile eventually. 'I am scared about going it alone but I have you, and Josie, to help me out. Even if it's just for someone to talk things through with, I don't feel so alone anymore.' She held a hand to her chest. 'And I promise you faithfully, Cathy Mason, that I will do my best not to let him get to me. So half past two tomorrow?'

NINETEEN

While Cathy and Liz went to meet Josie at the flat, Jess and Becky sat in the back garden. Two sets of legs and arms were warming in the afternoon sun, two sets of brightly-coloured toe nails wriggling about.

'If I moved out, I don't think anyone would miss me,' said Jess matter-of-factly.

'I would,' said Becky.

'Yeah right.'

'I would!'

'I bet Cathy would be glad to see the back of me. I'm always bringing trouble home. I try not to but it just happens.'

'Me too, just lately,' Becky confessed.

'Yes, but you're not as bad as me. I'm a runner for Sam Harvey.'

'What's a runner?'

'I take drugs to people. They pay me cash and I take it back. Sam gives me a cut.'

'Of the drugs?' Becky was shocked.

'Sometimes.'

'But aren't you scared that you'll get hooked?'

'Sometimes,' she repeated.

'Do you like taking drugs?'

'Not if I end up like Cheryl. She was really nice looking at one time.'

'Oh?'

Jess got to her feet. 'Wait there.' She was back a few minutes later and handed Becky a photograph.

Becky peered at it but didn't recognise the girl sitting next to Jess at first. Then she brought it nearer and peered at it again. The girl was tanned, dark hair styled in an updo with just enough strands hanging down for it to look sexy. She wore make-up, her full red lips pouted at the camera and she had huge dangly earrings. Her smile told of happier times. More noticeably, she looked healthy.

'Is that Cheryl?' Becky said in disbelief.

'Yep.' Jess flopped down beside her again. 'That was only taken the summer before last. She was a real stunner until she got hooked.'

'Aren't you scared of looking like she does?' Becky recalled how thin Cheryl had been the last time she'd seen her: wasted even, her skin the colour of milk, her eyes dark puddles of oil.

Jess shrugged. 'But what else is there to do around here if we don't get high?'

'Plenty.'

'Like what?'

'Maybe we could go out and not get bladdered.'

'Like going to the flicks or out shopping?'

'Or working together?'

Jess turned slightly to look directly at her. 'Now you are talking silly! Me, working. What would *I* do?'

'I thought maybe we could get a job in a bar. We could say we were eighteen.'

Jess pointed to her temple. 'You're mad, do you know that? Why would I want to work my arse off for a pittance?'

'Don't you ever have dreams, goals and all that?'

'Of course I do, but being brought up on the Mitchell Estate soon knocks it out of you. Just like it will with you in time. It sucks living around here.'

'Maybe we could be waitresses or something?' Becky wouldn't be put off.

Jess tutted. 'I'm not being anyone else's slave.'

'It was just a thought. It's ages yet until we go to college.'

'That's *if* I bother with college.'

'What do you mean?'

'Just because you're thinking of doing the same course as me, it doesn't mean that I'm definitely going to enrol.'

'That's a bit mean.'

'I meant I'm not sure I can be bothered.'

A stroppy silence fell between them.

'We could just do more things together,' Jess ventured. 'You know, look out for one another.'

Becky smiled, secretly pleased. She'd enjoyed having someone of her own age around to confide in, have a laugh with, go shopping with and discuss boys.

'Like bessie mates?'

'Yeah. Would you want to?'

Becky nodded. 'I might. What about you?'

They looked at each other and shared a shy smile.

'So what shall we do tonight?'

'I fancy stopping in and having a laugh with Cath,' Jess surprised Becky by saying. 'What about you?'

'It's a deal.'

*

'Is this it?' Cathy sounded exasperated as she looked around the tiny flat.

'Yes.' Josie wasn't put off by her tone as she followed her back into the living room. 'This is it. What do you think, Liz?'

Cathy didn't give her time to answer before replying. 'And you want to swap my house with its range of rooms for this tiny shed?'

'Of course she does.' Josie prodded Cathy lightly in the chest. 'Don't take any notice of her, Liz. She's just feeling low because you're moving on.'

'No, I am not!' Cathy snapped, furious with Josie. How dare she jump to conclusions at her expense!

Liz touched her lightly on her forearm. 'She's winding you up. Even I can see that.'

Cathy relaxed a little and licked her tongue out at Josie as a means of apology. If truth be told, she was still smarting over the quickness of everything. If she took this property, Liz would have to be moved in by next weekend or pay rent until she did. The property had to be occupied as soon as benefits were registered against it. But, as Josie had rightly guessed, Cathy had started to feel lonely already.

'It's okay, I suppose,' she offered reluctantly. 'Preston Avenue is one of the better streets on the estate.'

Liz gazed around the square living room with its dowdy wallpaper and blood red skirting boards and gulped back tears. It was a far cry from her beautiful home in Douglas Close. But the maisonette was much better than moving in to one of the high-rise blocks, her biggest fear.

'It'll do just fine.' She smiled at Josie. 'A lick of paint and a fair bit of elbow grease and it will be home in no time. When can I have the keys?'

'Are you sure?' Josie searched Liz's face for the slightest glimmer of doubt but didn't see anything. 'You can stay at Cathy's for a while longer.'

'I'm sure,' nodded Liz.

'I need a few days to sort out the doors and such. How does a week on Monday suit you?'

'What do you think, Cathy?' Liz twirled round to face her. 'Can you put up with us for that long?'

'Suppose I'll have to,' she muttered. Then she winked at her. 'I am going to miss you, though.'

'See,' cried Josie. 'What did I tell you?'

'I just love having you and Chloe around,' Cathy stated. 'Much more than anyone else I've had to stay.'

'I'm sure I'll be in your kitchen just as much as mine,' Liz soothed. She ran a hand over a bare wall, feeling the bumps and knocks of years gone by. 'Besides, you're going to help me to decorate, aren't you?'

Cathy tutted. 'Trust me to get lumbered with that one!'

Driving Rose home after she'd attended her afternoon luncheon club, Cathy was still smarting about Liz.

'I'm really going to miss her,' she told Rose. 'It's been great having her around.'

'Nothing like having an ancient decrepit like me, then?'

Cathy smirked as she changed gears. 'You know what I mean. No one can replace you, you old hag.'

'I like Liz, too. And Chloe's a little darling. Such a sweet girl, despite her circumstances.'

'And I hope she stays that way. This estate can twist anyone round if it gets under your skin.'

They stopped at traffic lights. Cathy hummed along to the radio.

'I'll still worry about them when they've gone,' she said.

'They're not far. You can visit every day if you like.'

'I bet I'd soon get on Liz's nerves.'

'Once she settles, you won't feel the need to visit so much.'

'I suppose you're right.'

Rose patted her lightly on the knee. 'And until then you'll just have to put up with me.' She pointed to the pink gift bag popping out of Cathy's handbag. 'Have you been treating yourself?'

'No, it's not for me. It's for Becky.'

Later that night when she was certain she could hear Jess in the shower, Cathy knocked on Becky's bedroom door.

'You going out tonight?' she asked.

Becky shook her head. 'Jess has a date. I hate playing gooseberry.'

Cathy marvelled at how mature she sounded. It was nothing like the young, frightened slip of a girl who had turned up on her doorstep at the end of March. Still, she knew she was vulnerable right now.

'I have something for you.' Cathy sat down on the bed and gave her the pink bag.

'What is it?'

'Open it and see.'

Becky reached inside and took out a small box covered with purple velvet. She flipped open the lid. Inside was a ring, a simple silver band with a tiny pearl and a moonstone.

'Do you like it?'

Becky pulled it out of the box. 'It's lovely.'

'When my husband died, I bought this.' Cathy held a silver necklace away from her neck and showed it to Becky. It had a small locket threaded through it. 'This heart reminds me of him. I feel like his love is locked away inside. When I feel sad, I clasp my hands around it and remember his love for me.'

'I've seen you doing that lots of times,' said Becky.

Cathy smiled. 'I thought you could do the same with the ring. When you feel sad, twirl it around your finger. When you're ready to move on, if you feel like it, you can take it off.'

Becky had tears in her eyes. Cathy touched her face gently.

'It's okay to be upset, Becks. It's okay to get drunk, take your anger out on your body, but sometime soon you will stop hurting. And then you will only have the memory.' She took the ring and slid it on to Becky's middle finger. It was a little loose. 'You can come with me to get it altered. I just wanted to buy it for you. I got you this as well.' Cathy opened another bag and took out a candle in a glass container. 'Whenever you feel sad, light this and think of your baby. I light one up every year on my wedding anniversary and to mark Rich's birthday.'

'What about –'

Cathy shook her head. 'I don't want to remember the day he died. I want to remember the happy times.'

Suddenly Becky was crying. 'I don't want to forget it,' she sobbed, 'but it hurts to remember it.'

'You have to think about it before it fades.'

'How long will that take?'

Cathy sighed, wishing she had the answer to that one. She still hadn't got over it yet.

'I don't know,' she said. 'Some people get through it quicker than others. Some don't get over it at all. You are the only one who can decide how it goes.'

Becky sniffed. 'I don't want to.'

'I know.' Cathy nodded. 'Believe me, I know.'

TWENTY

Josie and Liz were sitting together during a break in the latest self-assertiveness session. They'd both sat through a harrowing discussion, listening to Alison Bennett. Alison had fled from her husband four times so far. Each time he'd found her and each time he'd dragged her back to their marital home and beat her to within an inch of her life. But she'd still left again. After the last time, she'd pressed charges and he got eighteen months. Instead of looking forward to the six months she had left before he got out, she was counting down the weeks until he would find her again. She was certain that he would. Josie hoped that wouldn't happen to Liz. Despite her professional role, she'd become quite fond of having her around.

'So are you all set for the big move?' she asked her.

'I think so,' said Liz. 'Although I'm pretty scared after listening to Alison just then. What happens if Kevin finds me?'

'He will find you,' said Josie. 'There's no way he won't if he's as determined as he's always been.'

'I know that. I meant that I hope he gives me and Chloe time to settle in first. If he sees how happy Chloe is, then he might back down.'

Josie had no answer to that. 'At least the security pack is

in place now,' she said instead. 'I do wish I could offer you more in the way of safety but a personal alarm, property alarm and a reinforced front door is about my limit.'

'It's a start.' Liz nodded gratefully. 'And you never know, maybe Kevin will get bored after a while.'

'That is when he eventually finds out that you're not at Cathy's anymore. Oh, I nearly forgot. I have something for you.'

Josie rushed out of the room and came back dragging a black plastic bag behind her. She plonked it at Liz's feet.

'Curtains, cushions and covers,' she explained. 'One of my tenants, Dot, brought them in yesterday. Don't worry – she's one of my better tenants so they're clean. They're yours, if you like them.'

Liz opened the bag and looked inside, expecting to see some garish sixties flowers or gingham checks but was pleasantly surprised to see modern aqua blue, coffee and chocolate swirls on a cream background.

'They're really nice.' She smiled her gratitude. 'I'll take them, thanks.'

'There are a couple of framed pictures in there too, and some decorative candles.'

'I never checked to see if there were any curtain rails up.' Liz delved into the bag again and pulled out two church candles and an unopened bag of pot pourri.

'Two minutes ladies, and we'll get back together.' Josie waved a hand in the air to signify that the break was nearly over and then turned back to Liz. 'That's not a problem. I'll get Matt to come over, if not. He'll brighten any place up. And he's such eye candy.' Josie raised her eyebrows in a comical fashion.

Liz shook her head. 'Don't even think about it. I've had enough of the one I've left. I don't want to get involved –'

'Not you,' Josie interrupted. 'I would never suggest that after what you've been through. I was thinking more along the lines of Cathy.'

'Oh?'

'It's never right that she's on her own after so long. Rich died three years ago now. She gives so much of herself to other people that it's time she found someone to look after her for a change.'

'I wonder what's stopping them getting together. I know she likes him. She talks about him often – quite often, in fact.'

'I'm not sure, really.' Josie paused for a moment, her head cocked to the side like a terrier. 'Maybe we should think about setting them up. What do you think?'

'It's very kind of you to do this,' Liz said to Matt's thigh.

'I didn't have much choice,' Matt replied. 'That Josie is a right slave driver. Not that I mind, though,' he added hastily. 'As long as I get a cuppa and a chocolate biscuit as a reward, I'm content.'

Liz smiled. 'It doesn't take much to make you happy, then?'

'Man of simple taste, me.' He grinned. Then he glanced through the window. 'Hey, there's a pretty woman walking down your path.'

Liz followed Matt's eyes and smiled. Time to put operation Cathy into place. She rushed to the door.

'Cathy! How lovely to see you!'

Cathy smirked. 'I only saw you this morning, you dope.

What are you going to be like when you desert me and move in here? And after all I've done for… oh.'

Matt jumped off the steps and moved backwards, pretending to cower. 'Don't hurt me!' he cried. 'I promise I'll be good.'

'Hello, again to you, too,' Cathy grinned. She had a feeling that the elbow in the chest would be a standing joke.

As Matt took the box she was holding, Liz watched with interest. Was Cathy blushing? She sensed a sexual tension mounting but it was shot down by the arrival of Becky.

'Christ, this box is heavy,' she moaned. Spotting Matt, she hauled it on top of the one he'd taken from Cathy.

'Anyone for coffee?' Liz asked. She grabbed Becky by her shoulders and marched her across the room towards the tiny kitchen. 'You can help me.'

'But –'

Matt put down the boxes and climbed up the ladder again.

Cathy opened the lid of the top one and busied herself unearthing some mugs that she'd decided to give away. Sneakily, she stole another look at Matt. He had his back towards her, showing her his shapely, muscular legs and buttocks that fitted his jeans just so. As he reached up to secure a bracket, his white T-shirt rose up slightly to reveal bare skin at the waistline. Her hand reached out of its own accord and she pulled it back speedily. Her eyes continued upwards. No unsightly curly neck hair on show.

Matt must have sensed her staring and suddenly turned her way. Cathy was caught.

'How are you finding your new job?' she asked.

'It's great.' He pointed to another bracket on the floor.

Cathy passed it to him. 'The duties are really varied, keeps me busy. Mind you, I've heard your job keeps you just as busy.'

'Oh?' Cathy didn't know whether to be pleased that he'd asked about her or curious to know why.

Becky came through with a tray of drinks. 'Tea for the workers,' she said. 'Although from where I'm standing, there doesn't seem to be much work being done.'

'Cheeky,' said Matt. 'Men take their time to make sure things are done right.'

'More likely they take their time full stop,' Liz remarked as she joined them again.

'I can see that no matter what I say, I'll be outnumbered.' Matt jumped down to their level again. 'Three to one's not good for any man.'

'Especially when we hate men more than most women,' said Becky.

Matt opened his mouth to speak but thought better off it.

Becky laughed. 'Joking,' she admitted. 'I know all men aren't losers.'

'Most are,' muttered Liz.

'Now, now,' Cathy chastised. 'Don't give Matt a hard time. He's being a saint today. I know I'm a dab hand with a paintbrush but I'm hopeless with a drill. Some things you do need a man for.'

'Like sex,' said Becky. She giggled, still aiming for shock tactics.

'Not necessarily,' Cathy and Liz said simultaneously. Then embarrassment set in. They looked at each other, then at Matt, who now had the colouring of tomato ketchup, and burst into laughter.

'I'm getting back up my ladder,' said Matt. 'There are too many hormones at this level for my liking.'

He didn't notice the three women checking out his butt with each step up he took.

The next morning, Cathy couldn't believe her eyes when she found another note sitting on the doormat. In annoyance, she swiped the envelope up and tore it open.

'I'M COMING AFTER YOU'

She sighed with frustration. That was the third one now. She couldn't keep it from Liz any longer. But Liz was so happy about moving out. Did she really want to spoil that happiness? She knew it wouldn't take Kevin long to find out where she and Chloe had moved to but maybe by then he would have given up on this stupid note writing thing.

As she made her first coffee of the day, yet again she wondered if she was putting Liz at risk by not telling her about them. She decided it was time to speak to PC Baxter. Andy would know what to do. Maybe he could warn Kevin off with a stern word. That way, she wouldn't have to tell Liz, and Kevin would get his comeuppance and perhaps be more wary of leaving notes. Liz didn't need anything to distract her from the move. Kevin hadn't been around for a couple of weeks and Cathy had watched her soften a little more. Since she'd seen the flat and started to move her things in readiness for the move there this weekend, she'd seen a sparkle come back to her. It was a sign of hope. Who was she to dash it for her? Quickly she tucked the note away with the other two and made a mental reminder to catch up with Andy before the weekend.

She picked up the kettle and placed it underneath the water tap. Looking up, she noticed someone sitting on the bench in the garden. She peered closer: she was sure it was Cheryl. What on earth was she doing out there – more to the point, how had she got in? She must have climbed over the gate: a bit alarming as Cathy hadn't heard a noise. She sighed as she went outside.

Even from the end of the path, she could see Cheryl's neck was at a displeasing angle. She wondered whether to leave her there until she woke up or maybe try and wake her and get her into a bed. Luckily, hers was still empty at the moment.

'It's a good job it's summer,' she said as she drew level, 'or else you'd catch your death of cold, staying out here all night. What have you been up to since I last saw you, hmm? It must be over a fortnight since you told me –'

Cathy stopped. The hair on the back of her neck began to rise. There was no sound coming from Cheryl. Her lips were slightly tinged with blue, her eyes had rolled to the back of their sockets. Not wanting to think the obvious, she nudged her gently.

'I think we ought to get you to bed. It'll be far comfier than sleeping on this bench.'

Cheryl's head lolled forwards. Cathy gasped and jumped back. She caught her leg on the corner of the table and cried out in pain. It was then that she saw Cheryl's arm hanging down to the floor, a needle sticking out of one of her veins. The syringe was empty.

She took a moment to catch her breath before sitting down next to her. 'Cheryl?' she whispered. Images of horror films she'd seen came rushing into her mind but she pushed them to one side and lifted Cheryl's head. She was still quite warm to the touch but it was clear that she was dead.

'Cheryl!' she whispered again. Breathing deeply to keep her wits, she pulled the young girl into her arms and held her close. 'No. Please not Cheryl.'

And then she cried. She cried for the loss of a life that she felt responsible for. She knew deep down that it wasn't her fault but she wished she could have done more. Rose was right. There were some people that you just couldn't help, no matter what. But Cathy had always thought, up until now, that she could get through to anyone. Was she still good enough to do what she did? And if not, what would happen to Becky and Jess? Would they go off the rails too?

From that moment, Cathy knew that she wouldn't take anyone else in. Once the women with her now had moved on, she would give up the fight. She couldn't help everyone to alleviate her own guilt, to wipe out her own mistake. It didn't work like that.

'I'm so sorry, Cheryl.' Cathy hugged her closer still, the arm with the needle attached flailing around. 'I'm so sorry that I couldn't help you. I tried so very hard but I just couldn't get through to you. Please forgive me. I'm so sorry.'

Cheryl Morton's funeral was a huge affair. She had lived on the Mitchell Estate all her short life, so lots of people either knew her or knew of her. Her age brought out more folk and, with the fact that she had died of a drug overdose, it meant that over a hundred mourners turned up at the church on Davy Road.

On their way home Cathy, Liz and Rose called at Shop&Save. Liz drew the short straw, bagging the slowest queue at the three tills. After she'd packed her bag, she walked out into the aftermath of a rain shower. She trotted across the car park to rejoin Cathy and Rose.

Kevin stepped out from behind a parked car.

Liz jumped at the sight of him. Oh God, she was on her own again.

'I'm going to give you one last chance,' he said.

She moved around him and quickened her pace.

'I'm not giving up on you just like that.'

Fear intensified as he caught hold of her arm and spun her round to face him.

'Please, Kevin. Just leave me alone,' she said, her voice shaking.

'I can't.'

'You have to!'

'We could start again. I know we can make it work –'

'No!'

'Here, let me help you with those,' Cathy said, rushing towards them. 'I knew I should have waited for you.'

'Not you again.' Kevin frowned. 'I wish you would keep your nose out of my business.'

'Liz is my business too. I'm looking out for her while she lives at my house.'

'She won't be there for much longer.'

Liz felt her blood turn to ice. Had he found out she was leaving Cathy's house at the weekend?

'She's moving back with me,' he added.

'I didn't say that.' She let out a breath, thankful that he didn't seem to know.

'Why don't you just give it up?' said Cathy. 'You're not going to get her back.'

'We'll see about that.'

'Drop dead, you loser. And stop making empty threats. Come on, Liz.'

They walked on to the car.

'Try not to worry,' said Cathy quietly. 'I've had men turning up on my doorstep since I started this game but they don't hang around forever. Most of the time they just like the chase. You just need to learn to stick up for yourself.' Cathy held up a hand as Liz began to protest. 'I know, I know. It's easy for me to say that but the quicker you do, the more he'll lose interest, once the power of the relationship has shifted. They always do.'

Liz glanced around the car park but she couldn't see Kevin anywhere. Still she wondered if he'd really gone.

'You will get over things and move on,' Cathy told her knowingly. 'I've seen lots of women who have made more of their lives. Obviously it hasn't always worked out but most of the time it has.'

'I don't know what I would have done without you. You've probably saved my life.'

'Oh, get off with you. There's no need to be so dramatic.'

'You think I'm joking?' Liz shook her head. 'One day he's Dr Jekyll: the next Mr Hyde. You heard mostly his Dr Jekyll routine back there. It always won me over, made me think that I could answer back, maybe reason with him and be a person with an opinion. He'd use it to lure me into a false sense of security, even though I knew what he was capable of after the sweet-talking had finished. It still scares me to think what might have happened if I hadn't left him.'

Cathy gave her a quick hug. Even if she had any more comforting words, this wasn't the right time for them. Liz had suffered at Kevin's hands and nothing would erase that memory. Even if she never had to see him again, the pain would take an age to fade.

The next morning, Liz was in her room, packing up her and Chloe's few belongings. Cathy and Rose were helping too.

'So what do you think of the new maintenance officer, Liz?' Rose winked at her.

Liz grinned. 'He's very tasty. What do you think of him, Cath?'

'He seems nice.'

Cathy hadn't been able to stop thinking about Matt so she wasn't going to be drawn into the conversation as quickly as they imagined. She sensed what they were up to.

'Just nice?' said Rose. 'He's bloody gorgeous and I keep on telling you that if I were twenty years younger, I would have him.'

'Rose Clarke!' Cathy admonished. 'You're disgusting.'

'Well, I would, too,' Liz added flame to the fire, 'if my circumstances were different. He's adorable.'

'Adorable?' Cathy frowned. 'A puppy is adorable. A newborn baby is adorable. But a grown man?'

Liz roared with laughter. 'You're blushing again. You seem to do that every time his name is mentioned.'

Cathy grabbed one of Chloe's teddy bears and flung it at Liz. Liz ducked and it bounced off the wall behind her.

'I think you'd do well to grab him for some fun while he's still available,' said Rose.

'Why does the conversation always come back to my love life?'

'It's your lack of a love life we are discussing,' Rose corrected. Liz laughed. Cathy still ignored them.

'I think you should ask him out.' Rose sat down on the bed with a thud. She wiped her brow. 'He's not going to be single forever, a good-looking bloke like him.'

'But don't you wonder why he's still single, if he's as good as you seem to think he is? He must have some excess baggage.'

'Of course he must,' Rose agreed. She pulled a tissue from her pocket and ran it over her neck. 'But so do you.'

'We've all got excess baggage,' Liz chirped in. She sat down beside Rose. 'That's what makes us who we are. There isn't any harm in it.'

'There is if he's a serial killer,' muttered Cathy.

'Or a cross dresser,' giggled Liz.

'Or a – Rose?' Cathy crossed quickly to her friend who had turned the colour of wet putty. 'Are you okay?'

'Oh, it's nothing,' Rose insisted. 'I've just come over all queer. I'll be fi–fine in a minute.'

Liz got to her feet. 'I'll get you a glass of water.'

Rose smiled up at her. It was then that Cathy acted.

'Call an ambulance,' she said.

Liz stopped in her tracks and turned back abruptly. 'Oh, God,' she whispered and dashed out of the room.

'Mumpfhgiggeh,' Rose tried to speak but her mouth had dropped to one side. A faint glimmer of saliva formed at the corner. Cathy reached forward to wipe it away. Quickly, she grabbed the pillows from the bed and shoved them behind Rose to stop her from falling.

'Rose. Rose! Don't you dare leave me!' Cathy looked on helplessly. There was nothing she could do. She knew the warning signs from the current spate of advertisements on the television: F.A.S.T.

Face.

Arm.

Speech.

Time to call 999.

Rose was having a stroke.

TWENTY-ONE

It had been five days since Rose had been admitted to the City Hospital. Cathy walked slowly along the vast maze of corridors heading for the stroke ward, thinking of the job satisfaction in knowing that you had helped someone live out their last moments in peace. And not all of them died, she admonished herself. Mentally, she prayed Rose wasn't going to be one of those statistics just yet.

Careful to protect the flowers she'd brought from the shop in the foyer, she pushed open the door to the ward. Rose had been moved to a side room shortly after her arrival. She lay tucked up in the bed, her eyes closed and her mouth covered in an oxygen mask. Cathy gently ran her fingers over her friend's hands. Every vein was covered in pinpricks, mottled blue and purple bruises forming.

She'd been surprised to see the room free of visitors when she'd arrived. She'd expected at least one of Rose's three daughters to be sitting by the side of her bed. They were never usually far away.

'Rose?' Cathy spoke in a whisper, even though there was no one around to listen to her. 'Can you hear me? The girls send their love. Rose? Please do something to tell me that you're still with us.'

But Rose never moved, never acknowledged she knew

she was there. Cathy wondered if the stress of attending Cheryl's funeral had contributed in any way. She hoped not.

She glanced through the partially opened window in front of her and wondered if she'd been wrong not to tell Rose about Simon. Heaven knows she'd been desperate for someone to talk to. Perhaps it would have gone some way towards easing her pain. But how could Rose stay impartial when she had children of her own? She wouldn't have understood the reasoning behind what Cathy had done. No, she shook her head, she had been right not to burden her.

For the remainder of her visit, she recollected as many anecdotes as she could. She tried her best to smile but all the time she felt her happy face slipping. Finally she let go of Rose's hand, placed it underneath the sheet and tucked the blanket around her. With great care, Cathy bent down to kiss her forehead.

'I'm going to miss you so much, Rose, you old doll,' she said, tears streaming down her face.

'You must have heard the kettle boiling,' Cathy said to Andy as she opened the front door to him later that afternoon. He followed her through into the kitchen.

'Sorry I couldn't ring after I got your message. I've been busy on a bit of business,' he explained as he sat down at the table. 'How's Rose?'

'It's not looking good at all.'

Cathy didn't want to think about Rose dying, even though she realised it might not be long now. Instead, she retrieved her diary from the drawer and showed Andy the hand-delivered notes.

'It does seem a bit suspect,' he said after studying them.

'They're obviously from the same person: they all have a threatening tone to them. Even so, we have no proof unless there are fingerprints that we could match up to our database.'

'It's him.'

'The ex-husband?'

Cathy slid a mug of tea across the table and sat down opposite him. 'I think so. But what about you?'

Andy nodded. 'It's more than likely. You don't think they're for either of the other girls? Jess or Becky?'

'No. I think what needs to be said to them would be said direct.'

'You mean with a punch and a slap rather than a grown-up taunt.'

Cathy grinned. 'Precisely.'

Andy read the notes again, spreading them out on the table. 'Do you want me to warn him off?' he asked.

'Will it work?'

'Well, I can't be certain of it.' He held up a hand for silence as a voice came through on his radio but then continued to drink his tea when he realised it wasn't for him. 'But sometimes it does the trick. I'll mention harassment warnings to see if he gets the message.'

'Thanks.' Cathy felt her shoulders relaxing as her problem was shared. 'Will you keep it to yourself, though?'

Andy raised an eyebrow inquisitively.

'I haven't said anything to Liz.'

'Ah.'

'I don't want to worry her,' Cathy spoke out defensively. 'She's trying to forget him and move on, not be reminded of his every move.'

Andy nodded. 'No, I'm with you on that one. If we can sort it out without her knowing, then it will be better all round.' He pointed to the notes. 'Keep these safe for now and leave it with me. I'll see what my wonderful persuasive tactics can do.'

'I want you to do something for me,' Danny Bradley said as he tucked his shirt back into his trousers.

Becky rearranged her skirt and climbed back into the front of his car. She pulled down the visor and applied a generous layer of strawberry burst. The sickly scent invaded the small space but it didn't make it smell any better.

Since Jess had copped off with Mickey Grainger, and was now seeing him three nights a week, Becky had become a regular in the back of Danny's car. After her talk with Cathy, she'd stopped sleeping around but Danny seemed to always be available when she was tired of waiting for Jess. And Austin Forrester had gone slightly off radar. Twice Danny had picked her up on her way to the shops and both times Austin hadn't been around.

Danny watched her for a moment before he spoke. 'You like sex, right?'

Becky rolled her eyes. 'That's so obvious,' she fibbed. She didn't so much like the sex, as the attention that it gave her but he didn't need to know that.

'I'm doing a job tonight and I need to make sure the security guard is... kept busy.'

Becky flicked her eyes to his. 'You want me to have sex with a security guard?'

'No... yes... no... well, actually whatever it takes for me to get in and out unnoticed.'

'Get stuffed!' Becky folded her arms and turned away. 'I'm nobody's whore.'

'You're a whore when you want to be,' Danny smirked. 'Austin's told me how you've been giving him the come on.'

'I have not!' Becky turned back so quickly that she cricked her neck. She rubbed at it angrily. 'I so have not.'

'All right, keep your hair on.' Danny lit a cigarette. 'I just need you to flirt with him really. There's money in it for you, if you do.'

'How much?'

'Twenty quid.'

'I'm doing nowt for a twenty.'

'Thirty then?'

Becky paused. 'How come you're not including your new best friend, Austin?'

'That's none of your business.'

'It is if you want me to do a job for you.'

Danny exhaled loudly. Becky wafted her hand in front of her face as the smoke engulfed her.

'All I need you to do is keep the guy on the gate busy, long enough for me to get in and give you a signal when I'm out.'

Despite her misgivings, she was still curious. 'What are you going in after?'

'Someone's given me a tip off that there's money to be had. If you can keep the guard sweet once I'm in, it'll be a doddle. Then do the same while I get out again.'

'I don't know, Dan.'

Danny leaned across and pulled her top down lower to show a little more cleavage. 'Use these,' he said. 'Shove them in his face and he'll probably come in his pants. I reckon any bloke would.'

Becky had huge doubts of that working. 'What if he's old and manky?' she asked.

'Then use your mouth.' Danny sniggered snidely. 'You're good at one thing. I'll give you that much.'

'I am not going down on some old man just so you can rob somewhere!'

'Fifty quid?'

'Not for a hundred!' Becky opened the car door and scrambled out.

'Becks!' Danny shouted after her. 'Come back!'

'Piss off and do your own dirty work,' she yelled before disappearing through an alley and back into the estate.

Hidden behind a row of industrial bins a few yards away, Austin watched the drama unfold. It had been a good idea to steal a car and follow them tonight: he'd sensed something was going down with Danny. Danny had been way too preoccupied that afternoon. Four times they'd driven past Cookson's Factory. On the third, Austin had asked Danny if he had anything planned. But Danny had flatly denied it.

He grinned when he saw the indignant look on Becky's face as she marched off. He was looking forward to getting to know her better. By now, he could tell that she was the trusting sort, very much what he had in mind to occupy his time while he waited.

Austin had seen enough of Danny's attitude with Becky over the past week to know that he only saw her as a quick shag whenever he fancied getting his leg over. He hated how Danny made a fool of her, one put down after another when she wasn't around. She was a sweet girl really. She could do far better than hang around with that prick.

As Becky made her way home, Austin watched Danny roll a balaclava over his face and, with a quick glimpse around to check the coast was clear, sling a rucksack over the fencing away from the main gate and climb over after it.

Austin threw his cigarette to the ground, stubbed it out with his heel and followed him. When he got to the fencing, he pulled himself up and jumped to the other side. Grinning, he followed after Danny. What a stupid bastard he was. He'd handed things to him on a plate.

TWENTY-TWO

As usual when Cathy had things on her mind, she found herself up early, sitting in the kitchen drinking tea while everyone in the house slept around her. Despite wanting to think about a certain good-looking, dark-haired man who kept trying to invade her thoughts, she couldn't get the image of Rose out of her head. She pictured her wasting away in that hospital bed. Every now and then her face morphed to that of Rich's, even though, strangely, he had been nowhere near a hospital when he'd died.

Cathy didn't want her friend to leave her but she knew that time was running out for Rose. She would miss her knock on the door, followed by a smile and a jokey remark. She'd miss chaperoning her – her own personal taxi service, Rose used to tell everyone – to the shops, into town, luncheon clubs, bingo, to the cemetery once a week.

It felt as though she'd always been there for her. Most of the time, Cathy was okay to carry everyone else's problems around like a packed-to-the-brim-holdall but sometimes she needed to unpack her own worries. Who was she going to turn to when Rose had gone?

Along with that, the house was going to be so different after today when Liz and Chloe moved out. She was going to miss Chloe belting around as only an eight-year-old can do and asking for bunches in her hair as 'Cathy doesn't pull as much as Mum.' Yet she couldn't tell anyone that. Liz had made a momentous step towards gaining her independence. Who was she to come over all self-pitying and sulky because she was going to be left alone again?

It was then that she thought of Matt. Cathy really liked him and she knew the feeling was mutual, but was that all there was to it? And as much as she didn't want to make a fool of herself, she also didn't want to think of anyone taking Rich's place. Rich hadn't left her for someone else. He'd died. Of course he'd want her to move on and stop being lonely but she couldn't. Not yet anyway. Gently, she pushed Matt to the back of her mind again. It was the only space she could muster for him right now. Because at the forefront of it was Simon.

'Morning,' said Liz as she came into the kitchen. 'I can't believe it will be my last one waking up here.'

'Morning, traitor.' Cathy smiled as she pulled out a chair for her to sit on.

'Have you been up long?'

'I couldn't sleep.'

'Thinking about Rose?'

'Among other things. I didn't expect you to be up yet, though.'

Liz yawned and stretched her arms above her head. 'Chloe kept me awake for most of it. She's as excited as if it was Christmas Day. Now she's fast asleep and *I* am wide awake.'

'And are you all set?'

'I'm still scared to death about it,' Liz admitted candidly. Then she came across all shy, blushing as she spoke.

'Talking to you is like having my own personal counsellor. You're like my fairy godmother really. Even after knowing you for such a short space of time, I'm going to miss you so much.'

Cathy was touched. 'I'm not far away and always at the end of the phone.'

'At least I have Chloe on side. She's been an angel, as usual. I don't know what I did to deserve such a good little girl.'

Cathy smiled at the memory of Chloe when she'd first seen the flat. She hadn't taken any notice of the peeling wallpaper, the smelly kitchen cupboards, the overgrown jungle of a garden, the rubbish that had to be removed before they could move in. Even having her own bedroom again had been second best. The main thing that had swung it for Chloe was that her best friend, Emily, lived three doors away.

'I know,' Liz agreed. 'She can't decide where to put her bed in her new room. That was mainly why she couldn't sleep last night.'

'What time is your furniture arriving?'

'Anytime from nine until midday. I'm so grateful for Josie's help.'

Josie had put Liz in touch with a place that sold second-hand furniture. For a small fee and proof that she was claiming benefits, she could take away as much as she wanted. Josie had warned her that sometimes the donations weren't up to much but other times she'd seen people come away with some wonderful items. Liz had trotted off with a list and apart from a coffee table had got the lot: double bed, single bed, wardrobes, drawers, small table and chairs that folded up out of the way, bookcase for Chloe and a wall unit for the living room, washing machine, cooker, small television and a nearly-new, grey, dralon three-piece suite. Not exactly the colour she would choose but the quality was superb. And although most things weren't up to much in the fashion stakes, everything was clean and tidy. She'd even spotted a mirror and a couple of table lamps.

'Praise the Lord for decent people who donate what they no longer require,' she added with a grin.

'I'm going to miss you so much,' Cathy said suddenly. 'It's been great having you around.'

'Even though I brought along an eight-year-old maniac and a wayward husband?'

'Works both ways.' Cathy nodded. 'Didn't I say welcome to the mad house when you first came to stay?'

Liz faltered. It seemed such a long time since she'd first arrived at Cathy's house yet just the mention of her vulnerability was enough for all the fear to come back.

'Do you think I was right to get away, Cath?' she asked now, in a voice similar to Chloe's when she was at fault.

Cathy sat forward and covered Liz's hand with her own. 'Of course! It took a lot of courage to do what you did. Why do you think it was wrong?'

'I thought I could forget him if he wasn't around to remind me. But the memories came with me. Not to mention the man himself. I can't stop thinking about him, yet I know that I don't want to be with him anymore. It's like his ghost is following me around. Watching my every move in case I do something he disapproves of. Every time I go out, I keep looking over my shoulder, expecting him to pounce on me. Do you think he'll ever give up?'

Cathy shrugged. 'I don't know, Liz. My experience over the years hasn't taught me how to anticipate these things because every man I've dealt with has been different. I've only had a couple who have gone on for a while, though. Maybe Kevin will get fed up eventually.'

'You're such a good listener,' Liz told her, which brought her neatly onto the subject that was intriguing her. 'I think you would have made a great mum. It's a shame you and Rich didn't have any children.'

Cathy endeavoured not to look too sad as she tried to explain some of the pain in her heart. 'We did try for years before he died but nothing happened.' She went off into a world of her own, her eyes glistening as she thought about what might have been. Especially if she had told him about Simon. Why hadn't she told him!

Liz realised that she'd touched a nerve. She smiled at Cathy to make amends. 'Thanks for listening to me going on. I'm still getting used to everything changing. It's good to have someone to confide in.'

Cathy stood up and suddenly Liz was hugging her.

'You're only moving five minutes away,' she said, wiping away a tear. 'You can come back as often as you like.'

'Don't say that!' said Liz. 'If you say it too many times, I might have to stay here. It will be much – what's the matter?'

'Sorry.' Cathy had gone to turn the radio up. 'There's something going on at Cookson's Factory down the road. I'm sure I heard that someone's been murdered.' As the broadcaster moved on to the next story, she switched on the television to see if the story had caught the morning's news.

*

Becky heard Liz go downstairs but didn't want to get out of bed just yet. But ten minutes later, when Liz came back up to her room, she stretched and decided that she might as well get up.

'Morning, Cath.' She yawned loudly before plonking herself down beside her at the table.

'Morning.' Cathy kept her eyes on the television.

'What's up?'

'Someone local's been murdered. I'm just looking to see if it's anyone I know.'

'Cathy!' said Becky. 'That's so morbid.'

'Everyone's interested in something when it happens on their doorstep. It's a local factory – Cookson's. It's not far from here. A security guard was shot last night.'

Becky gulped. She knew exactly how far away it was. Cookson's Factory was where she'd left Danny last night.

They sat in silence, both engrossed as they watched *Sky News*. The man was reported to be in his forties, had worked at the factory for nine years and was rumoured to come from Stockleigh. He'd been shot twice, once in the chest and once in the leg. The reporter was saying there'd been an anonymous tip off by a member of the public.

A few minutes later the news bulletin changed to another story. Cathy stood up.

'Suppose I'd better get ready for my shift at the den,' she said. 'Do you want me to leave this on?'

Unable to speak, Becky nodded. She began to shake. This time it was she who kept her eyes peeled to the screen. But they soon filled with tears as it all became too much for

237

her. Her skin tone changed to a sickly grey colour, wide eyes pools of horror.

'What's the matter?' asked Cathy. 'Are you ill?'

'I know who killed that security guard,' she cried.

'Oh, dear God!' Cathy caught her breath. 'I might have known one of you girls would be in the thick of things!'

'No! Danny Bradley wanted me to help him but I wouldn't. I left him there, I swear!'

Cathy sat down again. 'Tell me everything,' she said.

When the phone rang twenty minutes later, Cathy took it into the hallway while she spoke to Andy Baxter. Becky dragged her knees up to her chest and balanced precariously on the chair. Stupid, stupid cow. What was wrong with her? First there was the business with Uncle James. Then there was the trauma of losing her baby. Now Danny Bradley had murdered someone. Would she always attract trouble, no matter where she went?

'Was that the police?' She looked up as Cathy came back into the room, trepidation plain to see in her eyes.

'Yes. They already have Danny in custody. Andy says he can't say much right now but Danny was found injured on site. He claims that he had nothing to do with the shooting, and he has come up with some cock-and-bull story. He says he was hit over the head and passed out. When he came round, the gun was in his hand. What the hell were you doing –?'

'He had a gun?' Becky stood up, her eyes widening in horror. 'He had a *gun*!'

'Yes, a flipping gun! Have you any idea who you've been messing around with? He's a troublemaker and –'

'He had a gun?' Becky repeated.

Cathy pursed her lips. 'Don't come all innocent with me and tell me that you didn't know.'

'I didn't! Oh God, I – what happens if they think I'm involved? They'll lock me up too and then I'll get hooked on drugs and end up dying like Cheryl. I –'

'Becky!' Cathy placed her hands on the young girl's shoulders to calm the hysteria that was mounting. 'If you're telling the truth, you have nothing to worry about.'

'But if I grass him up, I'll have all the Bradley family coming after me. They're a bunch of nutters.' She began to hyperventilate. 'What if –'

'Becky, calm down!' Cathy looked her directly in the eye again. 'Danny's prints were all over the gun. And they've found his rucksack. Andy says he'll need to talk to you.'

But Becky could only register one thing.

'No.' She shook her head furtively. 'He's a bit scary at times but he hasn't got murder in him. He must have panicked or something.' She shook her head again. 'No, not Danny Bradley.'

Cathy relaxed a little as she realised the situation wasn't as serious as she'd first thought for Becky. Danny Bradley was hardly in a position to plead not guilty. Maybe Becky's evidence wouldn't be needed in court. All she could do was put him there just before it happened and the incident itself did that anyway. Suddenly, despite the seriousness of the situation, she was finding it difficult to stop herself from smiling. Danny's mother, Gina Bradley, would be furious. She couldn't wait to see the look on her face. She needed to call Rose immediately. She wouldn't want to miss the –

Cathy stopped short. Rose was still in hospital.

'What?' Becky caught Cathy's sorrow.

'Oh, nothing, really. I was just thinking about Rose.'

'She will be okay, won't she?'

'No,' Cathy replied truthfully. 'Sue, her eldest daughter, rang me last night to say things weren't improving. I don't think she'll be with us for much longer.'

The rest of the day turned out to be a mixture of hard work, laughter and tears. Cathy said her goodbyes to Rose, the hardest thing she'd done in a long time. She joined the others afterwards at Liz's new flat and by mid afternoon she and Chloe were moved in. Copious amounts of tea and chocolate biscuits had been consumed. Liz and Cathy laughed as Jess and Becky struggled to shift the settee into its place and they both collapsed into it afterwards. And even though numerous clips of the goings on at Cookson's Factory were watched, neither Cathy nor Becky mentioned they knew anything about it.

Yet amidst the laughter, Cathy was on alert, waiting for the phone call. It arrived shortly after eight thirty that evening.

'Is that you, Sue?'

'Yes, Cathy,' said Rose's daughter. 'Mum died half an hour ago.'

Although she thought she'd be devastated when she replaced the receiver, Cathy found herself flooded with relief. Tears fell with mixed emotions. Happy tears as she recalled joyful memories. Sad tears because she'd lost such a precious friend. Even still, she prayed in silence her thanks to the Lord who'd taken away Rose's pain.

At the family's request, Cathy had stayed away when she

knew Rose was near to the end of her life. To her Rose would always be family, but that still didn't give her the right to invade such an emotional, such a personal time. Besides, Rose had spent ample time with her since they'd met, so who was she to complain.

She poured a large whisky and took it out into the garden. Looking up to the sky, she smiled to herself as she let her tears fall. Rose would be with her husband, Arthur, now and she knew she would be checking in to see if Rich was okay.

In respect, Cathy raised her glass in salute to the woman who she had loved more than her own mother.

'God bless you, Rose Clarke,' she whispered. 'I'm going to miss you so much.'

TWENTY-THREE

Becky was on her way to the shops to get a few things for Cathy when she heard footsteps behind her.

'Hey, gorgeous!'

She swivelled round to see who was addressing her and smiled, her heart giving a flutter when she saw Austin running towards her. She hadn't seen him since Danny had been charged last week.

'I heard about Dan,' he said. 'Are you okay?'

'No. It's doing my head in. People keep thinking I was involved.'

'But you weren't, were you?'

'No!' Becky sounded horrified that he would even think that.

'Hey, just checking.'

Austin gave her a smile that made her insides do something most peculiar. She leaned on the garden wall of a nearby house.

'Bet you never thought he'd do someone in.' Austin sat down too. 'Want to talk about it?'

Becky shook her head. She still didn't think it was possible, even now. At first she'd blamed herself. If she'd flirted with the security guy, he might not be dead now. But eventually she'd realised that this was Danny's fault.

'I didn't even know he had a gun,' Becky admitted. 'I've never seen it.'

'He showed me lots of times.'

'Did he?'

'Yeah. He bragged about how he'd use it one day. I just thought he was all talk. Just goes to show how wrong I was. Do you miss him now that he's banged up on remand?'

'Not anymore. He's evil to do that.'

'I know that he should have treated you better.'

'Really?'

'Yeah. He had the chance to be your man and he blew it. I would never waste an opportunity to get to know you better.' Austin reached for her hand. 'I think you're beautiful.'

'Really?' Becky repeated, this time with a giggle.

'Can I say something? You won't get upset?'

Becky shrugged.

'I always thought he was too good for you.'

Becky smiled. 'Really?' she said again.

Austin grinned back. 'Really.'

'Oh.'

'So how about you and me going out some time soon?'

'Oh, for crying out loud,' Cathy muttered to no one in particular, shaky fingers having a battle to fasten the buttons on her black woollen jacket. She couldn't believe it was the second time in just over a fortnight she'd had to wear it. Finally managing to squeeze the top one through its buttonhole, she pulled out the collar of her white shirt to complete the look. No matter how difficult it would be for her, she would have to put on a brave face today. Rose had been a good friend and there was only one way to pay her respects.

It was hard to think that a week had passed since she'd died. Cathy had spent so much time with Liz and Chloe that even Becky and Jess had started to hang around. They'd had quite a few girls' nights in with pizza and wine and she'd really enjoyed it. It had helped to block out that neither here-nor-there feeling after a loved one dies and before they are buried or cremated.

As she rummaged in her jewellery box for a necklace to wear, her hand fell upon Rich's watch. She picked it up, held it to her wrist. The hands displayed the time as twelve fifteen, the battery long ago run out. She touched its face lightly, remembering the time she'd given it to him. It had been his thirtieth birthday. Rich had gone mad; said she shouldn't have spent so much money on him. When she told him that she loved him enough to spend every penny she had, he'd laughed. He'd said he meant that now she'd have to spend far more for his fortieth birthday. Sadly, she never got that chance.

She placed the watch back carefully, chose a cheap necklace with a clear glass pendant and fastened it behind her neck. Putting it straight in the mirror, she couldn't help but think back to the day she'd laid Rich to rest: the hymns they'd sung, the bright clear sky even though a bitter wind blew, the vicar's tribute to her wonderful man, the flower arrangement she'd ordered for him, the large congregation that came to say goodbye. Even years later, she could remember it like it was yesterday.

Cathy shook her head to rid herself of its confusion. There was no time to think about Rich now or else she'd start crying again. Quickly, she grabbed a few tissues and pushed them into her pocket.

There was a knock on the half open door. Josie stepped into her room. She took one look at Cathy, walked over and hugged her tightly.

'We'll do Rose proud today,' she said.

'I miss her so much.' Cathy let her tears fall again.

'I know you do.' Josie wiped gently at Cathy's cheeks before linking her arm. 'Come on,' she said. 'Let's go and say goodbye to our friend.'

When Cathy arrived home shortly after midnight, Jess and Becky were asleep in their rooms. She made a cup of tea and sat down with a thud, thinking about the day. Rose had been a well-liked and well-known woman around the Mitchell Estate. The service was perfect for her. Her family chose some really meaningful words to remember her by. There had been at least fifty people congregated in the tiny chapel at the crematorium. Cathy had recognised many of them from her trips to collect Rose from the bingo hall or her luncheon club. Josie said she recognised many of them from helping out at jumble sales and raffles to raise money for her domestic violence courses.

While she was there, she'd also managed to catch Andy Baxter who had attended the service but was unable to come back for the wake. 'I've had a word with Kevin McIntyre,' he told her before he left. 'He denies sending the notes but I still explained what would happen should there be another one. I also told him I'd be keeping an eye out for his wife, making sure no harm came to her. I think he caught my meaning but only time will tell.' Cathy sincerely hoped so.

This was a new beginning for Liz and Chloe. And it was as she arrived home that she decided this was to be a new beginning for her too. Losing Rose so suddenly without a chance to say goodbye made her realise that she didn't want to leave this world with things left unsaid if it was possible not to.

It might be hard if he didn't want to see her and it might not be easy to trace him after all this time but she was ready now. She would find a solicitor.

And then she was going to find her son.

In the city centre the next morning, Liz crossed over at the traffic lights on the high street and made her way to the shops. She had a few bills to pay, she needed a small piece of netting for the bathroom window from the indoor market and Chloe had asked for the latest *Bratz* magazine. Although she'd had a few expenses lately, she reckoned she could run to that. Chloe had been a good girl: she deserved a treat.

It had been ten days since she'd moved into the flat and so far it had been uneventful. The place was beginning to look welcoming at last and even though she'd spent a great deal of time at Cathy's after Rose died, she was beginning to feel like she could make it into a home for her and Chloe.

Bills paid and netting purchased, she decided to catch the bus home rather than walk the half hour back to Preston Avenue. The day was lovely and she held her face up to the sun for a moment, still relishing her freedom. It was good to be out on a day like this. Maybe she should take Chloe to the park again this afternoon – that is if she could tear herself away from Emily's house, which is where she'd left her earlier. They'd become inseparable since the move.

When she looked back down again, Liz gasped. Kevin was walking towards her. He was with a young woman: she looked no more than a teenager. They were laughing about something, the woman talking enthusiastically with her hands.

Liz's legs felt as if they were made of something heavy. In desperation, she looked around for somewhere to hide but it was too late. Kevin had already seen her. The look he gave her was one of surprise, then pure delight. She dived into the nearest shop, all the time feeling his eyes following her. Much to the astonishment of the till assistant, she pressed herself up against the wall.

Kevin looked into the doorway as he went past, his arm now slung around the girl's shoulders. Liz gulped, her hand covering her mouth as she began to dry-retch. She could hear their laughter taunting her. As she stood like a statue, paralysed by fear, Kevin pulled the woman closer and gave her a squeeze. Then she heard giggling.

They walked further away and Liz's breathing took on a life of its own again. She moved across to the window, staying hidden behind a post, continuing to watch until they were out of sight.

'Are you okay, love?' the till assistant asked with genuine concern. 'You look like you've seen a ghost.'

'I – I…'

'Ex-partner was it?'

Liz stared at her with wide eyes but the woman smiled.

'Don't worry, I'm not psychic. I just followed your gaze. Would you like to sit down for a while, just until you get your colour back?'

'No, I'm fine.' Liz's breathing was calming down now;

she wanted to get home as soon as possible. 'But thanks for your concern.'

With that she was out of the shop, heading for home on foot, in the opposite direction to Kevin McIntyre.

TWENTY-FOUR

'I thought you'd be thrilled to see him out with someone else,' Cathy tried to soothe Liz as she listened to her ordeal. 'It means he might be moving on.'

Liz paced the room. 'But what if he does the same things to her that he did to me?'

'That shouldn't concern you anymore.'

'I can't just switch off after what he did.'

Cathy sighed. 'Sorry, I didn't mean that to sound harsh. What I meant to say is there will always be victims in this world. Maybe he won't hit her –'

'You think it was my fault that he treated me like that!'

'– until he gets to know her better,' Cathy finished off her sentence.

Liz lowered her eyes. She should have known that whatever Cathy said would make sense. As soon as she'd got back to the flat and bolted the door, she was the first person she'd contacted. Cathy had been there in minutes. Now she was here, Liz was doubting her words.

'Men like Kevin will always get the upper hand with their women,' Cathy continued regardless. 'The woman he was with has two choices, just like you did. You chose well. Maybe she will too. But that doesn't mean that you have to feel sorry for her. We make our own mistakes.'

'Yes, but what if he hurts her like he hurt me?'

'You got over it, didn't you? You got away from him.'

'It still doesn't make it right.'

'Of course it doesn't. But in my experience, a lot of women around here are regularly abused by their husbands. It's part and parcel of their lives.' Cathy raised her hand when she saw Liz was about to interrupt again. 'I'm not saying that it's right. But some of the women don't know any better. They've watched their mothers being punched and kicked by their fathers. They've seen man after man come along and abuse them. None of them chose it, but sometimes it's just a way of life for them. Heartless to hear, I know, but some of the women think they deserve it. I –'

'Oh, how can you say such things? I never thought I deserved it!'

'Will you let me finish before butting in, woman? Their men drag them down; make them feel insignificant, like they have done wrong. That's what Kevin did to you, didn't he?'

Liz nodded reluctantly.

'He made you feel that you were worth nothing. Like no one else would want you. Now imagine that you confided in your mother and she told you that it was your duty to take a good beating every now and then as par for the course. What would you do?'

Liz didn't know what to say to that.

'Nature versus nurture, Liz. That's what I meant. It wasn't intended to make you feel that you didn't do your best to get away. You are one of the lucky ones. There are too many women out there who go unheard.'

'What would you have done if Rich had hit out at you?'

'He did.'

Liz gasped. 'What did you do?'

'I hit him back, twice as hard. That's what Josie meant by the shenanigans going on when Rich was alive. He gave me a backhander twice but, luckily for me, Rich was remorseful. And boy, did I make him pay.'

Liz's lower lip started to tremble.

'I'm sorry. I didn't mean it to sound like I was making fun of you.'

'You didn't,' said Liz. 'I'm just so scared.'

Cathy hugged her. She glanced around the tiny living room that she'd helped Liz to decorate. The walls were coloured pale aqua, woodwork a slightly darker shade now. To lighten it up, there was a huge mirror hanging over the fireplace. It made more of a focal point than the cheap pine fire surround that had taken hours to strip of its dark chocolate gloss paint. Add to that the curtains and paraphernalia that Josie had given to her and the overall feel of the place was warmth. She decided to use its relevance.

'Look around you, Liz. Look what you've created. You have such a lovely place here, a new, safe home. I bet it feels like that already?'

Liz sniffed before nodding. 'It's getting there.'

'And you?'

Liz nodded again. 'We're getting there too.'

'You'll be okay here.' Cathy hugged her again, trying greatly to ease her pain. But when they pulled away, Liz stood with tears running down her face.

'Things will get better, right?'

*

251

'Off out with lover boy again?' Jess stood defiantly in Becky's bedroom door, watching as she applied her make-up.

'Yep,' said Becky.

'He only wants you because you spread your legs so easily.'

Becky turned her head slightly, enough to stare back. 'Don't be so nasty. You're only jealous.'

'I know, sorry,' Jess confessed. She threw herself down onto Becky's bed. 'Now that Danny's off the scene, it's left me with no one but the local idiots. Bloody marvellous.'

'So Mickey Grainger's off the scene too?'

'Deffo. I'm not going anywhere near him now I know he's been shagging around behind my back.'

Not long after they'd become an item, Jess had caught Mickey snogging the face off Lucinda Chapman as she'd been on her way to the toilet in The Butcher's Arms. She'd pulled them apart but instead of taking her anger out on Mickey, she'd punched Lucinda in the eye. A fight had erupted – Becky had become embroiled in it too – but Jess hadn't spoken to Mickey since, despite the constant barrage of text messages and phone calls from him.

'That's precisely why I'm going out with Austin,' Becky replied, trying to keep away from the mention of Danny Bradley. Despite everything, Jess still had no idea that she'd gone all the way with Danny and she intended keeping it that way. Otherwise their newly-formed friendship would be doomed before it had really got going.

'You've only been out with him a few times,' said Jess. Suddenly her demeanour changed. 'Just be careful, Becks. I've heard a few things around the estate about him.'

'What do you mean? What have you heard?'

'He gave Trevor Watson a right good pasting the other night. Apparently it was because he looked at him the wrong way.'

'Oh, rumours schmumours,' Becky repeated one of Jess's favourite slang terms. Satisfied with her eye shadow, she started applying mascara. 'And Trevor Watson is a right knob anyway. Everyone knows that.'

'And he slapped one of the Bradley twins because they wouldn't move out of his way.'

This had Becky's attention. 'What were they doing hanging around him? Wait 'til I get my hands on them, the stupid slags!'

'Bleeding hell! You're changing into a monster.' Jess sounded horrified. 'Chill out, will you?'

'Says the one who told me to toughen up.'

'Yes, but that was only to wise up to how things work around here. Not to get into fights over a loser.'

As Becky glared at Jess for the first time since they'd met, Jess was the one who felt vulnerable.

'I will do what I have to do to survive this shit life,' said Becky, sounding sixty and not sixteen. 'And if that means getting a pasting every now and then, that's what I'll put up with.'

Jess frowned. 'Do what you want, but Becks?' She waited for her to look up again. 'I'm here if you want to talk, yeah?'

Becky glanced at her watch, checked her appearance one more time and grabbed her key.

'Time to go,' she said and pushed Jess out of her room. Austin would be waiting around the corner for her.

*

'You smell gorgeous,' Austin told her when she slid into the passenger seat of his car. He pulled her into his arms and kissed her with a passion that left her breathless.

Becky smiled. Who would have thought Austin had a kick in him like that?

'Where are we off to?' she asked, as he started the engine.

'Let's go somewhere quiet and then we'll see. I fancy a good time. You up for it yet?'

'Absolutely.' Becky's smile widened. This was her fourth time out with Austin and, despite what she'd said to Jess, they hadn't gone all the way yet. On their first date, she'd pulled out his shirt and run a hand over his bare skin. But he'd stopped her when she tugged at his belt. 'What's the hurry?' he'd said. The next time she tried it, he moved her hand away again. At the third attempt, she started to wonder if he was gay, wondering what type of man refuses sex offered to him so willingly.

Then she began to wonder if it was her. Did he really fancy her or was he just playing about? So his mood now delighted her. She stretched out her long legs, crossed them at the ankles and rested her hand on his thigh.

In no time at all, they were turning around the back of the White Lion pub.

Austin parked up. 'Okay then, little girly,' he teased. 'Why don't you do your best and blow me away.'

Becky's smile dropped. Why were men only interested in themselves? Didn't she deserve some good loving too?

Austin spotted her expression. 'A favour for a favour?' he licked his top lip suggestively.

She shrugged, having no idea what he meant. All Danny had ever wanted was his own good time. He hadn't been bothered whether or not she had enjoyed herself, even though he always said he'd be the best she'd ever have.

She undid his belt and slid her hand around his erection. He gave a moan and pushed her head down towards it.

Becky hadn't known how to give head until she'd met Danny. Over a bottle of vodka, she'd made her confession to Jess and she'd shown her what she did by using the bottle neck. She'd also shown her how to put on a condom sexily but Becky had rolled around with laughter. She had, however, tried it out numerous times on a banana until she was a dab hand at it.

Idly as she moved up and down on him, she wondered what Jess was up to tonight. Part of her felt really bad about taunting her earlier on. It was through her that she'd met Danny, then Austin, so maybe it wasn't fair to exclude her. And now that they'd become friends, Jess's threats didn't bother her anymore. Maybe tomorrow she should find time to have a few girlie moments. Life didn't have to be about men all of the time.

Austin cursed as he pushed his hips up out of the seat. Becky laughed inwardly. It gave her such a kick to see that. Finally she'd realised that sex could be used to her own advantage. She could make any man go weak at his knees if she gave him a blow job. No more being taken advantage of.

Austin was inching his fingers up the side of her thigh. She sat upright and gave him a smile as his fingers moved up further. Becky gasped as he ran his nails gently up and down, up and down her thigh. Goosebumps erupted over her skin and everything began to pulse all at once.

'Wet and horny,' Austin whispered, not taking his eyes away from hers. The intensity made Becky gasp again. Touch me, she begged inwardly. Touch me now.

As if he read her mind, Austin pulled her over on to his lap. His hand dived between her legs, his fingers easily slipping into her wetness. She bit her lip to stop from gasping again. Austin kissed her then, his tongue matching the rhythm of his fingers.

Suddenly Becky broke away. She felt her back arch. Ohmigod, what was happening to her? With his spare hand, Austin pulled her top down and licked her nipple. Round and round with his tongue. She felt waves building up inside her, threatening to take her into unknown territories. Why had she wasted her time with stupid Danny Bradley when she could have been doing this with Austin? Her breathing quickened and she let out an involuntary groan. Embarrassed, she looked down at Austin, his eyes still locked on hers. She noticed that her chest had coloured, the nipple being worked on right now as erect as he'd been minutes earlier.

Another groan escaped. God, what was he doing to her? Just as something peculiar started to happen in her stomach, Austin stopped. Everything.

'Get out of the car.'

'What?'

'Relax. I'm not going to drive off without you. I'm getting out too. It'll just be more comfortable for you.'

Once they were out, Austin pushed her onto the bonnet.

'Hitch up your skirt and rest your feet on the bumper.'

She quickly did as he said.

Austin shook his head. 'Take your knickers off first.'

Becky took them off. She didn't have time to do anything with them before Austin had his face between her legs. Becky's eyes closed as he moved his tongue over the edge of all her senses.

'Oh my God,' she whispered. She held on to the side of the bonnet as feelings inside her erupted like never before. Faster and faster, dizzier and dizzier.

'Oh my God,' she said again and a wave of pleasure finally washed over her. This time she arched her back fully, her toes scrunching up inside her shoes. It took all of her strength to stay on the car. 'Oh my God,' she moaned. 'Oh my God. Oh my fucking God!'

Austin stood up and pushed himself into her and she wound her legs around his waist, holding on to him for dear life. The pleasure was turning to irritation as every nerve exploded in her body. No, please, it's too unbearable. But just as quickly the pleasure was back and she began to ride him, begging for the waves again.

As she arched her back for the third time, Becky suddenly realised that she had just relinquished her power.

TWENTY-FIVE

'I can't believe you've thrashed me,' Matt said as they zigzagged through the milling crowds in the foyer of Super Bowl and then out into the night.

'I promise I wasn't fibbing when I said I was useless at it.' Cathy grinned, failing to hide her delight: she had beaten Matt four games to two, including five strikes.

Matt folded his hand around hers. 'You'd better not relay any of this to Josie. She'd beat me up for lesser things.'

Cathy tutted. 'You mean our friend who set us up?'

There had been talk about a crowd of them going bowling. Josie said she'd invited Andy Baxter and his wife and Suzie Rushton from the community house. Liz had said she'd try to get a babysitter and Jess and Becky had said they'd come along too. But during the day, one by one they'd cried off until there was only Josie meeting them at the Festival Park. When Cathy had arrived ten minutes early, she'd spotted Matt in the foyer. Josie hadn't answered her mobile when Matt tried to contact her. They'd then waited a further half an hour before realising that she wasn't going to show. Embarrassment turned to laughter and they'd decided to go it alone. And it had been great. Cathy hadn't enjoyed herself so much in a good while.

They fell into a steady pace along the path which led to

the car park. Matt stopped as they drew near a burger van.

'Fancy a hot dog?'

'Why not?'

They joined the small queue and within minutes had put in their order.

'How long have you known Josie?' Matt asked as they waited for it to be prepared.

'Since she started working on the Mitchell Estate.'

'So were you a naughty girl then? Josie only deals with unruly tenants –'

Cathy thumped him playfully on his arm.

'Or so I heard.'

'My husband had a flat and once we were married, she helped us to get a bigger place. We didn't have any children so we were bottom of the list for a house. Josie persuaded one of the old girls to do a tenant swap with us for the flat. We had a downstairs flat with hardly any garden to maintain so it was perfect for her.' She smiled with affection. 'I've always admired Josie for the work she does.'

'She is remarkable,' Matt agreed. 'I suppose she's always been that passionate?'

Cathy nodded. 'Yeah. Not many things get her down, although I thought we'd lost her last year when the community house opened. But luckily for us, she splits her time between there and the office.'

'She still does support calls?'

'Yes. She wanted to keep in with the women on the estate. She's a born helper. Anyway, less about Josie. What really brought you here? Marriage break up?'

Matt looked on in astonishment. 'How did you know?'

'It was just a lucky guess.' Cathy grinned. 'Any kids?'

'No, we never got around to it.' Matt sniggered harshly. 'We were always too busy arguing to think of the better things in life. And I'm not sure that I want children now. I'm forty-five.'

'That's not old.'

'It's old enough to be set in my ways and not to want anything tiny holding me back.'

Cathy frowned. He seemed so sure about it that it was almost too sad to hear.

'And you don't have any regrets about moving?' she asked, deciding to change the subject. 'Now that you've been here for a while, I'm sure you must be as mad as the rest of us?'

Matt laughed. 'I still don't think the Mitchell Estate is that bad.'

'It bloody is.'

'It was strange at first, I must admit, but now I wouldn't want to be anywhere else.'

'You're definitely as mad as the rest of us then,' Cathy teased.

'I must be. But the best thing about moving here so far is that it's given me a chance to get to know you.' Matt moved towards her and lightly kissed her lips. Then he moved back, staring intently at her.

Cathy pulled him close again.

'How did the date of the century go?' Becky asked as soon as Cathy got home. She and Jess were huddled together on the bottom step of the stairs.

'I'll kill that Josie Mellor when I get my hands on her,' she told them. 'She set us up!'

The girls only had to glance at each other before bursting into laughter.

Cathy turned her head sharply. 'Did everyone know?' she asked, feeling the start of a smile.

'Yeah.' They spoke in unison.

'I will definitely kill her when I see her.' Cathy grinned as they stared at her, waiting for more details she presumed. 'But it was worth showing up. I had a great time.'

'And did you have a snog?' Jess followed her through to the kitchen. Becky was right behind her.

'Never mind, young lady.' Cathy busied herself making coffee.

'Well, did he try to feel you up?'

'Jess!' said Becky. 'People as old as Cathy don't get felt up.'

'What do you mean, people as old as me?' Cathy came to her own defence. 'I'll have you know I haven't reached forty yet.'

Becky grinned. 'You know what she meant. Sex for us teenagers is a boy seeing how far a girl will let her go.'

'You should know that one,' whispered Jess.

Becky glared at her but relaxed when she saw her grinning too. Now that they were getting on much better, the snide remarks had stopped. But every now and then, Becky couldn't fathom out what was intended and what wasn't. This time she saw it was meant as a joke.

'Did you go bowling eventually?' Becky asked.

'Yep.'

'And did you get a strike?' Jess taunted.

'Yep.' Cathy bit her lower lip to stop from smiling at the double meaning of the sentence. But then she decided to back it up. 'Five times actually. I had a hot dog as well.'

Jess and Becky smirked at each other.

'Is *that* what you called it in your day?' Jess teased. 'We'd call it –'

'I had a hot dog of the *food* variety, you cheeky mare. In *my* day, we never did anything untoward on a first date. Yes…'

Cathy paused. The night had been fun, even though it had felt really strange to kiss another man after so long. All at once, it had made her realise how lonely she was. So when Matt had suggested they meet up again, she'd agreed without hesitation.

'Yes, I do admit to going on a date with Matt,' she said sweetly. 'And what's more, I'm going out with him again.'

In the shadow of the garden hedges, Austin stood finishing his second cigarette. He stared at the house, watching them all in the kitchen. A few minutes later, he saw Becky in her room. She was dancing around like a five-year-old, her hair flying behind her at every step.

He grinned at her childish antics. He could hear the music blaring from here. But she wasn't a youngster anymore. He'd certainly made her into a woman earlier that night. She'd been so loud: he must be keeping his reputation intact.

His eyes flicked to the right as the light went off in the kitchen and another went on in the next room. He saw an older woman, long dark hair; watched her rearrange a few magazines on a coffee table and plump up cushions before drawing the curtains. Then the light went out again.

Cathy Mason, he presumed, as he lit another cigarette

and took a lengthy drag. Although they'd yet to be introduced, Austin wondered what she'd think of her young charge having her legs spread over a car as he made her scream out obscenities? Would she think Becky was so innocent then?

He glanced up again. Becky had a hairbrush in her hand now, pretending that it was a microphone. Surprisingly easy to seduce, she had just made his stay around here all the more enjoyable. He couldn't believe his luck. Something nice to do to while away the time and stay inconspicuous until he could unleash his plan. It wasn't long now until the fifteenth of August, the most important day of his life.

Even though Cathy had enjoyed herself immensely that evening, she ended up having a fidgety night in bed. Images of Rich and Matt flashed up intermittently and she tossed and turned in her bed. First she'd be kissing Rich and then pushing him away. Then she would do the same with Matt. Then she would wake up breathless, wrestling with the duvet, pummelling the pillow to stop from screaming out.

What was wrong with her? The first man she'd shown any affection to and she was reacting like this. She should be remembering Matt's touch, Matt's tender kisses. Surely after three years she had nothing to feel guilty about? But she couldn't help feeling at fault – which left her with one burning question. Was she really ready to go out with Matt?

Finally, she could bear it no longer. Even though it was only five thirty, she got up. It didn't make sense to try and force sleep. Besides, she had to keep her wits about her this morning. Today might turn out to be a very big day once she'd been to see her new solicitor. After finally plucking up the courage to search for Simon, she'd made an appointment and given details over a few phone calls. She was going in to the office to meet him and provide him with a bit more information.

Going downstairs, she noticed there was another note waiting on the doormat. Annoyed, she ripped it open.

'STINKING WHORE'

Cathy sighed. How dare Kevin write that about Liz, especially after Andy Baxter had warned him of the consequences if he sent any more messages.

Although she could be grateful for one thing, she supposed. Obviously Kevin didn't know that Liz wasn't living there anymore. She hoped he'd moved on when Liz had seen him out with that young girl in town but it looked like he was back on the scene. She would have to brace herself for another torrent of abuse. Kevin wouldn't give up until he knew where Liz had gone. She could keep him off the scent for a few days, a week at the most, but he'd want to see Liz. Come what may, there was no way Cathy would ever tell him where she had moved to. But Kevin would then probably go back to following her. It wasn't hard to catch her out. He only had to look out for her on the school run. All the same, maybe she should warn Liz that her ex would be on the prowl now. Stupid, selfish bastard!

She tucked the note away in the diary with the others. Why couldn't Kevin accept that Liz didn't want that kind of life anymore and leave her and Chloe alone? What was it with some men these days, she wondered? Why did they think they had the right to interfere in a woman's life and leave her with nothing but turmoil? She sat down at the table with a thud and rested her head in her hands.

Actually that was a bit harsh on Matt's part, she realised. All he was responsible for was making her feel guilty because she'd had such a good time. Why couldn't she shake the feeling? Did she lead him on last night and now regret it? She truly hoped not. He was far too nice for that.

Cathy sighed again. In the space of a few short hours, her life had turned upside down. Bloody Josie Mellor! Wait until she got hold of her.

'It's your fault,' Cathy told her later that same morning when she collared her in her office. 'You started this whole sorry fiasco.'

'*You* needed a helping hand,' said Josie. 'You shouldn't have to be alone at your age. I know Rich wouldn't have wanted that.'

'Talk to the dead, can you?'

'Oh, Cath, I'm sorry. I didn't think that you'd –'

'No, that's right, you didn't think!'

Josie raised her hands in surrender. 'You're right. I was a nerd head. I just thought that you and Matt were a good fit. He's single, a nice guy and so bloody attractive. You're single, a nice woman and well… I knew he would find you attractive. You deserve some fun, some loving in your life. What are you so afraid of?'

'Afraid of?'

'Starting again, in case it doesn't work out? In case it doesn't measure up to you and Rich?'

'Our marriage wasn't perfect, as well you must remember,' Cathy replied.

'You see?' Josie smiled encouragingly as she picked up a bundle of files. 'So don't make out that it was all sweetness and light and that you will never find another Rich. No one is expecting you to do that. I just want you to find a Matt.'

Despite herself, Cathy smiled. She knew that Josie was right – she had been over-analysing her marriage. But she was wrong about one thing.

'I'm not afraid,' she told her. 'I just feel guilty after... after...'

'Cathy Mason, surely you didn't give out on your first date?'

'No. I meant I haven't been kissed by anyone else for years. That's the reason behind all this crap I've been tormenting myself with.'

'Then it's about time you caught up and moved on.'

Cathy spotted the clock. 'Christ, will you look at the time. I'm going to be late!'

'Yes, where are you off to, dressed up all posh?' Josie asked as she rushed to the door.

'Oh, I'm just going into town.' Cathy was non-committal. 'Nowhere in particular.'

Rushing through the pedestrian only shopping area an hour later, Cathy got to her appointment with ten minutes to spare. She sat down in the roomy reception area and reached for a magazine. Steele, Barrett and Co had been the first solicitors she'd come across in the local phone directory. Now that she was here, she recalled looking inside it many times on her trips into town.

She casually flicked through a gardening magazine as she recalled what Josie had said about Matt. She knew she'd put Rich on a pedestal and left him there too long. Would he really have wanted her to be alone forever? Not likely. And Matt was a nice guy to mess around with. It didn't have to be anything serious.

A door opened to her right and a man she was sure wasn't old enough to have passed any exams, came towards her. If first impressions really did count, he had to score top marks. All smart pin-striped suit and shiny black shoes, his hair, although cut in a choppy style, looked like he'd spent hours getting it just right. He strode towards her, his large hand outstretched.

'Mrs Mason?' He shook hers firmly. 'I'm David Barrett. Come on through. Zoe, could we have drinks, please?'

The office she was ushered into was vast, modern and tidy. Even its minimalist décor seemed inviting. Cathy sat down, realising that if the business was as good as the overall appearance of everything she'd seen so far, this was going to cost her a fortune.

'Mrs Mason, I did some digging around after you called to arrange this meeting,' Mr Barrett started once he'd settled into his seat. 'I know the details you gave me were scarce but no one can change their date of birth, now can they? Unless they don't want to be found, that is.'

Mr Barrett laughed a little. Cathy smiled faintly to play along with him but she didn't find it funny. What planet was he on? People changed their identity with plastic surgery these days, so changing a date of birth to get lost in the system would be a doddle.

She looked up as Mr Barrett had paused. He had the most captivating of eyes, but Cathy could see apprehension in them. She held her breath, studying his face, desperately looking for some sort of clue. What was he going to say?

'What is it?' she prompted.

'Mrs Mason, I've managed to track down your son.'

TWENTY-SIX

'But how?' Cathy's hand clutched her chest. 'I only gave you a few details. Where is he? Does he want to see me? Oh, don't be so pathetic, Cathy. Of course he doesn't want to see you. Not after all these years.'

Mr Barrett held up his hand for her to stop but she continued as if not seeing it.

'And abandoning him like that as a –' She sat forward. 'He does want to see me, doesn't he?'

'Mrs Mason.' Mr Barrett spoke straight yet with a soothing manner. 'I'm sorry but, no, he doesn't want to see you.'

'What?' Cathy faltered, trying hard to keep her composure as the man sitting before her shattered her dreams.

'I tracked down his adoptive parents. He was with them until he was ten. They told him about you then. They thought it best to be honest with him from an early age but it backfired. He started to become disruptive, uncontrollable. Eventually they had no choice but to put him back into care. He spent the rest of his years in a council run home and that is all they can tell me. He rings them quite often – usually once a week – but he does have a tendency to go off radar for long periods too. During his last call, they told him you were trying to contact him but he said that he didn't want to see you. I could keep on digging, if you'd rather hear it from him?'

Cathy felt like she'd lost the ability to speak.

'People change, Mrs Mason,' Mr Barrett added, noting her distress. 'He was only sixteen when they last saw him. Would you like me to continue with my enquiries?'

Without remembering how, Cathy got into her car and began to drive. The sky was an inviting clear blue but her mood was sombre. Passing the city's central park, she decided to pull over and take a walk.

With every step she took, she didn't notice anyone who passed her by. The flowers were out in bloom, the perfectly mowed lawns and the preened hedges were wasted on her. All she could see was her baby being taken away, Mr Barrett's words running continuously through her mind.

She carried on until she found herself by the side of the lake. Spying a bench that was as empty as she felt inside, she sat down. Before long, tears poured down her face. She'd dreamt of this moment and now it had happened, it had all turned out wrong. Why wouldn't Simon see her, let her explain the situation? Let her explain that she thought she'd done the best for him.

It hadn't even crossed her mind during last night's thoughts of Rich and Matt. She'd thought the meeting today would be a matter of formality, sorting out further details or finalising others so that Mr Barrett could then begin his search. Cathy didn't think for one minute that he would have acted so quickly.

For three hours she watched the world go by while inside she was breaking. Her mind replayed every single detail of the time when she had given Simon up for adoption. Even now she could clearly recall the tiny curls of hair stuck to his face as he took his first few breaths and found out that he could scream. She could still see his tiny squashed nose, his long, yet perfect fingers which wound round her thumb so tightly. Like that one treasured photograph, she only had a memory. She couldn't remember anything else because he had been taken away.

But all too well, Cathy remembered that feeling of inadequacy and longing. How she cried as the nurses looked on. She'd wanted to scream at them, make them understand that she wasn't in a good place, that she couldn't look after him. That she was scared, alone, vulnerable.

Now it was just like losing him again. After all this time, all the years she had yearned to see her son's face, longed for forgiveness, he didn't want to know, and she couldn't blame him.

For a while, she found herself hating Rich. If he hadn't been sent to prison, this would never have happened. And she should have been able to talk to him, air her concerns. Things might have been so different then. Why hadn't she trusted him? If he loved her as much as he said he did, then surely he would have understood her dilemma?

But she knew she couldn't blame Rich for any of it. It was all her fault. She'd chosen not to tell him because she didn't want him to leave her. She couldn't risk losing him so instead she'd stayed quiet. She was the stupid one.

Cathy jumped back to reality as a man too old to be riding a bicycle rode past, narrowly missing her feet as he wobbled about perilously. It was the first week of the school summer break and the park was busy. Children ran around the outside of the lake. Mothers fed the ducks with their toddlers. A group of boys with nets and buckets were shouting so loud they would frighten off anything they might catch. A man was walking towards them, no doubt to tell them to be quiet. She began to cry again. How could life go on all around her?

She must have gone off in a daze again because the next thing she saw was a stout man wearing green overalls standing in front of her. He had kind eyes and a warm smile.

'Are you okay?' he asked gently. 'You've been sitting there for hours.'

'I'm just admiring the beautiful view,' Cathy said, knowing that he'd see right through it.

'Troubles are better when they're shared. Haven't you got anyone to talk to?'

'Sometimes the words won't come out, no matter how many people are waiting to listen.'

The man sat down beside her, not close enough to cause offence. 'Whatever you have done, or indeed what someone else has done, can always be rectified.'

Cathy sniffed. 'If only it was that simple. I've ruined someone's life.'

'I doubt that. We humans do a pretty good job of ruining life for ourselves.'

They sat in silence for a minute or two before he put his hands on his knees and pushed himself up straight.

'I was just about to have a coffee before I leave for the day.' The man smiled warmly. 'There's a spare one going, if you'd like it?'

Cathy burst into tears. His kindness was more than she deserved. She wiped at her eyes quickly.

'Thank you but I just need to go home. I need to hate myself for a while longer yet though.'

'Don't make it too long, then, hmm?'

He tipped his cap, a gentlemanly gesture that Cathy admired in him immediately. Manners didn't cost anything and they were hardly ever reciprocated nowadays. God bless the older generation. As she watched him walk away, her thoughts suddenly turned to Rose and she burst into tears again. How she wished Rose was here to help her through this mess.

Finally she headed home. Just before five thirty, she parked in the driveway and switched off the engine. How the hell she was going to get through the rest of the evening she didn't know.

'Cathy! Where have you been?' Liz cried as she came through the front door. Jess and Becky followed quickly behind her. 'The girls rang me when you weren't answering your phone so I came around. We've all been trying. Have you switched it off?'

'You look like shit,' said Jess. Liz nudged her sharply.

To their amazement, Cathy walked past them into the living room. All three trouped behind her and watched as she poured a large drink of whatever was first to hand and knocked it back in one go.

'We've been really worried about you,' said Becky.

'I've only been gone for a few hours.' Cathy looked at them, each in turn. 'Surely you can survive without me for that long? I'm not responsible for everyone. I can't be responsible for – responsible for –'

She began to fill the glass again but her hands started to shake uncontrollably. Liz took the bottle from her.

'Cathy, what's going on?' she asked gently.

Cathy looked up. 'I... I...' It was no use: if she started to speak she would cry. She picked up her bag and left the room.

'Cathy!' Liz called after her.

Upstairs, Cathy closed the door quickly so they couldn't see the tears streaming down her face. It was all she could do to stop herself turning back to them. She couldn't tell them. She felt so ashamed. But she needed to talk to someone.

In the safety of her bedroom, she switched her mobile phone on and dialled a number. A welcome voice rang out.

'Hello, Josie Mellor speaking.'

Josie was there almost immediately.

Cathy sunk into her embrace. She knew she'd never find the right words to explain what had happened. And how could she tell anyone? She was going to show herself for what she was: a fraud, a fake, a useless human being.

But she *had* to tell someone. The secret was eating her up, churning her insides. She took a deep breath before she began.

'I went to see a solicitor today. He's been trying to track someone down for me and...' Cathy looked at Josie as she said the words she'd never spoken to anyone before. 'I lied when I said I couldn't have children. I had a son, fathered by another man.'

'What?'

'I – I was so lonely when Rich was in prison. And so young and bloody naïve. Three years was such a long stretch. When one of his friends started to call around more

274

than was necessary, I began to look forward to his visits. One day he kissed me and... I kissed him back. One thing led to another...' Cathy clung to Josie as she continued to speak. 'Two months later, I found out I was pregnant.'

'So you had the baby?' Josie sounded puzzled. 'I had no idea.'

'Neither did he. I didn't tell him.'

'But how did you –?'

'How could I tell him? It was my fault that I got into such a mess. If Rich had found out, I would have lost him.'

'No, surely not.'

'Of course I would! Rich was a right Jack-the-lad back then. It was only prison that changed him for the better as he swore he'd never go back once he got out. Imagine how he would have felt if I'd turned up on his release. "Oh hi, darling. This is Simon. He was born while you were inside. No, Rich I wasn't unfaithful, not once."'

'Your son was called Simon?' Josie said without thinking.

'Yes.' Cathy began to cry again. 'And I let him down. I let him down so badly.'

'So you had him adopted?'

Cathy nodded. 'I always thought that one day I might meet up with him. But I've just found out that he... he doesn't want anything to do with me, ever. Now I won't be able to t – t – tell him how much I – I loved him. How I made the biggest mistake of my life: how I should never have given him up.'

Josie grabbed a handful of tissues from the cube by the side of the bed and passed them to Cathy.

'How come Rich never found out?' she said, wiping at

her eyes too. 'You can hardly explain a bump like that away.'

'I kept it hidden for a long time with baggy clothes. Then when it came to the time that I couldn't hide it any longer, I stopped seeing him. I told him that I was ill, kept in touch by phone and letter. I still don't know to this day how I got away with it. I guess he must have trusted me. I rang a friend I'd made when I was in care. She was the only person that knew about Simon; the only person I knew I could trust to help me out and keep quiet. I knew she wouldn't judge me either. Tina let me stay for two months, until I'd had him. Then I came back home and started to see Rich again.'

'I can't believe he didn't find out, given how quickly rumours fly around this estate.'

'He wasn't suspicious about it, I suppose, because no one he knew saw me around so he *could* think I was holed up somewhere with a dreadful bug. And Terry Lewis – that's the father's name – kept his mouth shut.'

'He would, the low life.' Josie knew of Terry and his family. 'He'd be scared of what Rich would have done to him.'

Cathy sniffed before blowing her nose loudly. 'I couldn't risk losing Rich if he found out the truth.'

'Oh, *Cathy*. Is that why you didn't have any more children?'

'No! I knew I could get pregnant so I assumed there must have been something wrong with him. It might have been me: some sort of complication at the birth, though I can't recall anything. That's why I didn't push the fact that he didn't want to go for tests. If he'd ever found out –'

'And you've kept this to yourself for all those years?'

Cathy nodded. 'I was a coward, afraid to face up to my responsibilities.'

'No, that's not how it was,' Josie disagreed. 'You were young and frightened. You did what you thought was best at the time.'

'No. I did what was best for me.'

'And what about now? You must feel better now that you've told someone about it?'

Cathy paused. How did she feel about it? Did she even feel at all?

'I feel like I've been robbed of the chance to say I'm sorry,' she said. 'In the back of my mind, I've lived for the day that I can see his face again. I prayed that his new family would love him but he became too much of a handful and they gave him away. How must he feel now? That must seem like a double whammy – the boy that nobody wanted.

'Every year on his birthday, I light a candle for the baby that I lost. Somehow I always believed I'd meet him when the time was right. It was selfish of me really. All I want to do is to say sorry to him, so that my conscience is clear. But it never will be. He hates me, Josie. He'll never forgive me.'

She started to cry again. This time it took her a long time to stop.

Cathy didn't sleep much that night. She'd switched off her mobile phone when a few texts arrived and she hadn't left her room since. Becky had brought coffee and toast up twice but she'd left them all untouched. Even now as a new day was breaking, she was still going over and over the events that led to the ache in her heart. She was so grateful that she had Josie to talk things through with. As usual, she'd been right there for her. Cathy knew she was lucky. Even with Rose gone, Josie was someone she could call a friend, no matter what her job involved. She was the salt of the earth. She would tell her whether she was right or wrong, even if it wasn't what Cathy wanted to hear.

It had felt so good to share her secret after all those years. Time after time, Josie had said she shouldn't blame herself for what had happened to Simon. Cathy told her how she'd often prayed that he would turn up, out of the blue, having tracked her down. There was no doubt that Rich would have been shocked at first but she'd always hoped that he would have accepted the situation, once he'd had time to digest the facts.

She began to cry again. Oh, why hadn't she told Rich the truth? She'd betrayed both of them, her son and her husband. But Rich had been betrayed the most. She'd been deceitful to him every day, until the day he'd been so cruelly taken from her.

She punched the pillow. Then again, and again.

Why, why, WHY?

Why had she lied to the man that had meant everything to her?

TWENTY-SEVEN

Jess popped her head around the kitchen door to find Becky sitting at the table busy clicking buttons on her phone. 'Do you fancy coming out tonight?'

'I can't.' Becky didn't lift her head up. 'I'm seeing Austin.'

'But I haven't seen you for ages!' Jess protested, sitting down next to her. 'You're always going out with him.'

'I wasn't supposed to be going out with him tonight. He said he was busy but he's just texted me, so I am now.'

Jess sighed dramatically. 'Can't you cry off and come out with me?' she begged.

Becky relented. Hadn't she said that she would spend more time with Jess? But just the thought of seeing Austin again made her insides go all peculiar.

'I hate being on my own,' Jess continued, watching Becky's finger hover over the send button. She grabbed her free hand. 'Please! Come out with me instead.'

'Okay, okay!' Becky pressed the delete button and began to write another text.

'Yay!' Jess punched the air. 'I've missed having you around.'

'I'll have to tell him that I'm sick or something. I don't want to get him mad.'

'You can't say that.' Jess shook her head quickly. 'If you do, we won't be able to go to the Butcher's Arms in case he's there. And you don't want to make him mad. He might give you a backhander.'

'He'd never do that to me. He's not a scrote like Danny Bradley. He knows how to treat a lady properly.'

Jess sighed. 'I hope we can get into the Butcher's. I heard it was raided last week because of us under-agers. We might have to stick to lemonade or have a drink before we go.'

'Whatever.' Becky started to write another text message.

'What are you going to tell him?'

'The truth – well, almost. I'll say I'd already arranged to go out with you.'

'That won't work. He'll be pissed off that you've dropped him for me then.'

'Austin doesn't own me.'

'We'll see,' said Jess knowingly. 'Guys on the Mitchell Estate always think they own their *ladies*.'

'He isn't from the Mitchell Estate, remember?'

'Where does he come from? Has he told you yet?'

Becky pressed the send button and snapped her phone shut. 'No. All I get out of him if I ask is somewhere further up north.'

'Don't you find it strange that he doesn't tell you?'

'Not really. We don't get much chance for talking nowadays.' Becky grinned, remembering what they'd recently been getting up to.

'Okay, okay. No need to get me all jealous and nasty. I haven't had a decent shag in weeks.'

Both of them shot to their feet as they heard the front door open. Jess reached for a tea towel as Becky turned on the hot water tap and quickly squirted washing liquid on top of the pile of dishes left to soak.

Cathy came through with two bags of shopping. 'That's what I like to see, girls.' She put them down on the table and smiled knowingly. 'And once those dishes are done, perhaps you wouldn't mind making me a cuppa before you finish off. I'm parched.' She pulled out a pack of vanilla slices. 'I have cakes too.'

'Have you been to the community house?' asked Becky.

'Yes. I've been with the rabble.'

'I bet they've missed you since you've been ill?'

After her devastating news, Cathy hadn't told anyone but Josie about tracking down and finding out that Simon didn't want to meet her. They'd spoken over the phone since but it had been nearly a week before she'd felt like getting back to her routine again. So she'd faked a sickness virus and stayed at home. She hadn't even told Matt yet; she wasn't sure if she ever would.

Before she'd left the community house, she'd collected a few leaflets for Jess. She handed them to her once they'd finished the dishes.

'What's this?'

'New college courses, starting this September. Thought you might like to know what days –'

'Have you seen the time?' Jess shoved the leaflet in her pocket. 'Must dash. Off to see a man about a dog.'

And with that she was gone. Becky followed after her.

Cathy smiled. She wasn't sure if she was more annoyed that Jess wouldn't take her advice or grateful for a bit of peace and quiet now they'd gone.

*

Later that evening, Cathy was having a girl's night in over at Liz's. Liz had made a huge bowl of chilli con carne for them to eat. Then Cathy had opened the bottle of wine she'd brought with her while Liz got Chloe into bed.

'I'm glad to see that you're feeling a little more settled,' Cathy said as she reached for the bottle and poured a drink for Liz. 'I do hope Kevin has finally given up now.'

'I hope so, although I'll always have my doubts.'

'Maybe he's with that woman you saw him with?'

Liz shrugged. 'Who cares as long as he's not anywhere near us? He told me about her, you know?'

'Really?'

'She's called Charlotte Heyburn and apparently she's a far better shag than me.'

Cathy stopped, her glass halfway to her lips. 'He said that? Was he trying to make you jealous? Make you see what you've been missing?'

'I don't know but I ignored him anyway. I haven't seen him since.' Liz lowered her eyes, not wanting Cathy to dig any deeper. It had been a traumatic experience when Kevin had collared her at the shops again. He'd waited for her to come out of Shop&Save, taken her arm and marched her over to his car before she'd had time to protest. She wouldn't get into the car with him and so they'd had a heated argument right there in the car park. That was when he told her about Charlotte Heyburn and a couple of others that he didn't even know the names of.

Liz chinked her glass with Cathy's. 'Here's to a better future for us both. So come on, spill. Have you done the dirty deed with Matt yet?'

'Don't be so nosy.' Cathy tried to look shocked but failed

dismally by bursting into laughter. 'I mean it! Don't be – '

Liz grabbed a cushion from the settee and threw it at her. 'I need details.'

'It's complicated.' Cathy sighed.

'Why?'

'Well, I know that Matt so wants to.'

'Hmm, that's a little obvious. He can't keep his eyes off you whenever you're around.'

'Really?'

'Don't try and change the subject.'

'Me? I would never be so devious.'

Liz picked up another cushion. Before she threw it, Cathy continued.

'Okay, okay. I'm teasing. Where were we? Oh, yes, I was telling you that he so wants to and...'

'And?'

'... I so want to.'

'And?' Liz was practically hyper-ventilating by now.

Cathy shrugged her shoulders in reply but it wasn't good enough.

'Bloody hell. It's like trying to get the truth out of Chloe. What are you so embarrassed about?'

'I'm afraid that I'll have healed up, I'll be totally useless at it, that he won't want to do it again – not to mention, all those embarrassing slurps and slips – that I have to touch another man's...' She ran a hand through her hair. 'I feel like I've forgotten what to do.'

Liz sat there, mouth agog. Then she smiled. 'Oh, Cath. They're only nerves. I'm sure they'll go once you get down to it.'

'You're so sure about that?'

Liz paused for a moment. 'Well, I'm no expert but they do liken it to riding a bike. Once learned, never forgotten.'

'But my bike is an old battered Chopper type from the seventies and I want to be a new type of mountain bike from the noughties – one with twenty-four gears that can cope with any terrain.'

'You have nothing to worry about on that score.' Liz dismissed her words with a flick of her wrist. 'Get it done and then let me have this conversation with you. I'm sure you'll be fine.'

'You reckon?'

'Yes, I reckon! Stop thinking about it or you'll never do it. There will never be a right time, a right frame of mind or a right state of happiness. Life isn't like that. You have to grab these opportunities…' She stopped then and grinned. 'I was going to say, grab them by the balls.'

Cathy grinned too. She raised her glass in the air. 'Right then, I'll do it.'

'What? Grab him by the balls?' Liz raised her glass too. 'Thank God for that. Now when shall I ring you for all the gory details? I still want to know everything!'

While Cathy was discussing the intricacies of her new relationship with Liz, Becky and Jess were returning from their night out.

'I've had a great time.' Jess slung an arm around Becky's shoulders as they approached the house.

'I really enjoyed it too,' said Becky. 'I couldn't believe that Phipps ended up getting barred for dropping his trousers again.'

'I think he should be arrested after seeing the size of his

prick. Did you clock it? It was *huge*. I don't think I'd like it anywhere near me.'

'He wouldn't put it anywhere near you!'

'Only because it's probably already been in you, you cheeky cow!' Jess went to push her but Becky moved out of the way.

'Ha, missed me!' she yelled before tripping and falling back into the flower border. She landed on the lawn with a thump. 'OW!'

Jess laughed. She pulled Becky up and they walked into the house.

'Cathy not home yet then? The dirty stop out. At least she won't know that we've been drinking.' She grinned. 'She must still be out with Matt the Magnificent.'

'She went over to see Liz, remember?' Becky followed her through to the kitchen. 'I'm glad she's seeing Matt though.'

'I know. She seems happier already. Although we still don't know why she was so upset last week, do we?'

'She seems to have got over it now.' Then Becky giggled. 'Imagine how pissed off she must feel that she can't just bring him back to her place because of us cramping her style.'

'I hadn't thought of that. Maybe we should make ourselves scarce some nights.'

They went upstairs a few minutes later. Becky had only just got into her room when she heard a tap at the window. She turned her head quickly. There was another tap. It sounded like a pebble hitting the glass. She looked down to see Austin in the garden. She waved before running downstairs to join him on the back lawn.

'Hiya, you!' She flung herself unsteadily into his arms. 'Have you missed me?'

Austin pushed her away. 'Where the fuck have you been?'

'I told you I was going out with Jess.'

'She's a right slapper: got a reputation for giving out. I don't want you mixing with her, do you hear me?'

Becky wanted to say so many things in reply but she was too drunk to get her head around it all.

'But –' she began.

Austin grabbed her wrists and pulled her nearer. 'When I tell you to do something, you do it. You don't argue. Got that?'

'But –' She stopped. Austin was staring at her in a scary way. 'What did I do wrong?'

'You went out with her when you should have been going out with me.'

'You were busy. You told me last night that –'

'I told you today that I had changed my plans.'

'But I'd already arranged to go out with Jess. Ow! You're hurting me! Let go!'

Austin squeezed her wrists tighter. He pulled Becky to within an inch of his face.

'You do not defy me.' He spoke through gritted teeth. 'Ever. Do you hear me? Or else I'll –'

'Stop it,' she wailed. 'You're really hurting me!'

Suddenly Austin let go and Becky was pulled into his embrace.

'I'm sorry, my little one.' He ran his hand over her hair, as if to soothe away her pain. 'I'm overreacting again. I just missed you tonight.'

'I'm s – sorry too,' she replied, glad to feel his arms around her once more. 'I won't do it again.'

'I know you won't.'

Luckily for Becky, she couldn't see his menacing expression.

Worse for wear the next morning, Jess and Becky came down for breakfast. Jess walked into the kitchen looking like an extra from a zombie film. Her hair was uncombed, remains of smudged make-up still clear around her eyes. Becky didn't look too much better, blonde hair like rat tails, luggy and unkempt. Cathy couldn't help but notice their demeanour.

'What were you two up to last night?' she asked.

'Oh, nothing much,' Jess fibbed, sitting down with a thud. 'We just hung around the square.'

'Really? I wasn't born yesterday. You both look like you've been dragged through a hedge backwards.'

'I'm thirsty,' said Becky.

As she reached up for a glass, Cathy pointed at her. 'What have you done?'

Becky stared down at her wrist where purple-black bruising had begun to appear. She frowned. 'I'm not sure.'

'Were you with Austin last night? Did he do that to you?'

'I can't remember.' Becky pulled her hand down by her side. She knew full well that Austin must have done it.

'She was out with me last night,' said Jess. 'Let me have a look, Becks.'

'It's nothing!'

But Jess looked anyway. She balked. 'I didn't do that, did I? I know I pushed you and you landed on the lawn –'

Cathy held up Becky's arm for further inspection. 'No, Jess. You wouldn't have done that. But someone did.' She looked Becky straight in the eye. 'Didn't they?'

'I – I said I can't remember.' Becky wouldn't meet her gaze.

'Fine.' Cathy sighed in exasperation. Whatever had gone on last night, Becky wasn't about to confide in her. She would just have to get it out of her in her own time.

But get it out of her she would.

TWENTY-EIGHT

The following evening when Matt pulled up outside her house, Cathy wasn't looking forward to the night ending. They had been out for a drink and the time had flown by. She had really enjoyed his company. So much so that she hadn't said a word of the prepared speech that she'd been going over in her head before meeting him.

Matt switched off the engine and turned towards her. 'I've really enjoyed myself tonight.'

'Me too,' said Cathy. All of a sudden shyness enveloped her.

Gently, Matt removed a stray hair from her face and ran a finger down her cheek and over her top lip. Cathy took a sharp intake of breath at his touch. His eyes bore into hers, causing her to shiver involuntarily.

'Matt, I need to tell you something. I –' She struggled to get her thoughts straight as his eyes pooled with lust. 'Things are complicated.'

'Aren't they always?' Matt moved an inch closer, his hand now cupping her chin. He tilted it upwards.

'It isn't that I'm not interested in you. It's just – I have some excess baggage to deal with. I need to move on from my past and afterwards I'm hoping that you might like to become part of my future?'

'You need me to wait for a while? Is that it?'

Cathy nodded, scouring his face for clues of his reaction. 'Would you be willing to take things slowly?'

He let her stew for a few seconds before replying. 'And then you'll be all mine for the taking?'

Cathy couldn't help but smile. 'If you'd like me to be yours.'

'Well, that depends.'

For a split second, Cathy felt herself physically droop until he continued.

'I'll need something to hang onto until I have your undivided attention.'

This time when he moved in to kiss her, she let him. When they finally broke free, he kept his face close to hers.

'So this time that you need?' He kissed the tip of her nose.

Cathy was still lost in the kiss. 'Hmm?'

'A day? Two days? A week? Two weeks?'

'I'm not sure.'

'You take as long as you need. I'll still be –'

'No, you don't understand.' She pulled him nearer again until their lips were a hair width apart. 'I'm not sure if I can wait that long.'

Two nights later, Jess was out with the recently dropped and acquired again Mickey Grainger and Cathy had another date with Matt. Becky sneaked back to the house with Austin. It seemed that they had the perfect love nest, if only time enough for a quickie.

'Why don't you want to meet Cathy?' Becky asked him as she opened the front door. 'I bet she'd like you.'

'I'm just not into meeting folks,' Austin replied. He picked up a photo frame and stared down at a couple. 'Is this her?'

'Yes. That was her old man. He died coming home from the pub. He was pissed up and he fell down some stairs.'

Austin put the photo back and pulled her into his arms. 'So what're we going to do while we have the house to ourselves?'

Becky grinned. 'Come on, I'll show you my room.'

They raced up the stairs like a couple of five-year-olds, all hands and giggles. Becky pushed open her door and flung herself flat out on her bed. She turned on to her back quickly.

'It's a bit cramped in here.' Austin nudged the bed with his knee. 'Isn't there a double bed we can use?'

'But I want to do it here.' Becky pouted. 'It's better than the back seat of a car you've nicked.'

'I know but it's mad to waste the opportunity.'

'We could use Liz and Chloe's old room. There's a double in there but we'd better be careful not to make a mess.'

'Come on then.' Austin pulled her to her feet and they walked across the landing.

'Who sleeps in there?' He pointed to a closed door.

'That's Jess's room.'

'And that one?'

'That's Cathy's.' Becky pointed to another door. 'This is Liz's old room.'

Austin stopped at Cathy's door. 'Let's be daring and do it in there.'

'We can't!' Becky shook her head. 'She'll go mad.'

He kissed her, feeling her resistance flowing away. 'I won't tell her, if you don't.'

'But, it's not right. We –'

Austin silenced her with his mouth. He pushed down the handle and stepped backwards, his free hand staying on her back, pulling her into him. Incapable of resisting, Becky giggled as he threw her down on Cathy's bed and then fell on top of her.

'I am so horny,' Austin said, unzipping his trousers. 'I might just come here and now if I don't get inside you.'

Becky pushed him away. 'No, there's plenty of time for that.' She sat forward and took him in her mouth.

'Perfect,' he replied. Austin groaned as Becky took him deeper. He looked around the room. It was just how he imagined it would be: tidy, clean and modern. And orderly, just like her life: Cathy Mason didn't stand any nonsense from Becky. And it seemed that Becky really respected her. Austin wondered what it would have been like to have someone care for him.

Suddenly he thrust forwards. 'Fucking bitch!' he shouted as he reached orgasm.

Becky wiped her mouth and glared at him. 'Fucking bitch?' she said, a little miffed.

Austin grinned. 'Did I say that? I meant oh, fuck. You certainly know how to give great head, Becks.'

Satisfied with his answer, Becky lay back on the bed. 'Now, my turn,' she smiled coyly, her index finger in her mouth.

Austin grinned and lay down beside her. 'I couldn't think of anything more appropriate.'

*

'I had such a good time tonight,' Matt whispered to Cathy as they stood on her doorstep. He stroked her hair away from her face and then kissed the tip of her nose. 'Again.'

Cathy smiled at him. 'Coffee?' she asked as she unlocked her front door.

'If it means another half an hour in your company, then yes. I just need to use the little boy's room.'

Cathy dived away from his searching hands and into the kitchen. The house seemed quiet as she filled the kettle with water. She stopped to listen afterwards but there was nothing. Then again, it was only just after ten o'clock. She knew both Jess and Becky had gone out before her.

Matt came back. His arms circled her waist and he ran his tongue over her neck. She shivered at his touch. It didn't go unnoticed.

He turned her to face him. 'Even though I enjoy coffee, I was wondering if you'd fancy making me breakfast soon.'

Cathy's heart felt like it had located into her throat. She could almost hear the roar of it inside her head.

'I'd really love to,' she said. 'But...'

Matt stuck out his bottom lip. 'But,' he pressed himself up against her so she could feel his erection, 'look what you do to me.'

'Typical man,' Cathy muttered.

'I –'

She looked up at him with a grin. 'Only kidding.' She thought back to Josie and Liz's advice. Then she kissed him. 'It's because of the girls.'

'Oh!' Matt's smile was back.

Cathy pressed her finger to his lips. 'One minute.'

Upstairs, just as she'd suspected, both Jess and Becky's

rooms were empty. For a moment outside her own bedroom door, she hesitated. Then she pushed it open. The room as ever was tidy but she left it like that. It was too soon.

Matt was sitting on the settee in the living room when she went downstairs. 'Everything okay?' he asked.

'It couldn't be better.' Cathy closed the curtains and then, very bravely she thought afterwards, went to sit on his lap. He smiled as his hands slipped around her waist again.

'The girls are out at the moment but we need to be prepared in case either of them arrives home sooner than usual.' In one swift move, she pulled her T-shirt over her head and threw it to the floor. 'I can't offer you my bed because –'

'I wouldn't ask,' Matt replied, his voice soft.

'– it's too soon.'

His hand slid up behind her neck and he pulled her towards him. 'This will do fine,' he whispered before his lips touched hers again.

Two hours later, Jess and Becky were home and in bed. They'd spent a fair bit of time ribbing Matt before they'd left him and Cathy in peace to fool around again. Now they were trying to say goodbye on the doorstep.

'I need to go,' Matt said as they kissed again. 'It's late and if I stay here much longer, I'll have to stop over. And what would the neighbours say then, Cathy Mason?'

'I don't give a stuff what the neighbours would say, Matthew Simpson.' She kissed him again.

'But you should be setting a good example for those girls of yours.'

'I do set a good example for them.' She ran her tongue

suggestively over his top lip and he groaned. They kissed again.

Matt broke free. 'I'm going now.'

Cathy stepped forwards. 'I'll walk you to your car.'

'It's only down the street.' He kissed her again. 'Go in and I'll call you tomorrow.'

As soon as she closed the door, Cathy ran to get her phone. Feeling like she was fifteen again, she texted Matt a quick message and grinned as she thought of him reading it outside.

Matt laughed out loud when he read the message. Cathy had certainly blown more than his mind! He texted back a message and then searched out his car keys. A noise made him turn quickly but before he could focus on anything, he was hit from behind, a sharp knock to the back of the head. He fell to his knees. An elbow came down on his back, followed by a fist upwards into his face. He bent forward to protect himself as he was kicked in the stomach. Instinctively he curled up into a ball, trying to guard himself from the punches raining down on him.

Finally it stopped. In the silence of the night, Matt struggled to get his breath.

'Keep away from her,' his attacker spoke. 'And if I hear you mention this to anyone, I'll get you again and next time I'll finish you off.'

Matt tried to speak but there was too much blood filling his mouth.

'Get in your car and drive away. And don't come back here or I'll be the death of her. Do you understand?'

Matt retched as he was kicked in the stomach again.

'DO YOU UNDERSTAND?'

'Yes!' Matt pushed himself to his feet. Holding onto his chest, he staggered to his car, fumbled with the lock and clambered in. As he drove off, he could see the silhouette of his attacker, a black shadow that would look the place in any crime drama. The shadow was still there when he turned out of Christopher Avenue.

TWENTY-NINE

Cathy woke up the next day feeling like the proverbial cat that had lapped up the cream. She stretched out lazily: the grin on her face just wouldn't subside. Matthew Simpson had brought back so many feelings that had long ago disappeared after Rich had died. She felt lustful, tingly and contented even. Like Sleeping Beauty, she'd been awakened from a very long sleep. Yet still she felt guilty.

She reached over to the framed photograph beside her bed and brought it closer. She ran a finger over the sharp jut of Rich's chin, looked into eyes that sparkled out from the image. It had always been her favourite photo. Rich seemed so happy, so... so alive, just like she was now.

'Please don't hate me,' she whispered. 'It's been such a long time without you. And I – I think you'd like Matt.'

She put the photo back before jumping out of bed. Then she sent a text message to Matt. After she'd taken a shower, she checked to see if he had replied but there was nothing yet. Impatient for an answer, she sent another and then went downstairs. She'd most probably see him soon anyway. She was due at the community house in an hour.

Before that morning's session, Cathy was searching out pens in the stationery cupboard.

'Need any help today?' she heard a voice behind her.

She turned to see Liz and handed her a box and two note pads. 'An extra pair of hands will do. Are you coming to join my session?'

'I am indeed.'

'Great.' Thinking back to their previous conversation, she couldn't help grinning but, alarmingly, she felt her skin start to redden.

'You're blushing!' said Liz. 'And by the look on your face... have you been up to something with our lovely maintenance officer?'

'Nothing that hasn't been done before. And you were right. It was like riding a bike.'

'You were definitely riding then?'

Cathy blushed even more. She hid a yawn as she checked her phone but there were still no new messages.

'You're not waiting for him to text you?' Liz giggled.

'Yes. Honestly, I feel like a teenager again.'

'I wish I'd made more use of mobile phones in my teens. It would have been so much fun to send and receive love messages.' Liz sighed. 'But, knowing my luck, I'd probably have been dumped by text.'

'It is good, I suppose, but it still leaves you hanging around waiting for a reply. I sent a message this morning and now I'm checking my phone every two seconds to see if he's got back to me. It's mad!'

'Perhaps he's in a meeting. Or maybe he doesn't do texting.'

Just then, Cathy's phone beeped. Both women gasped in anticipation. But Cathy tutted as she read who the message was from.

'That bloody Jess!' She shook her head in annoyance. 'I told her she had to help me out this morning. She's now saying she can't make it because she has to go into town. But she's sending Becky in her place. Un-bloody-believable. I can't even dock her any wages for not showing, either – as well she knows. I'll have to think of something else. She can't keep getting Becky to help out. It's only making coffee and doing a few dishes. It's not hard graft.'

'Well, I'd far rather work with Becky than Jess,' said Liz. 'She's a pleasure to be around, really gets stuck into whatever you give her. And talking of which, I've got a few hours working on the counter at Pete's Newsagents on the square. It's not much but I can fit it in around Chloe's school hours.'

'That's great news, Liz.' Cathy snapped her phone shut. 'I just wish I could engage the same enthusiasm out of Jess.'

Becky had sent a text message too. She'd replied to Austin's 'where are you' by telling him she was in Davy Road. Moments later, she heard a car pull up alongside her. Austin had commandeered Danny's heap when he'd been put on remand.

'Hey, gorgeous. Fancy a lift somewhere?'

With a smile, she slid into the passenger seat and threw her arms around his neck. He kissed her before starting the engine.

'Where are you off to so early?' he asked.

'I'm covering for Jess at the community house.'

'You shouldn't have to do her dirty work. Let someone else help out.'

'There isn't anyone else. And I don't really mind.'

Becky caught her breath as she felt Austin's hand creep up inside her skirt.

'But I'm lonely,' he whined. 'I was hoping that you might keep me company. That's why I came to find you.'

'Can I meet you afterwards?'

As Austin withdrew his hand, she felt a curtain come down between them.

'I suppose I'll have to occupy myself then,' he sulked.

'It's only for three hours.' Becky checked her watch. 'I should be there until one but I'll try and get off before, if you like.'

Austin didn't reply. They were only a street away from the community house now. Becky was stuck. If she didn't turn up, she'd get the wrath of both Cathy and Jess. But if she didn't spend time with Austin, he'd go into a sulk and maybe wouldn't want to meet her later.

She reached across to touch his cheek but he pulled his head away.

'I'll see if I can do two hours instead of three,' she suggested.

Still he didn't reply. He turned the corner and the car screeched to a halt. Becky shot forward in her seat.

'Okay, okay. You win.' She raised her palms then let them fall heavily in her lap. 'I'll come with you.'

Cathy's phone beeped and she reached for it again. Sighing heavily, it took all of her strength not to sling the phone across the room. Instead she began to stab at the keys as she sent back a reply.

'I take it that isn't Matt either?' Liz asked, trying hard to hide a smirk.

'No. Becky isn't bloody coming now.' Cathy pressed the send button before looking up. 'Honestly, kids these days.'

'Shall we go to your place?' Becky suggested casually to Austin. She was aware of the way his mood could change so quickly with a few choice words but she was curious too. Every time she'd suggested it so far, he'd refused.

'It's given out a good day.' Austin glanced up at the sky through the window. 'I've got a blanket in the back. I'm sure we can find a quiet spot somewhere.'

Becky had had enough of all the secrecy. 'Are you ashamed of me?' she blurted out.

'No.'

'Then why won't you tell me anything about yourself?'

'Nothing to tell. Been nowhere, done nowt.'

'But you clam up when I mention family. Or friends. Or... where do you live?'

'I told you, not far.'

'But why the big secret?' Becky chided, annoyed that he was dodging the questions again. 'You never –'

'For fuck's sake. Stop with the questions!'

Austin slammed on the brakes and took a sharp left. He screeched up the narrow street, crashing over speed humps, barely missing parked cars on either side. Becky held onto the door handle as he flew around another bend.

'Austin! I –'

The look he gave her silenced her immediately. The dark cloud had descended again. She held on for dear life as she waited for it to pass.

A few minutes later, he turned into the car park of the White Lion and drove round to the back.

'What have you come here for?' she asked. 'I thought we were going to lie out in the sun.'

Austin smiled then, as if none of the past few minutes had happened. He pulled the keys out of the ignition and turned towards her. 'Come on,' he said.

Becky scrambled out of the car, running to keep up with him. He pulled back the metal sheeting at one of the boarded up windows. She could see an opening small enough to crawl through. She looked at him incredulously.

'You live *here*?'

'Nowt wrong in it.' He mistook her wide-eyed look for one of disapproval.

'No, I think it's cool,' she replied. 'It's probably where I would have ended up if I hadn't been caught by that copper and sent to Cathy's.' She lifted her foot. 'Give us a leg up.'

Austin clasped his hands together and she stepped onto his palms. One quick push up and she was in. She jumped down onto the seating and then onto the floor. Austin was through after her before her eyes had adjusted to the gloom.

He grabbed her around the waist. 'Are you scared of the dark?' he whispered into her ear.

'Should I be?'

Becky pressed her body against his. He kissed her, pushing her backwards as he did so. She felt her feet slide over the odd beer mat. Before she knew it, her back was against the bar. She hooked one toe behind the trip rail. Austin had his hands inside her top, and then it was over her head and across the floor. She blanked out what it might have landed on – or in.

Suddenly she heard a noise. 'What was that?'

'Just the rats.'

'Rats!' She pushed him away and began to stamp her feet.

Austin grinned. 'Relax, I'm winding you up. There's no one here but us.'

He moved to her neck and down her chest as she gazed around the room suspiciously. Her eyes were more accustomed to the dimness now: tiny shafts of light coming through some of the smaller windows here and there. The floor was covered in dirty red carpeting. Crushed velvet curtains hung redundant in front of the windows, the stools around the many tables sat as if waiting for opening time and the regulars to troop in. Apart from a layer of dust, Becky reckoned the place would clean up pretty quickly. She wished it would open so that they had more choice on the estate.

She heard another noise.

'What was that?'

'I told you. It's just an old building.' Austin pulled down the zip to his jeans. Becky placed her hand over his as he undid his button.

'How do you know there's no one else here?'

'There wasn't when I left this morning.'

'But you got in through the window. Couldn't someone else do the same?'

'I thought you said the place was cool.'

'From the *outside*, yes. It gives me the creeps inside.'

Austin took her hand. 'If it makes you feel better, we'll check the rooms.' He headed towards a door on the right. 'Kitchen first: bedroom last.'

*

After a successful session with the teenagers in The Den, Cathy was clearing the room when her phone rang. Disappointed to see it wasn't Matt, she grinned when she saw who it was, knowing that she'd be calling to get all the juicy details of her date.

'Hi, Jose, what's up?'

'You don't know then?'

'Know what?'

'You haven't heard from Matt this morning?'

Cathy checked her watch: it was just gone midday. 'I texted him earlier but I haven't had a reply.'

'Oh.' Now Josie sounded really confused. 'Maybe I'd better tell you then.'

'Tell me what? Is Matt okay?'

'No, he was beaten up pretty bad last night.'

'But I was with him last night!' Cathy's blood ran cold. 'He left around quarter to one, I think. Oh, God. How bad is he?'

'Pretty messed up by the sound of it but he says it's only superficial. He called in sick this morning, said he'd most probably be off for the rest of this week.'

Cathy leaned on the wall. 'No wonder he didn't reply to my text.' Then another thought struck her. 'He's not in hospital, is he?'

'No, he's at home.'

'I'll ring him now and see if he answers. If he doesn't, I'll call around. No, I already have his address. Thanks.'

As soon as she cancelled Josie's call, Cathy rang Matt's mobile. It went unanswered before switching to voicemail.

'Matt? It's me, Cathy. Josie's just told me what

happened. I hope you're okay. Give me a quick ring when you get this message, would you?'

Now that she'd been there for two hours, the smell and the dreariness of the disused pub had started to become less eerie to Becky. They were dozing, lying together on the single mattress that Austin called his bed. Naked apart from her shoes, Becky ran the tip of her heel gently up and down his thigh.

'It's so cool in here and I love spending time with you.' She ran a finger up and down his chest. Getting no response, she glanced up. Austin was staring at the ceiling in a world of his own. She sat up and folded her arms.

'What's up now?' she asked. 'You've gone all moody on me again.'

'I'm just thinking.'

'About what?'

'Just things.' He took a drag of his cigarette.

Becky tried again. She swirled a finger further and further down his stomach. But he pushed her hand away. She fell sideways off the mattress onto the dusty floor.

'What did you do that for?' Her palm had landed on something dirty but she didn't know what. She grimaced, rubbing at it carefully.

Austin stood up and pulled on his trousers. 'It's all sex with you. I don't want to do it all the fucking time.'

'But I thought you liked having sex with me.' She pouted seductively and, ignoring the stained floor now, walked towards him on all fours. 'You do, don't you? You seem like –'

'Stop acting like a slut and get dressed.'

Sensing the cloud looming over them again, Becky covered her chest with one hand and grabbed her top with the other. What was wrong with him? One minute he would be doing really intimate things with her: the next he'd be looking at her as if she was a pile of shit. It was as if he were two different people.

She dressed quickly and stood up to tuck her T-shirt into her jeans. Daring a quick peep at him, she was glad to see he smiled at her. The nice Austin was back.

'Let's get something to eat.' He held out a hand.

Becky followed behind him in total confusion but happy that his hand was holding on to her at least.

Jess was coming out of the alleyway leading from Stanley Avenue when she noticed Austin's car coming from the back of the White Lion. At first her hand rose to wave but when she saw who was with him, she dived through an open gate into someone's front garden until he'd driven past. Then she emerged with a scowl on her face.

That was Becky she'd seen sitting in the passenger seat. She checked her watch. Half past twelve. The cow: she should have been covering for her until one. Which meant that Cathy would be on the war path when she got home.

Wait until she caught up with her.

Cathy drove to Matt's address, pulling up outside a block of six private flats. She glanced up at the one she thought might be Matt's to see if she could see any sign of life. But there was nothing. She parked her car and pressed the intercom. No reply from flat six.

She pressed it again: still no answer.

She stepped back, shielding her eyes from the glare of the sun and looked up at the window again. But she couldn't detect anything.

'Matt?' she shouted self-consciously.

Nothing.

She pressed the intercom again, leaving her finger on longer than last time. In desperation, she took out her mobile phone and rung him once more.

Cathy frowned. Since the last time she'd tried, Matt's mobile phone had been switched off.

'Maybe he's having treatment and can't use his phone,' Josie said when she called her.

'But you said he wasn't at the hospital.'

'Well, maybe he was hurting more than he thought and has gone to get checked over?'

'You can leave phones on in hospitals now.' Cathy recalled how annoying it was when she'd been visiting Rose. Having to listen to all those stupid ring tones and people telling relatives about their latest bowel movements or the colour of their urine was enough to make anyone ill.

'In some areas you can,' Josie replied. 'But not all of them. I bet he was having treatment when you called and he switched it off when he saw the signs. I know I used to forget to switch mine off and then be really embarrassed when it rang out. Those nurses can dish out evil stares.'

'But he could have rung me earlier on. I would have been straight up there, wherever 'there' is.'

'I'm sure he'll get back to you as soon as he can.' Josie tried to reassure her. 'He thinks a lot of you.'

Cathy thought of the intimacy they'd shared the night

before. She remembered how he hadn't wanted to leave. Something didn't add up.

'I just want to see that's he's okay,' she said.

And, she added to herself, to get all the details. Had it happened on his way home, or outside his block of flats?

Or had it happened outside her house?

THIRTY

'What are you playing at?' Jess flew at Becky the minute she got home that afternoon. 'You said you'd cover my stint, you cow.'

'And you shouldn't ask me to cover for something that you can't be bothered to do yourself. That's not what friends are for.' Becky pushed past her and into the kitchen.

'Cut the crap. I know who you were with and where you were. I saw you with Austin. Is he more important than our friendship?'

'I wasn't with Austin,' Becky lied.

'I saw you coming out of the car park of the White Lion.'

'What?'

'Gone round the back for a quick one, had you?'

'You're only jealous,' she replied, realising that she may have got away with it. Austin said she was to tell no one that he was squatting there or else they'd move him on.

'I'm not jealous of you.' Jess flopped into a chair at the table. 'What's happened to us, Becks? We were getting on really well. I can't believe you wouldn't cover for me.'

Seeing herself through Jess's eyes, Becky relented. She'd let her down and it wasn't a nice thing to do.

'I'm sorry. I was on my way,' she admitted, 'but Austin pulled up beside me when I got to Davy Road. He went all funny on me when I said I couldn't see him until after I'd been to the community house.'

'That's still no reason to cop out. Cathy's going to go mad with me.' Jess folded her arms, knowing she'd got Becky's attention; she'd learned over the weeks how to get under her skin, make her feel guilty. 'I miss having you around,' she added. 'Since you've met Austin, you're always with him. It's like you're joined at the hip.'

'Sorry,' Becky muttered.

'Is he always that intense?'

Becky shrugged, not meeting her eye for fear of giving her inner thoughts away. He *was* always that intense.

'You'd better hope that Cathy doesn't give me too much of a hard time when she gets home.'

Becky nodded. 'I am sorry. I should have thought of you first.'

Jess grinned and on impulse gave her a hug. 'You and me have got a lot to learn about friendship, but we'll get there.'

After tossing and turning in bed that night, Cathy flicked on the bedroom lamp and propped herself up. It was quarter past midnight. She checked her mobile phone again but the display showed no new messages. She sat up, hugged her knees to her chest and rested her chin on them.

What was going on? Matt still hadn't contacted her. She'd left him a handful of voice messages, along with half a dozen text messages. She'd even called back to his flat after the evening meal, pushing a note through the letterbox outside the building when she hadn't got an answer again.

She stared ahead, by this time not knowing what to think.

Was he ignoring her because he didn't like his appearance? She'd seen some bruises in her time so that wouldn't be a problem. Or was he ignoring her because he was embarrassed at being caught out? That was nothing to be ashamed of on this estate either.

But one thing kept running through her mind repeatedly. Was Matt ignoring her because he'd had his fun? Was that all she was getting? One quick 'how's your father' and 'I had a great time, thanks'. A one-night stand.

Cathy shook her head. She knew she was being irrational. Matt wouldn't ignore her. The signs were clearly there that he'd wanted to see her again. She reread the last text message he'd sent:

You really did blow me away. Can't wait for it to happen again... and to see you again of course, hee, hee. Mx

It didn't sound like he was giving her the elbow. There must be something wrong. But why would he let her worry like this? It just didn't make sense.

Sighing loudly she turned off the light, hoping that sleep would come to her soon.

The next morning, Liz woke up to another hot and promising day. She'd washed and pegged out a load of washing before Chloe got out of bed at seven thirty. At eight thirty, she kissed her daughter goodbye when Emily's mum called for her. They were going to Chester for the day. It was mid August and since the beginning of the school holidays, Chloe and Emily had become inseparable. It was heart-warming to see Chloe smiling.

Two more loads were done by lunchtime and just before she was due to leave for the community house, she decided to tackle a couple of bits of hand washing that she'd been putting off. She thought about this week's session as she scrubbed at them gently. It was going to be about self-confidence, something she was really looking forward to learning about. Last week they'd been given homework to do. They'd been asked to think about what they'd like to change in their lives if they were more confident and to write it down. Liz grinned as she recalled Chloe's look of astonishment when she'd told her. She hadn't been so happy at her reply though. 'You're far too old for homework, Mum,' she'd said in the grown-up way that only a child could.

After her initial reservations about the sessions, Liz had started to look forward to getting together with the women at the community house. The group she'd been with were really friendly, especially Suzie Rushton whom she'd bonded with immediately. Getting used to being with people again had been a huge hurdle, one she was still trying to conquer, but as Suzie had said, baby steps were all that was needed.

She folded one of Chloe's summer dresses in half and put it on the pile. As she reached over for the peg bag, she knocked a glass of juice over. It splashed onto her top, down the washer and onto the floor.

'Oh, bugger,' she cursed aloud: she'd only just put it on. Rubbing at it with a cloth made it worse. She glanced out of the window at the washing blowing slightly in the breeze. Perhaps her blue T-shirt would be dry now. In a tizzy, she yanked open the ironing board, unravelled the cord on the iron and plugged it in. She unlocked the door and went outside quickly.

'Hiya, Liz,' she heard someone say. 'You okay?'

'Oh, hi there.' Liz could just about see her neighbour, Jackie, over the garden fence. 'Enjoying the weather?'

'I sure am.' Jackie shielded her eyes from the midday sun. 'I can't believe we've had it for so long. Hardly any rain at all. It's been wonderful, hasn't it?'

'At least your peace won't be shattered.' Liz un-pegged the T-shirt as she spoke. 'Chloe's out for the day so she won't be chitter-chattering.'

'Oh, I don't mind that. I like your Chloe. She's a real angel.'

Liz laughed as she walked back up the path. 'You should see her when she's after her own way. She's a right little madam.'

'Are you off out soon?'

'Yes, I'm going to the community house.' She glanced at her watch again. 'Oh, Lord, I'm going to be late. I'd better get going. See ya.'

Liz ran into the flat and locked the door behind her. In her bedroom she slipped out of the juice-splattered top. As she pulled her head through the clean T-shirt, she caught sight of a shadow at the door. Before she had a chance to react, she saw Kevin blocking the doorway. He had a long-bladed knife in his hand. Fear she'd hoped never to feel again tore through her body.

'You – you shouldn't be here,' she managed to stutter.

Kevin stepped towards her. Liz moved back. She felt her heels hit the skirting board on the wall behind her. He stared at her unfalteringly.

'Please, Kevin... I ...'

Kevin touched the tip of the blade, glazed eyes never

leaving hers. Then he grabbed her by the wrist and pulled her nearer. In one swift movement, the blade was against her throat.

Liz squeezed her eyes shut. Oh God, he was going to kill her.

'I could waste you right here,' he said calmly. 'But I wouldn't want Chloe to see you if someone brings her home when they come looking for you.'

Looking for me? Liz gulped.

'So I figure, you walk out in front and I'll follow on behind.' He moved a smidgeon closer. 'Don't make a murmur, a sound, anything to indicate you are scared. You will smile why we walk down the path and then get into my car. Then we're going for a short drive. Do you understand?'

Liz's teeth began to chatter. She wasn't sure her legs would carry her that far. It took all of her strength to nod.

'Good. Let's go then, shall we?' Kevin stared at her with those dead eyes again. She had never seen him this calm, this desensitised before. It was as if he'd planned this down to the last detail. Cautiously, she stepped past him.

'Wait there a minute.'

Through the pine mirror on the chest of drawers, she watched as he searched in her wardrobe. She wanted to make a run for it but she knew better that that. She had to stay strong for her daughter.

Kevin pulled down her long black cardigan and placed it over his wrist and hand, concealing the knife altogether. Then he came towards her.

'You can go now.'

Liz arched her back away from him and started to move.

She unlocked the door, walked out of the flat and down the three steps to the path, all the time realising that he must have been watching her. When she thought he'd given up searching for her, he must have stayed hidden in the shadows, biding his time. Waiting for her to slip up, just like she had today. In her hurry, she'd left the door open while she'd rushed to get that T-shirt. Stupid, stupid, stupid!

When they got to the gate and it was locked, Liz realised that Kevin must have climbed over it – maybe lying in wait for a while. But where could he have hidden? Her eyes flicked to the small gap behind the bin stores. Was it possible he could have been there? And for how long?

She slid back the bolts and walked out towards the street. Kevin held onto her arm, the knife still pushing on her back, the tip of the blade staying in contact all the time.

Liz looked around the nearby gardens but apart from a man up ahead mowing his lawn, it was pretty much quiet. She'd have to do what Kevin said until she could get away.

As she got into the passenger seat of his car, she looked up to see Jackie watching from her front window. In desperation, Liz widened her eyes, hoping that this tiny movement would raise her suspicions. She didn't dare do anything else: one wrong move and she'd be dead, she was certain.

Jackie darted out of view and Liz gulped. She wasn't sure she'd seen her.

Oh, Chloe, my darling. I'm so, so, sorry.

THIRTY-ONE

Jackie Smythe had lived on the Mitchell Estate all of her life. At seventeen, she was married and had two children but the lout had done a runner three years later. At twenty-five, she married again. After two more kids, he left too and alcohol became her new best friend. Now in her late forties, the life she'd led had started to tell on her in more ways than one.

But Andy Baxter liked Jackie. She had a spirit about her that was needed to survive on the Mitchell Estate and since Josie had moved her from the notorious Stanley Avenue, Jackie had calmed her drinking down. At least, he assumed she had: he hadn't been called out for a disturbance at her property for some time now.

So when she said she was worried about Liz McIntyre, Andy had driven round to see her immediately.

'It might be something and nothing,' Jackie told him. 'You know I'm usually not one for interfering, but I can tell she's had trouble with a fella. The look that she gave me was like a frightened rabbit. She was trapped. I was trapped. I wanted to run out to her but I didn't dare in case he did anything stupid.'

Andy took out his notebook. 'Can you tell me anything else? Colour, make of car? What they were wearing etc?'

'It was some kind of Ford, navy blue. It was a four door, I think. I'd only just seen her in the garden. I was talking to her and –'

Andy raised a finger as his phone started to ring. 'Hello? Yes. When? Where? I'm on my way.' He disconnected the call and stood up quickly.

'What's wrong?' Jackie stood up too. 'You've gone quite pale for a copper.'

'There's something I need to check out.' Andy shoved his notebook back into his pocket. 'I have to go.'

Jackie was slightly annoyed that her request wasn't being taken seriously. 'You should finish with me before going off to deal with some scrote on the estate,' she cried. 'Liz could be in danger and as usual you don't give a shit.'

'It's not like that.' Andy handed her a card and headed for the door. 'Can you call the police helpline, give them my badge number, explain the situation and tell them everything – anything – you know. I'll follow up from there.' Before getting into his car, he shouted to her. 'You've been a great help, Jackie. Thanks.'

Cathy disconnected her phone. She tapped it on her bottom lip. It wasn't like Liz to be late for the sessions at the community house, let alone not answer her mobile. She looked to the door, any second expecting her to rush through, all apologies, and sit down at the back of the room.

'We're out of coffee,' Suzie shouted across to her. 'I'm going to see if I can pinch some from The Den.'

Cathy moved to the door. 'You stay here. I'll go and look. Do you want to get the group started?'

Andy had seen plenty of horrors since he'd started working on the Mitchell Estate but luckily not too many deaths – and all of them had died through natural causes. This body, however, wasn't even cold yet. Kevin McIntyre still had faint colour in his cheeks as he hung from the tree in front of him.

'When did you find him?' he asked PC Mark White when he reached him.

'About twenty minutes ago.' Mark nodded his head in the direction of an elderly man, a young Spaniel sitting at his feet. 'He does this walk every afternoon. When he went past earlier, he wasn't there. When he came back,' he pointed, 'he was hanging. Said it gave him the fright of his life.'

'Nothing prepares you for it, does it?' Andy looked around. There weren't many professionals at the scene yet, only two more police officers, but he knew that in less than half an hour, the place would be swarming.

He stared up at the body. There was only this one tree in the area that would support the man's weight and height: the rest were too small. Jackie Smythe had been accurate in her description of Kevin's clothes: jeans, blue and white striped T-shirt. A black baseball cap had been found a few feet away.

'He doesn't seem to have any ID,' said Mark. 'But I've seen his face enough times to know him. It's McIntyre, isn't it? Lived over in Douglas Close. We used to get called there on domestics. I saw him at Cathy Mason's too.'

'Yeah,' nodded Andy. 'Kevin McIntyre. He was last seen walking his wife out of her property a couple of hours ago.

Neighbour reckons she looked shit scared of him. They drove off in his car. I've just circulated details of it.'

'Fuck!' Mark rubbed at his chin. 'I remember her too. Small, nice-looking, really nervy. They have a young daughter, don't they?'

Andy nodded. 'I'm going to drive around the streets nearby. He can't have got far with her in such a short space of time. I've got to find her.'

'I'll come with you.'

'Hi, Josie, it's Cathy.'

'Hi, how're you doing? Have you heard from Matt?'

'No, but that's not why I'm calling you. Have you seen or heard from Liz this morning?'

'No, why?'

'She didn't turn up for this afternoon's session. I've seen her twice since last week and she said she was really looking forward to it. I've tried her phone but it keeps ringing out.'

'I'm at a tenant's house but should be done in an hour. Would you like me to call by her flat then?'

'No, I'll pop round anyway. My mind won't rest now until I've seen her.'

'You don't think anything's happened to her, do you? After we've just got her back on her feet?'

'I bloody hope not. I'll kill that Kevin McIntyre myself if he's done anything stupid.'

'I suppose you're off out with Austin the wonder boy tonight,' said a bored-looking Jess as she painted her toenails a bright shade of orange.

'Hmm-hmm.'

Jess tutted her annoyance. 'You two *are* joined at the hip. I thought you were into having a good time and going out with the girls before you settled down.'

'I am. It's just that –' Becky faltered then thought better of it. 'Jess, sometimes he scares me.' She told her what had happened the other day, when Austin had pushed her across the floor. But she pretended he'd made her get out of the car rather than tell Jess they were inside the disused pub. 'He made such a big deal about me using sex as a way to get affection.'

'Didn't stop him from having sex with you, though, did it?'

'He didn't want to know again.'

Jess laughed. 'You might have tired him out.'

Becky didn't laugh with her. Jess noticed.

'If he scares you that much, then why don't you finish things with him? There's plenty more where he came from. And,' she nodded, 'you should be looking forward to going out with him, not dreading what mood he'll be in when he turns up. He's a grown man, for God's sake.'

Becky sat in silence while she thought through what Jess had said. Maybe she had latched on to Austin on the rebound from Danny Bradley. After all, she'd been abused constantly for a few years. Maybe now she didn't really understand what was right and what was wrong behaviour. She mentioned this to Jess, being careful not to slip up about Danny.

'If you spoke to half of the women on this estate, they'd say that you should let your man do as he pleases with you, but I disagree.' Finishing her nails, Jess replaced the top on the polish and put it down onto the coffee table. 'I believe a fella shouldn't do anything that you don't want him to. IF you let him get away with his moody sulks, he'll do it more and more. Then you're in the circle.'

Becky looked confused. 'The circle?'

'The circle of violence. Once he smacks you and then makes you feel like you deserve it, his next step is to go on and on at you until you believe his messages. That's the logic behind Josie Mellor's courses, so I've been told.'

Becky paused for thought. Austin had scared her twice but he had apologised straight afterwards. Maybe she'd caught him at his worst.

Surmising that she was losing Becky, Jess continued. 'Has he ever hit you?'

'Not as such.' When Jess raised her eyebrows, she continued. 'He's grabbed me a few times but he's always been sorry afterwards.'

'Like those bruises on your wrist?'

Becky nodded.

'Those are typical signs to watch out for. Maybe you should stay away from him for a while?'

'I can't do that. He needs me. We'll make it work, you'll see.'

'You'd better be more careful then. If I saw you coming out of the car park of the White Lion, who else might have?'

Becky gasped. 'I hadn't thought of that.'

'Now if it was Cathy...' Jess left the sentence unfinished for more of an effect but she continued. 'Do you get down to it in the car or has he broken in to the pub?'

Becky blushed. She turned away but Jess had noticed.

'You go inside!' she said. 'Ooh, I'm not sure if I fancy that. Is it creepy?'

'Not really, but it's a bit smelly. And dirty too.'

'I used to go in that pub until it shut down. Which rooms have you been in?'

'Most of them,' said Becky. Suddenly the secrecy was too much for her. 'Jess, if I tell you something, will you swear not to tell Austin that you know?'

'I promise,' she said, truthfully. Austin might have caused a rift between them but Becky needed to talk.

'Austin lives there.'

'What, in the pub?' Jess was shocked. 'No way!'

'Yes way.'

'So when you go to have sex there, really he's taking you back to his place.'

Becky nodded. 'You won't tell anyone, will you?'

'No, but why have you told me?'

'He gives me the creeps every now and again. Just for a moment or two,' she explained as she saw Jess recoil. 'And then the real Austin comes back to me. But it's those times that scare me.'

'He'd better not touch you. If anything happens –'

Becky laughed nervously. 'Nothing is going to happen to me, you great nerd. I've told you, I can look after myself.'

Andy pulled up behind a blue Ford Focus. It was parked in Finlay Place, a row of one-bedroom bungalows for the elderly. An overgrown hedgerow followed the length of the pavement, the entrance to the adjacent playing fields was about ten feet away. The registration matched the one that Mark had taken down when Kevin McIntyre caused a commotion over at Cathy's house a few weeks back. But it was empty when they reached it.

Andy quickly put on a pair of latex gloves and checked the driver's door. Finding it unlocked, he flicked the boot release. Then, holding his breath, he lifted the tail gate. But apart from a towel and an empty petrol can, the boot was empty.

'I'm going to walk back to the body, see if I spot anything on the way,' Andy told Mark. 'Then I'll go over to the community house. You stay here until forensics arrive.'

Cathy was smiling as she chatted to one of the teenagers upstairs. Her face changed when she spotted Andy walking towards her. By the look of him, he'd had a shock. This couldn't be good. She ushered him into Josie's empty office and closed the door.

Through the window, Andy watched as the world went on with its business, as if nothing dreadful was unfolding. He hadn't been able to find anything on his walk back to the body so had come to see if Cathy had seen Liz.

'Andy?' Cathy touched him gently on the arm. 'What's happened?'

'Kevin McIntyre hung himself this afternoon.'

'Oh no! I can't get hold of Liz. Please tell me he hasn't hurt her.'

Andy had tears in his eyes as he spoke. 'That's just it. I can't tell you anything. Her neighbour said he left with her this morning in his car. We've found it over on Finlay Place, not far from where we found him hanging. The car was empty.'

'And Liz? What's happened to her?'

'We don't know yet.'

'You haven't found her?'

Andy shook his head. 'I walked Kevin's likely path back from the car to the tree where he hung himself but I couldn't see anything. It's mostly grass but I only did a quick scan. The guys are out in force now. I'm going back to join them.'

Cathy was lost for words. She'd known something was wrong when Liz hadn't shown up. She picked up her phone and tried the number again. It rang three times and then it was answered.

'Liz?' Cathy shouted excitedly.

'No, it's Josie.'

'Oh, I thought –'

'I've just got to the flat. I couldn't get her off my mind after I'd spoken to you so I called round. The back door was unlocked. I knocked but there was no reply so I went in. There's no one here. Her phone's lying on her bed and the iron's still switched on. It's as if she's vanished into thin air.'

'Oh, God. Josie, there's something I need to tell you.'

Cathy told Andy what Josie had said.

'I have to go,' he said. 'I'll keep you informed as soon as I hear anything.'

'And are you checking the hospitals?'

'Already onto it.'

His phone rang then. Cathy held her breath while he listened to the message. She could tell it was bad news before he'd said a word to her. The colour had drained from his face and he began to tap his toe on the skirting board.

'I'm on my way,' he said finally and disconnected the phone.

'Have they found her?' Cathy asked.

'They've found someone.' Andy thought back to Jackie Smyth's description of what Liz had been wearing: blue T-shirt, cropped jeans, strappy white shoes with a chunky heel and a white clip in her hair. 'Hidden well apparently, in the bushes at the edge of the walkway off Finlay Place, and on the way to where Kevin was found.'

'Hidden? What do you mean?'

Andy kicked the wall. 'Fuck!' He kicked it again.

'Andy, you're scaring me!' Cathy grabbed his arm. 'Tell me, please. I have to know. Is she alive? Andy! Is she alive?'

THIRTY-TWO

'Cathy!' Chloe greeted her as she was dropped off there by Emily's mum. She looked around the kitchen before twirling back to face her. 'Where's my mum?'

Cathy smiled at Chloe and took her bag and cardigan from her. 'She's not feeling too well this afternoon, pumpkin, so I'm going to look after you. How do you fancy something to eat with us? Jess and Becky are cooking.'

'Cool!' said Chloe. 'I can show you my new gymnastics moves. I've learned how to do a crab today.'

Cathy sighed with relief. It seemed Chloe didn't suspect a thing. At least they had some breathing space now until they heard from the hospital.

'That's great, honey,' she said. 'You can show us all.'

'Josie!' Chloe beamed as she came into Cathy's kitchen an hour later. 'We're making pancakes. Would you like one?'

'Oh, no, I've got to…' Josie noticed Chloe's smile drooping. 'Go on, then. Just a little one, though.'

'We're having fun, aren't we, Chloe?' said Becky. She was standing next to Jess, watching the batter mix in the frying pan change to something edible.

Chloe grabbed Josie's hand. 'Sit down,' she said.

'Just one minute.' Josie pulled her hand away gently. 'I need a word with Cathy first.'

'She's out in the garden,' said Jess. 'You go out to her. Me and Becks will look after this one.'

Josie smiled with gratitude. People were always the same in a crisis, she thought. They forgot about hindering and just helped all they could.

Cathy was sitting on the garden bench, watching the sun disappear behind the hedge. Actually she wasn't watching anything. All she could see was Liz's face flashing before her eyes. From what Andy had told them, it seemed that she'd been dragged out of sight, possibly left for dead. Luckily it hadn't taken too long to find her and she'd been rushed straight into surgery with internal bleeding. Cathy was blaming herself. How could she have let her move out to be attacked by that man? She should have insisted that she stay with her for longer.

'We let her down,' she said as Josie walked towards her. 'We knew he'd go after her and we let down our guard.'

Josie flopped down beside Cathy and they sat in silence, neither of them wanting to start a conversation.

'Will you stay for a while?' Cathy spoke eventually.

'Of course.'

'You're a good one.'

'I had thought you'd be saying that about Matt. What happened between you two? One minute you were all smiles: the next, it's as if it never happened.'

Cathy shrugged. 'He stopped returning my calls after we slept together. He must have had his fill of me and moved on to pastures new.'

Josie shook her head. 'Matt wouldn't do that.'

'You obviously don't know him as well as you think.'

'But wasn't everything okay until he was assaulted?'

'Who knows? I haven't seen him since then.'

'Not even at the community house?'

'Not in the last week. He's avoiding me completely. But I don't care anymore.'

'Now listen here, this is me you're talking to. I know you too well for bullshit. You were mad about him, even through your guilt!'

'He made a fool out of me.'

Josie shook her head again. 'That doesn't sound like Matt. Something doesn't ring true. I'm going to ask him in the morning.'

'You'd better not,' Cathy retorted. 'If anyone is going to ask him, it'll be me. I can do my own dirty work.'

'But what if –'

'Look, forget it, Josie.' Cathy stood up. 'I've got more important things to think about. Besides, he's a loser. He should have thought about what he was doing before he dumped me.'

'Maybe he did,' said Josie quietly, another thought crossing her mind as Cathy walked away.

It was seven thirty that evening before Cathy took a call from Andy. Jess and Becky were keeping Chloe entertained, watching television in the living room.

'Andy's on his way over,' Cathy told Josie who had stayed there, waiting to hear any news. 'I know it's late for Chloe but I said I'd get the girls to take her out.'

Josie's eyes filled with tears. 'That poor child.'

They hugged briefly before going into the living room.

'Right, young lady,' Cathy said to Chloe. 'As you are in my charge tonight, I think a chocolate treat is in order.'

'Can I ring my mum first?' Chloe asked. 'I want to see if she's feeling better.'

'Not right now, sweetheart. Let's leave her be for tonight. Now, I think I'll have some Minstrels and a Mars bar. What do you fancy, Jess?'

Jess stood up quickly. 'Ooh, I'll have to wait until I get there. I can never make up my mind.'

She nudged Becky who then reached for Chloe's hand. 'We'll race you to the end of the street.'

As the two girls disappeared through the door, Cathy handed a five pound note to Jess.

'She's so young.' Jess held back her tears. 'How could he… how could he do that to Liz?'

Cathy threw an arm around her shoulder and gave her a quick squeeze.

'Is Andy on his way over?'

'Yes. If there aren't too many youths hanging around, perhaps you can come back through the park? Keep Chloe out for about an hour – just in case.'

'Just in case? What? You mean…?' Jess shook her head vehemently. 'She won't be dead. She can't be! She's just injured, that's all. She'll be okay.'

'I hope so, Jess,' said Cathy. 'I really hope so.'

Andy walked up to Cathy's front door with a heavy heart. His shift had finished over an hour ago but it was what he'd seen during those hours that was playing on his mind. He really wanted to go home but he couldn't until he'd been to see Cathy and Josie. They were the only people that knew Liz well.

Cathy opened the front door before he got to it. He

walked in silence through to the kitchen where they joined Josie.

Andy gulped as he looked from one to the other. 'She made it but barely,' he said quietly. 'Her prospects are good if she can fight everything but it's still touch and go.'

Cathy held on to the edge of the worktop as she felt her legs go weak. Josie looked away unable to speak.

'It seems McIntyre drove her to Finlay Place and assaulted her. Then he must have dragged her out of sight. There was no way she could have got to where she was with the injuries she had.' Andy reached out a hand. 'Sit down, Cathy, before you collapse.'

'She fought back,' he continued once they were sat around the table. 'There are defence wounds on her arms, and her face has some vicious bruising appearing around her eyes. But the main damage was to her torso. She was found with a deep stab wound to her stomach. I might as well tell you now as you'll probably hear it in the news tomorrow. The doctors have done all they could – she was in there for four hours – but it's up to her now.'

'We should have done more,' Josie whispered.

'We couldn't have done anything else.'

'Can we see her?' Cathy looked up through eyes that glistened with tears.

'I'm not sure. You'd be better checking in the morning.' Andy handed a card to her. 'This is the ward phone number. I'll ring and tell them you're her next-of-kin, if you like? I hope they'll talk to you. But I do need to contact her family. Do you know of anyone?'

'She has parents in Devon,' said Cathy, 'and a sister, although they don't seem to give a shit about her.'

'They still need to be told.' Andy stood up and jerked his head towards the door. 'I'd better be going.'

'When is your shift over?'

'Finished. I couldn't go home without seeing you first.'

Cathy smiled her gratitude. Andy Baxter deserved an award for what he had to put up with in his day-to-day life. All those people out there who thought he had a 'bobby's job' should do a couple of shifts with him. She was certain they'd change their tune about police officers being paid too much money.

'When are you going to tell Chloe?' Josie asked once he was gone.

'It can wait until the morning. The last thing she needs right now is to be told – told –' Cathy broke down in tears, 'How could he do that to Liz, the selfish bastard!'

After shouting hello to his wife, Andy's first port of call was upstairs to check on his sleeping children. He took the steps three at a time. Six-year-old Natalie Baxter was curled up like a kitten. Her younger brother, Jordan, was splayed all over his bed. Before he left the room, Andy popped his tiny feet back underneath the covers.

For a moment he stood on the landing, holding back tears. The people who he loved were safe in their worlds. He prayed it would stay that way.

He went downstairs to find his wife. She was sitting on the settee. When she saw him, she flicked down the sound on the television. He smiled softly, tenderly touching her face. He kissed her gently, twice. Three times. Then he held her. There was no need for words and he wouldn't be able to find ones to explain how much she meant to him anyway.

While Cathy got Chloe ready for bed, Josie gave Becky and Jess an update before heading home.

'I didn't think he'd do anything like that,' said Jess afterwards, shaking her head. 'I know I was always ribbing her about him but I never thought he'd try to kill her.'

Becky sniffed. 'She was really nice to me when I lost my baby. I can't believe he'd leave her like that.'

Cathy appeared in the doorway a few minutes later. 'Chloe's settled at last,' she said, taking the whisky that Josie had poured for her. She knocked back the liquid in one go. 'I've put her into my bed for now.'

Jess frowned. 'She'll be staying here, won't she?'

'We'll have to see how things go with Liz,' Josie explained. 'But let's not think about that now. There will be lots of questions to answer in the morning.'

Becky drew her knees up to her chest, her arms hugging them tightly. 'Do you think she felt much pain?'

Cathy gulped. The million dollar question which no one would ever be able to answer. Despite knowing what the newspaper would report, she wasn't going to tell them the gory details that Andy had shared with her earlier.

'I doubt it,' she said. 'Andy reckons that her injuries would have made her slip quickly into unconsciousness.'

'But she probably felt everything while he kicked the shit out of her first.'

None of them had an answer to that.

Once Josie had gone, Cathy checked in on Chloe before going back downstairs to Jess and Becky. She found them sitting in silence. The television was blaring out a comedy but both of them seemed totally lost in their thoughts.

'I thought you two would be off out by now,' she said.

'Don't feel like it,' said Jess.

'Me neither,' said Becky.

'Coffee?' she asked. 'Or maybe a little something stronger? I know I shouldn't encourage you but a little tot in a hot drink won't hurt. And it may help you sleep.'

'Coffee,' said Becky.

'Something stronger,' said Jess at the same time.

'Let's do both, then.'

Cathy flicked on the kettle. As she waited for it to boil, she stared out of the window. It was still hard to take in all that had happened. Was it only yesterday that she'd found Chloe's tennis racket at the bottom of the cupboard and put it in the outhouse ready to return it? Why couldn't she have done that this morning? Then Liz might not have been attacked.

Her mobile phone beeped. Cathy slid up the cover.

'*I'm really sorry to hear about Liz. Matt. x*'

In temper, Cathy slid the cover shut abruptly. How dare he try to get around her now, after what had just happened with Liz. That was sick, to use it to his own advantage.

But then again, maybe he was genuinely upset. Matt knew Liz too, not as closely obviously, but in circumstances such as these it didn't really matter. To even know a person who had been beaten up so brutally must be upsetting enough. Maybe she shouldn't be too harsh. It did, after all, show a human side to him, a side that she hadn't seen too much of admittedly. What had happened between them, she wondered again. Why had he just dropped off the face of the earth after they'd had sex? She'd been so convinced he'd enjoyed it too. She'd never be able to fathom that one out.

The kettle flicked off and she cursed loudly. 'Fuckity fuck!'

Now was not the time to think of herself.

After a restless night, Cathy was awake early. Chloe lay sleeping soundly beside her. It pained her to think how she slept so peacefully now, oblivious to what was going on. How she didn't know that her life would be very different when she awoke.

She gazed at her, wanting to pick her up and squeeze her hard; wanting to protect her from what had happened; keep her wrapped up away from hurt and anger. Even though it was warm, she pulled the duvet up and over Chloe's bare arms. She gulped back tears.

How could she tell her what had happened? Chloe had only just started to accept that she and Liz were on their own now. Last week, Liz had been saying how much brighter she seemed since they'd moved into the flat. Now it was all going to be shattered. She hoped and prayed that Liz would pull through, for her daughter's sake.

She must have dozed off because when she woke up next, Chloe was sitting up beside her, playing with her baby doll.

'Hello, missy.' Cathy prodded her gently in the arm.

Chloe turned to face her. 'Hello.'

'Did you sleep okay?'

'Yes. Can I ring Mum this morning?'

'It's still early yet. I think we need to get you breakfast first. What do you fancy? Toast with marmalade?'

'Yuck!' Chloe shook her head. 'I don't like marmalade.'

'Peanut butter?'

'No!'

'Jam?'

Chloe giggled. 'No!'

'How about I spread a cheese triangle over it?'

Chloe nodded enthusiastically. Cathy pulled back the duvet. 'Right then. Race you downstairs!'

Later as she waited for the bread to toast, Cathy contemplated what to say. She glanced at the clock: half past seven. Maybe she should ring the hospital first and get an update. But what would happen then if anything had happened to Liz? She'd have to tell Chloe and she wouldn't want to do that. Without realising, she banged the palm of her hand on her forehead three times.

'What's the matter, Cathy?'

Cathy turned to see Chloe looking at her strangely. She dropped her eyes. *Oh Chloe, I'm going to break your heart.* She gulped. But it had to be done. She slid over the toast, knowing that it had been impractical to cook breakfast beforehand. Chloe wouldn't be able to eat after what she was about to tell her.

'Is my mummy sick a lot?' Chloe's bottom lip began to tremble.

Cathy sat down beside her. 'I – I – Chloe, a terrible thing happened yesterday. I didn't want to tell you until I was sure of everything. Now that I am, I think you should know about it.'

'Has my dad hurt my mum?'

Cathy cringed. How much violence towards her mother had Chloe seen to ask that?

'Yes, he has,' she said. 'Your dad found out where you

were living and he was angry with your mum. So he – he got a little too rough with her and he – he…' Cathy couldn't hold back any longer. She began to cry. 'Chloe, do you know where heaven is?'

'Yes.' Chloe started to cry too. 'Is my mummy in heaven?'

'No!' Cathy could have kicked herself. What on earth did she say that for? Now Chloe would be thinking the worst no matter what. Stupid, stupid! 'But she's very poorly in hospital. Very poorly indeed.'

'So she might go to heaven and be with the angels?'

'She might but we don't know yet.'

'But I don't want her to be with the angels. I won't be able to see her. Mum told me Rose went to see the angels and I can't see her!'

'Chloe, your mum is poorly but she might not go to heaven,' Cathy reiterated. 'Your mum loves you very much and she is a strong lady. She would never want to leave you.'

'I want my mum. I want my MUM!'

Cathy pulled her onto her knees and cradled her while she sobbed. Tears ran down her own face as she held onto her little body as it jerked and shook. She wished there was some way that she could soften the blow but there wasn't. Life was cruel: it was a fact. But how would someone as young as Chloe get through this? She prayed that Liz would survive. She had to. The child had been through enough already. It wasn't fair to put her through much more.

Suddenly Chloe pulled away. 'Where is my dad?' she asked. 'Is he in heaven?'

'Yes.' Cathy's heart sunk. 'He's in heaven.'

'But that means I have no dad and no mum to look after me. What about me?' Chloe covered her hands with her ears and began to scream. 'I want my mum. I want my MUMMY!'

Cathy let her vent her anger. After a few seconds, she fell back into Cathy's arms again. She snuffled into her chest for a while.

'My dad loved my mum too much, didn't he?' she whispered.

Cathy wiped at her cheeks. 'Yes, honey, he did.'

THIRTY-THREE

Cathy could hardly breathe as she sat next to Andy in a small room off Liz's ward later that morning. She'd left Chloe with Jess and Becky, saying that she would come straight home if they texted her. She hoped Chloe would settle with them. So far, there had been no text.

'What if she's beaten up so badly that she doesn't recognise anyone?' Cathy shuddered. 'What if her brain has been damaged?'

'She's in good hands,' said Andy. 'Let's wait and see.'

They glanced up as a middle-aged woman came in to the room. She was heavy framed with a round face and thick black hair tied back in a pony tail. She pulled up a chair and sat directly facing them both. Cathy didn't like the solemn look on her face. She braced herself for bad news.

'I'm Dr Morgan.'

'Is Liz… is she okay?'

The woman nodded. 'Elizabeth – Liz is out of imminent danger for now.'

Cathy sighed dramatically. Then she burst into tears.

'She came through surgery well and we've since carried out a few tests. We're still waiting on some results but thankfully she has no damage to her brain.'

'Is she conscious?'

'Yes, but she'll be in a lot of pain today so I've given her something to help. She might not be particularly lucid until tomorrow. As well as the knife wound she has a cracked rib, a dislocated shoulder and a gash on her wrist. Her left foot is badly sprained and three of her fingers are broken. She obviously fought to survive. You have the attacker, you say?' She looked at Andy for confirmation.

Andy nodded. 'He's lying on a slab in the morgue.'

'Ah.'

'Can we see her for a few minutes?'

'No longer than that.' Dr Morgan stood up. 'But remember what I said. She may wake up and talk to you but she won't recall anything.'

They followed the doctor through into the ward and on to where there were four bays. Cathy paused at the foot of one of them, staring at the still figure lying in the bed, wires and tubes coming from her attached to all kinds of machines. Beeps, lines and flashes. It was a sight Cathy would never forget: it would be etched on her mind forever. She stayed at the foot of the bed, not wanting to go any nearer, not wanting to get in the way. The ward had a surreal quietness to it – almost as if no one dared to speak. A nurse checking a chart smiled and urged her to step forward. All at once, she was at the bedside.

'Hi there,' she whispered. Her hand hovered in mid air over Liz's swollen cheek before she thought better of touching it. 'It's me – Cathy.'

'Most of her injuries are superficial,' said Dr Morgan. 'They will heal in time. And now that you're here, I'm sure you'll help with her recuperation.'

*

Back out in the waiting room, Josie came rushing in half an hour later.

'Sorry, I couldn't get here earlier,' she apologised. 'The traffic's terrible and it took me an age to find a parking space. Have you seen her? How is she?'

'She's going to be okay.' Cathy burst into tears with relief. 'She's poorly but she'll get better.'

The two women hugged.

Josie looked at Andy over Cathy's shoulder. 'Did you manage to contact her family?'

'Yes. Kevin's too. His father hadn't seen him for years. They'd had an argument when he accused Kevin of mistreating Liz. He was quite angry at first, blaming himself for not doing more. Far different than when I spoke to Liz's mum. She just went on and on about how she'd told her that there was something not quite right about Kevin. And then she started moaning about the time it would take to drive up from Devon and how she wasn't even sure that she would. Not once did she ask about Chloe. I had to hold my tongue a few times.'

They sat down on a row of chairs. The waiting room was spacious but open. Relatives of loved ones in intensive care sat around too. Young and old. It was heartbreaking to see how everyone held their breath when a door opened and a doctor appeared. Hopes dashed or tears of joy. Fifty-fifty.

'And how's Chloe?' asked Josie.

'I have to make cakes with her later,' Cathy spoke matter of factly.

'You haven't told her, then?'

'Oh, yes, I told her. But she doesn't believe that Dad has gone to heaven and she just wants to make cakes for when

Mum is better. I suppose if it takes her mind off things…'

Cathy shrugged, her eyes brimming with tears again.

Even though she was unable to do much but sit around in the waiting room, Cathy stayed at the hospital for most of the day. Chloe had been looked after by the girls but now she was back to take over, Becky had slipped out to see Austin. They were inside the White Lion, lying on the filthy mattress that she was so used to now. She rested her head on his chest.

'Don't you think it's sad, though?' she asked him. 'Chloe's only eight. I can't stop thinking about it. What would have happened to her if they'd both died? I –'

'Shut up with your rattle, will you?' Austin sat up and reached for his cigarettes. He lit one and took a long drag before lying back again.

Becky cuddled into his side. 'But it's such a shame.'

'How do you know she didn't deserve what she got?'

'That's not a nice thing to say.'

'I'm not a nice person.'

Becky smiled, even though she was a little unnerved by the tone of his voice. She tried to boost his mood.

'Of course, you are,' she replied. 'I think you're fab.'

'I'm not what you think I am.'

'How would I know? You still won't tell me anything about your parents.'

Austin took his arm from her shoulder and placed it behind his head. 'There's nowt to tell. My mother abandoned me when I was born and I never knew who my father was.'

'Haven't you ever wanted to find them?'

Austin smirked. 'You obviously don't know me at all.'

'But I want to.' Becky sat up on her elbow to face him. 'You just have to let me in. There's something eating you up. Maybe I can help if you talk about it?'

'I told you, all right. There's nowt to talk about. But I will say one thing.' Austin turned towards her. 'Everyone will know my name soon.'

The look on his face made Becky's skin crawl. 'What do you mean?'

'It's my birthday at the end of next week. My twenty-first, my coming of age. The day that I get to be a grown-up.'

'Why didn't you say?' Becky whined. 'It doesn't give me much time, does it? I'll have to go shopping, get something special for you. We have to celebrate.'

Austin nodded, looking happy for the first time that day.

'Yeah, let's celebrate,' he said. 'The day's going to end with a bang anyway. One way or another.'

Becky frowned: he was talking in riddles again.

Austin jumped up and pulled on his jeans. 'Come on, let's go. I've got things to do this afternoon.'

'Yeah, I've got lots to do now.' Becky stood up and flung herself into his arms. 'Austin Forrester, I love you. And I'm going to make this birthday one to remember.'

Austin smirked again. 'You don't need to go to any trouble. I'm capable of doing that all by myself.'

Josie and Matt were sorting out a store room that had gone haywire at the community house. There were all manner of things stacked on shelves, not to mention the floor.

'Have you heard off Cathy lately?' Josie asked. Despite

being warned by her, she was determined to get to the bottom of what had happened between the two of them.

'No.'

Matt stepped up onto a low stool and then handed a box down to Josie. She took it from him and put it on the floor. She looked up at him, willing him to continue but he remained silent. She decided to move things along.

'What went on between the two of you?' she asked bluntly. 'I thought you were getting on really well.'

'We were.' Matt handed her another box.

'And?' Josie said impatiently as he handed her another.

'And nothing.'

Josie sighed. 'Look, Matt, quit messing around. We sleep with someone and move on to the next conquest when we're sixteen, not our age.'

'I never did that!' Matt sounded appalled.

'No?'

'NO!'

'That's what Cathy thinks.'

'Does she?' Matt ran his hand over his chin.

'What's going on?' Josie questioned gently. 'One minute you're whistling all day, can't wait for your date with Cathy. You sleep with her –'

'She told you that too?'

'Yes. She said she had a great time and couldn't wait to see you again. In the meantime, you go off sick, beaten up by some useless cretin, and you and Cathy are no more. It's weird.'

'It's – it's complicated.' Matt sighed.

'I must admit, I can't understand why you haven't contacted her to see how she was after Liz was attacked.'

'I did! I've sent dozens of text messages. I even called a few times, right after it had happened, but her phone either rang out or it was disconnected after a few rings.'

Josie suddenly thought of something. 'This man who attacked you. You didn't get a look at him at all?'

'No, I didn't.'

'What about his build? His hair? Even his shoes?'

Matt shook his head. 'I curled up in a ball. The bastard kicked the shit out of me.'

Josie frowned. 'Do you think it could have been Kevin McIntyre that attacked you?'

'Kevin McIntyre?' Matt paused. 'You mean he thought I'd been seeing Liz and was warning me off *her*?'

'What do you mean, warning you off?'

'The guy who beat me up. He told me to stay away from her.'

'But he didn't know that Liz had moved out then so he could have been on the watch for her. Can you recall any tone to his voice? Any accent?'

Matt tried to remember. He shook his head.

'Anything else that he said?'

'He said, "Don't come back or I'll be the death of her." Fuck.' Matt froze. 'I could have stopped Liz being attacked, couldn't I?'

Josie shook her head. 'No one could have stopped that from happening. You mustn't blame yourself. Kevin –'

'But if I had reported the attack, perhaps the police would have checked up with him!' Matt stepped back onto the floor. 'It was my fault!'

'No, it wasn't!'

'I thought he'd hurt Cathy, if I didn't stay away. You

don't know how much it's pained me, not being able to see her. I wanted to, so badly. But the way he hammered into me, I was scared he'd beat her too. And, maybe I was naïve in believing him but I don't know the estate like you do, nor its tenants. I didn't want anything to happen to her. What a wimp I've been.' He caught his breath while he looked at his watch. 'I'm going round to see her. Right now.'

'No,' said Josie. 'She has too much to think about at the moment.' She paused. 'But she needs someone like you. More than she will ever know. More than she'll ever admit. You just need to convince her of that.'

'I will.' Matt nodded fervently. 'You don't think it's too late?'

'I don't know. Just give her time, yeah?'

While Chloe stayed with Cathy, each day Liz became just that little bit better. She was moved from intensive care to a routine ward shortly after she'd been admitted, where she recuperated well. Finally ten days after the attack, she was on the mend and told she would be discharged shortly. That afternoon, she was sitting by the side of her bed when Cathy arrived to visit.

'Hello, you.' Cathy smiled, pleased to see her up and about. 'How are you feeling today?'

'I'm feeling good,' said Liz. 'I had a better night's sleep and I'm hoping to go home the day after tomorrow.'

'Really? Oh, that's great news!' Then Cathy's smile dropped. 'Are you sure you want to go back to the flat? You can always come and stay with me for a while, until you find your feet again.'

Liz shook her head slightly. 'I could stay with you but –'

Cathy gave Liz's hand a quick squeeze. 'You don't have to explain anything to me. Although I'm always here to listen whenever you need me.'

Liz's silence told Cathy not to pursue the matter. But it was after they'd settled down to their usual routine of vending machine coffee and afternoon TV that Liz started to talk.

'I ran out to the garden for ten seconds and left the back door unlocked,' she said quietly. 'Stupid, stupid! I can't believe I did it.'

'But you weren't to know he'd climbed over the gate.' Cathy pulled her chair closer.

'He must have been waiting for me behind the bin stores. One minute I was changing into a clean T-shirt – I'd spilt orange juice down the one I was wearing – the next minute I turned around and – and he was there in front of me. Well, I just went into panic mode. Before I knew it, I was up against the wall and he'd cornered me. All I could think of was that the iron was on and if he reached over and grabbed it…' Liz shuddered, tears spilling out of her eyes. 'He had a knife anyway. He covered it up and made me walk out to his car.'

'Why didn't anyone help you?'

'There was no one around – and to the outside world, he was just a man walking down the path with his wife. I hardly know anyone, anyway. Luckily for me, Jackie from next door noticed my distress.'

Cathy sat quietly while Liz cried for a moment. She half thought she wouldn't be able to tell her any more for that day so was surprised when she spoke again.

'He drove me across to Finlay Place. He made me get out of the car and took hold of my hand, squeezing it so hard that my fingers went numb. All the time he was hurling abuse at me, shouting at me, saying I shouldn't have left and that what he was about to do was all my fault. All I kept thinking was that if I didn't antagonise him, he'd let me go. He tucked the knife in his pocket and covered it with his jumper. Then he marched me across the playing fields. As we were walking up the path, I realised there was no one around to shout out to so I decided to make a run for it. If I could just get back to one of the houses behind me, maybe I could get away. So I shook off his hand and ran. But he caught me.'

Liz's sob was enough to tear a hole in Cathy's heart.

'I – I thought he was going to kill me,' she cried, clinging on to Cathy's arm. 'He stabbed me with the knife and I dropped to the floor. He kept on hitting me. I tried to crawl away but he kicked me in the back. It was a rage I hadn't seen in him before. He grabbed my arm and turned me to face him. I thought I was a goner.'

By this time, Cathy was crying openly too. She held Liz close to her as she finally broke down.

'I said one word that stopped him, Cath. I shouted out Chloe's name.'

'You were so brave,' Cathy whispered into her hair.

She was too. Cathy couldn't begin to imagine how she would have reacted in that situation. Everyone thought she was strong because she could stick up for herself and the women she looked after but, in reality, she would have gone to pieces if she'd had to go through what Liz had.

Liz pulled away then and they sat in silence with their own thoughts. Shortly after, Cathy looked over to see she was asleep. She left the ward quietly, deep in thought, only to find Matt sitting on a chair outside in the corridor. It stopped her in her tracks. He was the last person she'd expected to see. The awkward look on his face matched her discomfort at the sight of him; a few yellow-green bruises were all he had left to suggest he'd recently been attacked.

'Can we talk?' he asked.

'No, I don't think so,' she told him sharply. 'I think it's a little too late for that now.'

THIRTY-FOUR

A porter wheeled a bed past with an elderly patient lying in it, a nurse carrying his belongings. A man with his leg in plaster to the knee hobbled past on crutches. A male cleaner mopped a floor. Visitors coming and going: staff in varying uniforms walking up and down. Everyone around them was oblivious to Cathy's personal trauma.

'You have some nerve,' she told Matt. She made to move past him but he touched her arm.

'Please! Let me explain.'

'Do you think you can say anything to take away the hurt and humiliation you caused because you thought of me as nothing but your latest conquest?'

Matt looked uncomfortable. 'Josie told me that you thought that.'

Cathy glared at him. Not only had he been ignoring her but he'd been talking to Josie about the situation!

'I might have known,' she hissed quietly, aware of their surroundings. 'Pray tell me, what lies did you tell her?'

'She made me realise how stupid I'd been but I did have my reasons.' He pointed to a row of empty chairs. 'Just give me five minutes to explain. Please?'

The look that he gave her could have melted her heart had she been in the right frame of mind.

'Five minutes,' she told him.

Ten minutes later, Cathy's head was in turmoil after he'd told her Josie's opinion about things.

'But why didn't you stand up for yourself more?' she questioned

Matt bowed his head before raising his eyes to meet hers. 'I admit that he got to me. I've never been a fighter and I was terrified when he said he'd hurt you. Yet since I've had that conversation with Josie, I can't get it out of my head that it was that man, Kevin, who thought I was after his wife. I could have prevented Liz's attack.'

Cathy instinctively touched his hand. 'You mustn't blame yourself for his actions,' she told him. 'He would have done that anyway. He wasn't of sound mind.'

'But I should have done something to protect her.'

'Actually I think I could have done something too.' Cathy told him about the notes that had been pushed through her letterbox. How she had chosen not to tell Liz about them.

'I should have shown them to her,' she said afterwards.

'Most people would have done the same in your position.'

'I doubt that very much.'

Matt smiled shyly. 'Maybe neither of us should blame each other and realise that Kevin McIntyre would have got to Liz regardless.'

'That's what Josie said. But it doesn't make me feel any better.'

'I think we should listen to her.'

Cathy paused for a moment while she looked into Matt's eyes. Honest, earnest eyes that were telling her so much more than what he was saying. Matt had kept away from her because he feared for her safety as well as his own. He'd taken a beating, had been scared enough to think that whoever attacked him would do her harm. He might not be as hard as Rich but he cared for her just as much.

She kept her eyes trained on his as a porter wheeled a young boy in a wheelchair past them. 'Would it help if I said I was sorry?' she asked.

Matt shrugged like a petulant child.

Cathy knew that he sensed victory and shrugged her shoulders too. 'Well, that's that, then.' She stood up but he pulled her down again.

'Of course it would help.' He grinned. 'I think it would help more if you said that you were willing to try again. And then much more if you kissed me too.'

'Don't push your luck, matey.' She sighed loudly. 'Let's hope this is the last time anything happens for a while.'

'Hospitals and funerals; suicides and attacks. You get the lot, don't you?'

'What, me in particular?' said Cathy, knowing full well what he meant.

'Actually, yes!' Matt smiled.

'Well, let's hope things calm down for a while.'

'At your house?' Matt scoffed jokingly. 'Things will never be quiet with your lot.'

Becky had been out shopping in preparation for Austin's birthday in the morning. Luckily, she had managed to save up a few pounds from the pocket money Cathy gave to her for completing chores around the house.

By four thirty, she'd bought him a striped shirt and a

cheap CD player with rechargeable batteries. She was fed up with sitting in silence in the pub and if they were going to celebrate properly, they'd need some music. She bought a couple of CDs, chocolates and nibbles, a bottle of fizzy wine and two bottles of vodka.

By five thirty she was in her room, rolling out wrapping paper on her bedroom floor. Of all the presents she'd got, she hoped he'd like the shirt best. Maybe she could get him to put it on tonight rather than save it until tomorrow.

She broke a strip of tape with her teeth and fastened down one corner of the paper. But when she pulled again, the roll came to an end.

'Shit!' She rushed downstairs to search through the drawers. Cathy must have some more somewhere.

'What are you after?' Jess asked as she walked in.

'Sellotape,' Becky cried. 'I've just used the last of the roll I found this morning. And I can't find any more.'

'What do you need it for?'

'To wrap up presents.' She kept her back towards Jess as she continued to rummage. 'It's Austin's birthday tomorrow. He's twenty-one so I'm making a special effort. I want everything to be perfect.'

'He doesn't act like he's that old,' Jess taunted.

Becky turned her head to stare at her. 'Don't start that again.'

'You're all alone in that pub. No one can hear you scream.'

Becky laughed then. 'I'm not that scared of him. He's just a lot more streetwise than Danny Bradley. I suppose you could say he's more of a man.'

'We all knew Danny's background though, didn't we?

352

He's been raised on the estate, part of the scratty Bradley family. He was bound to do something stupid sooner or later. That's why he murdered that security guard. It was in his genes.'

'I know exactly what's in Austin's jeans.' Becky giggled this time.

Jess laughed too. Then her expression became serious. 'All I'm saying is be careful, Becks. You've only known him for a few months. To be honest, I've never felt safe with him. And I can't understand why he won't tell you anything about his past.'

'But that's where you're wrong,' Becky said triumphantly. 'He's been telling me about his parents. His mum gave him up for adoption. He's never known who his father is. He's not sure if he has any other family because he hasn't wanted to find any of them. Doesn't that tell you that he needs to settle down with someone who loves him?'

'You mean you, don't you?'

Becky nodded. 'He makes me feel special. He's fantastic at sex. I've nearly passed out some times, he – well, he always thinks of me. Not like Danny Bradley. He's all mouth when it comes to –' Suddenly she stopped.

'You cheap slag!' Jess cried out when she realised what she was about to say. She grabbed hold of Becky's hair and tried to punch her face.

But Becky fought back. Her first punch landed on the side of Jess's face.

'You told me that Danny never screwed you!' Jess slapped Becky. 'You lying bitch!'

'Girls!' said Cathy as she walked into the room. She threw down her bag and keys. 'GIRLS! Pack it in, will you.

I could hear the both of you the minute I got out of my car.'

Jess swung for Becky again but Becky lashed out with her feet. She caught Jess on the shin. Jess let go of her then.

'Ow! I'll bloody kill –'

'I said break it up!' Cathy pushed herself between the two of them. 'Right now.'

Jess pointed at Becky. 'She started it,' she accused.

'I did not,' said Becky, trying to catch her breath. 'It was you. You grabbed my hair.'

'Only because –'

'Girls!' said Cathy. 'You're supposed to be friends!'

'Friends don't shag each other's boyfriends, do they, Becky?' Jess pushed past Cathy and ran upstairs to her room.

Cathy stared at Becky. 'Care to tell me what's been going on?'

Becky shrugged her shoulders, her reddening cheeks giving away her embarrassment. 'Do you have any more tape, Cathy? This roll has finished.'

Back in her room, her head and cheek stinging, Becky wrapped Austin's remaining presents. Then she preened and perfected herself while ignoring Jess's taunts every time she walked past outside her room. Stuff her, she thought. She'll come round eventually.

At seven, in eager anticipation, she raced out of the door and down to the end of the street where she could see Austin waiting. They drove straight to the White Lion.

'Mmmmmmmm!' Becky stretched out on the mattress half an hour later. Every nerve in her body had just been set on fire. The smile on her face had grown to full capacity.

'You certainly know how to make me feel like a woman.'

'I thought I'd give you something to remember me by.' Austin lit a cigarette.

Becky sighed. 'You're talking in riddles again. I'll never be able to work you out, will I?'

'It will all become clear soon.'

'Maybe the birthday boy would like some more loving first?'

Afterwards, Austin swigged back more vodka. He wiped his mouth with the back of his hand and burped loudly.

'Two more hours,' he said.

'Until your birthday?'

'Until I can unleash my plan.'

'What plan?'

Austin flopped down beside her, ignored her question and handed her the bottle. 'Let's get wasted.'

Cathy was catching up with *EastEnders* when Jess appeared in the doorway.

'Can I talk to you?' she asked.

'Sure you can.' Sensing the urgency in her tone, Cathy pressed the record button and patted the space next to her on the settee.

'I'm worried about Becks,' Jess started. 'Ever since she's been messing about with that Austin fella, she's gone all strange.'

'Worried about her?' Cathy frowned. 'You were practically trying to rip her hair out from the roots earlier.'

Jess shrugged. 'That was boy talk. She's crazy about Austin now. But he's said some really creepy things. He scares me when I see him. His eyes are so cold.'

'Not everyone is going to fancy you, Jess,' Cathy teased.

But Jess didn't find it funny. 'She told me that one minute he's nice and the next he can get real nasty.'

Cathy caught her breath. 'He's not hitting her, is he? Oh, dear God. Not after what happened to Liz.'

'You remember those bruises on her wrist? He did that. I don't know exactly how but she told me. He could have held her down or something.'

Cathy shuddered involuntarily, a sense of déjà vu taking over.

'What do you say you know about him?' she asked.

'He's been into care. That's about it. Becky doesn't know where he comes from, why he's come here, how long he's staying. She doesn't know anything about him really.'

'And you want me to try and talk to her? See if I can figure out this Austin fella?'

Jess nodded. 'You always have a knack of getting things out of us. Even when we *don't* want to tell you anything.'

Cathy smiled. 'Okay. I'll give it a go but even though you think I'm good, there are times when I know you girls hold back on me.'

'Becky?'

'Hmm?'

'Becky. Wake up.' Austin nudged her awake. 'It's midnight.'

Becky opened an eye. The few candles she'd lit earlier flickered in the gloom, disorientating her slightly. Then she realised what he'd said.

'Shit!' She sat up and pulled her top over her head quickly. 'Why didn't you wake me? Cathy will kill me.'

'Don't I get my presents before you run off?' Austin asked.

Becky shuffled over to the carrier bag that she'd brought with her. Despite trying to get him to open anything earlier, Austin had declined. She pulled out a brightly coloured parcel and shuffled back to him.

'Happy birthday.' She planted a kiss on his lips. 'There are two pressies for tonight and two for tomorrow. Oh, it is tomorrow.' She giggled.

Austin sat up, back against the wall and brought up his knees. She rested her chin on them as he ripped open the present. He pulled out the shirt and held it up.

'Nice,' he said. 'At least I'll look well dressed for the final act. And clean, for a change.'

'Clean? Final act? You scare me when you talk like that. What do you mean? The final act of what?'

'Shut the fuck up.' Austin's face went dark again.

'But what's wrong now?'

'I said shut the fuck UP!'

He leaned forward and punched her in the face.

Becky fell backwards. Dazed, she placed her hand to her mouth. Before she could register that there was blood on her fingers, he punched her again. This time she disappeared into blackness.

THIRTY-FIVE

When Becky came round, Austin was tucking the new shirt into his jeans. He threw her clothes onto the mattress.

'Get dressed.'

She lifted her head a little and then put it down quickly as the room began to spin. She squinted at him. What the hell had happened to her? Was she drunk?

'Austin, I don't feel well,' she murmured. 'What did –?'

And then she remembered what had happened. She tried not to panic. He was stronger than her, capable of anything. She needed to gather her composure. This was what Jess had warned her about. Jess had said he'd hit her eventually but she hadn't believed her.

'I said get DRESSED!' Austin pulled her roughly to her feet.

Becky struggled to get into her jeans, twice missing her foot hole. He threw her shoes across the floor towards her.

'Hurry up, for fuck's sake.'

'I'm trying my best.' She began to cry, feeling her lip beginning to swell.

Austin took hold of her arm, squeezing it hard. 'I said hurry up!'

She slipped her feet into her pumps but she still wasn't quick enough. He grabbed a fistful of her hair.

'Ow!' She yelped like a puppy, trying to ease away his hands. But he was already dragging her out of the room. She lost her footing halfway down the stairs: he continued regardless. She scrambled back to her feet when she reached the ground floor. The pain in her head had intensified now.

Austin pushed her through the door into the lounge area. Apart from two further candles alight on the bar, the room was in darkness. But Becky could make out two chairs, side by side in the middle of the floor. He shoved her into one of them. Instinctively, she got up and ran towards the door. But he was quick on her tail. He yanked her back by the hair and pushed her back down again with a thump. From underneath the chair he produced a piece of rope.

'I knew I'd have to do this,' he said with a huge sigh. 'You always were a wild one.'

'Noooooooooooo!' Becky fought hard but he held her down with the weight of his body. He took hold of her hands and tied them behind her back. Then he grabbed for her feet. She kicked out in defence. He slapped her hard again: her head lolled to the side with the force. It was enough to quieten her while he carried on. The next piece of rope went around her waist and secured her to the chair.

'Please,' she whispered, her teeth starting to chatter. 'Let me go home.'

'Sorry, I didn't quite hear you.' He brought his head down to her level and cupped his hand around his ear.

Becky felt dry but she still managed to speak. 'I want to go home.'

'Home?' Austin threw back his head and laughed. 'What about my home?'

'I – I –'

'You wanted to know about my background? Now you can sit here and listen.' He laughed at the irony of his own joke. 'Well, you can hardly leave until I say so.'

He picked up the other chair and placed it a short distance in front of hers. Facing her, he straddled it and began to talk.

'You think you were hard done by when your mother died? I never knew my mother. The bitch abandoned me as soon as she had me. I think I know why. But I am going to find out for definite soon anyway.' His eyes burned into her as he spoke. 'It was the not knowing that got to me. Can you imagine what that was like? Always wondering why the fuck she gave me away.'

Austin wiped at his brow. It was then that Becky saw he had a gun. She sat still, trying not to panic while he continued.

'I was fostered out for a few years and then social services told me I was too much of a trouble maker to be adopted so they put me back into a home. Well, that was all I needed, the stupid fuckers. I was wound up, like a wooden top. I was always in trouble for fighting but I became top dog. No one messed with Simon.'

'Simon?' Now Becky was really confused.

'By the time I was sixteen and out on my own, I was into all sorts – drugs, alcohol. I tried glue a few times but didn't like it much.' He grinned. 'It made me look too much of a mess: put the girls off kissing me. And you know what that meant? No sex.' He nodded slightly. 'There is a reason why you and me like sex so much. It's because for a few moments in our pathetic lives, the pain of not being loved is replaced by someone wanting to be with you, someone wanting you to feel good.' He aimed the gun at her face. 'You ought to be careful of that, once I'm gone. You need to be more picky.'

Becky whimpered and squeezed her eyes shut. He was going to kill her! She started to shake. The room went quiet. When she opened her eyes again, the gun was back down by Austin's side. But his words were still up in the air.

'What do you mean, when you're gone?' she asked, struggling to find her voice. She coughed to clear her throat.

'Don't interrupt me. I haven't FINISHED yet!'

Becky jumped. Out of his view, she tried to loosen her wrists but it was no use. The rope was fastened too tightly for her to budge it.

'They kicked me out of my hostel eventually and I ended up living rough. That's when I first had an idea about finding her, my mother. It took me a while to track her down. All I had on my birth certificate was a surname and an area but my social worker helped me. I didn't tell him the reason why I wanted to find her though.

'But when I did find out her address, I ended up losing my temper and getting banged up for assault. It was only a two-month stretch the first time. Second time I got six months but they let me out after three. I came straight here and that's when I did my first kill.'

Becky began to cry then. 'Please let me go,' she begged. 'You're scaring me.'

Austin snorted vulgarly. 'Don't worry, my pretty one, I'm not going to do you in. I like you, Becks. You'll be spared, but you will have to act quickly. There's a knife over on the bar, in between the two candles. If you get the chance, you should try to cut yourself loose.'

Becky's eyes flitted around until they landed on the knife. Austin was talking in riddles again. What did he mean if she got the chance? Panic engulfed her. She breathed deeply to keep it at bay. Inwardly she urged herself to focus, try to work out the clues he was giving to her.

'I didn't get caught for the murder,' Austin went on. 'It was made to look like an accident so no one came after me. I just wanted her to hurt, like she'd made me hurt. I took away the one person she loved more than herself. And I would have got to her sooner if I hadn't gone into a fucking rage as I watched her at his funeral being all upset and teary-eyed. Afterwards, I went ballistic. I got pissed and when I came out of the pub, there was a lad walking towards me. I felt so angry and he was, well, he was in the wrong place at the wrong time. But I got caught. Fucking CCTV cameras. I did three years for GBH. That's why it's taken me until now to finish off what I started.'

Austin seemed to have slipped into a trance. He was waving the gun around now as if he'd forgotten its existence. Becky stayed still as he pointed it down towards her stomach. One false slip and he could kill her.

'What about the people who fostered you?' She tried to keep him talking.

'Yeah, they were okay actually but they couldn't cope with me. I don't blame them. I only blame her. I've always kept in touch with them just in case she tried to contact me. They told me all about the phone call from her solicitor when I rang. I nearly ran then, Becks, even though I was so close. The bitch was messing with my head. She wanted to see me. She thought she had the right to contact me after all I'd been through.'

Austin looked up again. Becky could see pain behind the anger but she knew she couldn't help him.

'I began to watch the house.' Austin smiled, almost kindly. 'You weren't supposed to be part of the plan, but you were there. Why not have a bit of fun?' He waved the gun around the room again. 'Then I found this place. I had to get rid of the loser who was stopping here though. I didn't want to share so I dumped him in the canal.'

Becky froze as she vaguely recalled something happening just before she'd arrived at Cathy's house. 'The homeless boy,' she whispered. 'That was *you*?'

'Yep.' Austin nodded. 'This place was perfect to hide in and he was cramping my style. He had to go.'

'Stop!' Becky cried. 'Please! I don't want to hear anymore.'

Austin moved forward quickly and sat down heavily, straddling her lap. Becky moved her head to one side but he squeezed her chin hard. It brought tears to her eyes. The whole of her face felt like it was on fire.

'You were the one who went on and on about knowing everything. Well, now I'm telling you everything.' Austin stopped for a moment, his breathing heavy. 'It was when I saw you that I knew I could get my plan going. But you were off screwing Danny Bradley.' He laughed nastily. 'It was easy to get rid of him too. What better way than to set him up for murder.'

Becky's eyes filled with tears. Austin squeezed her chin harder and she groaned.

'I was following you when you stopped outside the factory. I watched you storming off in a strop. I remember laughing at you: you went marching off in such a mood.

That's when I had an idea of how to get you for myself. I followed Danny into the warehouse.'

Becky gulped. 'You murdered the security guard, didn't you?' she tried to speak properly.

'Yes, the girl has got it!' Austin threw a punch into mid air. 'And from then on you were mine. I gleaned every bit of information that I could from you. Don't worry. I know I used you but I did like you. It wasn't a chore. It was quite good fun actually. You're a right little goer.'

Becky's shoulders dropped. Slowly the clues were falling into place. The first man he'd murdered, the homeless man and the security guard. It seemed like Austin wouldn't stop until he killed who he had come after.

'You've worked it out,' Austin grinned excitedly. 'Haven't you?'

Becky nodded. 'Cathy is your mum.'

THIRTY-SIX

Austin clapped slowly but significantly. He stood up and threw the chair across the room. 'Give the girl a round of applause.'

'Austin, I –'

'Shut up!'

'But Austin, I –'

'I SAID SHUT UP!' Austin cracked her across the face again.

This time Becky did as she was told.

After their earlier conversation, Cathy and Jess had spent the rest of the evening together. Just recently Becky had been home on time but when eleven o'clock had come and gone, Jess had asked her not to be annoyed because it was Austin's birthday. Cathy had said she'd give her the benefit of the doubt; she'd even laughed about it with Jess over the times she'd done it for her.

Then Jess had gone to bed at eleven and she'd thought nothing more of it until Becky hadn't arrived home at midnight. She waited another ten minutes but still there was no sign of her. Finally she sent her a text message to express her annoyance. But she didn't go to bed. Instead she dozed on the settee, half listening out for a knock on the door.

Now it was nearing eight thirty the next morning. She sat in the kitchen with a cup of coffee, wondering what to do next. Becky hadn't replied to the text message. Cathy had rung her mobile phone too but it had gone unanswered. It was so unlike her. Concern had long ago taken over from annoyance but even still. Some of the girls she'd had to stay had sneaked back in the next morning, not even thinking how worried she might be because no one had ever cared for them before. Today's date playing heavily on her mind, she decided to take a quick look around Becky's bedroom.

Upstairs, her eyes quickly skimmed around, trying to see if anything looked untoward. Becky's belongings were strewn everywhere: make-up left as she'd used it, hairdryer on the floor after she'd sat in front of the wardrobe mirror, used tissues scrunched up in a pile on the drawers. Two pairs of shoes looked like they'd been discarded at the last minute for a better choice, along with a denim skirt and a T-shirt thrown on top of the bed.

Cathy stood still for a moment. There was nothing unusual about the room. She opened the wardrobe door and sighed with relief when she saw the rest of Becky's clothing still there. At least she hadn't done a runner.

She sat down on the bed and wondered if she was over-reacting. Maybe it was Becky's way of rebelling, growing up. After all, she'd been the same at her age. No, actually, she'd been far worse. But she had also been more streetwise.

Absent-mindedly, she picked up the greetings card standing on the window sill. On the front was a sepia picture of a young boy and girl. They were holding hands and walking along a dusty lane into the distance. She opened it and read the message written inside.

'TO BECKY, HOPE YOU ENJOYED YOURSELF LAST NIGHT. HA, HA. LOVE A.'

Cathy's shoulders suddenly relaxed. This Austin, whoever he was, didn't sound like he was a deranged victim if he wrote messages like that. He obviously cared enough to buy a card in the first instance and it was some kind of joke they were sharing.

Then images of other words flew across the front of her mind.

'I'M WATCHING YOU.'

'YOU WILL NEVER BE SAFE.'

Cathy rushed downstairs to the kitchen. She pulled out the notes that Kevin had sent to Liz and looked at them carefully. Her hand covered her mouth as the reality sunk in.

'I'M COMING AFTER YOU.'

'STINKING WHORE.'

The handwriting on the card sent to Becky was the same as the handwriting on the notes. She'd – no, everyone – had thought that Kevin McIntyre was responsible for them. Everyone had thought they were meant for Liz.

Austin had written the card. Austin had written the notes. But he'd sent that card to Becky with affection so the notes couldn't have been meant for her. Now she knew they weren't meant for Liz, could they have been for Jess? But Jess didn't really know Austin so why would he watch her?

She sat down at the table. Again she read the notes.

'I'M WATCHING YOU.'

'YOU WILL NEVER BE SAFE.'

'I'M COMING AFTER YOU.'

'STINKING WHORE.'

Cathy cast her mind back to the strange goings on over the past few months. Her car had been vandalised. When the house was burgled, she had automatically thought it was Cheryl. But the only thing smashed up had been a photograph of her and Rich – maybe Cheryl's bedroom had been trashed to make it look like it had been one of the girls. Could it have been Austin? Then there were the notes.

Today's date was the fifteenth of August.

It all fitted into place.

The messages were meant for her.

'Jess!' Cathy barged into her room. 'I need to talk to you.'

'I'm here,' Jess shouted through from the bathroom. 'I've been up ages actually. I'm going into town to –'

'Becky didn't come home last night.'

Jess opened the door. 'What?'

'I've texted her and rung her but there's been no reply.' Cathy paused to catch her breath. 'Have you any idea where she would be? Please, Jess. This is no time to think you're betraying a trust. I need to know.'

'Austin's squatting in the White Lion.'

A look of fury crossed Cathy's face. 'You knew where she was and you didn't tell me!'

'I didn't know she wouldn't come home!' Jess looked on sheepishly. 'I would have said something. I would!'

'Okay.' Cathy tried to hide her panic. 'I'm going over to look for her.'

'I'll come with you.'

'No, I need you to stay here in case she comes back.' She wiggled her mobile phone in her hand. 'Will you ring me straight away if she does?'

Jess nodded. 'I'm sorry. Becky's grown up so much lately that I thought she could handle herself.'

'I'm sorry too, for snapping at you.' Cathy gave her a reassuring hug. 'We all make mistakes,' she added, praying that her one big mistake wasn't about to catch up with her.

'Anyone home?' Matt waved his hand in front of Josie's face to get her attention. 'What's up with you? You look like you're miles away.'

Josie looked up with a frown. She was listening to a voice mail on her office phone.

'Cathy's left me a message to say she'll be late for this morning's session. Becky didn't come home last night. She reckons she's out with that lad she's been hanging around with.'

Matt raised his chin in recognition. 'That Austin fella? I saw her with him last week. He was in a clapped out Vauxhall. I remember when I had one of those back in the days. I added extras to make it look like an SR. Can you remember those, Josie?' He paused. 'I'm not helping, am I?'

But Josie didn't seem to be listening. 'Matt, have you and Cathy ever discussed her past?'

'I know she was widowed three years ago and I know about the baby that she gave up for adoption, if that's what you mean.'

Josie smiled. 'She's trusting you, then?'

'She was upset the other night because it's his birthday this week.'

'Did she tell you that she'd tried to make contact with him?'

'Yes. And that he didn't want anything to do with her. I wish he'd give her a chance. He'd love the Cathy we know, despite her mistake. And she was only young. Surely he can't hold that against her?'

Josie ran her hands through her hair and then rested her chin in her palms. 'Oh, I don't know. But something's not right. I just can't put my finger on it.'

Matt smiled. 'You really care for her, don't you?'

Josie nodded. 'I care for them all. They're like my extended family.' Suddenly Josie sat upright. 'Oh fuck! It's him, isn't it?'

Matt looked on in bewilderment. 'Josie, you've lost me.'

'Austin – I'm not sure but I think he could be Cathy's son. She could be in danger. And if Becky didn't come home...' Josie picked up her car keys. 'I'm going over to Cathy's.'

'Wait, I'm coming too,' said Matt.

Becky hadn't got a clue what time it was but she reckoned that it must be morning. The room was a tiny bit lighter and she could see more than the shadows, which didn't help in the slightest. Every part of her body felt stiff from sitting in the same position for hours. Behind the double doors that led through to the kitchen, she could hear Austin banging about. Every now and then he'd come out, pick up a couple of stools and take them back into the room. When he next appeared, she tried to talk to him. She said the first thing that came into her head.

'Austin, I need to pee.'

'You're not getting me on that one. That's the oldest trick in the book. Even if there was a working loo, you'd only try and do a runner.'

'But, please, I –'

'Piss in your pants,' he told her cruelly without even looking her way. 'I had to do that loads of times when I was young. My foster brother used to tie me up in a chair and keep me there for hours.'

He disappeared into the back room again with another stool in each hand. Becky's eyes were sore. One of them was swollen now but she could still see out of it. In desperation, she glanced around the room. She couldn't see anything sharp except for the knife on the bar but she'd never reach that. She couldn't even stand up because her feet were tied together. One slight move and she'd topple over. That was the last thing she needed to do, to rouse his suspicion.

The double doors banged open again and Austin reappeared. Dust was smeared down his face and his shirt had dirty marks down its front. Much to Becky's dismay, the gun was tucked into the waistband of his jeans.

'Everything's in position now,' he said. He held his arms up high as if saluting the air. 'Just one more thing to fetch until Mummy dear shows up.' He checked his watch. 'Not long now, I'm sure. She's bound to work things out soon.'

'What time is it?' Becky asked.

Austin switched on the CD player that she'd given him last night. As the music pumped out its beat, he turned the volume up, louder and louder until the bass reverberated around the room.

'It's party time!' he shouted. 'And now for my party trick.'

He ran out of the room, laughing like a hyena. He was back moments later with a canister in each hand. He raised them high in the air before twirling round, letting the liquid pour out and splash over everything around him. As some dropped into Becky's lap, she let out a scream.

It was petrol.

THIRTY-SEVEN

Cathy pulled up erratically in the car park of the White Lion and scrambled out of her car. She glanced at the metal sheeting at the windows and doors but couldn't see any clear way in. She raced around the back. As she got nearer to the building, she heard the music. For a split second, she thought the pub had re-opened. But then she heard a scream. She pulled her mobile phone from her pocket and dialled Andy's number. As she waited for him to answer, she heard another scream. Shit: his phone went through to voicemail. There was no time to call anyone else. She would have to go inside.

At the first bay window, she ran her hands over the metal sheeting but couldn't feel anything out of place. She tried the next bay window: nothing there either. On the third attempt, she was almost in tears with frustration when she noticed the jemmied corner. She climbed up onto the thin window ledge and pulled it up. The glass had been smashed, scattered over the seating inside. She stepped in carefully. Then she froze. Although she didn't know what he looked like, she was half expecting Austin to be waiting there with an axe, ready to chop her head off. But there was no one there.

Her heart racing in time to the music's up beat tempo,

she edged towards its source. It took every ounce of courage but when she got to a door, she peeped through the tiny diamond window at the top. Knowing the layout of the pub having been there many times before it closed, she knew it was the lounge. In the dim light, she could make out a few tables and chairs, a long forgotten dartboard hanging forlornly over on the far wall. Then she saw Becky. Her back towards her, she was sitting on a chair, another empty one beside her. Cathy could see her hands tied behind her back. There was a man standing over her, waving his hands around. From where she stood, he seemed to be dancing. Her breath came in shallow bursts. For the first time ever, she was looking at her son.

She moved away from the door, hoping to calm herself while she thought what to do next. Should she just walk in and announce her presence? But what would he do when he saw her?

Should she go and get help or could she talk to him, see if he would let Becky go?

Would he hurt Becky?

Cathy held back a sob as she realised she had no idea how he would react. She'd never spoken to him; she didn't know anything about him. She couldn't judge his character.

But it was Becky who decided for her. When Cathy heard her screaming again, she pushed open the door.

'She isn't here,' Jess told Josie and Matt as they came down the path towards her. 'I took Chloe to her friend's house and when I came back there was no sign of her. What shall – ?'

'We haven't come about Becky.' Josie moved past her. 'It's Cathy we need to talk to. Is she in?'

'I meant Cathy.' Jess frowned. 'What's going on?'

Josie had no time to answer questions. 'Do you know where she was heading?'

'The White Lion.'

'But it's boarded up.'

'Austin broke in. Becky told me he's been sleeping rough in there.'

'Shit!' Josie paused. 'Did Becky mention anything else about him?'

'She told me he'd been abandoned at birth; that he hated his mother. She said –'

'It is him!' said Matt.

Josie nodded. 'He's holding Becky because he knows that Cathy will go looking for her.'

'What's going on?' Jess repeated. 'Tell me! I –'

Josie held up a hand in dismissal and spoke to Matt. 'What if I was wrong about Kevin McIntyre beating you up? What if it was Austin and he was warning you against seeing Cathy?'

Matt gulped. 'If you're right, then Austin is out to hurt Cathy, maybe Becky too. We need to get to them quickly.' He disappeared down the path towards his car.

'You think he's going to hurt them?' said Jess. 'Why would he do that?'

'I – I can't tell you,' said Josie, not wanting to betray Cathy. 'I'm going with Matt. You wait here –'

'I'm coming with you.'

'No. I need you to –'

'I'm not staying behind again. They're all I have! I have to know if they're all right.'

'But I need you here in case we have to call the police.'

'The police! You don't think –'

'Come on, Josie,' Matt urged her. 'We need to move fast.'

'Look,' said Jess, 'I'll wait outside and if I don't hear from you in ten minutes, I can ring the police. But I'm not staying here.'

Josie nodded and they ran to catch up with Matt. Within seconds, they were heading towards the White Lion.

When Austin spotted Cathy walking into the room, he ran to switch off the music. It left an eerie silence bouncing around the walls. He held out his arms as if to welcome her.

'I knew you'd come.' He smiled as if happy to see her, his demeanour saying otherwise. 'You've remembered what day it is.'

Cathy couldn't speak. She was mesmerised by the man standing in front of her. His dark hair, his medium build, his good looks in a devil-may-care sense, the scar down the side of his face. A carbon copy of her eyes stared at her but on him, they looked mean, moody and menacing. In dismay, she noticed his long fingers curled around the handle of a gun. Tears sprang to her eyes. She wanted to reach out to him, but she knew it would be too antagonistic.

'HAVE YOU REMEMBERED WHAT DAY IT IS?' Austin bellowed, bringing her out of her trance.

'Of course I've remembered,' she replied. 'I gave birth to you twenty-one years ago, at two twenty-five in the afternoon. I would never forget that.'

'You forgot me as soon as I was out of your belly, though, didn't you? Please, after all this time, tell me why you gave me away?'

'I was too young to cope with you. I –'

'LIAR!'

'I was! I swear.'

'You didn't care about me.'

'No.' Cathy took a tentative step towards him. 'I've thought about you every day. You were always on my mind. I called you Simon.'

Austin's face contorted with rage. 'Do you think I'd want to stick with that name after you'd given me away with it, you stupid bitch?'

'Please, let me explain. I –'

'DON'T SPEAK TO ME!' He pointed the gun at her.

Becky screamed again.

Cathy's face creased in anguish yet she dared to take another step forward. 'I tried to contact you,' she said. 'Just recently, through my solicitor. He told me –'

Austin crossed the room and brought the butt of the gun down onto her forehead. She hit the ground with a thud.

'Cathy!' Becky began to cry again. 'Austin, this has gone beyond a joke now. Please let us go!'

'This isn't a *joke,* you silly bitch.' Austin grasped Cathy under each arm, dragged her across the room and sat her on the chair next to Becky. He pulled out another piece of rope from underneath the chair, pushing her head back as it lolled forwards. He turned to look at Becky for a moment. 'Now you have someone to keep you company while I decide whether or not to let you burn in hell with her.'

'No!'

'She obviously cares about you because she came here but she never gave a fuck about me. So maybe we should all go out of this world together.'

'Austin, please!' Becky wriggled about in her chair, hoping to loosen off the ropes. 'You said you wouldn't hurt me!'

'Oh, dear.' Austin grinned as he bound Cathy's legs to the chair. 'I lied.'

'There's her car!' Josie pointed it out as they approached the disused pub. Matt pulled up beside it, got out and raced across the car park.

Josie turned to Jess in the rear seat. 'Wait here,' she told her. 'Give us ten minutes and if we're not back, call the police.'

'But –'

'Just do as I say!'

After looking over each downstairs window, Matt pointed to the side of the building. 'There's no way in at the front. I'll try around the back.'

When Josie reached him, he was at the far window.

'Over here!' He pulled up the metal sheeting and climbed through.

Josie stood for a moment wondering what to do. Should she go in or should she call the police and wait outside?

'Come on!' Matt whispered loudly.

She didn't hesitate this time. Within seconds, she was through.

'What shall we –?'

He put his finger to his lips and they listened. Becky's crying could just about be heard above the ranting of a man.

'What are we going to do?' Josie whispered.

'I haven't got a clue,' said Matt.

Josie moved in front of him.

'No, I'll go first. Wait!' Matt sniffed sharply as he got nearer to the door.

Josie sniffed too. 'It's petrol.'

'We have to go in.'

THIRTY-EIGHT

Josie followed closely behind Matt as they entered the lounge, shielded by him but trying to take in as much as she could about the room and the situation. They moved slowly forward into the main area. She could see Becky and Cathy, their hands and feet bound, ropes tying them to the chairs. Cathy's head had been lolling to the right but now she seemed to be coming round.

Austin was standing in front of them. Behind him, the door to the next room was ajar. Josie could see tables and stools piled up like a bonfire; curtains, cardboard and newspapers thrown on top. The whiff of petrol fumes more apparent as they inched their way forward, she realised his intentions. He was going to torch the place. She gulped, hoping she could keep her fear concealed.

'Ah, the cavalry has arrived.' Austin pulled his legs together sharply, stamping his right foot and saluting them both. Then in a quick move, he brought his face down millimetres from Cathy's. 'I wish you'd told me that you'd invited other people. I thought the party was going to be an intimate affair with just the three of us.'

'Please.' Cathy's voice was no more than a croak. 'Let Becky go. She has nothing to do with this.'

'That's where you're wrong.' Austin shook his head.

'Because I know that you care about her, don't you?'

'Yes,' Cathy whispered.

'DON'T YOU?'

'Yes!'

'That's better. Now, all I need –' He turned his head towards Josie and Matt and pointed the gun at them. 'Come any closer and I'll blow your fucking brains out.'

Matt froze in mid step. Josie walked into him with a thud.

Austin sighed loudly. 'Can't you see that I'm busy?' He circled the two chairs. Then he stopped in front of Cathy and held the gun to her forehead.

'No!' Matt stepped forward.

'I told you to stay where you were! But if you do insist on joining in, pull up a chair, why don't you? You can watch the show for free. You can even join in, if you so wish.' He flashed them a smile, using the gun to point out the seating. 'Sit.'

As they sat down, Josie wondered if she should reach for her phone and see if she could alert the police. They were several feet away: maybe Austin wouldn't see her. But she didn't dare provoke him. There was no telling what he was capable of in his frame of mind. All she could do was hope that Jess would ring for her. And... stuff it.

She decided to try and talk him down.

'Austin, I'm Josie,' she began, 'and I'm one of Cathy's closest friends. She told me all about you. How she made a mistake when she gave you up. How she wished she'd never been so stupid. She's always wanted to meet you, to apologise, get to know you so that you could become a part of her life. Please, can you give her a chance to explain?'

'She doesn't deserve a fucking chance!' Austin bellowed across the room before lowering his voice back to normal. 'And she needs to listen to me first.'

'I'm listening,' said Cathy. 'But I want to talk too. I need to tell you how sorry that –'

'You left me in care to rot!' Austin moved to the middle of the room again, the gun down by his side. 'Because of you, I didn't have a decent start in life.'

'I thought you'd be better looked after by someone else. Someone more stable, who could give you a good grounding. I couldn't do that on my own.'

'But you had a man then. Why didn't you want me?'

Cathy began to cry. 'Because I –'

'SAY IT!'

She shook her head.

'JUST FUCKING SAY IT!'

'Because I didn't want to lose him!'

'That's right.' Austin nodded. 'You thought more of him than you did of your own son, didn't you?'

Cathy couldn't look him in the eye. She knew he was right. She'd tortured herself for years over the same thing. But she had to lie to him to make him understand.

'No,' she said. 'I – I was just too young to realise how important you were.'

'But I knew how important Mr Mason was to you, didn't I... Mummy?' Austin bent down to her eye level. 'Which is why I can now take great pleasure in telling you that he didn't fall down the stairs on that fateful night. I gave him a helping hand – well, a helping shove, actually.'

Cathy frowned. The knock on her head was making it hard to think. What did he mean by that?

'Once upon a time there was a man called Rich Mason,' Austin continued. 'He loved his wife, Cathy, and she loved him. She loved him so much that she didn't tell him she had given away her baby.'

'It wasn't like that. I –'

'You didn't want him to know about me.'

'NO! It wasn't –'

'He knew who I was before I pushed him.'

Cathy felt bile rise in her throat. It was all she could do to keep it down. Oh, God, this couldn't be true. Not her son, who she had longed to see again for twenty-one years. No.

But she had to ask.

'You… you killed my husband?'

'Of course I killed him. I wanted to take away the one thing that you loved, that would cause you the most pain. So I took his life in return for the life you refused to give me. It was easy really.'

'No!' Cathy sobbed loudly, images of Rich rushing to the front of her mind.

'Austin,' said Becky. 'Please don't –'

'I watched him for a few weeks, learned his routine: what nights he went to the pub, which way he walked home. I must admit, the steps at Frazer Terrace were an added bonus.'

'No!'

'On the night I killed him, I hid behind some hedges until he'd staggered past. Then I called him back. I told him who I was.' He pointed the gun at Cathy. 'Told him you were a fucking BITCH. When he lunged towards me with his fists flying, I pushed him and down the steps he went. One, two, three, four, ten! But he didn't die straightaway.'

'No more. Please!' Cathy couldn't bear to listen to him but she didn't have any choice. She had to sit there while he told her everything.

'When I got down to him, he was lying in a huddle on his side. He'd taken a knock to his head, there was blood everywhere. His leg was twisted underneath him. I remember his arm hanging funny too. He spoke to me then.'

'You mean he was alive!' Cathy gasped.

Austin nodded. 'Right until I kicked him in the head a couple of times. I'm not stupid, though. I only kicked him twice so that it wouldn't be noticed. And I could hardly make much more of a mess.' He laughed.

'Austin.' Becky tried again, wanting to say something – anything – to calm him down. 'I think –'

'There were others too. Tell them who, Becks, if you're so desperate to talk.'

'He killed the homeless boy dumped in the canal and he killed the security guard at Cookson's. It wasn't Danny Bradley. He set him up.'

As everything clicked into place, Cathy felt distress like never before. Suddenly everything she stood for seemed like a lie. Her son, standing in front of her, was a killer. She wanted to hate him for what he'd done but she couldn't. She couldn't blame him because she had set the ball rolling.

In silence, she watched him cross the room to the double doors. She watched him flick open his lighter. Glancing over at Matt and Josie, she urged them to help. But what could they do? Austin had a gun. They'd all witnessed how unstable he was. She couldn't blame them for sitting this out. She tried one last time to talk to him.

'Why now?' she shouted. 'Why come back now?'

'Because I watched you with him and it made me sick. And then you made me even angrier at his funeral. I could see how much you cared about him. You should have loved me that much!' Still, he kept his back towards them. 'There was so much rage inside me that I stormed off: ended up kicking someone half to death. I got caught and did time, three years. While I was in there – every fucking day I was locked up – I thought of what I would do to you when I got out. It kept me sane, working out my revenge.'

He flicked the lighter and ignited the flame. For a second, he turned back to them all, a smile on his face, his eyes darker still. Then he threw it into the room.

The flames took hold almost immediately. Cathy gulped. My God, she had created a monster. A demon that was not only hell bent on destroying her but was prepared to take everyone she cared for down with her too. Feeling helpless, she writhed around, trying to free herself.

'If you want to survive, I'd leave now,' Austin turned towards Josie and Matt. 'The room back there will go up pretty sharpish. I reckon the smoke will become unbearable first and then… what the fuck are you doing?'

Josie looked up sharply. All the while Austin had been talking, she'd been trying to send a text message to Andy. She'd typed a letter at a time and was about to press send. Before she could finish it, Austin ran over and swiped it out of her hand.

Matt spied his chance and reached for the gun. As they grappled, Josie ran over to retrieve the phone. She pressed send on the message, willing it to go faster. When the screen was clear again, she dialled 999. But instead of putting the phone to her ear, she left it connected and slid it underneath one of the tables. There wasn't enough time: she could see the flames catching hold in the other room, smoke starting to bellow out.

'Help me, Josie!' cried Becky, wriggling in her chair.

Matt tried to knock the gun from Austin's grip but he was too strong. Austin struck it across his face. As he fell to the floor, Becky screamed.

'No, Austin! Leave him alone.'

'Matt!' Helpless to do anything, Cathy screamed too.

Josie stayed poised. She had no choice. Austin had turned the gun on her.

'Did you send a message?' he asked.

Josie nodded. 'The police will be here in minutes.' She hoped that he believed her. How was she to know if Andy was able to read the message straight away? Or if the operator had taken the call seriously and was busy trying to locate them – or if it had been dismissed as a nuisance call.

'You stupid bitch.' Austin took hold of Josie's arm and threw her at Cathy's feet. 'You are not going to spoil my party!'

'Austin, I –' Cathy tried one more time to reach him. The smoke was getting thicker now. She began to cough.

Austin glared at her. She blinked back tears as she saw the hatred he had for her.

'I'm sorry,' she managed to say.

But he wasn't listening anymore. 'I don't care about you,' he replied. 'Today is all about me. It's my birthday and I promised I'd go out with a bang. This isn't quite how I'd planned it as I was going to make sure you were dead first. But I figure it will hurt you more this way. And hey, I'll make sure you'll never forget the date.'

'Austin – Simon. I can assure you that I will never forget your birth date. Ever.'

'But this way I can make absolutely sure.' He turned the gun and aimed it at his forehead. 'It was because you made me do this.'

'Nooooooo!' Becky screamed.

Austin gave Becky one final look. 'Bye, Becks.' He winked at her.

And then he pulled the trigger.

Cathy cried out as Austin's body hit the floor. What was left of his face fell towards her: remnants of hair attached to a bloody mass of tissue. She squeezed her eyes shut tight to rid herself of the image. But even then, she knew it would haunt her dreams forever.

Josie covered her mouth with her hand and ran over to the room where the fire was. She managed to close the door, hoping to contain the flames and gain them a few minutes extra before the lounge was completely full of smoke.

'He left a knife,' Becky shouted over to her. 'Over there between the candles.'

Josie raced across to it and hacked at the rope around Becky's chest until it was loose. She undid her hands and handed her the knife.

'Cut your feet free and then untie Cathy,' she cried, coughing. 'Then you'll have to help me drag Matt out.'

'He poured petrol everywhere,' Becky spluttered, hacking away at the rope.

'I know. We'll be okay if we hurry.' Josie touched Cathy's shoulder. 'Are you all right?'

Cathy nodded. 'Please help Matt.'

Josie ran over to him. Blood poured down his face from a gash over his eye and he was out for the count. Coughing again, she slapped him about the face to stir him.

'Matt! Wake up!'

Moments later, Becky was at her side.

'We'll have to carry him,' she told her.

They picked him up and slowly moved across to the exit. Flames were licking at the door behind them, singe marks visible where the fire was taking hold. The smoke was increasing as quickly as the relentless noise from the roar of the fire.

'I'll get his legs,' Cathy said as she reached them at last. She picked up one foot but just as quickly dropped it in order to wipe her eyes. 'I can't see,' she spluttered.

Matt groaned.

'Matt!' said Josie. 'Thank God. I was beginning to wonder how we'd get you out.'

In the next room, the air was clearer. It gave them vital seconds to catch their breath and they headed towards the window. But Cathy dropped behind.

'What about Austin?' she said.

'There's nothing we can do for him now,' shouted Josie.

'But I can't just leave him in there. He'll burn to death!'

'He's already dead!'

There was a bang. Behind them, one of the doors swung open. Josie ran to close it again. She peered through the window.

'We can't go back in there. It's too dangerous.'

'But –'

'He's gone, Cathy,' said Josie again. 'And we need to go too. Come on. COME ON!'

Becky climbed through the window to find Jess waiting on the other side.

'You're here!' she exclaimed. 'I rang the police.'

They helped Matt through and then Josie followed. Stepping down to the car park, she bent over, resting her hands on her knees as she gasped for air. When she stood upright and turned to see where Cathy was, she wasn't there. Two police cars arrived in quick succession but she ran back to the window.

'Cathy?' she shouted. 'Cathy! You need to come out. Right now!'

'I can't leave him! I can't leave him again.'

Without thinking of her own safety, Josie climbed back inside. By now the smoke was coming underneath the doors in that room, enough for her to feel threatened. Cathy was on her knees staring at the door, one hand raised in front of her. Josie grabbed her arm and pulled.

'We have to go!' she said. 'Now!'

Cathy looked up at her, pain etched on her face as tears slid down her cheeks. 'I let him down,' she cried, gut-wrenching sobs coming from deep within. 'He was my son and I let him down.'

'But you helped a lot of other people because of it.' Josie coughed again. 'Come on!'

'I let him down.'

'Come ON!' Josie pulled her up and across to the window. Andy was climbing down from the seating. He helped them both to get back outside before jumping out himself. They ran across the car park to safety.

When Matt saw Cathy, he struggled to get to his feet. As she got to him, she fell into his arms.

'I let him down,' she repeated over and over.

To the sound of sirens getting closer, they walked to the front of the building.

'We made it,' laughed Becky, throwing her arms around Jess. 'We fucking well made it.'

Then she burst into tears.

THIRTY-NINE

It took a couple of weeks for the dust to settle down after they all escaped the fire. Austin's body had been burnt beyond recognition when the fire had finally been put out. Due to the amount of rubbish inside and outside of the property, it had burned for hours. The investigation had taken place, the cause of death had been established and the building was due to be demolished as soon as possible.

Once the bruises had started to fade and the media attention stopped, everyone could reflect on their stories. Cathy, Josie and Matt were sitting around the table in Cathy's kitchen.

'You were so brave coming after us,' Cathy told them both. 'If you hadn't worked it all out, Becky and I would have been toast. Literally!'

Josie smiled. She knew that joking was Cathy's way of dealing with the reality of how close they'd all been to death.

'We could all have been toast if it wasn't for Austin,' she concurred. 'In his state of mind he could have booby-trapped doors, windows, anything to make sure we didn't have a way out. And if he hadn't left the knife, then we would all have struggled. And,' Josie pointed at Matt, 'you need to lose some weight. You're too heavy to be carried.'

Cathy patted Matt's tummy gently. 'You leave my man alone, Josie Mellor,' she told her. 'I like him exactly the way he is.'

'Yeah.' Matt pinched an inch of the skin around his waist. 'These are my love handles, if you must know.'

Josie held up her hands in mock surrender. 'I just meant that the next time you get stuck in a fire, don't –'

'*Excuse* me,' Matt interjected. 'I'll have you know, the next time I get stuck in a fire, I want to be the one doing all the rescuing. I missed out on all of the action.'

Cathy blinked back tears as she looked around her kitchen. Everything could have been so different. Liz was on the mend now too. Apart from the mental scars, most of her injuries would heal fully over the coming months. She'd moved back into her flat as planned but Cathy had insisted on cooking her a good meal every evening until she was able to stand for longer periods.

Jess and Becky arrived a few minutes later in a burst of colour and laughter.

'Guess what?' said Jess as she and Becky came into the kitchen. 'I've got a job.'

Cathy stared at her wide-eyed. 'You?'

'Yes, me.' Jess folded her arms. 'Why are you so surprised? You're always on at me to get off my arse and do something.'

'I have one as well,' said Becky. She sat down next to Matt.

'It was Becky's idea, if you must know.' Jess sat down too. 'She saw the advert. The place is called Sparks.'

'That's the new bar opening in Stockleigh,' said Josie.

'Yeah, that's the one. We walked in as bold as brass, lied

that we'd worked in a bar before. They took one look at us and wanted proof of age. We looked a right pair of stupid mares.' Jess giggled. 'But they took pity on us and we're collecting glasses. It'll be boring but we'll make it fun. We start tonight, eight 'til midnight. That's okay, isn't it, Cath?'

'That's fine by me as long as you look out for each other.'

'And fine by me as we'll get more time to spend alone,' whispered Matt loud enough for everyone to hear.

Becky and Jess rolled their eyes at each other. But Josie beamed. It was great to see the two of them together at last.

Ten past ten that evening, with Jess and Becky doing their first shift at Sparks, Cathy was relaxing in Matt's arms. They were curled up on the settee. An empty bottle of wine stood next to a half empty tub of peanuts on the coffee table. The sound from the television was low in the background as they sat silent with their thoughts.

Cathy slipped her hand up inside Matt's T-shirt and ran her fingertips gently over his stomach. She was just about to go in for the kill when something he said stopped her in her tracks.

'Have you ever thought of fostering children, Cath?'

'What's brought that on?' she replied after a moment.

'I've been watching you with Chloe.' Matt paused to collect his thoughts. 'And the way she responded to you while you looked after her. She's a great kid. I often wonder what mine would have looked like.'

'Definitely ugly with green teeth and spotty skin.'

'Cheeky.' He paused before speaking again. 'Would you, though? Consider fostering?'

'I'm not sure. I doubt it's easy looking after other people's children.'

'I agree it would be a challenge but if we did it together…?'

Cathy didn't know what to say. Since she'd started seeing Matt again, she'd quickly got used to them being an item. So for him to talk about something so important, so soon, felt really special. Here was a man who she hadn't known six months ago, who knew all about her history, and he was now saying that he'd like to be a part of her future.

'It's something to think about, to look forward to, maybe?' he added. 'I'm sick of dwelling on the past.'

Cathy looked up, only to find him staring intently at her.

'Are you sure you want to be a part of my mad life?' she questioned. 'I can't ever promise to know what tomorrow will bring.'

'Even more reason for me to stick around.' Matt kissed the top of her hair. 'You need someone to look after you for a change.'

Cathy smiled. 'You're not the only one who maintains things around here. I haven't got time to be looked after. I am the looker-afterer.'

Matt laughed. 'There's no such word.'

'Even so. But say that thing about looking out for me again.'

'Cathy Mason, I am here for *you* whenever you need looking after.'

'Mmm, I like the sound of that.' In one quick movement, she straddled his lap as she'd done on that first night they'd slept together. 'Fancy staying over?'

Matt kissed her tenderly. 'I thought you'd never ask.'

COMING IN OCTOBER 2012

The Estate, Book Two

Behind a Closed Door

Housing office Josie Mellor loves the community spirit of the notorious Mitchell Estate – when it doesn't involve benefit cheats, aggression, or vandalism, that is. A natural problem-solver with her tenants' best interests at heart, Josie throws herself body and soul into finding the culprits when a spate of burglaries causes havoc on the estate, and deadly violence erupts.

But Josie has secrets of her own. Trapped in a loveless marriage, she struggles to escape her controlling husband. As Josie's home life deteriorates, she realises only a thin line separates her from the people she's trying to help. Can Josie save herself and return the estate to relative normality, or will both she and her tenants become victims of violence?

BEHIND A CLOSED DOOR

Of all the shenanigans that occurred on the estate, nothing sent shivers down Josie Mellor's spine more than a no-response call.

'Josie, it's Trevor. The alarm's going off at number five, Nursery Lane. No one's answering.'

'But that's Edie Rutter!' Josie grabbed her car keys, the phone still against her ear.

'Her son can't get there for about an hour,' Trevor continued. 'Any chance of you checking on her for me?'

'I'm already on my way.'

Josie took five minutes to drive to Edie's home. She banged on the front door and lifted up the letterbox to shout through.

'Edie! It's Josie. Are you there?'

She looked through the window but could see no one in the front room. She raced around to the back and stood on her toes to look through the kitchen window. There didn't seem anything amiss although she couldn't see the floor from where she was standing. She moved to the bedroom window, took off a woollen glove and gave it a firm rap.

'Edie?'

Cursing her short legs, Josie moved aside a terracotta plant pot, jumped up onto the low wall and looked inside. Screwing up her eyes, she tried to focus through the pattern of the netting.

In desperation, she began to lift up some of the pots around the tiny patio area. At her third attempt, she found what she was looking for. Moments later, she unlocked

Edie's front door and stepped in. Please God, she prayed, don't let it be gruesome. Let her be asleep.

The television was on low as she stepped into the tiny porch. Through the slightly ajar door, she could see a foot in a pink slipper. Pushing it open, her hand shot to her mouth. Wide eyes stared straight at her. Edie was lying on her back, her head turned towards the door. There was a pool of blood around her ear, her arm reached out in front of her.

Josie gagged. There was no life in Edie's eyes but she could see so much fear. The buzzer for the lifeline system still hung round her neck. Josie had fitted it when Edie's husband had died. Alfred Rutter had left Edie broken hearted and distraught – leaving Josie with the job of visiting her regularly to see that she was coping. She picked up another slipper that had been left behind as Edie had fallen and carefully knelt beside her.

'God bless you, Edie Rutter,' Josie whispered into the silence of the room. It was then that she noticed the mess. The living room was littered with Edie's possessions. The lamp and its occasional table lay on its side. Photographs were ripped from their frames and discarded, glass shards sprinkled like confetti. The mahogany sideboard stood with its doors wide open, its contents slung across the carpet.

A noise behind her made her jump.

'Fucking hell, Andy, you scared the shit out of me! Couldn't you have knocked to let me know you're here?'

'Sorry, the door was open. I heard the call and then I saw your car outside.'

Tears streamed down Josie's cheeks. Her hand shook as she pointed at Edie. 'She's dead. And I don't think it was an accident.'

Andy took off his police helmet and a glove. He checked Edie's neck for a pulse. Then he held his palm in front of her mouth. Finally, he closed her eyes.

'What the hell happened in here, Andy?' Josie asked. 'It's one thing to rob the old dears but another to take their lives as they try to defend what's theirs.'

'There are some nasty bastards out there. We can't protect everyone, no matter how hard we try.'

'How long do you think she's been there?' Josie glanced at the clock on the mantel piece. It was only nine thirty-two. 'All night, maybe?'

'Early hours, I suspect. She must have come round enough to raise the alarm before she died.'

Josie pointed to the poker lying on the rug, knowing better than to touch it. 'There's no blood on that though.'

'She caught her head.' Andy pointed to the corner of the tiled fireplace. 'Someone could have pushed her.'

'So there won't be any evidence on that?'

'I doubt it.'

'I'll let the office know what's going on,' Josie added a few moments later when they were still stood like zombies.

'Yeah, me too.' Andy reached for his radio. 'Get the team out, set the wheels in motion.'

When Josie didn't move, Andy placed a hand on her shoulder. She looked up at him with tears in her eyes.

'How can anyone do that?' she asked. 'Even if it was an accident, someone left her there to die. It's so cruel.'

Andy sighed. 'Aren't you forgetting something?'

'What?'

'This is the Mitchell Estate.'

ONE

Josie Mellor threw her car keys onto her desk and collapsed in a huddle on her chair.

'What is it with me and dead bodies lately? That's two in as many months. I was hoping after Mrs Rutter that I wouldn't have to witness that again.' Her voice held a tremor as some kind soul pushed a mug of tea under her nose.

'Your two-fifteen's here,' Debbie Wilkins shouted over. 'I've put her in interview cubicle one. She seems a bit stressed.'

'A bit stressed?' Josie retorted. 'She ought to try finding dead people and dealing with the aftermath. I don't know which is worse, being the first one to find her or waiting for the police to show, knowing there's a dead body sitting at my feet. And before I can take a minute to catch my breath, I've got to deal with all *this*.' She pushed aside the pile of phone messages on her desk since she'd left it two hours ago. 'I'm sure our tenants think I have the answers to all their problems.'

'Poor Vera Barber,' Debbie said as she joined her. 'Do you think she had a heart attack and fell?'

'It's hard to tell. It could be a number of things, given her age.' Josie sighed. 'I really liked Vera.'

Debbie caught her breath. 'You don't think it could be connected to the murder last month, do you?' she asked.

Josie shook her head. 'Nothing's out of place and there's no sign of a break-in.'

'That doesn't mean anything,' said Debbie. 'He could be a clever git. He might think he needs to do it differently this time. Make it seem like a normal death to cover his tracks, so as not to get caught.'

Josie had been distraught when Mrs Rutter, another one of her elderly tenants, had been found dead with head injuries in her bungalow a few weeks ago. The place had been trashed; a huge sum of money among other things had been stolen. But Mrs Rutter's daughter had been particularly upset that a pearl necklace with a clasp in the shape of a butterfly was missing. It had been a family heirloom for years. There had been no leads at all, not even with the press coverage it had received for a couple of weeks afterwards.

The aftermath of that death had been much worse than dealing with Vera Barber. Josie was still having nightmares; the image seemed to be imprinted on her mind.

'It doesn't seem fair, does it?' Josie could feel tears forming again. 'People shouldn't die all alone. I met her son at Mr Barber's funeral. He thought a lot of his parents. Not like some of the families on the estate. Some of them wouldn't give a toss whether their mother was left lying covered in a pile of her own crap because she wasn't capable of looking after herself. All they'd be concerned about is what benefits they'd lose rather than the death of a parent.'

'Cluck, cluck, Mother Hen,' Ray Harman chirped up. 'It's a good job everyone has Josie Mellor.'

Josie pulled a face at Ray. 'Yes, it is, because if it was up to you, there would be no Mitchell estate, right?'

Ray nodded long and slow. 'You got me.'

'Oh, I got you a long time ago, you smarmy git,' she muttered under her breath.

'You've only yourself to blame though. If you would insist on spoon feeding the morons, then what do you expect?'

Josie ignored him. She'd known a lot of people like Ray Harman during her eighteen years working for Mitchell Housing Association. Ray had been a housing officer for longer than Josie, yet he didn't mince his words when it came to job dissatisfaction. Between the two of them, they covered the sprawling estate, along with Doug Pattison, the maintenance officer. Doug looked after reporting all the repairs needed to the properties but would always offer to help out if Josie didn't feel safe going to a visit alone. Ray, however, would be far too busy checking if garden hedges were an inch higher than they should be or whether Ms-Anderson-at-number-fifty-two's skirt needed to be an inch higher than it was.

Josie picked up two folders from her desk and wiped her eyes again. 'Right, then, I'd better get started on the next one. As the saying goes, no rest for the wicked.'

A few minutes later, she put on her broadest smile as she walked into the glass-walled cubicle.

'Hello, Kelly.'

Kelly Winterton's face scrunched up with indignation.

'And, you,' Josie turned her attention to the young child sitting next to her, 'you must be Emily. Am I right?'

Emily nodded shyly.

'Do you remember me? I've met you before, at your house, and it's very nice to see you again. Now, if I give you some pens and a colouring book, do you think you can choose a picture to fill in with some bright colours, while I speak to your mummy?'

'Have you got a red one?' asked Emily, wide brown eyes looking up expectantly. 'Please.'

Josie gave her one of the folders and watched her face light up when she saw the packet containing felt tipped pens of every colour. Along with her mittens, her coat and scarf came off in a flash and she got down to work.

'Now, it's your turn.' Josie pushed a thick form across the table towards Kelly. 'You'll need to fill in the bits I've marked with a cross while I go through your options.'

Kelly remained silent while she chewed on her nails.

'As the tenancy is in Mr Johnstone's name only, and due to his recent trip to Her Majesty's Services, number one is to stay where you are now, at Patrick Street, while we set eviction proceedings in motion.'

'Eviction proceedings!' Kelly cried. 'What do you mean? He's only been sent down for six months!'

Josie flicked over a page and pointed to a box. 'Mr Johnstone isn't entitled to housing benefit if he's in prison for longer than thirteen weeks. And as he won't be able to pay the rent himself, we'll try and get him to give up his tenancy. Six months will give him a bill of at least two thousand pounds to pay when he gets released. And a criminal record – which will work in our favour. But we don't do evictions willy-nilly. We have a duty of care to offer you something else. And we have to follow procedures, take Mr Johnstone to court first, so it's likely to take a while. You can stay at Patrick Street, if you wish.'

Josie had Kelly's full attention now. 'But what if he only serves three months, half his time? Scott will keep his nose clean. You know him.'

'Not my rulings, I'm afraid. And if he doesn't assign the property straight back to us, for every week he's inside, he'll be liable to pay when he does get out.'

Kelly sat forward. 'Well, I'll claim benefits, then. I live there too.'

'Are there any bills in your name?'

'How the hell should I know?'

They sat in silence until Kelly sighed loudly.

'I don't think so,' she replied.

'In that case, you have no proof that you've been living there. You're registered with the benefits agency from 18, Christopher Avenue.'

Kelly frowned. 'No, that's my mum's address. I left there five years ago, when I shacked up with Scott.'

'Not according to our records.'

'But he filled the forms in for me!'

Josie raised her eyebrows questioningly.

'I had my money paid into my own account,' Kelly snapped. 'I didn't have to ask him for it if that's what you're getting at!'

'No. What I'm trying to tell you is that he lived at Patrick Street claiming as a single man. You were, unbeknown to you, maybe, claiming as a single mother.'

'But why would he do that?'

'To get more money. Lots of couples scam that way.'

Kelly shook her head. 'He wouldn't do that. Not to us.'

'Oh, he would,' Josie told her. 'And he has.'

For a moment, Kelly sat quietly while her brain tried to work out the logistics of the conversation. She wondered how long the eviction process took but didn't dare ask. Even she realised the rights must be different when a prison sentence got handed out.

'Mummy, look at my picture,' said Emily, getting to her feet. She thrust the drawing book at Kelly. 'I drawed a car.'

'Drew, Emily,' said Kelly, taking it from her. 'You *drew* a car. It's very good. Can you do another one while I finish off, please?' She looked up at Josie and spoke quietly. 'And my other option?'

Josie pointed to another box. 'You could have your own tenancy. It would have to be another property, though. It couldn't be Patrick Street because that's in Mr Johnstone's name.'

Kelly quickly wrote down her national insurance number. 'Would Scott be able to move in with me when he gets out?'

'Yes, but you'll have to declare it to the benefits agency. No more single living.'

'*I* didn't know that I was.'

Josie turned the form over to the back page. 'If you do decide to have your own tenancy, there are two flats ready to view.'

Kelly narrowed her eyes. 'You never said nowt about moving into a flat!' she hissed.

'There are only the two of you. And, with you being classed as homeless now, you don't have much of a choice, I'm afraid.'

'But I'm not homeless! You're forcing me to leave my house. And there are three of us. You're forgetting Scott.'

404

Josie leaned forward, aware how vital it was that she gained Kelly's trust. 'Look,' she said. 'I don't feel good about doing this but Mr Johnstone played things really clever. By keeping your name off any of the household bills, as well as the tenancy agreement, it means that you can't prove you've been living there for the past twelve months. Therefore, you're not entitled to stay. If he won't sign the forms, we'll start eviction proceedings for non-payment of rent. Eventually the property will come back to us.'

'But you know how long I've been living there!' Kelly's eyes pleaded to Josie to give her a break. 'You could vouch for me!'

'It's not that simple. For all I know, you could have been staying over for a couple of nights whenever I've visited.'

Kelly sat back in her chair again. She folded her arms. 'So, I'm fucked, whichever way I look at things?'

Josie didn't flinch. She was used to tenants swearing at her when she told them something they didn't want to hear. Unlike some of the violent ones who'd come within an inch of her face to do so, Josie sensed that Kelly wasn't using it for the benefit of annoying her. Her anger seemed to be directed at the system.

'The other thing I need to tell you is that both flats are on the top of the estate.'

'You mean on the 'hell? Jesus Christ! It gets fucking worse!' Kelly kicked the table leg in temper. Emily jumped but with a quick, reassuring smile from her mum, continued to draw.

'It's only just off Davy Road,' explained Josie. 'And watch your language please.'

Kelly could feel herself breaking. Everyone knew that

the top of the estate was the worse place in the city to live. The Hell Estate, it was called. She didn't want to live there.

As Kelly's head fell into her hands, Josie's heart went out to her. The application form told her that she was twenty-four and Emily was four. From her appearance, Josie could see that Kelly was capable of looking after herself. She could spot no obvious indications of self-neglect; no dark bags under her eyes, no sallow, spotty skin, so she wasn't doing drugs, always a good sign. Kelly's dark brown hair was cut in a short and spiky style, and her iconic elfin face wore just the right amount of make-up to make Josie feel fifty-seven instead of thirty-seven. She wore stylish clothes, all clean and pressed, and her daughter was spotless.

'Both flats need decorating,' Josie forged ahead regardless of Kelly's silence, 'which we will give you an allowance for, but it probably won't cover the cost of all you'll need. I take it from your earlier comment that you'll be claiming benefits?'

Kelly slapped her hand down hard on the table top. 'Don't you look down your nose at me, you snotty cow, with your high and mighty attitude! Just because you work here doesn't mean that you're better than me. I used to have a job before I had Emily, but Scott wanted me to stay at home with her when she was little. What's wrong with that? Don't you think bringing up a kid is worthy of a job title?'

At the sound of her raised voice again, Emily rushed over to her mum. Kelly lifted her onto her knee.

Josie tried to keep her cool even though she could feel her hands shaking. 'You need to calm down, Kelly.'

Kelly hugged Emily and looked down into her innocent face. 'If you must know, I hate living off handouts. It makes me feel like crap.' She looked up again with a glare. 'Don't you think I wish I could get a job again? But it's been too long. Who'd take me on? I've got no one to look after Emily. And if I did, I'd get a pittance that won't be worth getting out of bed for.'

'Don't knock yourself too much, Kelly. You have as much chance as anyone.'

'But what can I do?'

'Lots if you put your mind to it.'

Kelly stared at Josie, ready to protest again, but realised that she wasn't patronising her.

Josie pointed to the last empty box. 'You need to sign here as well. I also need to do a property inspection.'

'But I don't want to move out!'

'You don't have to move out straightaway. But you will be evicted and then I won't be able to help you.'

Kelly's shoulders drooped even further. 'I don't have a choice, do I?'

'Yes,' nodded Josie. 'You could always try and find yourself another property to rent. But you need to decide soon what is right for you, and Emily. I can't hold the flats for too long. There are other people on the waiting list.'

'Mummy, can we go now?' Emily pushed herself off Kelly's knee. 'I want to see Nanny.'

Kelly smiled down at her. 'Sure we can, poppet. You get your coat on. I won't be a minute.'

Josie sighed. Underneath the hard exterior she could see a frightened young woman. Yes, she lived on a rough estate and mixed with a few rough characters but this wasn't the east end of London.

Already she could feel herself warming to Kelly's plight

as she watched her fasten up Emily's coat. Josie knew she could help her. It would be hard work trying to pierce Kelly's durable shell, but persistent was her middle name. How many hostile people had she befriended over the years? Not every one had been a success but she had a feeling that Kelly could be one of them.

'I can help you through this,' she offered.

'I don't need your help,' Kelly replied curtly. 'I don't need anyone's help. I can manage on my own.'

Hmm, thought Josie, maybe not! Even so, she wasn't perturbed by the tone of her voice.

'I'm sure you can,' she agreed. 'Now, you just need to sign here and we're done. Then there are the flats to view.'

Join Mel's mailing list at www.melsherratt.co.uk to keep updated on future releases of murder and mayhem on the Mitchell Estate.

ALSO BY MEL SHERRATT
TAUNTING THE DEAD

You can't always take the truth to your grave...

Statistics say nine out of ten murders are committed by someone the victim knows. So when Steph Ryder is found dead with her head caved in, Detective Sergeant Allie Shenton begins investigations close to home, starting with the victim's family and friends.

As each one tries to cover up their actions on that fateful night, Allie becomes convinced husband Terry Ryder has something to hide. Powerful, ambitious and charming, Allie's attraction to the successful businessman grows with each interrogation, risking both her job and marriage. But he's not the only one she's investigating. Secrets and lies begin to escalate as quickly as the body count. Can Allie uncover the truth before her life not only falls apart, but before she ends up a victim, too?

ABOUT THE AUTHOR

Ever since she can remember, Mel Sherratt has been a meddler of words. Right from those early childhood scribbles when she won her first and only writing competition at the age of 11, she was rarely without a pen in her hand or, indeed, her nose in a book.

A self-confessed shoeaholic, born and raised in Stoke-on-Trent, Staffordshire, Mel used her beloved city as a backdrop for her first novel, TAUNTING THE DEAD, and it went on to be a #1 best seller. SOMEWHERE TO HIDE is the first book in a new series, THE ESTATE.

You can find out more at www.melsherratt.co.uk

or on twitter at @writermels and on Facebook

Printed in Great Britain
by Amazon.co.uk, Ltd.,
Marston Gate.